A Mother's Testament

Durnyam Mashurova

Translator's Introduction

A Mother's Testament is a largely autobiographical story of life and times in a Uighur village from the 1930s to the turn of the twenty-first century. The village of Bolshoy Chigan and the nearby town of Zharkent are situated in the far southeast of Kazakhstan, a stone's throw from the border of China's Xinjiang region, where most of the Uighur people have lived in modern times. This border was formerly an external border of the USSR and was not easy to cross until the *perestroika* period of the late 1980s.

Told as a series of episodes to a fellow passenger on a long flight to America, the narrator, Mehriban, gives emphasis in her tale to the womenfolk of the village and the hardships they endure. Later, the story becomes self-referential as she describes being moved to write about these women's lives, resulting eventually in a book called *A Mother's Testament*—the purpose of which is to preserve the memory of the "holy mothers" for future generations. Mehriban sees this both as the fulfillment of an obligation toward the spirits of these women and also as part of an inner gift that has been granted to her. In doing so, she comes into her own spiritual inheritance and is able to bridge the apparent differences between old and new and between East and West.

We have chosen to retain a number of Uighur terms in the text, most of which refer to food, clothing, and household items, as well as to occasions such as weddings and funerals—situations that recur throughout the story and are described in considerable detail. A glossary of all such words, together with occasional Soviet, Russian, and Islamic terms, is given at the back. The inclusion of these words gives readers a taste of the linguistic environment in which the characters lived, as well as giving an ethnographic dimension to this memoir of past lives.

It is especially worth pointing out the forms of address used between the members of an extended family and among people living in close proximity in a village. In traditional societies, these tend to be highly elaborate and precise, with labels of seniority and gender encapsulated in pronouns that can also be suffixed to a person's name. For example, *apa* means "mother," and a person of any age will use it when speaking to his or her mother. It may, however, also be appended to the person's first name. For example, Gyuli-apa, and used by others to address the same woman. In this case, it is simply a term of respect when addressing an older woman. All these particles are included in the glossary. Another occasional feature is the *-m* ending common in Turkic languages that indicates possession and thus dearness: *bala*, 'son," becomes *balam*, "my son", and Aisha becomes Aisham, "my Aisha."

A final point is that these forms of address can be used loosely. One may address any older woman with *apa* or *ana*, meaning "auntie," whether or not she is formally related.

The novel was originally written in the Uighur language and was subsequently translated by the author's son David Mashuri into Russian. This English translation has been made from the Russian version, and it is hoped that sufficient flavor of the original has been maintained.

Robin Thomson
Hawick, 2014

1

THE TRAVELING COMPANION

"Would you like something to drink, ma'am?" the stewardess asked. I glanced at the tray of drinks and chose an orange juice. As I did so, the crew asked us to fasten our seatbelts. A minute later the captain's voice came over the loudspeaker system. "Ladies and gentlemen, we would like to welcome you on board this KLM flight number 0410 from Almaty to Amsterdam. The scheduled flight time is seven hours and twenty minutes. Our arrival time in Amsterdam will be 10:40 local time. The captain and crew would like to wish you a pleasant flight."

I was always a little nervous as I waited for the moment when the undercarriage lifted from the ground, the aircraft sailing softly up into the ocean of the sky. Its wings would bear me from one continent to another over the course of many hours. I looked around and noted that not all the seats in the first-class cabin were occupied. Once we were airborne, the smiling stewardess offered me drinks once more.

"No, thank you, I'm a little tired. I think I'll sleep for a while," I replied. I let my seat back and settled into it comfortably. On the screen in front of me, the KLM airline logo was proudly displayed: a white swan soaring upward from water. Today this white swan would bear me to Amsterdam and then to America. I was on my way to meet my readers. My childhood dream of becoming a writer had come true, and the ugly duckling from some obscure village was now spreading its wings. But surely this must be a fairy tale? Even today, I found it hard to believe.

Beneath us, dazzling white clouds drifted in a limitless blue sky. Enchanted at this sight, I began to doze. When I opened my eyes again, I noticed a woman sitting in the seat next to me. Gray-haired, wearing a sporty white outfit, she turned to me. "Hello. How are you?" she said, smiling.

"Very well, thank you," I replied.

When I meet somebody, I always study their appearance. In my neighbor's eyes were signs of sadness. Judging by the deep wrinkles on her face, she must have been over sixty.

"Where are you going?" she asked.

"I'm going to Los Angeles."

"That's where I'm going too."

"I'm catching a connection to Chicago."

"So are you traveling on business, or are you visiting?"

"I'm going to appear on Oprah Winfrey's TV show."

"Wow!" A smile broke out on my companion's face. "That's impressive. Oprah is hugely popular in America."

"I've been wanting to meet her since 2001. And now, at last, I will."

"How amazing! What will your show be about?"

"Oprah read my book about the lives of Uighur women and got very interested in the subject."

"So you're a writer?" The gray-haired stranger gave me a look of respect.

"Better to say a beginning author." I grinned. "I write about what I've seen and what I've experienced. My book consists of tales about people I've known. They have interesting and sometimes tragic lives."

"I'd love to hear more about the Uighur. Would you tell me about them?"

"It's a long story," I warned her.

"Well, we've got more than twenty hours ahead of us. That's time enough. But first, let's introduce ourselves. I'm Ruth."

"And my name is Mehriban."

I looked out of the window and thought for a moment. Where should I start?

2

A SPRINGTIME FAREWELL

It was the month of May. In our village the apple and apricot trees were blossoming, and the air was heady with sweet scents. Fed by the spring rains, the grass had grown high and was bright green. One night, I was awoken by a storm—peals of thunder and violent flashes of lightning, followed by a torrential downpour. No sooner had this died down, the telephone rang. My heart began to pound with unease. I lifted the receiver to my ear.

"Mehriban, Gyuli-*ana1* has died." This fateful news arrived with the dawn. The clock said half-past five, but I knew I would be unable to go back to sleep. I went over to the window and pressed my forehead to the cold glass. The news had shaken me.

Death, of course, comes to us all sooner or later, but I had hoped that old Gyuli-ana would be able to overcome her illness one more time. But why was I still standing here thinking? I had to go and help relieve the suffering of my relatives.

------

[1] For explanations of italicised words - mostly Uighur expressions - see the glossary at the end of the book.

I dressed quickly and went out into the street. The houses and gardens had been washed clean by the rain, and everything seemed to breathe freshness. Yet this only made it harder for me, and my chest ached from my loss.

People were already crowding along the street to Gyuli's house. The elders were sitting in the yard on long benches. The sounds of weeping and keening made my shoulders sink even lower. Her son Yadikar was unable to contain his sobbing. "Oh Mama, you looked after us; you gave to us all your life! Why did you leave us so soon, Mama? Forgive me, Mama!"

The grandchildren, who like their father were wearing white bands around their waists, also keened, "*Moma*, our own dearest grandmother, you were solid gold! And now you've gone away and left us."

Nor did the neighbors standing around them hold back their tears. And since Gyuli-ana had been known and respected far beyond the boundaries of the village, the street and the yard were soon full of people. Death forces us to feel our frailty and dependency, and when somebody departs this world forever, we try to be closer to one another.

I went inside to the inner room where the women were sitting. Their heads were covered with white mourners' shawls. Scarcely had we greeted each other before my two cousins, Selimyam and Saniyam, came over to me. We hugged each other and wept together. One after another we lamented, "Oh, mother! How much you labored all your life long! In the heat and the cold, in the garden and in the house! You raised us, you nurtured us, and then you were nanny to our own children. You really loved life! But now you'll never see your grandchildren marry! You cannot now rejoice in the good life, our beloved *ana*, our priceless, irreplaceable mother!"

Appak-ana, the wife of the village imam, who sat on a *korpya* in the center of the room, said, "My children, stop weeping now and pull yourselves together. Nobody in this world lives forever. We will all leave by the same road. Allah said, and may it be so, that the child will lament its mother, but not the other way round. May heaven protect us from the grief of a mother who weeps for her child!"

Soon more relatives arrived from the nearby village of Pidzhim. Our neighbors, my sisters, and their woman friends resumed their keening and sobbing. May their crying reach heaven, may it help the soul of the departed to find the straight path to the Most High God!

Then came an announcement. "Quiet please, everybody. They are now ready at the cemetery. Who will go in and wash the body of the deceased?" At this, the crying stopped.

Selimyam spoke up. "Mama's wish was that her friends Mervan, Mariya, and Zaynap would wash her for the last time. And let Sepiyam-*hada* bring and pour the water."

The women mentioned went out into the yard and began by performing an ablution, as if before the ritual prayer. Next, they went into a separate room and sewed a garment for the deceased out of white material. Once this was completed, the oldest of them, Mervan-hada, wrapped everything they had prepared in white cloth.

"Good," she said, "now let's go in and say *Bismillah*, then wash our friend's body and comb her hair before she is laid to rest. We'll give her the best of farewells." She went into the room where Gyuli had been laid.

They fetched two buckets of water and a *kapak-chumush* for pouring it. Once they had washed the body, they dressed it in a shirt, tidied the hair, and wrapped the body in the white cloth. Now the children, relatives, and close friends came to pay their respects. Gyuli had changed: her eye sockets had grown deeper, all her features had become sharper, and her face suddenly seemed small.

We whispered our farewell. "Mother, may your resting place be paradise." We quietly went outside.

The men gently lifted the shrouded body, carried it out to the yard, and placed it on a covered stretcher. A prayer was recited, then the men carried Gyuli off to the cemetery. The sound of keening grew stronger as they went. The women accompanied the procession as far as the cemetery gates, then washed their hands and returned to the house. I looked over the rooms with their subdued occupants and felt a lump in my chest. Another wave of crying and ritual lamentation broke over us. As is our custom, the eldest daughter Selimyam then stood up and asked:

"My dear friends and relatives, tell us, what kind of person was my mother?"

Mervan-ana replied, "Gyuli was a good woman. She never hurt anybody; she was gentle, unassuming, and hard-working. Everyone in the village respected her highly. When I think of how much we went through together…" The old woman broke into sobs.

And it was true. Gyuli-ana was one of the oldest among us. Today, the number of old-timers left in the village can be counted on one hand, like precious beans in a thin soup.

Now Zaynap-ana spoke up. "Selimyam, child, that's enough crying. Calm yourself. Let's choose who will take care of the *kazan* and who will stay in this house for the next seven days to care for the family." She pulled her shawl a little tighter.

"Dzhanyam and Halidam, my mother loved and respected you very much," Selimyam addressed her neighbors. "Would you be willing to work at the *kazan* for seven days?"

"Of course, we will be happy to fulfill your mother's wishes." The two women rolled up their sleeves and went over to the hearth straight away.

Old Zaynaphan, stroking her aching knees, added, "And I will make *zhit* for the seven days."

Selimyam turned to the others. "Dear friends of my mother, relatives, and elders of our community, please stay with us, any of you who can, for this period of seven days."

Sighing, the younger women, neighbors, reluctantly declined, unable to leave their work, their homes, and their animals for a whole week. Many of the older people were also distressed that they could not stay, but how could they neglect their grandchildren, whom they looked after every day? Free time was precious.

Now Dzhanyam entered the room holding a tray piled high with freshly-baked *nan* from the *tono* oven. She went up to each woman in turn and said, "Take some of this *nan*. It has been held over the head of our deceased mother." Each took half of one of the flatbreads, and when they had all sat down, Halidam came in. She also had a tray, on which was a quantity of tea leaves wrapped in newspaper, together with some needles and thread. Going up to the older women, Halidam said to each: "Take a handful of tea, a needle, and some thread."

They did so, and then she addressed the younger women. "And you take some as well, and tomorrow, when you do your *namaz*, remember our Gyuli-ana." Each of the women took a handful of tea and a needle and thread and wrapped them, together with the piece of *nan*, in their shawl.

"Why do they give out *nan* and tea after someone has died?" a young woman asked the elderly Zaynaphan.

"If a neighbor borrows bread, tea, or a needle and thread and does not manage to return them while she is alive, then on the day after her death, her relatives give out all three, to ensure that the soul of the deceased is free of debts," she replied. "This is an ancient custom of ours, daughter."

Noticing that some of the older women were preparing to leave, Selimyam stood up and said in a trembling voice: "My dear ones, thank you—all of you—very much for coming to pay your respects to my *ana*."

Appak-ana, filled with compassion, responded, "You are all deserving children who have acted respectfully as you buried your mother. Those of you who remain, I wish you the best of health. Let me say a prayer." All the women sitting in the room lifted up their hands and passed their palms over their faces.

After the prayer, Appak-ana continued, "Selimyam, I'm not feeling too well. Allow me to go home. But on the seventh day, I will come back and pray with you all again." The old woman got up to leave.

Since our tradition forbids any close relative of the deceased to leave the house, Selimyam-hada asked one of the young girls to go with Appak-ana and put her in a taxi home.

Old Zaynaphan stood up, took the jug for ablution, and went out into the garden. Then, going into the *chayhana*, she filled a large bowl with flour, took a tea bowl and placed a little salt in it, dissolved the salt in some cold water, and poured this onto the flour, then began kneading the mixture into dough for *zhit*. Nine-year-old Guncham, watching every movement of the old woman, asked her, "*Moma*, why are you making *zhit*?"

"These breads will be fried in oil while we remember and pray for the person who has died."

"*Moma*, let me help you."

"No, daughter, it's better for you to watch. One day you will have to make *zhit* yourself."

While Zaynaphan-ana was frying the thin *bread*, Mervanam-ana went out into the yard and gave instructions to two younger women. "Daughters, would you place a table in one of the rooms for when the men come back? Put a tablecloth on it. As soon as Zaynaphan finishes making the *zhit*, she'll come and put them and the other food out on the table."

By now, it was hot in the house. The woman beside me, Pashahan, and I went out into the yard. I looked at the house. On one side of it was a canopy up which a vine now crept, with new shoots appearing in tender green. On the other side of the house stood the *chayhana*, decorated with a carved floral pattern. On a high shelf in a corner of the *chayhana* were two *kazans* that had been scrubbed up until they shone. Not for nothing did the villagers say that Yadikar had golden hands. The yard was tidy and attractive. Around the *chayhana* Gyuli-ana had planted rose bushes, whose swelling buds now glittered with dew. For the whole of the summer to come, the yard would be pervaded by the fragrance of roses—Gyuli's final farewell. Not only in her garden, Gyuli used to work incessantly, but she and her children had it no worse than others, and her children grew up to be hardworking and honest.

There was a creak as the gate opened and the men returned from the cemetery. Yadikar was in front; he looked as though he had aged. He stopped in front of the entrance to the house and lamented, "So I have entrusted my *ana* to Allah. Without you, this yard is bereft, my dear mother, my source of joy and wisdom."

To Yadikar's lament was added the voices of his sisters. The women came out; once more the yard was filled with weeping, and not even the men could hold back their tears.

The weeping died down, and the men were invited to the room prepared for them. The *zhit* was consecrated with a prayer recited from the Qur'an, and everybody prayed for Gyuli-ana. They drank their tea in silence.

When they had finished drinking tea, Yadikar addressed the mullah. "Mullah, father, would you please pray for our mother."

"Very well, son, I will do as you ask. I will say prayers for forty days," he replied.

After the closing grace, everybody got up from the table and began to say good-bye to one another. The friends, in-laws, and close neighbors appointed to rememorate Gyuli-ana for seven days stayed behind in the house. We talked softly, sometimes reducing our voices to a whisper. At times of sadness the familiar world can seem quite different: the eyes see more sharply, and feelings are felt more keenly. In the evening, when it was time for the meal, Dzhanyam and Halidam brought long low tables into the room and announced, "The daughters-in-law of Mervanam-ana have brought you *suyuk ash.*"

The daughters-in-law, Pashahan and Memanhan, served the soup into bowls and placed one of these in front of each woman, then broke a large *nan* into pieces that had been baked in the *tono* and placed it on the table. Meanwhile, the men assembled in the *chayhana.* They were also each given a bowl of *suyuk ash.* After the meal, *aktyan-chay* was served. As they drank their tea, they conversed at leisure. Afterward the women silently cleared the dishes from the tables.

After their tea, the most respected of the women, who were sitting in the places of honor, took turns to invite one another to lead prayers, as was part of the memorial ceremony.

At last, Maryam-ana turned to Pashahan and Memanhan and said, "Daughters, may your hands never be tainted! You have given us such delicious food! Thank you." She raised her hands for prayer.

According to Uighur custom, when a person dies at home, their relatives do not prepare or serve any food or drink; instead, this is brought in by friends and neighbors. This goes on for seven days. The two women chosen to work at the *kazan* prepare the food, wash the dishes, and perform the other kitchen tasks for that week. The same women also serve the food to the others who have elected to stay for the seven days of remembrance. As the close of the seventh day, the people who washed the body are presented with the best clothes of the deceased as a token of thanks, while the neighbors who served in the kitchen are each given a blanket or *korpya*, a block of soap, plus tablecloths, spoons, and a large bowl filled with rice. Significant events always become covered over with small, commonplace happenings, and these help to heal the wound of loss. Life goes on and takes us forward with it.

• • •

It is customary in Uighur villages that money be collected from each household and a large *kazan* purchased, along with two hundred trays, spoons, plates, and bowls, plus tablecloths and benches. These items are then used for *nazyrs*, weddings and other communal events. At the end of each occasion, they are washed, put away, and stored, ready for the next event.

Before we knew it, it was time to prepare for the seventh day *nazyr*—the wake for Gyuli-ana. On the appointed morning, people brought tables and benches into Yadikar's yard, where they were arranged under the vine canopy in two rows. Cloths were spread on the tables. On one side of the yard, men were butchering meat, while on the other side, women peeled carrots. These people included relatives, neighbors, and friends. Dzhanyam and Halidam, aided by other women, baked ten batches of *nan* in the *tono* and arranged them on the tables. The sight of these people, who had put aside their own affairs to support the family that had been afflicted by grief, was heart-warming. But ordinary people are like this—friendly and responsive to need.

Two days earlier, Yadikar had gone to visit Nizamdun, a cook well known in the village who was always ready to help, be it for a wedding or a wake.

"*Aka*, can you please prepare a special *plov* in honor of my deceased mother? Tomorrow we will kill a large bullock. Do come and see. If we need extra, we will also slaughter a sheep."

"Don't worry, brother, I will come and check everything," the cook answered.

The day before the *nazyr,* Nizamdun came to boil the meat of the bullock. He inspected the sliced carrots and estimated the quantity. He took a handful of rice, examined it, and let pour back into the sack. Only after this did he sit down with the others to drink a bowl of broth.

And now the day of the *nazyr* had arrived. Early that morning, Nizamdun had set to preparing the *plov* in two large *kazans.* By his calculation, each person would require roughly a hundred grams of rice, fifty grams of meat, eighty grams of carrot, thirty grams of oil, thirty grams of onion, and various seasonings. Normally, before starting to cook the *plov*, Nizamdun heated the oil to a high temperature and fried the meat together with the onion and carrot. He examined the type of rice, estimated the amount of water required and brought this to the boil in a separate *kazan*. While it heated up, he washed the rice carefully in warm water. Finally, he placed the rice on top of the fried meat and vegetables and poured in the boiling water. It was a perfectly ordinary recipe, but Nizamdun's *plovs* were particularly delicious; the guests always ate it with relish and complimented the cook.

By midday, more than three hundred men had gathered in the yard. After washing their hands, they took their places. The mullah said a prayer and blessed the *zhit*. Women poured tea for them and then began to serve the steaming *plov*. The men ate unhurriedly, in serious mood, talking quietly among themselves. The day was calm and sunny.

Toward two o'clock the men began to disperse. It was the women's turn. After they had washed their hands, the oldest women went into the house, while the younger women sat down under the canopy. Once again, they were first given bowls of *sin chay*, then, once this was complete, the fragrant *plov* was served on deep plates called *tavak*, after which the milky *aktyan-chay* was served.

By this time, sunset was approaching. The memorial meal was over, and the crockery was cleared from the tables. They gave thanks. Yadikar's wife Hushnyam, and his sisters Selimyam and Saniyam, brought four bundles of clothes into the room and placed them in front of Mervan-ana, Zaynaphan-ana and Maryam-ana, who had washed the body of the deceased, and

Sepiyam-ana, who had poured the water. Once again, the daughters wept a little, then said to the four helpers, "Please accept these things of our mother and do not be offended if anything isn't quite right."

Hushnyam then turned to Dzhanyam and Halidam. "Dear neighbors, you've worked so hard in the kitchen all these seven days. Thank you." Selimyam and Saniyam now put in front of them everything that they had prepared.

The two women declined, however. "No, no, what are you doing? We are close neighbors, almost relatives, you could say. And we helped you out of respect for your mother."

Appak-ana, sitting in the place of honor in the center, said, "Selimyam and Saniyam, you took good care of Gyuli, you kept an eye on her and took her to the doctor. But her days on this earth have ended. There is a day and an hour appointed for all of us. Yadikar is a deserving son who made his mother proud, even after her death. May the place where Gyuli lie down be soft, and may her soul be at rest. Good health to you all! And never let your mother's light, the light of your family, ever go dim." After saying these words Appak-ana raised her hands to lead a prayer, and the others followed her movements, bringing their palms toward their faces.

Afterward, Zaynaphan-ana spoke. "Dzhanyam and Halidam! May you have long lives! Thank you, dear neighbors, for everything. We will pray for your well-being."

All the women raised their hands to their faces.

The seventh day *nazyr* for the deceased Gyuli-ana was now over, and the relatives departed. The neighbors took Selimyam and Saniyam back to their homes. Hushnyam and her daughters began the cleaning up. Once everything was tidy, Yadikar went into his mother's room. Looking at the empty bed, he felt a wrench in his heart and once again he began sobbing violently.

His own young son Tairzhan came up to him, looked at his grandmother's bed and asked, "Papa, why did *moma* die? Her friends also got ill, but then they got better again. Why didn't *moma* get better?" He collapsed on the bed and cried.

Yadikar was at a loss as to how to answer his six-year-old boy. He stroked his head, wiped away his tears. "Don't cry. Your *moma* never liked it when you cry. I'll take you to her tomorrow."

The child looked up at his father. "I loved sleeping next to her so much. She used to tell me all kinds of stories. Who's going to tell me stories now?" He hugged his father.

"Your *moma* is in heaven, and she's watching us. If you want to make her happy, be a good *dzhigit* and remember what she told you."

Next day, as promised, Yadikar took his wife, little Tairzhan, and his daughters Unchyam and Guncham to the cemetery. Unchyam made a bouquet of her grandmother's favorite peonies and placed it in a jar of water. The cemetery was situated in a hollow below the mountain. The family walked up to the mound over the grave and stopped. Yadikar squatted down and said a prayer. They all whispered, "Amen," and passed their hands over their faces. Unchyam placed her bouquet of peonies on the grave.

Tairzhan had never been in a cemetery before. He walked about the mound that had been built over his grandmother's grave. He could not have imagined the amount of suffering and grief that had been her portion before she was laid out in the dark earth.

• • •

When I had finished my tale, I added, "So, where can children learn about grandmothers and mothers like Gyuli-ana, except from books? This is why I have written my book."

Ruth nodded agreement. The aircraft was droning along, trying to catch up with the sunset, but the wing was already bathed in pink light.

I looked at Ruth. "I don't know how much you know about what happened to us in the 1930s. The truth was covered up for decades. Almost all of our history from that time is a blank. So I had to rely on eyewitnesses for many events from that period. They remembered how some men were labeled as 'enemies of the people' and thrown into prison or tortured. Their wives and mothers, left at home with the children, had no easier a time; they were often forcibly relocated to unfamiliar places. The mothers held themselves together heroically for the sake of their children. Each of them, down to the last, hoped that their menfolk would come home. So what happened in our village is what happened all over the country."

"And what is the name of your village?" Ruth asked curiously.

"It's called Bolshoy Chigan. It's divided into two parts, the upper village and the lower village, by the Great Silk Road. There used to be not more than fifty families there, but it has gradually grown. And what used to be clay adobe huts have been replaced now with modern, good-quality houses. People have a better life there today. Before, we had only an outdated primary school, but now we can boast a ten-year combined school on three floors. Its classrooms are bright, and it has a sports hall and an assembly hall. The streets have proper asphalt, and there are flowers everywhere. The one thing that hasn't changed there is the ability of its inhabitants to work hard. They labor on the land, which they love and understand. But I want them also to know and understand our history. That's why the heroine of the book is Gyuli-ana, one of the women from the village."

"So was it her death that inspired you to start writing?"

"It wasn't just that. It was also that for many years, nobody could write or speak about the repression. Only decades later were the archive documents declassified and the truth became known. The times had changed. So, I decided to portray the suffering of thousands of people through the lives of an ordinary Uighur family."

"Will you tell me your story? From the start?" Ruth declined the tray of drinks proffered by the stewardess, while I took a glass of water.

"If you aren't tired yet," I smiled at my traveling companion, "then I'll start at the beginning."

$$3$$

EXILE

Gyuli was a fair-skinned girl who was not particularly tall. She was gentle in her movements and in her speech. Her eyes exuded a bewitching spark. She wore a modest white dress with little blue flowers that suited her very well. Gyuli would throw her long hair down her back, keeping her slender neck erect. One day, her mother sent her to visit old Hadzhyar-ana to take her some presents. As she was coming home, Gyuli bumped into a young man. She gave him only a single glance, flushing flushed red because this swarthy *dzhigit,* with his broad forehead, returned that glance. His face showed admiration. That fleeting encounter was to bring big changes to the lives of both Gyuli and Tairzhan.

It was not acceptable in those days for young people to meet and get to know each other without their parents' consent. Normally, the parents decided whom their children should marry to continue the family line. Once a decision was made, matchmakers would be sent to the girl's house; if her parents approved of the young man, the wedding would quickly follow. This is what happened for Gyuli. They held the customary Muslim marriage ritual of Nikah, after which Gyuli and Tairzhan set to building a house of their own.

Tair invited his friends to help with building the house. They worked day and night, and soon they had erected a small cottage with two rooms; they covered the roof with poles and coated the walls with adobe. Young Gyuli worked feverishly to make the house orderly and cozy inside. In the center of the living room, on a small piece of *koshma*, she placed a low table, a *dzhoza*, and around this, she spread out some *korpya* for sitting on. She placed a chest on the opposite wall, and on top of this she stacked several more *korpya*. The rooms were small, cozy, and warm. This was where Gyuli and Tairzhan spent their sweetest and happiest days.

The pair worked unceasingly. After five or six years, they bought a cow. Now Gyuli had sufficient milk and butter to feed her two small daughters, Selimyam and Saniyam. The young couple were in love with life, and they lived it with relish, not noticing how the happy days were flying by.

Tair's friends Dzhelil, Kudryat, and Adil also started families at about this time. Tired after long days of work, they would spend the long winter evenings together, talking or playing the *dutar*. The life and soul of the company, however, was Tair, who sang well and had candid and contagious laughter.

When the warm weather returned, the working life of the *kolkhoz* also resumed. Tair and his comrades went out to work in the fields. They dug *aryks* and cut and gathered hay. They sat boys on the horses and set to plowing. All the hot summer days were spent watering the crops. Each day, the young people got up before dawn to work on the harvest, cheerfully and companionably, like one large family. Their joking and laughter made the heavy work go easily.

At the hottest point of the day, when sweat poured down their faces and necks, the reapers, burning with thirst, would erect an area of shade out of branches. They sat down on the grass and ate melon and watermelon and drank sour milk. Often Tair's friends would ask him to sing some soulful song; his weary fellow villagers would listen, sigh, and look up at the sky. Sometimes they joined in, and then the surroundings would resound with their strong voices. And so, laboring from dawn to dusk, they scarcely noticed the passing of yet another summer.

In 1937, Tairzhan and Adil graduated college in the neighboring town of Zharkent. Tairzhan began working for the *kolkhoz* as an accountant, while Adil became a veterinarian.

Autumn brought cold winds together with incessant rain and early frosts. Alarmed, the villagers were forced to bring in the cotton as a matter of urgency. Every morning, the *brigadir* would ride through the village on his horse, pausing at every house to call out, "Hey, people, get up! Don't just lie there! The cotton's going rotten!"

Anybody who did not go out to the fields went hungry. This was because, rather than being paid in money, the workers were paid each day with a spoonful of *talkan*—ground roasted wheat. People who had not worked in the field that day would not receive their daily *talkan*. Forced to work in the rain in thin clothing and worn shoes, people caught colds and often fell ill for a long time. But the cotton had to be harvested at any cost.

One rainy autumn evening, Dzhelil came to see Tair. They had barely sat down at the table when Shavdun barged in, muttering "S*alam aleykhum.*" Shavdun was a cunning young man and nobody's fool. Many people disliked him, but no-one had yet been able to prove his guile. Gyuli made tea and put on the table everything they had in the house. Meanwhile Kudryat and Adil also turned up.

"Looks like we've got a complete *kolkhoz* meeting tonight," joked Tair.

"Well, what can you do at home when it's raining like this? We thought we'd drop by and persuade you to play some *dutar* for us. We could sing and talk," answered Kudryat.

Little Selimyam ran out from the other room. She looked at the visitors and said "*Assalam!*" and put her right hand on her heart and bowed slightly to the seated guests.

"Little one, may grace be upon you for your kind greeting," said Adil.

Noticing that the three-year-old Saniyam was about to follow her elder sister, Gyuli took them both away, saying: "Come on; let's go in the other room. There are visitors here; this is no place for children."

The men were talking, as ever, about *kolkhoz* matters, about the illnesses that were spreading as a result of the raw, damp weather, and about the indifference of the bosses to the hardships the people were suffering. Tair grew passionate and said many things that were entirely just. Dzhelil, however, a man of few words, said quietly to him, "It's no use saying these things, *adash*. Let's hear you play to us instead."

Tair realized that Dzhelil was hinting at the presence of Shavdun, not wanting to talk of such matters in front of him. He picked up his *dutar* and began to pluck the strings, and at once everybody perked up. Seeking to improve the mood of his guests, Tair sang a song before playing a folk tune. Again, Selimyam came out of the inner room. "Why not let our little one dance for you?" suggested Gyuli, coming out after her.

Selimyam had been waiting for those very words. She bowed and then began dancing. She did it with enthusiasm, forgetting herself, and the men clapped in time to the music. After this performance, everybody's mood had become more cheerful. The group of friends sat and talked a little longer, and then they made ready to leave.

"That was wonderful. Tair, Gyuli, thank you so much. You've raised our spirits. But it's late now, so we had better be going," said Kudryat.

Outside, the rain was still pouring. "Tair doesn't mince his words," they said to one another as they walked home. "He's so open and direct."

They often used to meet at Tair's house for heart-to-heart talks, or to discuss what was going on around them. But rumors had begun to reach the village of disturbing events. At first, people responded with astonishment and disbelief.

In a single night, however, the rumors were suddenly confirmed, when five or six men were declared "enemies of the people."

After seeing his friends out, Tair had gone to bed and fallen asleep before he became aware of strange noises. As he woke, there came a loud knock at the door and a voice, yelling, "Open up! Open up, I said!" The rough voices of the nocturnal strangers frightened Gyuli. A hard lump rose in her throat as she wondered who it could be, coming here at midnight.

Tair got up and opened the door. Two men in military uniform entered. One of them took a document out of his pocket, showed it to Tair and, knitting his brows, said, "Tair Husanov, we have orders to take you away with us."

"Bring some warm clothing," the other man added.

Tair felt dread spreading through him. Sweat broke out on his brow. He could not believe that what was happening was real. For a moment, an oppressive silence hung in the room; only the sound of the unceasing rain could be heard. Through his mind flashed the thought, "So this is what being 'arrested and taken away' means," but he did not say anything out loud. He dressed in silence. The soldiers ordered him to walk in front of them. As he crossed the threshold, he turned and saw Gyuli and Selimyam, who was holding onto her mother's skirt with one hand and wiping her tears with the other. In that moment, Gyuli's expression and his daughter's eyes meant more to Tair than the whole world.

Gyuli cried out in a breaking voice, "Tairzhan! Tair!" and froze, leaning against the wall.

Behind the soldiers, the door slammed shut. The rain was lashing at the ground.

Everything in Gyuli's eyes went black. She broke down in tears, holding her daughter tightly to her. The house already felt cold and abandoned. Worrying thoughts crowded into her mind. "What is Tair guilty of? Where are they taking him? Where will I have I go to find him?" But no answer would come to these unending questions. She lay Selimyam, who had fallen asleep on her lap, carefully down beside her little sister. She sat down beside them and looked at the two children sleeping so peacefully and began to sob softly. A little while later, she came to her senses and said to herself, "Crying isn't going to help. I've got to do something. I have no right to be weak. Not for my own sake, but for the sake of my daughters and for the child I am carrying. I need to be tough and persistent. Tair is not dead; he is alive, and one day he will come back. We will live happily again. But for now, I need to keep the house and feed and bring up the children." She tried to comfort herself, talking in this way.

When Soviet power had come to their region, there had been unrest. The White Guard stormed into the towns and villages, shooting Communists and Komsomol members and taking men prisoner. Later, Soviet power became established in Zharkent, and the process began of removing the *kulaks* and wealthy peasants—and those of only average means as well. They took everything. Arrests and shootings began. They took grain and animals from the inhabitants of Bolshoy Chigan, and there was nowhere to hide.

The sole exception was Tudmet, an *aksakal* who stood up against this arbitrary dispossession.

"What are you doing?" he demanded of them, shaking his fist. "What rich *kulaks* are there here? All the village families have seven or eight children. If you take away their animals, how are they going to survive? They are hardly feeding themselves as it is, and you will kill them outright!"

At that, two Red Army men beat the old man and took him to the edge of the village. They tied him to a tree, saying, "You have opposed Soviet authority, and that makes you an enemy." Then they shot him, without trial or investigation. This appalling injustice, together with the brutality that was everywhere, put fear into ordinary people. Many abandoned their homes and became refugees. Some of the Uighurs made it across the border to China—to Ghulja, Shuiding, Chilpanze and Dashigur. They had to submit to their fate and struggle hard to make ends meet in a foreign land.

The parents of both Gyuli and Tair had also crossed into China and settled in Dashigur. There was no possibility of writing to them. All of Gyuli's family that remained in the Bolshoy Chigan was her sister Maysimyam. She and her family lived on the same street, and the two sisters were very close and took care of one another. So Gyuli, having had no sleep all night long, took her children and rushed to her sister's when it was barely light. Seeing them arrive so early, Maysimyam became worried. "Goodness, it's Gyuli!" she exclaimed and pulled her tearful sister toward her. "What's happened?"

Gyuli could not answer and instead burst into tears again.

"Why are you crying? What's happened then? Tell me!" Maysimyam turned her sister's face toward her.

Gyuli sat down on the steps. "Last night two soldiers came and took Tair away. I don't know why!"

This sinister news made Maysimyam go cold. Just then, her husband Kurvan-aka came out of the garden, cool and unflappable as he always was. He came up to the two women and looked down from his full height at the crumpled Gyuli. When he heard what had happened, Kurvan-aka told them all to go indoors. "In these times, you mustn't talk candidly even with your own family," he said. "I love Tair as my own brother. But now he has paid the price of always telling the truth. You have to think ten times before saying anything. Truth can be bitter, and it's not to everybody's taste. That's how he made enemies. Gyuli, you've got to stand firm! Crying won't get you anywhere. They'll interrogate Tair, and in a few days, they'll let him go. And if they don't, we'll still see him again. Think about your children—look how afraid they are."

Meanwhile, Maysimyam had prepared *aktyan-chay*, which she now brought and poured into bowls. The subdued relatives drank the tea in silence.

Finally, Gyuli, exhausted, went home. A single thought thumped in her mind. *How can I get news of Tair?*

Word that Tair had been arrested spread through the village at lightning speed, and soon Dzhelil, Kudryat, and Adil were at Gyuli's house. Reflecting on what had happened in the night, they recalled their conversations of the previous evening in that very house and exchanged glances. They knew who had informed on Tair—Shavdun.

The three friends resolved to visit the prison in Zharkent. They had to find out everything they could about Tair.

"If you see Tair, tell him that all is well at home. Ask him what he needs." Gyuli stood up and pressed her hand to her heart. "If they don't release him today, I'll go tomorrow myself."

The men set off. Left alone, a deep melancholy settled onto Gyuli. The dark thoughts gave her no peace, and images flickered in her mind, each more disturbing than the last. She sat down, not knowing what action to take. At length the door opened, however, and in came her friends Zaynaphan, Mervanam and Mariya. They greeted her, hugged her, and sat down on the *korpya* spread out on the *koshma*. "Gyuli, cheer up! We're here, and we will help you. You're not alone," said Mervanam.

"There's nothing I need at the moment," Gyuli answered, unnerved.

The smartest and most resolute of the three, Zaynaphan fetched some brushwood from the yard and lit a fire, not allowing Gyuli to come near the hearth. Maryam poured water into a pot, a *kora*, and set it on the oven; gradually, it heated up until the water came to the boil. Zaynaphan now prepared *aktyan-chay* with the butter Mervanam had brought.

"Yesterday, I baked a large pumpkin in the *tono*. It was really sweet. So, I've brought half of it for you to try." Maryam placed a laden tray on the table.

"And I've brought an *apkur* of homemade curds," Zaynaphan added.

As they talked and drank their tea, Gyuli again began to feel anxious. "My dear friends, I'm so grateful to you," she said, holding back tears.

"I'm sure Tair will come home any day. Then this nightmare will be over," said Zaynaphan gently. "But you mustn't let yourself go to pieces in your situation. Remember, you've got a baby on the way."

"If God wills, you'll give Tair a fine son, and they'll go out to work together," Mariya added by way of support.

"Your Tair is very hardworking. Look, his yard is neat and tidy, he's got in a stock of hay, and he's laid in firewood for the winter," complimented Mervanam.

Gyuli smiled to hear these admiring words about her husband. "He built his own storehouse, you know, and keeps the vegetables in it." She pointed to a place to the right of the main door.

"If only we had husbands like that," whispered Zaynaphan.

Mervanam grasped the small of her back with her hands. "Oi, girls, something isn't right with me today. But remember, Gyuli, if your cow stops giving milk, I'll give you milk for your children. We'll all share whatever we have, right?" The other women nodded. "So now let's say the prayer."

After they had prayed, the women got up from their places. Gyuli went out to see them into the street.

"Let's hope our husbands will come back from Zharkent with good news," said Zaynaphan. And on that note, they parted.

As evening approached, Tair's friends came back to Gyuli. They evidently had no good news to give her from Zharkent. Gyuli did not take her eyes from them for a moment. Dzhelil quietly said, "Gyuli, we went to the prison, but were unable to see Tair. We sent a note in to him with your message. Tair sent a reply straight away. He said, 'They interrogated me today, and are accusing me of some pretty hefty offenses. But it is all lies. I don't actually know how I'll get out of here. And ask Gyuli to make me some warm clothing.'"

Gyuli felt weak all over her body, as though something inside her had broken away. The men, unable to give her comfort, sat with her for a few more minutes and then went home.

The days passed grimly. To obtain warm clothes for Tair, Gyuli went to visit the old woman shepherd Ryszhan-apay and explained the situation. The *apay* gave her a sack of wool, with which Gyuli knitted mittens, socks, and a scarf. She went to the prison every day but was unable either to see Tair or to leave food for him. She would come home again in tears. Whatever could she do? How on earth could she get her husband released? Nobody could give her an answer. Nobody could help her.

Then one day some news arrived. Tair had been tried and sentenced to five years' imprisonment and would be sent to a labor camp. When she heard this, Gyuli spent the entire night in preparations. Into a large sack she put a pullover, several shirts, and everything she had managed to knit, and on top placed a packet of *talkan*. Kurvan-aka contributed a pouch of tobacco and his favorite boots with puttees. Gyuli put the sack of things in a corner. Alone, as she waited for the dawn, she stroked her swelling belly and said softly, over and over again, "You will be five, son, by the time you see your *dada*." She looked at her two girls, sound asleep, then, going over to the window, came to a standstill, staring intently into the darkness of the yard outside. Her thoughts were heavy and bitter. After a while, Gyuli lay down next to her daughters and fell asleep.

Dawn had scarcely broken when Gyuli woke with a start and began to dress her sleepy daughters. Kurvan-aka and Maysimyam drove up in a two-wheeled cart harnessed to a donkey. Gyuli went outside holding the sack, which she loaded onto the cart. She then also seated her two girls, who had fallen asleep again, on the cart. By the time they set off for Zharkent, it was almost light.

The closer they came to the prison, the more people they saw. They were all heading in the same direction. Finally Kurvan's cart drew up by the gloomy hulk of the prison building. People were standing all along its iron perimeter fence. Clutching at the grating, they were looking out for friends and relatives, weeping and talking to one another—women with sacks, children, gray old people, stooping old women—and all were staring anxiously through the bars of the fence, trying to identify their particular relative or friend among the dense huddle of the captives.

Kurvan-aka, Maysimyam, and Gyuli with her daughters elbowed their way with difficulty through the mass of people. Gyuli spotted Tair at once. He was standing at a distance and was almost unrecognizable— unshaven, emaciated, with sunken eyes. There was nothing left of the old Tair she had known. With trembling hands, he rolled up a cigarette and started to smoke. Seeing her haggard husband, Gyuli felt nauseous; her heart constricted, and she could not take in enough air to breathe properly.

Meanwhile Kurvan-aka, who had experienced many things and learned to keep control of himself, called out in a stentorian voice, "Tair! Tair!"

Tair raised his head at the familiar voice, recognized the group of visitors, and made his way to the lattice, elbowing the other prisoners aside and putting his hands through the bars.

"Tair-*uka*, be strong! Don't worry about Gyuli and the children; we'll take care of them." Kurvan-aka squeezed the hand of his brother-in-law firmly.

Tair, just keeping control of himself, uttered, "Thank you. Please keep an eye on my family."

Gyuli pushed her daughters forward toward their father. Tairzhan kissed them through the grating and moved his hands over their faces. Next, he threw his wife an ardent look. Gyuli choked with pity for him. Her voice was inaudible when she said, "Tair, I've brought you some warm clothes. Try to come home as soon as you can. We will be waiting for you." Then she shouted out, "My love, we'll be happy again!"

Selimyam and Saniyam, holding onto their father's hands, repeated their mother's words tearfully, "Papa, please come home."

Now a man in uniform began issuing orders. "Fall in!" Hanging their heads, the prisoners fell into ranks. A strong wind was building and whirling up dust. Tair did not take his gaze from Gyuli. She could see how much he was suffering. Looking at his eyes, Gyuli thought, *My Tair, my one and only, will we ever see each other again?* Her heart was racked with pain and her face was wet with tears.

The crowd of prisoners moved away and disappeared, but the people who had come to see them off as they went to begin their sentences remained at the fence for a long time. Mothers, wearing white dresses, wailed, "Oh Allah, what offenses have we committed? What are these sins for which we are suffering? Will we live to see our children?"

The slow journey home and the steady thudding of the wheels of the cart on the stone road filled Kurvan-aka with bleak thoughts. What were these times that had come upon them? He thought again about how the White Guard came first, who brought shootings and confiscated the grain, driving away all sense of life. And then came the Soviets, and with them more executions, taking away everything that the people had meanwhile managed to reestablish. Anybody who opposed them was killed without trial or investigation. And now, yet again, they were capturing innocent people, calling them "enemies of the people" and sending them away to God knows where. Half a year earlier they had taken his brother Abdumanap, an honest worker at the *kolkhoz*. Nobody now knew whether he was alive or dead. Whom could he ask? Where could he have searched? And hundreds of other families were likewise weeping blood-stained tears for lost relatives.

Kurvan-aka sighed deeply. His own parents had worked themselves to the bone all their lives for wealthy *bays*. They had exhausted themselves and died young, leaving five children orphaned. His sister Adalyat lived near him in the village. His brother Abdumanap had been arrested. His sister Rozihan was living in Dashigur, across the border in China. And now he could see, as though right before his eyes, his little sister Patam—tall, big-eyed and pretty. When she was seventeen, she married a young man called Elam. Soon she was pregnant. When she was near her time, however, there was unrest in the village. Patam and Elam went to her older brother and said, "*Aka*, a group of us—a total of eighteen people, all relatives and close friends—have decided to cross to China. We'll be leaving in a few days."

Crossing the border was difficult at that time. People hid in the deserts near the frontier, sleeping under the open sky and fleeing pursuit on horseback. Some made it across. Others fell afoul of the Red Army and were shot, their bodies left where they fell for predators to deal with.

Kurvan-aka worried for his beloved *sinnim* Patam. He held her close to him and said to her, "God willing, we'll see each other again. Take care of yourself and your child-to-be. May you have a good journey. If you get to Dashigur, please give Rozihan our sincere greetings. Allah is merciful; he has taken care of you." Tearfully the brother and sister embraced one another. A few days after the group had set off, a rumor came back to the village. "Somebody has come across from the Chinese side. It seems he saw eighteen dead bodies in the desert."

All day, Kurvan-aka could find no solace, and in the evening, he went to the house where the arrival from China was staying and tried to extract the details from him. Yes, it transpired, one of the villagers shot at point-blank range was his Patam. And with her died her unborn child. Kurvan-aka began to cry out uncontrollably, falling to the ground and scraping at the earth with his nails. Did these murderers have souls at all?

When he now remembered Patam, he was again wrought with pain and choked on his grief. Tears poured from his eyes and disappeared into his black whiskers. He saw his sister lying somewhere in a pool of blood, her body not laid to rest. Then he sighed and shook his head. Life had to go on, even for those who suffer. He cleared his throat loudly, forced himself to calm down and admitted to himself that he was not alone in this torment. How many people were being made to drink from this bitter cup? They lived in savage times.

He came out of his reverie as they reached home. "Whoa there, you wretched creature!" He reigned in the donkey and drew up at the paddock.

Seeing Gyuli, Maysimyam came running over to them and invited them in for some tea. And Gyuli, who had not eaten a scrap since the previous day, now felt hungry. When Gyuli got up from the table after tea, she clutched at her lower back with both hands. Maysimyam, sensed what was to come, said , "Let me come and stay with you tonight. I think your labor is about to start."

She was right. Next morning, Gyuli was woken by birth pains. Maysimyam ran anxiously to the house of their aunt Hadzhyar-ana. Without even asking her how she was, as was proper, she said, "I need your help. Gyuli's gone into labor."

"Oh, Allah, show us the way! Has her time come, or has something just startled her?"

"It's her time," Maysimyam answered impatiently.

"*Bismillah*…" The old woman stood up, straightened the shawl on her head. She took a light *chapan* from its hook, put it on, put a pair of galoshes on her feet, and came out, locking the door behind her.

Hadzhyar-ana was already seventy. She had delivered many of the children of the village. She was lean, not very tall, and kept up with Maysimyam easily, saying to herself as she went, "I was the midwife to both of Gyuli's daughters. God willing I'll be midwife to the third."

When they arrived, Gyuli was walking round the room in circles. Her daughters watched her anxiously from the doorway to the inner room. When Hadzhyar-ana saw Gyuli, she exclaimed: "O Allah, O merciful Creator! Open up the way for us in this and let the birth go easily!" She felt Gyuli's belly gently. "When did the labor start?"

"Early this morning."

Maysimyam lit the stove and set water to boil, then unrolled some clean rags that Gyuli had prepared for the baby. She took her young nieces away to her own home at a trot, then came running back. Gyuli groaned incessantly, now pacing about and now sitting for a moment. After a while the labor began in earnest.

"Right, everything's ready to go," said the midwife, touching Gyuli's belly. "O Allah, these are not my hands, they are the hands of the holy mothers," she exclaimed, getting down to her task.

"It's a boy! It's a boy!" announced Hadzhyar-ana as she cut the umbilical cord.

Now that the suffering behind her, Gyuli felt immense relief. Tair had always longed for a boy. Now his dream was fulfilled.

The old woman washed the baby's ears, mouth, and nose. Then she dried him, wrapped him in his swaddling clothes, and showed him to Gyuli. "May Allah grant your son many years of life. May he be happy, prosperous, and may he support his parents in their later years!"

Maysimyam kissed her sister on the forehead, washed her face and hands, and handed her a large bowl of *aktyan-chay.*

"Hadzhyar-ana, you must be tired. Please have some tea and then lie down and rest," said Maysimyam gratefully, handing the old woman two cushions.

Wiping away the tears and sweat from Gyuli's face, Maysimyam looked down at her. "Don't worry, my dear. You and your children are alive. We will pray to Allah for Tair's return. Our *ana* is resting beside you. I'm going to rush home now. I've got a handful of flour there for this very occasion. I'll make some spicy *suyuk ash* and bring it over." She stood up, tossed some wood into the stove, and hurried home. Gyuli, after finishing her tea, fell into a slumber.

When Maysimyam returned with the evening meal, Hadzhyar-ana and Gyuli were sound asleep. Maysimyam set the *dzhoza* and poured the food into bowls. First to be woken by the aroma was Hadzhyar-ana.

"O Allah, I was sleeping so deeply. Have you already made supper?" The old midwife leaned her elbows on the cushions and sat up. "You'd better wake Gyuli and get her to eat. If she doesn't produce milk, the baby'll be restive."

Maysimyam woke her sister, placed a pillow under her back, and put a bowl of the soup in front of her. Gyuli's hands were weak and shaking.

"What a wonderful sister, always a support—in life and in death," the old woman observed as she started to eat. "You're like a mother to Gyuli. Now Gyuli, *kizim*, you need to eat something. You need strength, and the boy needs milk."

At that moment, Selimyam and Saniyam burst in from outside. They rushed to their mother and kissed her. They looked at the baby. Saniyam frowned. "Why is he so small?"

"But he's so sweet!" exclaimed Selimyam. "Mama, can I pick him up?"

Maysimyam picked up the sleeping infant first. "Selimyam, you must hold him with both hands. Don't drop him. If you want him to grow up into a big strong *dzhigit*, you must look after him well."

The sisters looked tenderly at the newborn baby, holding him close to them and trying to rock him to sleep. As she looked at this moving spectacle, Hadzhyar-ana smiled. "Gyuli, your boy has two wonderful little nannies."

After their meal and an unhurried conversation, Hadzhyar-ana turned to Maysimyam and said, "All seems well with Gyuli, so I'll go home. It's already getting dark," and started preparing to leave.

"Thank you so much. Sorry for causing you so much trouble. Why don't you stay with us for a day or two at least? After all, I'm your daughter too," said Gyuli, lifting herself a little from the cushions.

Indeed, once Hadzhyar-ana had also delivered Gyuli herself, and so in a certain sense was a mother to her. So now the midwife agreed now to stay for twelve days while Gyuli regained her strength.

On the twelfth day after the boy's birth, Kurvan-aka invited one of the elders, Zair-buva, to come and name the child. Kurvan-aka gave Gyuli five rubles of his own because the birth of a son had been one of Tair's wishes.

They drank bowls of tea, as was their custom, and then Zair-buva announced, "We will call your son Yadikar. It is in keeping with his father's name."

Gyuli nodded her agreement. It was an attractive, sonorous-sounding name. Zair-buva took the newborn baby in his arms and read out the appropriate *sura* of the Qur'an. Then he intoned the *azan* into the baby's ear, lifted him up high, and raising his voice, pronounced, "I congratulate you on receiving your name, Yadikar, who have been sent to us from heaven." He lay the baby down again on the *korpya*, wrapped him, and again took him in his arms.

Everybody present at the table turned to Gyuli and congratulated her.

• • •

Winter arrived, covering everything in a veil of snow. It fell from early morning to late at night, and the whole of the village turned white. The following morning the villagers busied themselves, clearing their yards and their flat roofs of snow. Snowdrifts appeared on the roads. After Gyuli had put everything in order in her yard, she decided to visit old Hadzhyar to see how she was.

"*Assalam*, Hadzhyar-ana! How are you?"

"Oh, it's you, Gyuli! Well, as for me, everything's well. But how are you managing with your three children, *kizim*?"

"We're doing fine, *ana*. The children are in good health. Look, I've come to take you home with me. Why do you want to spend the winter here on your own in this cold? We can live together and help each other out."

Thank you, my dear, but while I've got the strength I think I'll stay here. If I get unwell I'll come to you." And the old woman saw Gyuli out.

In the winter, the villagers lit their stoves and took the ashes out, fed hay to their animals, and cleared away the dung. They ate any leftovers from the summer harvest. On winter days, the streets were largely deserted, though you might occasionally see children taking carts to collect water or pulling a sledge laden with firewood.

All winter, Gyuli burned the firewood and *kizyak* that Tair had laid in during the summer months. She did not let the children be cold and ensured that the *kang* was warm at all times. Gyuli's friends were afraid to be seen visiting her for fear of being spotted by the informer. They came in the evenings, under cover of dark and with great caution. Gyuli, meanwhile, had grown thin and drooping and bore no trace of the beautiful woman who had lived so happily with Tair.

And today, as darkness fell, Tair's friend Kudryat came together with Zaynaphan to see her. "Have you had any news or letters from him? How is he, wherever he is?" they asked.

But ever since Tair was sent to the camps, there had been not a single letter. This worried them all. Her friends had told her about other *kolkhoz* members who had also been arrested as "enemies of the people." Gyuli was shaken. "What is this?" they asked one another, "Who could have informed in this village?" But none of them had an answer.

That evening, Gyuli could not sleep, tortured by thoughts. *Look at me; I live with our children in a warm house, but what about Tair? What if he's caught cold and become ill? Is he being properly fed or is he hungry?* And although she was lying on a warm *kang*, free to stretch her legs or to pull her children to her, sleep would not come.

She was also preoccupied the cow. Zaynaphan and Kudryat had noticed the cow that day, heavy with calf, and said to her, "She'll calve any time now. Make sure the calf doesn't freeze." For this reason Gyuli had got up twice in the night and gone out to the cowshed, candle in hand. But the cow was peaceful. She came back into the house. "Thank goodness Tair sealed the doorways with *koshma*, otherwise the cold would get in." She lay back down, pulled her baby son to her, and finally drifted off to sleep. At dawn she got up, washed herself, raked the ashes out of the stove, and took them into the yard. She looked in at the cowshed and found the cow licking her new calf.

"Thank God, the calf's well. My cow's a good one. This is for the children's sake," she whispered to herself, tears in her eyes. At that moment, she heard a cry from the street.

"Gyuli!" Going out into the yard, she saw the stooping old Hadzhyar, shaking with cold.

"*Assalam, ana!*" she called out, going over to her. She could see that things with the midwife were not good. "Come into the house, quickly," she said, opening the door and ushering her in. She closed the door tightly behind them.

Hadzhyar-ana clambered onto the *kang* straight away. "I went to bed a couple of days ago. That way there'd be no need to light the stove and no ashes to clear up. And then I thought I'd go to my daughter instead. So, you see, I've wasted no time and come early in the day."

"It's good that you're here, *ana.* I'll light the stove. You lie down and rest." Gyuli lay the old woman down beside her sleeping children. She then lit the stove and made tea.

Old Hadzhyar sighed. "What was I doing, lying there getting ill in that cold house when I have such a caring daughter?"

Selimyam and Saniyam woke up and cried out with delight. "Look, it's *moma!* Our *moma* is here!"

Hadzhyar-ana pulled some dried apple and dried apricot out of her pocket and held them out to the girls.

"Eat, my little ones." She stroked them on the head and kissed their foreheads.

"*Ana*, do you know, just as you arrived here, our cow gave birth to a calf," Gyuli said.

The midwife nodded. "Allah grants riches for children. And I have no children or grandchildren of my own, so I'll help you all now."

Gyuli's house was a warm and friendly place. The old woman forgot about her infirmity. Life had hardly spoiled her. Hadzhyar married when she was very young but was unable to have children. She and her husband divorced, and she lived for some years by herself. Later she remarried, this time to Tair's uncle, Mohammed-aka. Yet no sooner had they established a home of their own together than the White Guard descended on the village, rounded up the Komsomol members and Communists and shot them all. Among the dead activists was Mohammed-aka. Since that time, Hadzhyar had lived alone.

Gyuli had just finished washing the dishes when Maysimyam's eldest son came in and said, "*Kichik-apa*, our mother is calling for you."

Unnerved, Gyuli finished breastfeeding the baby and turned to her daughters. "If Yadikar cries, rock him gently to sleep in the cradle. I'm going to see your *chon-apa*. Don't make any noise. Your grandmother is asleep."

When they entered her sister's house, Maysimyam said to her, "They're sending my husband to Talgar for training."

"What's he going to learn? Is that far away?"

"They say it's a long way. The others going from here are Pahardin, Savut, and Imyar. When they finish their training, they'll come back to the village on tractors. Then we'll be working the land with tractors, not horses and bullocks. They can be used for sowing as well."

"That's excellent news. It will be easier for people."

Kurvan-aka entered. Tall and strongly built, he smiled at Gyuli. "You need to keep an eye on your sister! Look after the children together and help each other out. Something with Maysimyam isn't right. She keeps falling asleep on her feet. This morning she went out to milk the cow, and while she was there she fell asleep. It's a good thing I went out and found her. I don't know what to do. I can't turn down my tractor training. We're leaving tomorrow."

Gyuli looked nervously at her sister's face. It was as white as a wall. "Kurvan-aka, don't worry. I will stop by every day and see how things are. There are a lot of us in the village with illnesses like this."

"I've already told my sons, Tursun and Turgan. They are already big enough to look out for the younger ones and help their mother."

"Would you bring me medicine for my illness when you come back from town?" Maysimyam asked her husband.

"Of course, I'll find it and bring it. And I will come back as a tractor driver. There are new times ahead. From now on we'll be working on machines."

"So there'll be no need for people? If so, how will we manage to live?" asked Gyuli, disturbed.

"Well, it won't happen overnight. It'll be a gradual process," smiled Kurvan-aka.

Maysimyam and Gyuli gathered everything the men would need for their journey. After a while, Maysimyam's eyes began to close, and a sluggishness came over her movements. Concerned, Gyuli said, "What's this all about? Hadzhyar too is sleeping and never getting up. Have we been infected by sleeping sickness or something? Surely we aren't all just going to fall asleep and expire?"

From gossip she heard at the well, Gyuli found out that two or three people were suffering from the sleeping disorder in every house. Most of the people affected were advanced in age. It was said that in the next village, several people had even died in their sleep.

Soon after Kurvan-aka's departure, Gyuli and her sister brought out some tomatoes they had in store along with some dried peppers. Gyuli then set off to sell them in the Zharkent bazaar and use the money to buy flour and meat. At the bazaar, she told a milk seller she knew that she was looking for a remedy for sleeping sickness. The milk seller pointed to a short, stout woman of about fifty who was selling knitted items. "That Russian woman over there can cure illnesses. We call her Mama-Finya. Go and ask her."

"But I can't speak Russian, so how can I talk to her?"

"Don't worry, she knows Kazakh, Uighur, and Tatar as well."

After she had sold her produce, Gyuli went over to the Russian woman. She was wearing a large woolen shawl, a sheepskin coat, felt boots, and warm mittens.

She did not seem to be bothered by the cold; her cheeks were ruddy and red. It seemed as though everybody at the bazaar knew her. People were constantly calling her by name and greeting her. Gyuli also greeted her. "I've come to ask you for help." And she told her about her sister's condition.

Mama-Finya nodded, understanding the situation. "Daughter, this illness is caused by hunger. You should give your sister a bowl of boiled milk every morning, stirred forty-one times with a spoon. Go on doing this for forty days. If you have sugar or honey, then all the better. Give her grated carrot to eat and boiled beetroot. If you've got some meat, then make a broth with beetroot, onion, carrot, and potato. She needs proper nourishment. Don't worry. Your sister will get better."

"Eh, Mama-Finya, if we had food in the house do you think we'd be falling asleep from weakness?"

"Daughter, you must drink the milk in the mornings too, or you'll end up like your sister."

When the healer learned that Gyuli had children, she nodded toward some of her knitted socks. "Choose the ones that are the right size for your little ones."

"No, thank you," said Gyuli, "I've only got enough money for flour and meat."

"Go on, take them. I'm not asking you for money," the woman said to her. And despite Gyuli's protests, she thrust a present of them into her hands.

Shivering with cold in her thin *chapan*, Gyuli only just made it home. Coming into the warm room and seeing old Hadzhyar sitting on the *kang* with the girls, however, she felt better.

"Look at you. You're blue with cold! Go and take your coat off and climb up on the *kang*. I'll light the stove," said the old woman as she bustled about.

Still shivering, Gyuli looked at her son lying in the *beshchuk*. "Did Yadikar cry?"

"He cried a little, then I gave him a spoonful of water, and he quieted down."

Once Gyuli had drunk a bowl of hot tea, she stopped shivering. "Thank heavens you're here, *ana*, so I don't have to always worry about the children. Look, I managed to trade and get some flour and meat."

When the girls heard this they shouted out: "Mama, make us some *laghman* today!"

Woken by the noise, Yadikar started crying. Gyuli sat down beside the *beshchuk*, picked him up, and unwrapped him, talking baby talk all the while. She watched him as he sucked at her breast. How like his father he was! The same eyebrows, eyes, and lips. Yet the father of little Yadikar was probably trudging somewhere far away, knee-deep in snow in a blizzard. She shuddered and whispered, "O Allah, keep my Tair safe."

"So, how was dinner, Yadikar?" Gyuli patted the child gently on the back. "Now I'm going to put you back to bed. Let's see you sleep a bit longer, all right?"

Yadikar puckered out his little lips and began to babble amusingly.

"He came in to the world with ease, so he'll grow up big and strong. If God wills, he'll be crawling by the spring," said the old woman, not taking her eyes off them.

Selimyam and Saniyam observed what was happening attentively. Gyuli put down the baby and handed them the woolen socks. "These are for you from an old Russian woman." She then told them about Mama-Finya.

Cheered by the gifts, the girls quickly pulled the socks on and began to show off in front of the old woman, who was like a grandmother to them.

"I'm going to take some of these things to my sister," said Gyuli. She divided the flour and meat equally and set off to see Maysimyam.

When she arrived, Maysimyam was sleeping on her warm *kang*. She raised her head when she heard Gyuli's voice. "Is that you back already? Well, goodness, half a day has already passed. You walked to Zharkent in this cold?"

Gyuli put the flour and meat down on the table. Maysimyam could not conceal her delight. "Today at least, I can make something filling for the children."

Modangul, who was washing dishes, added, "Mama, Mahinur and I will wash some greens and we can make a nice *laghman*."

At that moment, Tursun-zhan and Turgan-zhan came in carrying firewood. The sight of the provisions on the table cheered them also.

Gyuli smiled sadly to see how much happiness a handful of flour and a piece of meat could bring, and how the children in both houses had become so animated. "Today the children will go to sleep on a full stomach, but tomorrow we leave to Allah." She remembered what the Russian woman had prescribed her.

"Sister, I've found out how to cure your sleeping disease." Gyuli told Maysimyam everything that Mama-Finya had advised her.

"Well, really! If it's just a matter of milk, then I'll definitely drink it as she says."

Tursun looked at his mother in her weakened state, then turned to Gyuli and said, "*Kichik-apa*, I milk the cow every day. Now I'll start boiling some every day and give it to mother. God willing, she'll be better by the time Father gets back."

"I'm going to make *laghman* today as well," said Gyuli, getting up.

Tursun and Turgan saw their aunt to the gate. A strong snowstorm was blowing outside. Gyuli wrapped her face in her shawl and walked quickly toward her house. After a few seconds her figure disappeared into the whiteout.

When she entered her yard, Gyuli filled a basin with *kizyak*, piled some firewood on top, and went inside. And so what if the blizzard kept blowing outside, blinding her eyes. Her children, satisfied by the food they dreamed of, would sleep soundly, and that was enough. For both sisters' households, today was a festive occasion.

The blizzard relented the next morning. People set to clearing their yards of snowdrifts, feeding the animals, chopping wood, and lighting their stoves. Having completed their tasks, Tursun and Turgan went over to Gyuli's to fetch water for her from the well. Gyuli helped them load the small wooden barrel onto the cart. As the brothers set off home and she closed the gate behind them, she saw her neighbor Rihanbuvi coming toward her. The two women greeted one another and then Rihanbuvi said, "You know my aunt's daughter, who lives in the upper village?"

"You mean Zorabuvi, Shavdun's wife?"

"Yes, that's her. Well, I'm afraid she died this morning."

Gyuli raised her hands and passed them over her face. "Was she ill?"

"She was helping with the cotton harvest in the autumn in the rain. She caught cold. She was forever complaining about a pain in her side. And she died of it. She was only twenty-one. She's left two little boys. I just came to tell you." Wiping her eyes with her shawl, Rihanbuvi began to hurry away.

Gyuli saw her to the gate, and then went back inside, shaking her head in regret. Evidently, sorrow came in both heat and cold.

Hearing the bad news, Hadzhyar began to lament. "And now all the responsibilities will fall to Zorabuvi's elderly mother. Oh, the poor thing! Both her sons have gone over to China, and Zaynaphan only stayed here for her daughter's sake. How will she bear this hardship now, in her old age?"

It is a general rule that if one of the villagers has suffered misfortune, the others cannot simply sit at home. So today, despite the heavy frost, Hadzhyar, Maysimyam, and Gyuli went over to Shavdun's house. Women were wailing in the yard. The men standing nearby were blue with cold. One of the oldest men in the village, Mahmut-aka, asked them to light a fire. They did so, and once it took hold, the men were able to warm themselves.

The women went inside the house, greeted one another and went up to the elderly Zaynaphan, embracing her. Old Hadzhyar held her grieving friend close to her, stroked her head, and comforted her. "Dear friend, crying won't bring her back. And you can hardly stand on your own feet anymore, you need to take care of yourself."

"I didn't want to abandon my daughter. I lost my sons for her sake," wailed Zaynaphan in her thin voice. "I thought she would be there to see me out… but she's gone, and still so young! It would be better now if she was weeping for me instead!"

An old woman sitting in the place of honor raised her hands for prayers, and they all fell silent. After the prayers, the conversation resumed. "I didn't let her go out to the fields," Zaynaphan said, shaking her head. "But Shavdun, once they made him the *brigadir*, he started forcing her out. In the fields, in the cold and mud, my *kizim* caught cold. Three months she endured that pain in her side—and today, see, they've laid my little dove out cold in the middle of the room."

Again she began crying bitterly. Hadzhyar-ana kept saying to her, "Zaynaphan, calm down. Death comes to old and young alike, it makes no difference. It's clear that this is our destiny." She straightened Zaynaphan's shawl and stroked her gray hair. The other women in the room looked with pity at the old mother as she grieved for her daughter.

The men dug the grave, even though the ground was frozen. Some women washed the body of Zorabuvi and combed her hair. And so another of Allah's children was committed to the earth.

On the way home, Maysimyam sighed deeply and said to those about her, "Is the only purpose of this life for us to suffer and then die?"

As they walked, the women talked about the two children Zorabuvi had left behind, now orphans. They also knew that the person to blame for Zorabuvi's death was her own husband, Shavdun. But none of them wanted to say so out loud.

• • •

The villagers were tired of the cold winter months and longed for spring. When spring finally came, the whole world awoke once more from beneath its snowy cover. The gardens turned green and blossomed, the sun shone radiantly in a clear sky. The morning crowing of the cocks, the barking of dogs, the neighing of donkeys, and the warbling of birds all heralded the return of life. When nature was reborn and showed its beauty once more, the human soul felt lighter. It was as though winter had brought only sorrows and grief, but the spring brought joyful changes.

Kurvan-aka and his comrades finished their course at Talgar and returned safely to their village. They then went to Zharkent to collect their tractors. Toward evening, the old men sitting on stumps saw two tractors rumbling toward the village and raising clouds of dust. They jumped from their seats, shouting out, "Oh, Allah!"

Mahsum, a joker, called out, "Hey, people, watch out! The iron tractors are coming! Get inside or they'll knock you flat!"

Some small children and old people, believing Mahsum's words, went running home. But Tursun and Turgan, seeing their father at the wheel of one of the tractors, ran out to meet him. "It's Father, he's driving the tractor!"

When they started plowing the land with the tractors, everybody, young and old, came running to see. The villagers watched with rapturous astonishment at this miracle. And so the spring work began happily and in a new way that year.

Every morning, the women set off with *ketmens* on their shoulders to dig the main *aryk*. Maysimyam, now recovered from her sleeping sickness, set off to work in the kindergarten. Gyuli was barred from working at the *kolkhoz*, however, as she was the wife of a so-called "enemy of the people."

"If I can't work on the *kolkhoz*, how will I feed my children?" she asked the management.

The chairman of the *kolkhoz*, Imyar-aka, replied dryly, "I'm just not allowed to employ you. That is an order from above."

The dismayed Gyuli turned to growing vegetables on her vegetable patch. Around the arbor that Tair had built, she and the girls planted pumpkins and climbing flowers. There had been a time when all the family had sat in this arbor and enjoyed sweet conversation and food. As she remembered that happy time, her eyes filled with tears.

One sunny day in spring, the mail carrier, Masim-aka, came up to her house on his old black horse and called out her name. Gyuli emerged from the garden and froze when she saw him. How long had she been waiting for this! She greeted Masim-aka and asked joyfully, "Have you got a letter for us?"

From his ragged cloth satchel, Masim-aka pulled out a letter. "It's from Tair."

Gyuli seized the envelope and rushed inside, her heart beating wildly. She took out the thin sheet of paper and began to read:

My dear family, greetings! How is life with you? If you are alive and well, then I will be happy. Gyuli, my dear, I hope that you have had your baby, and all went well? I think about you and the children every day. I know that it is hard for you but remember me, and things will be easier. If God allows, we will see each other again. It was hard for me to be parted from my home and village. They brought me and the other political prisoners to Siberia. Here it is very cold, we have knee-deep snow, and all around is the endless taiga. All day, from morning to evening, we fell trees. The work is very heavy, but there's nothing for it—we can't escape our fate. But for the sake of seeing you, I will endure it all and survive...

Gyuli read each word, trying to extract all the meaning. When she reached the end, her shoulders shook. She held the letter to her breast. Now old Hadzhyar and the girls came in. Seeing Gyuli with the letter, she asked with concern, "Daughter, it looks as if you've had bad news?"

Gyuli responded almost inaudibly, "I've had a letter from Tair." She burst into tears again.

"Mama, when will Papa come home?" asked Selimyam impatiently.

Gyuli started to read the letter again, out loud. When she finished, the old woman said gently, "Well, that's good. Tair's alive and is working with the others. This is a trial, and we must be patient. Let's look forward to celebrations in our street."

Six months had now passed since Tair's arrest. One day Gyuli became agitated, without knowing why, as though sensing trouble. She could not concentrate on anything. Later that day, after the cow had come home from pasture and they had lit the lamp in the house, there was a loud knock on the door. Two men in uniform entered.

"Would you be the wife of Tair Husainov?" one of them asked in a steely tone.

Gyuli's arms and legs were shaking. "Yes, I am," she whispered. They made her feel guilty.

One of the officers held a document out in front of him and began to read loudly, "The family of an enemy of the people is not permitted to live in a border zone. You are required to relocate within a period of twenty-four hours or you will be arrested." When he finished reading, he handed the paper to Gyuli.

"Get yourselves ready. A truck will come by tomorrow. It will take yourselves and two other families from this village to Chilik."

"Where am I supposed to go with three small children? What am I guilty of?" Shaken, Gyuli shifted her gaze from the officers to Hadzhyar. The old woman waited for the two strangers to leave, then began tearfully to curse everybody and everything. But Gyuli's eyes were dry. "Hadzhyar, I hope they won't keep us in Chilik for long. Meanwhile, you can live here in my house. My sister's boys live nearby and will help you. But I've got to leave." She started to gather items of clothing.

Sobbing, the old woman began to help Gyuli. Soon afterward, Maysimyam appeared, having heard the appalling news. She brought a few items of food. Clasping her sister to her, Maysimyam began to sob. Still Gyuli did not shed a single tear.

"Don't cry, sister, I'm not going alone. There are three families going from here."

Hearing of the latest misfortune, Mervanam and Dzhelil, Adil and Mariya, and Kudryat and Zaynaphan came to comfort her. Again, Gyuli did not weep.

"The others going with you are the families of the bosses who were arrested in December. They are also "enemies of the people," said Adil.

"What are these times that have befallen us? It's all very well if Party workers and bosses are guilty, but what's that got to do with ordinary villagers? All we know about is how to use a *ketmen* to dig ditches. It makes your heart bleed!" cried Kudryat angrily.

When her friends heard that Gyuli had had a letter from Tair, they began asking her about it. All but breaking down in tears, she told them what he had written.

"But there must be better times on the way. Sooner or later we've got to be able to laugh and sing again. But for now, it's a matter of fighting for our lives," sighed Adil.

"Gyuli, nobody will make you happy where you're going," added Kudryat. "We hope you are able to find work, bring up the children, and one day can come back home."

The women friends simply sat and wept.

Eventually Gyuli's friends bade their farewells, left food for her, and went home. Maysimyam kissed her, her daughters, and Yadikar repeatedly. She left in tears.

Next morning as the sun rose, three families—twelve children and four women—were loaded into the back of a truck and driven away to Chilik. Not a single person came to see them off.

• • •

The roar of the aircraft filled my ears. Ruth, who had been listening to me with her eyes half open, now seemed to come to life. Straightening herself up in her seat, she sighed. "But what are those children guilty of? They're innocent victims of a policy."

The flight attendant came to our seats to see whether we needed anything. But we were still deeply immersed in that distant time. I recollected the years past, and Ruth tried to comprehend the pain and terror felt by these people she did not know.

After a pause, I looked at Ruth.

"I'd like to hear what happened next," Ruth said.

4

WOOL AND CLAY

During the journey, the mothers, surrounded by their crying children, gripped by the most morbid sense of foreboding, tried to make sense of their desperate plight. Among them was Alahan-hada, the mother of seven children. Her mother, the elderly Rozihan, was in tears the whole way. Alongside Gyuli was Tadzhigul with her two children. From time to time, she would be overcome by bouts of coughing.

"Where are you from originally?" Gyuli asked her.

"I'm from Donmiallia, just outside Zharkent. We were a peasant family. My husband's parents crossed the border. They arrested Askar, my husband. They accused him of having contact with China, although he never received so much as a letter from there." Tadzhigul broke out in a fit of coughing that prevented her finishing. She put a handkerchief to her mouth to try to stifle the coughing.

Gyuli gave her some water and saw that the handkerchief was stained with blood. "I see you really are unwell. How will you manage away from home?"

"If I can just survive until Askar comes… I don't want to leave the children complete orphans."

Tadzhigul looked at her son, asleep in her arms. For the rest of their journey, Gyuli tried to help her wherever she could.

The three families, none of whom had ever traveled further than Zharkent, were taken to the settlement of Chilik. They were dropped outside the Kolkhoz Workers' Club, where many women, old people, and children had already arrived from various districts—all families of "enemies of the people." There they were left to fend for themselves. The local inhabitants had learned from bitter experience and were wary of helping the new arrivals, so they avoided them. There was no work here for the mothers, nor was there a chance of education for their children. The mothers begged for help, but their appeals went unanswered.

Their first task was to find some kind of shelter. Gyuli, with her three children, and Tadzhigul with two, settled in a half-ruined building with a single room. They did what they could to make it habitable, washing it out and putting the stove and *kang* in order. Gyuli took to walking through the village in search of some kind of work; the food they had brought from home had already run out. So she was delighted when, walking around the periphery of the village, she discovered clay. Her mother knew how to fashion *tono* ovens from clay; she and her sister had used to help her when they were small. The women would now mold these ovens and sell them in order to feed their children.

Tadzhigul seized on the idea. The two women began heaping clay into sacks and dragging them to the house. Gyuli ripped open a quilt, which was stuffed with wool, made long ago by her mother. While she tore the wool up into small pieces, Tadzhigul and the girls fetched water from the *aryk*. After combining the wool with clay, Gyuli added water and began to puddle the mixture until it became a homogeneous mass. The heat and the heavy work caused her to sweat profusely, but there was nothing for it; they had to earn money and feed the children.

To make a *tono* oven, it was necessary to turn the clay mixture they had prepared twice a day, morning and evening. They sprinkled a little water over the place where the clay had been and covered it with old sacks to prevent it drying out. After six or seven days, the clay mixture could be considered "ripe." Now they would dig a hollow in the ground to suit the size of oven required, in which they laid the first layer of the mixture. Small pebbles were placed on top of each layer. They would become very hot when the oven was fired. They added another layer each morning and evening, with a slightly smaller diameter each time. The result was a dome-shaped oven with an opening in the top—a *tono*. Now the oven was built, it had to be thoroughly dried out in the sun. Anybody who bought an oven was advised to carefully light a fire of dry dung bricks in it for six consecutive days, as this would cure the inside of the oven properly and give it a protective coating of carbon. Only after following this procedure should they fire the oven with wood to bake their *nan* flatbreads.

Despite the laborious work and the heat of high summer, Gyuli did not wait for the first oven to dry before she started on the next. And, one by one, she began to sell the ovens to the local women.

Selling the *tono* became a profitable undertaking for Gyuli. She was happy because this gave her an income with which she could support her family.

One day on her way home she bumped into Alahan, the mother of seven.

"Good heavens," Alahan exclaimed, "how thin you've become! Have you been ill or something?"

"Not at all, my dear Alahan, I'm in good health. It's just that I've been making clay ovens in this heat. And thanks to that, I've been able to go to the bazaar and buy flour, meat, butter, and vegetables. How are you? How are you managing to feed your children?"

Alahan remarked that Gyuli had not only lost weight but was also sunburned. Her eyes had become sunken, and she had wrinkles that extended to her temples. She had aged by ten years.

"Gyuli, come and see us this evening," Alahan said to her. "I'll teach you some lighter work."

Gyuli nodded agreement and went home. Scarcely had she opened the door before she heard Selimyam's voice:

"It's Mama! Mama's back! We're hungry! Tadzhigul-hada has fallen over again." The girl was holding Yadikar, whom she now held out to her mother.

Gyuli put down her sack and picked up little Yadikar, then went to see Tadzhigul. She felt the other woman's forehead.

"I'm already feeling better, sister. Please don't be angry with me for being such a burden," she began.

"Don't you ever say such things! It is important that we are here for each other."

"Well, you know the saying: I've no strength, but can't tell you where it hurts," Tadzhigul said, trying to smile. "My sight went dark, and I fainted."

"Let me go and make some noodle soup, or we'll all be fainting with hunger."

Selimyam and Aminam rushed to peel vegetables. Instead of squabbling, Gyuli's and Tadzhigul's children looked after Yadikar, played together, and did domestic tasks. Yadikar could already crawl and was even trying to stand up.

The keen aroma of grilled, seasoned meat so taunted the ravenous children that they would have jumped into the big metal *kazan*; they did not take their eyes off it for a moment. As soon as the noodle soup was poured into the bowls, the children fell upon the food greedily.

"Sister, I will remember your kindness for the rest of my life. You have taken care of me like a mother."

"Enough words, *hada*. Eat up. You need to build up your strength," Gyuli replied.

While they were eating, Selimyam said, "Oh yes, *apa*, an old woman came today asking for a *tono* and she said she would come by tomorrow with a cart. She said to make sure you were home. *Apa*, if you sell one and buy some flour, will you make us some *nan*?"

"Yes, my little one, I'll make *nan*, and I'll buy you clothes for winter."

Gyuli remembered that Alahan had invited her to visit. She ought to go and see what kind of light handicraft she had in mind for her.

After dark, Gyuli made her way stealthily to where Alahan lived. It was quiet all around, with only the occasional soft whistle of the night birds. She entered the house to find grandmother Rozihan surrounded by her grandchildren.

"Ah, Gyuli, is that you? Alahan's been waiting for you. Come in, sit down."

Greeting her, Gyuli went in and sat down beside the old woman. Alahan brought some Uighur tea and started to talk about her life and situation.

"Two of my older sons work on the plantation, harvesting melons. The foreman, Akhmat-aka, tells everyone that they are his relatives. Two of my daughters knit clothing, and I help them if I have spare time. I also managed to bring a hand-operated sewing machine from home. I sew all sorts of things on it—dresses, suits, quilted jackets. I cut down old clothes for the children. People give me vegetables or flour for this."

"Tell her about Big Dzhanyat," old Rozihan threw in to the conversation.

"Big Dzhanyat lives on the next street. One time she brought her old coat to me and said, 'My daughter's getting married. Would you turn this old coat inside out and alter it for her?' I worked sewing that coat for four days, and when I gave it to her, she did not even say thank you. Today I sent my daughter round to her, but she threw her out of her house grumbling, 'I'm sick of these orphans!' But that's life—you do meet ungrateful people like this."

"If you haven't experienced something like this, daughter, you'll never understand somebody who has. They say the full man doesn't understand the hungry, and for a good reason," grumbled grandmother Rozihan.

Alahan now leaned toward Gyuli. "And the light work I was talking about is yarn and knitting. In our house, mother combs wool and spins thread and the girls knit."

"When you get to my age, spinning isn't easy. Afterward your hands ache all night," complained Rozihan. "Gyuli, I can teach you to spin."

"I'd be very happy for you to teach me a little."

"It's easier than making ovens," Alahan remarked.

"I'll go to the bazaar tomorrow and buy some wool, then I'll come here for a lesson," Gyuli promised.

"Are you getting letters from Tair?" the old woman asked.

"I've only had one, from Siberia. I wrote back straight away, and now I'm waiting for a reply."

"It's a harder life in those penal colonies than we have here. May Allah grant him strength and patience." Alahan drew breath. "I haven't had any letters from my husband at all."

They went on sitting together, drinking tea and sharing their burdens and concerns.

"It's getting late, I'd better go," Gyuli remembered suddenly. "Tadzhigul's very ill, and I'm worried about her."

"May Allah grant health to us all, and may He preserve us," said Rozihan, raising her hands in prayer.

From that time onward, Alahan often sent her sons to Gyuli with a melon or watermelon, asking how she was.

The days passed in their appointed order. Gyuli and Tadzhigul had a single aim: not to allow their children to die of hunger. The children were growing fast and were doing everything they could to help their mothers.

Every evening an old woman selling milk would pass their window. Catching sight of her, Selimyam would shout out, "*Apa*, the old woman's here who sells milk!" and rush outside. Aminam, who was her age, would run along beside her, and behind, with short, mincing steps, came Saniyam, holding on tight to the hem of her sister's dress.

The girls nurtured Yadikar. He grew stronger and stronger on his legs and was already starting to talk. Tadzhigul's son Omar was a quiet, shy boy.

This year Selimyam and Aminam would have gone to school, had they not been branded as belonging to the families of enemies of the people. This injustice outraged Gyuli to the core. But she herself was secretly teaching her children to count and to read and to write the letters of the alphabet. Imitating her mother, Selimyam took it on herself to teach the younger children. Her sincere desire to help and to be seen as a grown-up greatly pleased Gyuli and Tadzhigul. And in a short time, the children started to know the illusion of a normal life.

The hot summer reached its end; now autumn arrived and plunged the world into gold. But with it came new worries. Gyuli and Tadzhigul began to lay in a stock of firewood, collecting brushwood from the land outside the village, sawing up dry branches and stacking them. In the evenings, they knitted. Gyuli, having mastered the craft, also taught Tadzhigul to knit. By the dim light of the lamp, the mothers held heartfelt conversations and knitted children's clothes. On bazaar days, they sold the clothes, and the proceeds sustained them. They were grateful to Allah that this winter they would not go hungry.

One evening as they sat at their knitting, Gyuli gave Tadzhigul a worried look. "The good days are ending. The wind has changed, and there will be snow soon. We need to save up for a stove, or the children will catch cold."

"Why don't we give up milk? We can survive on tea. That way we'll save money," Tadzhigul replied.

"But if the children get nothing but tea and a scrap of bread, they'll be completely emaciated. Look, they're already just skin and bone."

"So let's buy a stove, and then there'll be money for food again."

Without reaching agreement on the matter, the two women sighed.

"Whose fault is it that there is no happiness in our lives and that our families have been scattered about the earth like millet?" said Gyuli. The two women lay their work aside and sat without speaking. After a while, they lay down beside their sleeping children and fell asleep themselves.

Life in exile from their village was becoming intolerable. Yearning to be allowed home, Gyuli and Tadzhigul began to haunt the doorways of various offices, begging and weeping, and in 1940, ten families were given permission to return. They were told to move to the village of Koktal, some seventeen kilometers from Zharkent.

• • •

"But why didn't they just let them go back to their own villages?" asked Ruth, shaken. "Why torture the children so much, children whose fathers had been sent to prison for no crime? How was it possible to trample the rights of people so much?"

"I think those politicians and officials had hearts of stone," I replied. "I'm not sure they could really be described as humans."

I looked out of the window. Dusk was gathering; the clouds below us were turning gray. We were brought dinner, but Ruth declined any food. I soon finished my meal and put down my fork and napkin. When I looked round, Ruth was giving me a questioning look.

"Would you like to hear more?" I smiled. "Well, then, we'll carry on."

5

THE SCENT OF THE HOME COUNTRY

In Koktal, Gyuli and Tadzhigul again shared a house and were well used to helping one another. Alahan, with her mother and her children, also managed to make the move. Things were a little easier here, as they were allowed to see their relatives and friends.

Tadzhigul's parents and relatives began to visit and bring food. When they learned from their daughter how Gyuli had helped her and the children, they vowed to pray for her good health every day.

Gyuli's sister Maysimyam also soon came to Koktal with her elder son, Tursun. She gasped when she saw how Gyuli had aged and grown thin over the past two years. The two sisters held each other and wept for a long time.

"Well, the worst is behind us," said Maysimyam eventually. "At least the children are healthy. Life in the village is slowly getting back to normal as well."

Gyuli asked about Hadzhyar.

"She's still living in your house," said Maysimyam. "She's planted the garden and is keeping chickens.

My sons built her a chicken coop. She's getting quite old, but she's still coping by herself."

"How is she managing with the animals?"

"After you were sent away, people from the government came and announced that all animals owned by enemies of the people now belonged to the *kolkhoz*. We wept and made a fuss and eventually persuaded them to let us keep the calf. It turned out to be a heifer. She calved just a few days ago. Hadzhyar-ana does not have the strength to milk her, so Turgan does it. And so, thank God, we're alive and well. And now, you tell me about your ordeals."

"What haven't I gone through in these two years?" said Gyuli quietly. "Look at me, and you'll see. I lived only for the children and worked round the clock to put bread on the table. I endured it all for the hope of coming home." Tears were running down her cheeks.

Now Selimyam and Saniyam came rushing and shouting into the house and threw their arms around their aunt. Little Yadikar huddled up to his mother and watched Maysimyam in silence.

Tursun picked up Yadikar. "Well, well, Yadikar, what a big *dzhigit* you've become already!"

Maysimyam, meanwhile, was doting on the girls. "My my, mama's little helpers, how you've grown!" She kissed and hugged them repeatedly.

Tadzhigul offered them all tea. They sat down at the table, talking excitedly, and their anxiety faded. The two sisters kept looking at each other and talked unceasingly. Maysimyam and her son spent the night with Gyuli and returned home next morning.

Gyuli threw herself into work of all kinds in Koktal to provide for the children. At the same time, she also applied in writing to all manner of official posts for permission to return home; she longed to go back to the little house she and Tair had built and had been happy. Another year passed. Then, in springtime, the three exiled families were granted permission to return home. The women and their children joyfully loaded up a truck, and by evening they were back in Bolshoy Chigan. Old Rozihan lifted up her wrinkled hands and exclaimed, "Oh, my Allah, thank you! We've come home alive. There is nothing else for us to wish for!"

The sentiment that there is no place like home was surely true for most people if not all, and the older a person got, the more he or she appreciated it. Longing for home was most poignant for those who were forced to remain far away. And that evening, the three returning families would be able to breathe in the air of their native village and inhale the aroma of the food they had known since they were children. By the time they arrived, however, it was growing dark. They would have to wait until the next day before they could take a look around the village to see what had changed.

Gyuli jumped down, took some of the sacks containing their belongings, and started down the familiar little path to her house. Behind her rushed Selimyam and Saniyam, all the while outrunning each other and gripped by an irrepressible joy. They were the first to burst into the yard and began trying to outdo each other in banging on the door.

Inside, old Hadzhyar had dozed off. She got up and came to the door, worried by the unexpected arrival. Seeing the two girls, however, she stood, overcome, unable to believe her eyes. With shaking hands she pulled them to her. "Oh, my Maker! Is this really you?"

Now Gyuli caught up and also embraced the old woman. "Will you have us back, my dear?" She was smiling and weeping at the same time. "We've come home!"

Hadzhyar-ana came to her senses and began fussing about and chattering. "Well I thought I'd die without seeing you again. But here you are at last! My little nanny-goats have come home. Oh Allah! How long these three years have been!"

The excited group went inside. Hadzhyar sighed deeply when she saw how thin Gyuli had become, and even wept a little out of pity for her. Then she began fussing again and put everything on the table that she had managed to gather and preserve—milk, cream, curd, and *kurt*.

Soon the whole family was sitting and drinking hot, fragrant tea. They looked at each other over and over, smiling with happiness. Selimyam and Saniyam laughed and ran from room to room. Yadikar tried to run along after his sisters but fell, and then got up and got back to running after them. Gyuli looked round at the familiar walls, where every corner and every detail reminded her of her youth and her love, of Tair's tender glances and of the birth of her children. Soon, however, their warmth and happiness brought on tiredness, and they began to fall asleep. Their faces were softened by hope and joy, and they were protected in their sleep by their own home.

Early the next morning, Gyuli went out into the yard. Greedily she gulped in the cool fresh air of her home village. She paced about the yard, looking at everything closely. The crowing of cocks, the barking of dogs, the birdsong and the smell of smoke from the chimney in the morning silence gave the village a homey feel and heightened her sense of relief. She sat down on a bench in the arbor and remembered her father's words. "Love the land where you were born. Value everything, from the sky to the smallest blade of grass. Respect all people, and obey your father and mother, your husband, and your relatives." She wondered where her parents were now. Were they even alive?

As Gyuli sat there deep in thought, the old woman came out of the house with the *kumgan* for performing her ablutions. "You're up early, daughter. Couldn't you sleep?"

"I slept soundly in my own house," smiled Gyuli. "But now I can't get enough of this fresh air."

"The old people say, 'In your own home, the heart rejoices, and the feet are free.' I've planted pumpkin and convolvulus around the edge of the shed, and on the other side of the ditch I've put marigolds." Hadzhyar-ana proudly showed Gyuli her handiwork.

Gyuli washed herself, then went to the cowshed, bucket in hand. Just as she reached it, Maysimyam's son Turgan ran into the yard.

"I'll do the milking for you, *apa!*" he called out. When he saw Gyuli, the boy stopped and threw up his hands. "Why, *kichik-apa!* When did you get here?" He ran to hug her. "I'll tell mother, and then I'll take your cow out to the herd." He darted away.

Gyuli woke her daughters. No sooner had they put away their bedding and put the table in place when Kurvan-aka arrived with Maysimyam and their children. They all embraced and began smiling and gazing at one another.

Eventually they settled down. Kurvan-aka, sitting in the place of honor, glanced at Gyuli, then at her children, and said, "You've suffered a lot while you were away. Still, true heroes that you are, you held out through it all and have made it safely home. You should spend some time settling in and recovering—take ten days to rest—and then you will have to join the women working in the fields. We're at our busiest time at the moment. I'll tell the *brigadir*."

Gyuli nodded gratefully. "There is only one thing I ask of God, which is that our children never have to face such evil times as we had to undergo."

Rumors of the return of the three families sent to Chilik now spread all through the village. Gyuli's friends came by to welcome her home and to hear her tales of life in exile.

After just a couple of days, Gyuli started working, filling in the places where the plasterwork had come away with a mixture of wet clay, planting vegetables in the garden, and sowing seeds for flowers. Old Hadzhyar warmed herself in the sun and admired her hardworking daughter. "The old people say that work loves the young," she said. "Gyuli, when you came back, happiness returned too. Everything has started to shine in the house and in the yard."

"And thank you, *ana*, for looking after the house so well," Gyuli replied. "You've taken good care of it for these three years. Thank you, a thousand times, and may you live forever!"

"Well, in the meantime, Rihanbuvi and her daughter Saram and her children were living in my own house," said Hadzhyar-ana. But back in the spring one of the walls fell in. My house got damp all through and has completely collapsed."

"Don't worry about that. You'll come and live with us, won't you? You're like my own mother to me, after all."

"Hmm. Once I was considered to be the hardest-working laborer in the village, but look how decrepit I've become." Hadzhyar-ana looked at her wrinkled hands.

Gyuli stroked the old woman's gray hair. "*Ana*, you can grow old with dignity if you stay with us. You've never been a burden to anyone, and you always help other people. Everybody still looks up to you today." She kissed the old woman repeatedly.

From the henhouse came the voices of Selimyam and Saniyam. "*Moma*, we've given the chickens their grain. They're all pecking at it, but the white broody one won't move."

"Leave the white hen alone. She's hatching her eggs," warned Hadzhyar. "When she's ready, she'll get up by herself and will eat and drink."

The old woman felt lightness in her heart. God had not granted her children of her own, and yet, in her twilight years, she had been given these wonderful children. She was grateful to Gyuli for what she had said and felt happy.

"Gyuli, Maysimyam's invited us for tea today," she reminded her daughter, then bustled happily off to the chicken coop.

Maysimyam served her long-awaited visitors with large flatbreads fried in butter with onion and poured out fragrant *aktyan-chay*. Everything showed that her home life was falling into place. Now that Kurvan-aka had assumed his function of tractor driver and worked by the sweat of his brow, the *kolkhoz* management had begun to appreciate him. Yet he always remained his old self—taciturn, even-tempered, open, and direct. Life had not indulged him. When he had been a boy, Kurvan had had to give up school in order to help his parents. He respected educated people and did everything to enable his sons to continue their education in secondary school in Zharkent once they finished primary school. "Go on studying," he would say to Tursun and Turgan, "or you'll end up like me, breathing dust and overburdening your back."

When they were not studying, his sons joined the other young people working in the fields or digging *aryks*. In the villages, children as young as ten would go out to help the adults. When Tursun finished school, Kurvan-aka said to him, "*Balam*, there's a pedagogical college in Zharkent. You should go there and train to be a teacher. Then you will be respected. Teaching children is sacred work."

The son's wishes coincided with the father's desire, and Tursun entered the college. His parents were very pleased, and his sisters, anxious not to be left behind by their brothers, also did well in school.

Gyuli delighted in hearing this news and was pleased for her sister and brother-in-law. "I wish I could educate my children too, so that they could be of service to others," she said wistfully.

"You can do that now, Gyuli," said Kurvan-aka. "There's been a decree that from now on, "children are not answerable for the deeds of their fathers." Sepiyam's teacher told us about it. So now your girls are allowed to go to school."

Gyuli felt her spirits rise. Then Hadzhyar also broke into a smile.

Kurvan-aka went on. "It's been hard for us as well. We didn't manage to bring in the cotton in the autumn, so had to go out and pick it in the snow. The villagers were out there knee-deep in snow, half-clothed and without shoes, working their fingers to the bone. A lot of them died as a result. But as of this year—at last—we won't be sowing cotton. Let them grow it where it's warmer. We're changing over to wheat, oats, and maize. This will be a massive relief for everyone."

The next morning, Gyuli cleaned out the cowshed and then set to molding wet dung bricks on the wall, ready to dry out in the sun. While she was doing this, Shavdun rode up to her fence on his horse and announced, "From today you will take your *ketmen* and go out to the fields. Our women are digging the *aryks* and irrigating the wheat." He then turned his horse abruptly and rode off.

Shavdun looked haggard and was covered in dust. He had tried to avoid eye contact with Gyuli. Clearly, he had not recovered after his wife's death. Meanwhile Gyuli was secretly pleased to have been called to join the work brigade; she longed to be part of the communal work again and to be alongside her friends.

"Very good, my dear," nodded Hadzhyar when she heard about Shavdun's order. "If they've called you, then go and work. I'll look after the house and the children."

Gyuli told Selimyam and Saniyam to keep a close watch on Yadikar. He was a playful and curious little boy. His mother tied some lunch up for herself in a shawl, threw her *ketmen* over her shoulder, and went out into the road. Some of her friends were already coming toward her. Mervanam, Mariya, Zaynaphan, and other women were thrilled to see Gyuli join them, and they chattered cheerfully as they walked, scarcely noticing when they arrived at the work site.

Out in the field, all was a frenzy of brightness and color, and the air was laden with the scent of flowers. This multi-colored world was bewitching and stirring to the soul. How Gyuli loved this place! She could never get enough of admiring the beauty here. These vast fields, these trees with their spreading crowns of branches. The only thing missing was Tair. Gyuli kept seeing him every time she looked up, as though he were somewhere beside her…

Here, working again alongside her friends as they laughed, joked and sang, Gyuli felt her heart, long frozen, begin to warm through. Once more, the days rushed by barely noticed, and the horrors of the past years gradually began to fade. One Friday, however, Gyuli had a bad dream. She woke up in the night, shaken, and could not get back to sleep before morning. Inside her she sensed trouble. She did not, however, mention it to anybody.

• • •

"So what was her dream about?" asked Ruth with concern.

"I'll tell you about that later on." Mehriban smiled. She was pleased that Ruth wanted to go on listening.

6

A Letter of Parting

The days continued to pass in their endless stream. Once Gyuli and the other women had finished digging the *aryks,* they changed to irrigating the wheat. One hot day, as they took their lunchtime rest and were drinking tea in the shade of some trees, their *ketmens* laid aside, Tursun arrived unexpectedly and went up to Gyuli. "*Kichik-apa*, my mother has asked you to stop work for today and go home."

"What's happened? Is something the matter?"

"I don't know" is all that the boy said. It seemed to her, as he turned and hurried away, that he was hiding something from her. For several days, ever since her bad dream, Gyuli had remained in an anxious state, and now she sensed that trouble had found her. A sudden weakness came over her whole body and she looked at her companions helplessly.

"Go home, go on," they told her, "you should go and see what's happened. It must be something or she wouldn't have sent for you."

Mervanam got up and said to Gyuli, "Whatever it is, I'm coming with you." She straightened up her dress and the two women set off.

When they reached the house, out of breath, they were met by silence in the yard. The door to the house stood ajar. Gyuli crossed the threshold and found Kurvan-aka and the village elders, Mahmut-aka, Davut-aka, and Zair-aka inside. They were all sitting with mournful faces, and Gyuli felt her heart break loose and begin pounding convulsively in her chest. She was barely able to bid them good day. Then she saw Hadzhyar, sitting by the window with tear-stained eyes. Unable to utter a word, Gyuli dropped her gaze to the floor and froze in that position, biting on a corner of her shawl. Silence filled the room until it was broken by the soft, sorrowful voice of Zair. "Daughter, as you know, where there is life there is also death. We have received news that Tair has died. Be strong!"

It was as though Gyuli did not hear the last two words. Her face turned as pale as the wall, her lips went blue, and then she fell unconscious to the floor.

The old woman called out to Mervanam, "Get some cold water and splash her face."

The two women sprinkled Gyuli's face and began to rub her hands and shoulders. She came to and looked round, bewildered, and broke down in tears.

"Come now, my dear, be strong! Remember you've got three children."

The pain of loss was familiar and understandable for old Zair. He squatted down and began reading from the Qur'an. After this, they all expressed their condolences to Gyuli and to Hadzhyar and left the sorrow-filled house. Maysimyam came and tearfully embraced her sister. They wept together at length, clinging tightly to one another. The children came in, and without understanding what had happened, clung to their mother and cried with her. As she held them tightly to herself she wailed all the more.

"My poor little lambs! Your mother's suffering has still not come to an end. Your father has been taken from us. He's been kept from us forever! Oh, Tair, my love! And he's taken away the dreams we had together. Oh, Lord, did you only bring me into this world in order to suffer?"

"Gyuli, please, don't cry so loud, you'll frighten the children," urged Mervanam, though she was crying as well.

The tragic news spread fast round the village, and one by one, friends and relatives began to visit. Again and again the air trembled with groaning and weeping. When Gyuli saw Tair's friends weeping for him, she howled in despair. "I've lost my Tair, Dzhelil! How much he longed to come home. Tair, your children have become fatherless! My poor Tair, how much they tortured you, my Tair."

Old Hadzhyar looked tearfully toward Gyuli and tried to persuade her to calm down but was unable to restrain her own weeping.

The elderly Zaynaphan, who had come to give her condolences, thought back to the death of her own daughter and said tearfully to Gyuli, "We have to hold out through everything that we are sent, my dear. What can we do? Now you'll have to act as the children's father and their mother. And may God make it easy for you."

The other women spoke in agreement. Then when old Rozihan arrived with Alahan and Tadzhigul, who had been her companions during the difficult years in exile, another wave of lamenting filled the room. Each of them was also grieving for the suffering that had been their own lot.

Mervanam, Mariya, and the younger Zaynaphan, who had taken charge of the *kazan*, began to prepare *omach*, a soup containing pieces of dough. So, although Tair's body was somewhere far away, his people remembered him with a traditional *omach* and then went to their homes.

Tair's death struck Gyuli like a bolt of lightning. She could not come to terms with her loss, nor could she come back to her ordinary self. The dream she had continued to nourish, the dream that one day he would come home and live happily together, was gone. Ahead of her lay nothing but tribulations. Would she have the strength to face them, or would she, like Tair, eventually succumb and cease living in this world? Then what would become of the children? Horrified at having entertained such a thought, she said to herself firmly, "No, never think like that. I need to live for the sake of the children. They are Tair's and mine!" She looked up to the sky, where the bright, joyful sun was casting its golden rays generously upon all.

Less than a month after the arrival of the tragic news, the postman Masim-aka brought Tair's last letter. Gyuli had just returned from the fields, stoked the fire in the hearth, and had begun to prepare the evening meal.

She took the letter and pressed it feverishly to her heart, then opened the envelope with trembling hands.

Hello, my dear ones! How are you? Have you returned home safely? Gyuli, my love, you are a courageous woman, and I believe that you have great power of will. The very fact that you are bringing up our three children, despite all the hardships and humiliation, is heroism in itself. I am forever glad to have been able to spend those happy days with you in the house that we built together.

If you are wondering how it is for us here, then I will tell you that many have died, unable to survive the backbreaking work and the appalling conditions. And I, too, am lying down, seriously ill. For the sake of the children, and for your sake, I ask Allah for good health, but who knows what will be? Gyuli, if something should happen to me in these distant lands, please tell the children when they are a little older that their father was a prominent man, kind and brave and honest, but never was he an enemy of the people. All that is a lie.

The day will come when people will realize that we were pure and honest, that we worked for the people tirelessly. But for now, we—thousands of intellectuals along with ordinary uneducated people—have been made the victims of a loathsome policy. If I could come back home I would tell you how many good and worthy people have died because of this policy.

How much I long to come home, to see you and to talk with you, heart to heart! But with every day that passes I grow weaker. Gyuli, the

Tair you knew is no more. I am like a skeleton with skin stretched over it; my heart goes on beating softly, but the rest of my body died long ago. Gyuli, you are the dearest thing to me in this world. So now, although you are left without me, please bring up our three children. I ask Allah that you will be able to see them grow, mature, and achieve something in life. Kiss the children and hold them for me. Please give my greetings to my relatives and friends. And be happy.

It looked as though Tair had wept as he wrote the letter. Tears spattered the paper, together with drops of blood from when he had coughed, which made some of the words impossible to read. Gyuli reread the letter several times and stood fixed, deep in her thoughts. She then remembered the dream she'd had the previous Friday. In the dream, Tair seemed to be lying beside her. He said, "Why is there such an enormous distance between us? I was only just able to reach you. Gyuli, my love, I cannot live without you, and that is why I have flown to you, to take you with me." After saying this, he caressed Gyuli and kissed her.

She answered him sadly. "Tair, I would go with you without hesitating for a moment, but the children are still small, and I cannot leave them." She lifted her hand to touch him, but Tair had vanished.

Then Gyuli had woke, shaken, her heart beating wildly and her body shivering. Remembering the dream now, she let her eyes roam about the room. It felt to her as though Tair were here in the house.

"He's leaving this world physically, but Tair's spirit has come to us." Wiping her tears on her sleeve, she got up. She had no right to sit idle when the children needed to be fed.

That night, Gyuli could not sleep. Whenever she closed her eyes, she saw Tair lying withered and exhausted. The sight of him like that crushed her heart.

She rose early the next morning, washed, whispered "Bismillah" and filled a tea bowl with clear, cold water. She said a long prayer in remembrance of Tair, drank the water, and then, paying no attention to anything, went out into the yard.

From the cowshed there came the mooing of the calf. It was probably hungry. Gyuli's first task every morning was to check up on the animals and chickens. But today, like somebody with no obligations whatsoever, she heard neither the mooing of the calf nor the clucking of the chickens.

The sun rose higher. Gyuli went into the garden and breathed deeply of the cool morning air. Her gaze fell upon some trees in the garden that Tair had planted and upon the wattle fence of willow switches and thorny twigs that they had built together to enclose the garden.

"It's no use dreaming," she said. "I need to get busy if the children are to eat." She picked up the *ketmen* and began loosening the soil around the pumpkin and weeding among the potatoes, then brought water from the *aryk* to water the eggplant, tomatoes, and peppers. She was so occupied with her work that she did not notice how much she was perspiring. A sense arose in her that together with the perspiration, she was also sweating away her suffering and anguish, and she began to feel more at ease.

Old Hadzhyar came out carrying a cast-iron *chugun* and was pleased to see that Gyuli had had the sense to occupy herself with work. While she made tea, Gyuli went to milk the cow, took the cow out to the herd, then fed the chickens, cleaned out the cowshed, and managed to mold a few more dung bricks.

Now the whole family sat down to morning tea. "You must have got up with the sun," said Hadzhyar to Gyuli. "You've got so much done in the garden!"

In the last few days, Gyuli's face had become even more brown, and she had grown still thinner. Yet although her eyes concealed sorrow, she said, calmly and unexpectedly, "Yes, I couldn't sleep any longer, and then when I went into the garden there was so much work staring at me. So I did some before going out to the field. Selimyam, would you and Saniyam please weed the two onion beds in the vegetable patch? The onions have done well, but there are a lot of weeds. But make sure you weed them carefully and don't trample any of the onions, all right?"

"Of course, Mother. And you've sown *osma* and *hina* for us too?"

"Yes, the *osma* is next to the onions. I sowed the *hina* along the side of the *aryk*, and I think it's already started growing. And would you weed the flowers as well. Be very careful not to pull up the flowers with the weeds. Yadikar, you're not to go out in the street. Just play in the yard."

"Mama, I want to go and play with Arup next door."

Hadzhyar finished drinking her tea, swept the crumbs from the table into a bowl, and raised her hands for prayer. The others followed. Then Gyuli heard women's voices in the street and stood up. "Be good children now, and don't be a nuisance to your *moma*," she said, picking up the lunch that the old woman had prepared for her, placing the *ketmen* on her shoulder, and leaving of the yard.

Though they were poorly dressed and half-starved, the women and girls did not complain as they went out to the fields. Instead, they kept up their spirits with jokes and banter. And today, once they had properly irrigated the wheat, they all gathered together for lunch and began talking. "Boss, go and get some tea," called out Mervanam, seeing Shavdun riding past on his horse.

"Thanks. And you, you can have a rest, but don't forget about the water." He said nothing more and turned toward the village.

"Poor old Shavdun. He's got a lot older and so thin," said Adalyat sorrowfully, watching him riding away. Adalyat was a woman of medium height with a white face, attractive eyes and brows, and a name that suited her very well. It came from the Arabic name *adel*, meaning "just" or "fair." People respected her, maybe because she was a little older than the others, or perhaps because she looked after them all.

"Well, find him a suitable woman and marry him off," chuckled Zaynap.

"Who'd want him in the state he's in at the moment?" asked one of the others.

"Well, heaven knows, he's so pathetic because he's on his own. But get him hitched to a good woman, and she'll scrub him and dress him up, and he'll soon be the big *dzhigit* again," said Adalyat, demonstrating with her thumb up.

"It's so long since Zorabuvi died. Poor thing, and he's left with two children. But at least he's still got Zorabuvi's mother - how'd he manage without her?" said Maryam.

"Well," said Adalyat, playfully, "why not marry him to Saadat?" She gave a crafty smile and glanced inquisitively at Saadat. Saadat's eyes widened, and she hid behind Gyuli.

"What are you looking at me like that for? Isn't Shavdun your type?"

"No, he isn't. When I want someone, I'll find him myself," said Saadat. She got up, hurt, and went off with a friend to look for *segiz*.

"Just look at her," said Adalyat, finishing her tea. Then her look fell upon Gyuli, who was sitting opposite her.

Nobody dared to joke with Gyuli. Her face was serious and gloomy. Fearing that Adalyat might turn her attention to her next, Gyuli got up and tossed her *ketmen* onto her shoulder. "You go on and finish your tea. I'm off for a while."

Mervanam followed her. They walked along the *aryk*, directing water to where it was needed and gathered two large heaps of brushwood; these they tied up ready to take home with them. Mindful of the harsh cold of winter, Gyuli gathered a bundle of brushwood almost every day.

That evening, when she had returned home with the bundle of firewood on her back, she found old Momun, Tadzhigul's father, and her mother, the elderly Patam, waiting for her. Once they had exchanged the traditional greetings and asked one another after their health and family affairs, the old man said, "Gyuli, we've only just heard the news about Tair. Tadzhigul told us today, so we have come to express our condolences, to remember Tairzhan, and to pray for him."

"You can't change what fate deals you, so you will have to take courage and be patient," said Patam, wiping her tears. "It would have been wonderful if Tairzhan had come home to you, but what can you do? It wasn't to be. So, daughter, you need to be strong. Let your children carry the light of Tairzhan. Good health to them all."

Momun read from the Qur'an, remembered Tair, and prayed at length. The old woman and Gyuli thanked him and then started discussing household matters. While they did so, Selimyam set the *dzhoza* table in the middle of the room and placed a cloth over it.

"I've brought some things," said Patam, and put on the table a bowl of *zhutta*, four small *nan*, two packets of tea, material for a dress for Gyuli and a shawl for Hadzhyar. "Hadzhyarhan, Gyuli, please at least accept these little things. Don't be offended that we weren't able to come to express our sympathy at the proper time."

Hadzhyar and Gyuli stood up and thanked her. "Why, you didn't need to worry, Patamhan. We're grateful that you have come from Zharkent to give your condolences," said Hadzhyar.

Gyuli and Tadzhigul went out to the *kazan* and poured out the *suyuk ash* that the old woman had prepared for them. To the four eggs she had fried in the *kazan* she added beans, pumpkin seeds, and a little basil and coriander for seasoning. They then brought the tasty smelling *lapsha* into the room and served it into bowls. Maysimyam arrived, and Gyuli noticed that she had come alone and asked why Kurvan-aka was not with her.

"He only came home for a minute. He just had his dinner and went straight back out to the fields. They'll be plowing until dawn."

They ate unhurriedly, talking about past times. When the old Patam and Hadzhyar started discussing their relatives, it became apparent that they were related.

Wiping the sweat from his brow with a white cloth after the hot food, Momun began to speak about the death of Tair. "In my seventy years, I've seen much that is good and much that is bad. As far as I can see, these troubles have spared nobody. My own elder brother Akvyar, an *imam*, was condemned and then arrested. He was a believer and he never meddled in anything. All he did was pray to God and taught Islam in the *medrese*. But one evening in 1937, he was accused of issuing anti-Soviet propaganda. They interrogated him, they tortured him, and in the end, they branded him an enemy of the people and sent him to one of the Siberian camps. After some time, we received a document confirming that he was dead. My poor brother. In his declining years, he couldn't survive this torment. All this was a terrible ordeal, both for my brother's family and for us." He wiped his eyes with the kerchief; they had begun to shine with tears.

Moved by the old man's story, Hadzhyar now told them about her husband Mahammyat, tears also building in her eyes. "What didn't we suffer, all of us? How much patience we humans have! And Tair also was no stranger to me. He was the son of Mahammyat's sister. But now, here I am, grown old and living with Gyuli, looking after her children. I thank heaven for these times."

"You're right, Hadzhyar-han, helping each other out and talking peacefully over tea—this is how we can comfort one another. What could be better? Our Tadzhigul could hardly work on the *kolkhoz*. She's so weak she can barely look after the children. We have decided to take her and the children to Zharkent, where she can get treatment. God willing, Askar-zhan will come back home."

"And Gyuli, there is a saying. 'A good thing is never forgotten.' For three years, you did all you could to look after our daughter, and we will never forget that. May God grant that you will see your children's good fortune in life." Tears ran down old Patam's hollowed cheeks as she spoke.

Gyuli served the *zhutta* that Patam had brought on plates and poured hot, freshly-made *aktyan-chay* into bowls. They went on talking for a long time, discussing the things they had experienced and suffered. Each of them began to feel a sense of ease.

After the prayer at the end of the meal, the guests got up from their places. Tadzhigul embraced Gyuli tightly. "All good health to you, sister. I don't know whether we'll see meet again. God knows. Thank you again so much for everything."

Tadzhigul was very pale and thin. Every now and again she would cough and break out in sweat. Gyuli saw that the spark of hope in her eyes was fading. "Tadzhigul, sister, don't cry. You'll recover. Tell yourself you're going to live for the sake of your children. Then you'll get better."

But Tadzhigul's eyes were like a dying flame. The two women, who had overcome all the tribulations of three years of exile, both sensed that they would not see each other again.

Sometime later came the news that Tadzhigul had died. As though she had lost a member of her immediate family, Gyuli cried bitterly. "What sort of a treacherous world is this? They say that death is indifferent to young and old, but who's to blame for Tadzhigul, still so young, going down with an incurable illness? What have her parents done to deserve this? And her children, now left as orphans? What will happen to them?" She tried to puzzle these questions herself, then, finding no answer, she broke down in tears.

• • •

"My story isn't boring you, is it?" Mehriban looked over at Ruth.

"No, of course not! Far from it. The characters of your book are becoming real for me. I'm impatient to know what happens to them all."

"You know, we were brought up in the Soviet system, which taught us to show great respect to people who wear medals and decorations on their chests. This is because they fought at the front for our peace and safety, and we are well aware of this fact. And yet, just think how much effort was also expended by the women who stayed at home in the villages, who replaced the men in the fields, and how much their health was sacrificed, working outside in the rain, in the cold, and the knee-deep in mud.

"They grew wheat and carried sacks of grain on their frail shoulders, along with all the hardships of those times! None of them got medals or decorations, and many people now have no idea of how much they helped bring Victory Day closer through their hard work. They worked from morning to night and were paid only a scoop of roasted wheat per day. Yet, those women never gave up. On the contrary, they put their will to the test and held out. We are still amazed today by their resilience.

"Today's young people simply can't imagine the conditions in which those women had to live. For them, it's just a legend. Never real.

"The women had reasons to be grateful for their lot. They could sell vegetables from their plots and take eggs from their chickens to the shops, and they became skilled at buying meat and butter at the bazaar, and tea, salt, soap, and sweets in the shops. They thanked God for all this, saying they'd go through anything for the sake of the children, to ensure that they would never know war and could live in peace. There were women from our village like this, who were able to live through anything, regardless of what happened."

"I saw a film," said Ruth, "that highlighted the heroic efforts of Russian women during the Second World War. Your story has only confirmed what I learned. Please, keep going."

7

TROUBLING NEWS

The harvest looked promising in June 1941. The young wheat swayed in dense golden waves, and the villagers had hopes of a rich yield. Young people mowed the lush grass to make winter feed for the animals, and in the cool of the mornings, they gathered sweet clover. All around, the high-spirited shouts of the lads and girls rang out in song. The life of the village seemed at last to be running a peaceful course.

The high summer days also brought plenty of work at home. Apples and apricots swelled with juice, and the vegetables in the gardens ripened. Gyuli was working in the fields from morning to evening, so it was left to Selimyam and Saniyam to pick and dry the tomatoes by themselves. And Yadikar, now growing fast, was the family's best gatherer of berries. Old Hadzhyar did not sit idle either; she cut coriander and basil in the garden, washed it, and laid it out on a tablecloth in the yard to dry out.

"*Moma*, why don't we dry apples and apricots on the roof this year?" suggested the girls.

"No, I'm afraid we can't. There was a leak in the roof because of all the rain in the spring, and it might fall in if you climb on it."

The house, which was left without its proper owners for three years, now needed attention. For this reason, when it was announced that the harvest was to begin in a few days, Gyuli arranged with the *brigadir* to take two days off. Her first task was to fix the roof. She dug a small pit at the edge of the yard and prepared an adobe mixture of straw and clay. Then she called her nephew Turgan to help her, and between them they managed to cover the whole of the roof with the mixture.

Knowing that she would shortly be occupied from morning to night with work in the fields, Gyuli harvested everything she could from the vegetable patch and garden, loaded up a cart, and drove to the bazaar. The money she made selling her produce she spent on provisions, and on dresses and school things for the girls. Hadzhyar sewed them rag bags for carrying books. It was still a long time before school started, but even so, the girls tried on their new dresses every day. By now Selimyam had reached the age of nine and Saniyam was two years younger. They could hardly wait for September.

On June 22, the collective farmers went to help the young people mowing the grass. When the work was in full swing, the chairman of the *kolkhoz* appeared, together with a representative of the local government. The chairman seemed to be at a loss. He called all the villagers together and spent some time scrutinizing the gathering.

"Dear comrades, the war has started," the chairman said eventually, then was silent.

The farm workers, not fully comprehending, looked at each other in silence. The chairman cleared his throat. "Comrades! Early this morning the fascist German army treacherously attacked our motherland," he shouted. "Now there are rallies taking place, and men are being called up all over the country to fight against the enemy. The government has declared the Great Patriotic War."

The listeners held their breath, trying to grasp what they were hearing.

"The war has come, comrades," the chairman said quietly.

Now the local government representative spoke. "Comrades!" He looked round at the mothers and fathers, the *dzhigits* and the girls. "This is now wartime. From tomorrow, the men will start to receive call-up papers from the enlistment office. So be prepared! And as for all women and children, the work in the fields will be left to you. We need to ensure our soldiers are well supplied with provisions! Be strong! Be courageous!"

Noise broke out among the crowd gathered. There was worry on their faces. The men frowned and clenched their teeth while the eyes of the women were shining with tears. Hard times were coming for everyone. Would they be able to halt them?

"Comrades!" called Kurvan-aka, stepping forward, "The news of the war has shocked us all. But I suggest that we gather our strength right now and help the women with the haymaking as much as we can. Let's continue working until we get our call-up papers, and this will help our mothers, wives, and sisters to manage when we're gone. And it will help ensure that the harvest doesn't spoil and they aren't left hungry. Then we can go to face the enemy with an easy conscience."

The chairman and the government representative agreed with Kurvan's speech. A representative of the young people said that the boys would go to the recruitment office themselves and write declarations of readiness to volunteer for the front.

After the meeting, everyone who had been in the field hurried home.

From that day onward, the people knew no peace of mind. Weeping could be heard in all the houses. A few at a time, fathers and sons set out for the front. The first to leave from our village were Dzhelil, Adil, Kudryat, Arup, Mahammyat and others—ten men in total. The men who remained in the *kolkhoz* were asked to work day and night under the slogan *All for the Front, All for victory!* But the main burden of the farm work fell onto the shoulders of the mothers, children, and old people.

The harvest began in August—the toughest time of the year for the villagers. The mothers we know— Gyuli, Mervanam, Mariyam, Zaynaphan, Adalyat, Roshangul, and others—worked themselves to the point of exhaustion from morning to night. They set an example for the rest.

Each day they harvested not just a thousand square meters, but fourteen hundred. Because they exceeded the daily quota by so much, they were designated Leading Women. This, however, drained them severely. They went home in the evenings and collapsed with exhaustion. They would weep in despair and curse at all and sundry. But the morning would come, and the women would rise again at the crack of dawn, rubbing their aching arms, legs, and backs. They each would set about tidying their yard, milking their cow, and fixing new dung bricks to their wall. Then they drank a bowl of tea, picked up their sickles, and set off again for the fields.

Children were not exempt from the war effort either. They were forced to grow up fast and share the burden with the adults, gleaning the fields after the harvest. From early spring right through to late autumn, all who remained in the village, from seven to seventy, went to work in the fields.

Kurvan-aka could not understand why he had not been called up to the front and felt that perhaps he had done something wrong. One day at the evening meal he said, "They called Pahirdin up today. Tomorrow I'll go to the recruitment office as well and ask why they haven't sent me papers."

Tursun now glanced at his parents and then moved his gaze to his brothers and sisters. "*Dada, ana*, I got my call-up today. I leave for the front in three days."

Hearing this, everything went dark before May-simyam's eyes. She pressed her hands to her breast. "Accursed Fascists! You make mothers grieve! This war is depriving us of husbands and sons! What will happen to us?" She wiped her moist eyes with the tip of her shawl. "Will I see you again?" she addressed Tursun with anguish.

"Don't cry, Mama. I'm not going to the front alone," he said, trying to comfort her.

"And yet, they still take a child away from his mother. Mothers feel when a part of her heart has been torn away." Maysimyam sat motionless. The war had reached her own family and now loomed over it, over her village, and over her country.

Tursun was now nineteen. He looked every inch the *dzhigit*—tall, handsome, serious like his father, equally hardworking and a pure nature. Now the story of his love began. One of his fellow students at the Zharkent pedagogical institute was Saadat, who also came from Bolshoy Chigan. They became friends, then fell in love, and then swore that they would spend their lives together. So Tursun the *dzhigit* planned that once their studies were over, he would make a formal proposal of marriage, sending a matchmaker to Saadat's home. But then war came. No more studying for him, no more thoughts of marriage. He had to prepare to leave for the front.

8

ARDENT HEARTS

On the day before his departure, Tursun and Saadat met for the last time in the garden of her house. The young man and woman stood with their gaze fixed upon each other. The warm evening darkened into night. Tursun embraced Saadat tightly and kissed her lips; she laid her head on his chest as they stood together beneath an apple tree. They heard a nightingale singing, and they felt the beating of their own hearts. Tursun's arms were strong but tender, and there was a soft aroma of peach and honey in Saadat's hair.

"Saadat, do you know how many men and their girls are saying good-bye right now?"

"Damn this war! It's ruined our lives. I'm afraid, Tursun!"

"Yes, it's hard for us to endure."

"If something happens to you, I won't be able to live. I'll die." Her voice was trembling, and her eyes were filled with tears.

"Don't talk like that. We'll win and come home victorious. Then we'll invite the whole village to our wedding, and afterward we'll live together for the rest of our lives." He held her still tighter.

"I just hope so much that you're right."

"When I come back, you'll probably already be working as a teacher."

"No. I probably won't be able to finish my studying because of the war."

"Well, in that case, we'll both finish our studies together. Then we'll teach children and educate them. Other people's and our own." He looked into Saadat's eyes.

"That would be so wonderful," she sighed. Her reddened eyes moistened again.

"Come on, let's walk round the streets so I can say good-bye to them."

They wandered at length through the familiar streets and corners, holding hands, then at last returned to the garden. Saadat went back to the apple tree and took her bag from a branch, where she had hung it while they went walking. From the bag, she took out a *togach*—a small round *nan*—and turned to her *dzhigit*. "Bite off a piece. I will keep the rest until you come back."

Tursun looked at her tenderly. "Let's each eat a piece, and then we'll finish it—but only after the war. Shall we?"

That endless night of farewell, they each took one bite of the *togach*. Then Saadat wrapped the remainder in a kerchief, placed it in her bag, and again hung the bag on the branch. The full moon, an involuntary witness to their vows, now hid behind a cloud. They settled down beneath the apple tree. Saadat took a white handkerchief from her pocket and gave it to Tursun. Tursun unfolded it and saw a picture embroidered in colored stitches of a bird flying toward a bush, in which another bird sat waiting.

"That's a very wise piece of stitching." He grinned.

"The bird in the bush is me," Saadat explained, slightly embarrassed. "I hope that you will come home from the war and back to this garden. I will be waiting for you here. Just be sure to come back!"

"I shall keep this handkerchief close to my heart," said Tursun, as he folded the handkerchief and placed it in the inside pocket of his jacket.

Unable to part just yet, they sat for a long time under the tree, and after awhile, they found themselves overcome by tenderness, passion, and despair. Saadat melted into her beloved's arms and gave herself up to him. Afterwards, confused and ashamed, they could not look each other in the eye but sat a while in silence. The moon, emerging from the clouds for a moment, seemed to ask them, "What's life going to bring you now. What lies in store for you?" Then it paled a little and slid away through the night sky.

It began to grow light; the garden turned from black to gray, and then all its bright colors began to show. Now Tursun was more consumed by trepidation than ever. "Oh, Allah," he said, "will I ever see my home again, my father and mother, my friends, my sweetheart?" He pulled at a flower and placed it in Saadat's hair, then lay his head in her hands and closed his eyes. She felt two hot tears on her palms, and she also wept softly. Tursun kissed her again, took her wet face in his hands, and looked at her. She sank into his gaze, so full of longing and tenderness.

"Look after yourself, and whatever happens, come back," she whispered at last, before moving toward the house, looking back at him time and time again.

Tursun was just entering his house when he met his father coming out. "Have you only just come home? You've got to travel today. You should have gotten some sleep."

"I couldn't sleep," Tursun answered.

Kurvan-aka sat Tursun down beside him. Maysimyam also sat down with them. "Son, this war is like a wildfire that is consuming people's lives. But you're going there for our sake, for the sake of your motherland. So guard the honor of your parents. Remember where your home is and beat back those fascist reptiles without mercy. We will be waiting for you and for victory. I hope to be going to the front soon as well. But you're my firstborn, and if I don't come back, you will be the senior of the family."

Kurvan embraced his son strongly. Maysimyam came up to her son from behind and pressed herself to him. The war was taking her son. She could not contain her sobbing.

That day, the young men of all the villages between the ages of eighteen and twenty-one gathered at the military commissariat. They were registered and then began the long march to the railway town of Saryozek, two hundred kilometers away.

Sorrowful fathers and mothers, brothers, sisters, brides, relatives and fellow villagers accompanied the *dzhigits* as far as the Usek river. This crowd of followers then stood and watched for a long time as the line of draftees moved farther and farther away. Saadat was among them, watching until she couldn't see the men anymore. It seemed to her that as long as she watched him, her beloved might be protected.

• • •

After some time, a letter arrived from Tursun, addressed both to his parents and to Saadat. Tursun told them they had traveled from Saryozek to Kharkov on a freight train. They would receive training there for four months and then go to the front.

Soon Saadat had another worry. A month after Tursun left, she realized that she was pregnant. She began to suffer from a sense of heaviness in her body, dizziness, and nausea. Saadat felt guilty for what had happened in the garden on the night of their parting. If only Tursun had been able to make the marriage proposal and if only the marriage ceremony of Nikah had already taken place, her conscience would have been clear. She realized that others would soon see what was happening, and she was pierced by a sense of shame. No longer was she the cheerful girl student who was fun to be with. Her friends assumed that she was simply missing Tursun. But Saadat went out with the others to the harvest and did her best to hide the way she felt.

The first autumn of the war drew in, and though the war was far away, life in the village was lived fully in accordance with the laws of wartime. The villagers thought constantly about their men at the front. There was an immense amount to do. Some of them worked on the harvest, while others joined in the winnowing.

Small children went gleaning in the fields for leftover stalks of wheat, while the women loaded sacks of grain onto carts and sent them in convoys to Zharkent.

The old people encouraged the young. "Go and get busy! It'll be a lean time if there's no harvest!" Finally, with immense effort, the villagers brought in the whole of the harvest and submitted it to the authorities under their red banner with the slogan, "All for the front, all for victory!" Then, tossing their spades and pitchforks onto their shoulders, they returned home empty-handed.

Now that the work in the fields was done, the villagers started preparing for winter, drying the vegetables from their plots and storing them in cellars, laying in a stock of hay for the animals and gathering brushwood. Aware that there would be no help from the *kolkhoz* this year, each person had to rely on their own strength. If they were not to die of hunger, they would have to make their supplies last through until springtime. To general dismay, the price of flour at the bazaar had gone up. Still, maize could be used in place of flour. And so the people set to thinking about how they would cope with the difficulties ahead.

When the college term started, Saadat went back to living in college accommodations. After classes she did not mix with the others, instead concentrating on studying. She could not sleep at night because of the unhappy thoughts that crowded her mind. She would pray tearfully for Tursun's return.

It was not long before her rounded belly became obvious. She wrote to Tursun that she was pregnant and anxiously waited for his response. She did not know what to say to her mother, a widow with three children to look after. Her mother had placed high hopes on Saadat as the eldest in the family. Time and time again she would say, "Daughter, you must marry with honor, and only after you have your diploma. Make sure you don't shame me in front of other people."

"Whatever am I going to say to my poor mother? She's so ill. Will she be able to take it?" She struggled with these thoughts at length. Finally, a letter arrived from Tursun.

I have told my parents everything truthfully. Don't worry. They will send matchmakers to your mother. When the baby is born, my family will help you. We're going into battle now. I kiss you, my love.

It was a short letter, written in a hurry. That same day, Kurvan-aka and his family also received a letter from Tursun. When Turgan read it out to his parents, a change came over Kurvan-aka's face.

"I wouldn't have expected this of a son of mine," he said, tight-lipped. "Clearly all my guidance has been to no avail. How can we look Imyarahan in the eye? And those two want to educate children? Teachers are supposed to set examples for the rest to follow." He gave Maysimyam, who had grown very quiet, a menacing look. "So that's how you bring up your children, is it?"

"Don't get so angry, Kurvan. Remember, he's at the front. Don't curse him. It might come true." She said nothing more as he left the house.

She asked Turgan to read the letter again. As soon as he had finished, Maysimyam took the letter and put it in her pocket. "Do you also know this girl, son?" she asked Turgan.

Turgan took his mother in his arms and wiped away her tears. "Yes, Saadat-hada. She's very beautiful, and she's a good person. My brother's been seeing her for over a year. When they were in Zharkent together, they promised they'd marry and spend their lives together. Tursun has asked me to keep an eye on Saadat for him."

This calmed Maysimyam a little.

Kurvan-aka did not come home until it grew dark, and then he went to bed without speaking to anyone. Maysimyam, as though guilty of something, could not look him in the eye.

Kurvan-aka was a highly respected man in the village. He had been noted for his honesty and directness. Often, he would say to his sons, "I have had a hard life. But never once did I let my honor be compromised, never did I go against my conscience. So you, too, should never steal and never lie, never play with hashish, and never indulge in gambling." He had five children, but it was on his sons that he placed his highest hopes.

And now Tursun had done something inexcusable. Kurvan-aka tossed and turned in his bed until morning. Then at breakfast he said to his wife, "This evening we'll go to see Imyarahan. We don't need anybody from outside. We'll just take my sister and Gyuli. We can arrange everything ourselves. What lengths don't you go to for your own son!"

Sensing that her husband had cooled a little, Maysimyam sighed with relief. She went into the end room and opened the chest in which she had kept everything that would be needed for her son's marriage. Modangul followed her mother and asked her:

"Mama, what have you got in this box?"

"If we go to pay our respects to Imyarahan, *kizim*, we'll have to take her presents. I'm looking for a nice piece of material. I'll give her this white lacy shawl."

Maysimyam untied a small knot and showed Modangul a golden ring with a red stone set in it. "My mother gave me this ring for my wedding. I've kept it to pass down to our eldest daughter-in-law, the one Tursun will marry. And we'll give the nicest of these four lengths of cloth to Saadat, and another one to Imyarahan."

"Mama, how did you manage to collect all this?"

"I've kept them all for a long time, hoping that they will come in useful someday."

"And these other two pieces of material, who are they for?"

"One is for your father's sister, Adalyat, and the other is for Gyuli, your *kichik-apa*."

"But why do you wear a patched-up dress, Mama? You could sew yourself a new one from some of this."

"Daughter, your *chon-apa* and *kichik-apa* will also bring gifts for Imyarahan, so I have to give them something as a thank you. That's our custom."

"Are you taking them tonight?"

"No, today we're going to make Tursun's proposal of marriage to Saadat. First, we will listen to what she has to say, and then your father will discuss the day of engagement with her. On the day they agree, we must show our thanks by killing a sheep, giving out presents, and inviting people to tea."

Imyarahan will then invite the elders of the village. When Tursun-zhan comes home safe, if God wills, we will arrange a wedding and hold the Nikah ceremony." Maysimyam stroked her daughter's long black hair. "I hope that all of you can set up your own nests happily while your father and I are still alive."

Modangul hugged her mother and gave her a kiss. "*Apa*, you are wonderful. You're taking care of us and your future grandchildren too." Her tone became serious. "So you should wear this yourself." Modangul handed her mother a beautiful new shawl from the chest.

"No, *kizim*. We'll need that shawl later." Maysimyam put the shawl back and closed the chest.

At dusk, Adalyat arrived and greeted them with "*Assalam!*" Maysimyam invited her sister-in-law to sit in the place of honor. At once, Modangul put out the *dzhoza* and laid a cloth on it.

"No need to make tea for us, daughter. We've only come briefly," anticipated Adalyat.

"Really, *hada*, surely you'll have some tea with us? You don't come here very often," responded Maysimyam. "Gyuli's on her way here. Soon we'll all be going out."

Adalyat gave a sigh and shook her head. "You know, Kurvan came round yesterday. He told us about Tursun."

"I thought he must have gone to see you."

"Well, I said to him, "There's nothing you can do, *aka*. You'll just have to invite the elders for tea and then take the baby on as your grandchild. Then people will say that Kurvan did the right thing. And then when Tursun-zhan comes back, we'll put on a big wedding."

At that point Gyuli came in and looked questioningly at the women.

"Sit down for a while, Gyuli, we're waiting for Kurvan," said Adalyat.

While they were drinking their tea, Kurvan arrived.

"*Aka*, may all be well with you," smiled Gyuli.

"Thank you, *hada*. Today I wanted to go to the commissariat and ask to go to the front, but now there's all this fuss here. We need to sort this out first."

"Why are you in such a hurry to go to the war?" asked Adalyat reproachfully. "My son Mahmut is gone, and now I'm in a state of constant anxiety. It's like living in a dream. I've only had three letters from him."

Adalyat-hada had reason to be worried. Her only son had gone to the front on the same day as Tursun. Meanwhile, her husband Abdul-aka was in poor health and could not work on the *kolkhoz*; his daughters had to replace him in the fields. And in the last few years, Adalyat herself had suffered chest pains and shortness of breath from time to time. She and her husband were hoping that their son would take care of them, and when the time came, bury them. But now this accursed war had shattered their hopes, and Adalyat could think of nothing but her son.

It was beginning to get dark outside. It was time to set off to visit Imyarahan.

The marriage proposal was accepted. Kurvan-aka and Maysimyam slaughtered a sheep and invited the villagers to tea at Imyarahan's house. Their respect for Kurvan only grew when they learned that he had made the decision to help his future daughter-in-law. The chairman of the *kolkhoz* came up to him and shook his hand, saying, "You did right, brother, like a man."

Now that Kurvan-aka had fulfilled Tursun's request, he went to the war commissariat's office. His plea was declined, however. "We will call you when we need you, but for now, carry on working here."

A harsh winter set in. The troubles of the villagers did not cease. Every morning Kurvan-aka walked seven kilometers to the machine and tractor station in Zharkent, where the *kolkhoz* tractors were repaired. He came home very late in the evenings.

The women were now working on the farm in the daytime, and in the evenings, they spun, knitted socks and mittens, and sewed sheepskins for the soldiers at the front. Alahan was a skilled seamstress; she taught Gyuli, Zaynaphan, Mariyam, and Sariyam how to cut out and sew quickly, and they were soon declared the top team. Often the women would receive letters of gratitude from the front. The soldiers' encouraging words warmed their hearts and gave them a sense that every sheepskin they sent would keep a son, a husband, or a father warm. Despite the difficult times, people had not grown hard or lost spirit.

The villagers' food was meager—pumpkin, potatoes, and a pottage of cornmeal. Yet they were grateful. All they wanted was for the war to end and for their loved ones to return home alive. Students from the pedagogical institute in Zharkent would come to the village, give concerts, and tell the villagers about the situation at the front.

Kurvan-aka's second son, sixteen-year-old Turgan, was a first-year student at the pedagogical institute. He was a tall and slim young man who could bring people to the brink of tears when he sang the folk song "Ilahun" in his soulful manner. He had to sing this song more and more as time passed, when villagers started to receive killed-in-action notifications. One could not but feel their pain on hearing the grieving of mothers and fathers, old people and children, when such a letter arrived. The high spirits of their pre-war lives was now far away and more like something from a fairy tale.

The first notification came to the parents of Dzhelil Iminov.

The hero Iminov, Dzhelil fell during fierce fighting in the Ukraine.

So now Dzhelil's four children were orphaned. From this point, the villagers began to dread the arrival of the postman. Although the bloody fighting was far away from the village, it was echoed in the groans and weeping that issued from each house.

No more letters came from Tursun. Saadat was no longer embarrassed in front of the villagers, but her heart was heavy. She was expecting soon. She stroked her swollen belly and whispered, "You've got to meet your father, my boy. We'll wait for your father to come home when the war is won!" But then, when she thought about Mervanam, who had been widowed at an early age, she would be overcome with fear.

Harsh as the winter was, it passed into spring as though by appointment. The world turned green once again. Before the collective work began in the fields, each family prepared the soil of their own plots; and then, once more, the women in their teams took up their *ketmens* on their shoulders and set out to dig new *aryk* ditches and to clear out the old ones. From early morning to late evening, Kurvan-aka plowed and sowed. Sometimes his tractor rumbled up and down close to the village, and sometimes it was far away. The villagers kept in mind that they were laboring not only for themselves but for the men who had gone to the front.

That spring, Saadat gave birth to a boy. When her sister Rihanbuvi came running with the news to Maysimyam, she gave her a beautiful shawl and even wept for joy. "Thank you, daughter, for this wonderful news. May God bring my Tursun-zhan home and let him hold his son close to him."

That evening, Maysimyam prepared a tasty *korum shova* from a small piece of meat that she had carefully kept for an occasion such as this. She chopped the meat finely, fried it in a hot *kazan* with onion, garlic, pepper, dried tomato, and spices, then added water and boiled the broth a little. When the entire house was filled with the teasing aroma, she poured the broth into a small pot and wrapped a towel around it to keep it warm.

"Modangul, please will you take your father his dinner and tell him the good news at the same time. And on your way back, tell your *kichik-apa* that we've got a grandson," said Maysimyam to her elder daughter. She then took the younger, Mahinur, with her to her daughter-in-law Saadat's house.

Imyarahan opened the door to them. She was beaming with happiness.

"Congratulations!" Maysimyam embraced her. "I'm not coming into your house until twelve days are past. But please give this broth to your daughter."

Imyarahan was insistent, however, and finally Maysimyam was persuaded to go inside. Seeing her, Saadat got up from her bed.

"Lie down, *kizim*. I congratulate you with all my heart." Maysimyam kissed her daughter-in-law on the forehead and stroked her head. "With God's will may you and Tursun bring the child up to be a good man."

Imyarahan handed the baby to Maysimyam. "Congratulations, *svatka*. May your son grow up to be a noble *dzhigit*!"

Maysimyam took the child in her arms. He bore a striking resemblance to her son. Mahinur, sitting beside her, looked into the face of her baby nephew and whispered, "He's the very image of Tursun." She also held the infant for a while. Imyarahan, meanwhile, gave the nourishing broth to Saadat, who was still weak and pale after giving birth.

"Daughter, you should drink it up now while it's still hot. Get up your strength, and then you'll produce milk," Maysimyam said to her gently.

Maysimyam and her daughter sat and talked for a while with the in-laws and then returned home. "We've seen the child. Oh, Allah, he's so like Tursun. God give him good health!" she said to her daughters afterward.

At that moment, there was a creak and the door opened again. In came Cholpan, Adalyat's daughter. Her eyes were red from crying. Maysimyam and the girls stared at their unexpected visitor.

"My brother's come back," she said.

"Mahmut's back?"

"Yes. But he's lost an arm." Cholpan broke down in tears.

"Oh, Allah, when will this war be over?" said Maysimyam to herself. Then, thinking of her son fighting somewhere far away, her insides felt pierced by cold.

She looked at the weeping Cholpan. "Daughter, the main thing is he's alive. Come on, let's go and see him."

Adalyat's house was full of people. Adalyat did not know whether to be pleased about this or unhappy. Her son had come home from the war but was disabled. The people sitting with him expressed their sympathies to Mahmut and plied him with questions. The mothers asked him whether he had seen their sons, and the old men asked how the war was progressing and when would our side win. He answered their questions carefully and without hurrying.

Mahmut was now shorn of his previous youthful ardor. No longer did he resemble the tall, pale-faced twenty-year-old who had set out for the front. The empty sleeve of his soldier's blouse was tucked under a belt. The people listening hung on to his every word; images of brutal battles appeared before their eyes. After a while, the chairman of the *kolkhoz*, Imyar-aka, called in. He greeted them all and sat down next to Mahmut.

"Don't tell the old folk these stories, *uka*," he said, putting his hand on the young veteran's shoulder. "It's good that you've come back. We can't get enough strong *dzhigits*. The women, the old people, and the children are working themselves to the bone. Look, rest a little and recover, and then you can come and be the *brigadir* for the irrigation. There's so much to do. I'll always be there to help you."

A glimmer of hope appeared in Mahmut's eyes. "Thank you, Imyar-aka. I'll give it all I've got."

Two more men appeared in the village the following evening. They plodded slowly up the street, emaciated, exhausted, their eyes sunken. People came out of their houses to look at them but did not recognize them. Then one of the men said, "Don't you recognize us? It's me, Kasim, and this is Askar."

The women sighed and rushed toward the haggard wanderers. Kasim and Askar fell straight into their arms. The villagers took the pair to Kasim's house, where they were met with shouts and tears by grandmother Rozihan, mother Alahan, and the children. They lay them down, let them come round a little, and gave them something to drink.

Askar propped himself up on one elbow and glanced about the room, trying to see his wife Tadzhigul and their children among the people gathered.

"Make them some tea. They're dying of hunger," Rozihan ordered.

Alahan brought two large *apkurs* of *aktyan-chay*, and the old people contributed pieces of *nan*. They propped the two returnees up so that they could eat more easily. "Drink something hot. It'll bring you some strength back," Rozihan-aka kept saying.

"Thanks be to Allah! You've come home alive," said old Zair.

Alahan found some clothes for the two men. The villagers went outside, discussing what had happened. Kasim's children, Hasan and Husan, took the torn jackets and trousers from their father and Askar and helped them change into clean ones. Askar slowly got up.

"I'm going home to my family. They don't seem to know we're back."

Nobody had yet found it in themselves to tell Askar that Tadzhigul had died. Some villagers helped him walk to his house. The elders went into the house with him. Old Zair-buva sat down in the place of honor and sighed heavily.

"Askarzhan, you have come home, and that will be the greatest joy for your children. But you know the saying that life is always followed by death? We have had to bury Tadzhigul in your absence. She was a good wife and mother. But her time came very early. Try to be strong!"

Dropping to his knees, Zair-buva read a passage from the Qur'an, then all present said a prayer in memory of Tadzhigul. Askar clenched his teeth and did not speak. The tears ran down his sunken cheeks.

Finally he released his jaw. "Oh Lord above, why do you pour all this misery on me? Have I not suffered enough humiliation already? And now I've lost Tadzhigul as well."

The people sitting with him could only sigh.

"Take courage, son," old Rozihan said a number of times. "Allah will help you raise the children." She looked with pity on the frail Askar.

"You need to build up your strength," she said, getting up and turning to the others. "Come to our house. Alahan will cook you something to eat."

In the meantime, Alahan, her daughters, and the other women had prepared supper. Kasim and Askar, sitting at the table surrounded by their family and friends, seemed unable to believe what was happening. They ate, unable to eat their fill, and looked at those around them, insatiable in their hunger to see their loved ones again.

After the meal, the old men asked the two ex-convicts about their five years spent in faraway exile. Kasim pushed the empty bowl away from him and passed his hand through his hair.

"Well, what can I tell you? It was five years of brutality and survival. We were sent to a labor camp in Siberia. Fifty degrees below zero, and we were hungry, frostbitten, and in torn clothes. The political prisoners were kept separately. They had armed soldiers with dogs with them all the time. Anybody who collapsed out of weakness was shot where he fell, because this was considered an attempt to escape." Kasim looked down and linked the fingers of his two hands together tightly. "What else can I tell you? They shot political prisoners in front of the ordinary criminals. They didn't regard us as humans. People died ten at a time, mostly from cold and hunger. But they released us a month ago. We got as far as the station by train, and the rest of the way we walked. We slept where we could. There was no food anywhere. We just held on to each other and kept walking."

There was silence in the room. The villagers were drained of spirit. If it wasn't war, it was forced labor. Where could anyone hope to live in peace?

For several days after that, people from the village came to see Kasim. Again and again he told them about his ordeals in exile. His health was poor; a deep-seated cold sapped at his strength.

"Well goodness me, the whole village has been to see you to welcome you home. The only one who hasn't been is Shavdun," said Alahan with some surprise.

"He won't come. He was the one who got us sent away. He was the informer," said Kasim harshly, breaking into a fit of coughing. Beads of sweat broke out on his brow.

"Oh, Allah, what are you saying? Shavdun informed on you? Well if that's the truth, then God has already punished him. His wife Zorabuvi died. He's been left a widower with an elderly mother and his sons."

The sound of crying could be heard from outside. Alahan rushed out and saw that Tadzhigul's parents and their grandchildren had arrived to see Askar. Amina and Omar embraced their father, then began sobbing out loud. Alahan, glancing toward the garden, called softly to her mother-in-law. "*Apa*, come over here. Patam-ana and her husband are here."

They greeted each other and went into the house. Grandfather Momun and grandmother Patam looked with pity at the emaciated Askar.

"Let me read from the Qur'an," said Momun.

While the prayer was being recited, Aminam and Omar clung to their father, afraid to let go of him.

"Askarzhan, son, thank God you've come home. Now we don't have to worry about our grandchildren," said Patam.

"These are dark times. However did you survive in that hell?" added Rozihan.

"We thought about our families," Askar replied. "I was longing with all my mind to be with Tadzhigul. But she's dead, and my hopes are gone."

"We'll all be moving on to the next world sooner or later," said old Momun, glancing at the children sitting next to Askar.

The nine-year-old Aminam poured some water into the *kazan* and lit the flame in the oven. Alahan brought a whole *apkur* of milk with *kaymak* and prepared an excellent *aktyan-chay*. Patam put a plate of *manty* onto the *dzhoza* as well.

"Rozihan, Kayman, Askarzhan, come and eat. I'm not even sure what's happened. It's so long since I made *manty* that I could have forgotten how to." The old woman served the *manty* onto plates.

Alahan placed a large bowl of the tea in front of each person, then broke a large thin *nan* and placed a piece in each of the bowls.

"Sit down with us, daughter. Thank you for the tea. It's delicious. You're a wonderful neighbor. Tadzhigul always said good things about you." Patam smiled at Alahan approvingly.

Kasim broke into a fit of coughing and sweat appeared on his brow. "I saw Mahmut this morning.

He's only got one arm! That's the end of the fighting for him."

Grandmother Rozihan now joined the conversation. "We've already had three killed-in-action letters in the village now."

"And where we were in Zharkent, more and more people were getting them. Oh God, let them, whoever they are, just come home again alive and unharmed," sighed Momun-buva. "Anyway, it's time to get ready for evening prayers." He stood up, and the others followed.

"Come and see us again, Patamhan. Thank you for coming," said Rozihan, as she put on her overshoes.

"Thank you. We're going to be here for a few days to see Askarzhan recover a little."

After seeing the neighbors off, Patam-moma lit a candle, then consecrated the house, whispering something under her breath.

"*Apa*, is *dada* going to stay now? He isn't going away ever again, is he?" asked Omar once they were in the street.

"No, my boy. He's going to be with you now always."

"And you, are you leaving?"

"We're already very old. You need to live just with your father," said Patam, wiping away tears with the end of her shawl.

Aminam, Omar's sister, now burst into the conversation. "*Apa*, the apples and apricots in the garden have really come in, the spring onions are up, and Mama's flowers are in full blossom. You must come and see them! And I've seen Gyuli *chon-apa*. She was carrying a big bundle of wood on her back. She kissed me and told me I'd really grown. She said she'd come and see us in the next day or two."

"That's good! Tomorrow we'll make *porya* and invite Gyuli, Hadzhyar-han, and the children round."

When Gyuli got home she found Hadzhyar-ana and her friend Zaynaphan sitting under the awning in the garden. After washing her face and drinking a little water, she came into the arbor and greeted the two elderly women. Selimyam placed a bowl of *suyuk ash* in front of her.

"Will you share this with me?" offered Gyuli.

"No, thanks. We've just eaten. But you have your supper, daughter. You're working from dawn to dusk after all," said Hadzhyar, shaking her head.

"Well that's how it is for everyone these days," answered Gyuli, then, looking at Zaynap-apa, asked after her health.

"My soul deserted me after my daughter died. I cry all the time. I'm even worried about what's happening to my eyes."

"You can wear your eyes out with tears, but grieving won't help," said Hadzhyar-han.

"You're right, Hadzhyar-han. I'm living for the sake of the grandchildren. The elder one is already eight, and the younger is six. They can do everything at home by themselves."

Finally Zaynaphan-ana, a little embarrassed and looking now at her friend and now at Gyuli, came to the main purpose of her visit. "Gyuli, daughter, you're from a good family. You suffered terribly when Tair was taken from you, but you kept on looking after your children and knew no peace. And then you took in Hadzhyar like a mother."

Gyuli tried to work out what Zaynaphan was hinting at.

"Since my Zorabuvi died I've been getting weaker every year. I don't know if I'll have the strength to bring up my grandsons. Please don't be angry with an old woman, but I've come to offer you a marriage proposal from Shavdun. He's a widower too. You could be the mother to Shavdun's children, and he could be father to yours." Zaynaphan-ana looked shyly at Gyuli and then moved her gaze to Hadzhyar, hoping for support.

Gyuli said nothing for a moment. "Zaynaphan-ana, I love you as I love my own mother. I see you want to become related to us, but I'm never going to marry again. I want to dedicate myself to my children."

"But listen, daughter, you're still young," added Hadzhyar, "Don't let your life waste away. Shavdun's not a bad man. Give it some thought, then let us know."

"You're still strong at the moment, and you can be both mother and father to the children. But what if, God forbid, something happens to you?" persisted Zaynaphan-ana.

"Like the old people say, widows have three chances to marry. A woman should live under a man's care," Hadzhyar added again.

Gyuli cleared the bowls from the table, frowning. "I don't want to hear any more of this," she snapped before going off to the *kazan*.

The two old women exchanged glances in silence. Zaynaphan got up, wished them goodnight, and leaning on her stick, moved toward the gate. Gyuli rushed after her, hugged her, and said, "*Ana*, don't be upset. But I mean what I say. Look, it's dark now. Selimyam will walk you home."

Next day, as they were working in the fields, Shavdun rode up to Gyuli. "How's the irrigation going, Gyuli?"

"It's already finished. I've just got to cut off the water," she said, taking a large armful of grass and mud stopping up the branch of the *aryk*. Then she picked up her *ketmen* and set off along the path. Shavdun dismounted his horse and placed himself in front of her.

"Gyuli, my mother-in-law came to see you last night, and I know what you told her."

"That's how it is, and I have nothing to add. Please don't stand in my way," Gyuli said resolutely.

"I'm off to the front tomorrow. I wanted to apologize to you."

"What?" Gyuli took a step back.

"I know what I have done is unforgivable, and I am guilty beyond hope," the *brigadir* continued faintly.

Gyuli dropped her *ketmen* to the ground, not understanding him.

"Before the war started, the Party heads called me in and offered me work. I couldn't refuse them because they threatened reprisals against me and my family. I had to accept. To cut a long story short, it was me who informed on Tair. I can never forgive myself for this. Now I'm going to the front, and maybe I can expiate my guilt before Allah by dying."

Gyuli stood fixed, shaken. Then, swallowing a lump in her throat, she replied, "I would not wish what my children and I have been through even on you."

"I thought you were going to curse me," said Shavdun, bewildered at her resolve.

"I never curse anyone. But look, people who play with fire will get their fingers burned." She turned and walked away.

Clenching the bridle in his hands, Shavdun stood and watched her for a long time. Not so long later, Gyuli learned that he had been killed in action.

• • •

"So Shavdun did have a troubled conscience after all?" said Ruth thoughtfully.

"There's no forgiveness for him and his kind," said Mehriban. "What use is there in meekly confessing to having informed on someone when those action ruined lives and caused good men to die? How many mothers have been condemned to suffering because of informers like Shavdun? Some men go and defend and die for their motherland, while others creep and fawn, then do vile things and profit from other peoples' grief. And all for the sake of saving their own skin.

"I'd like to tell you about another cowardly informer who lived in the village," Mehriban said. "But you could meet someone like him anywhere."

"Do tell. I'd love to hear more." Ruth leaned back in her seat and closed her eyes.

9

A Soul like a Bird

When Shavdun was sent to the front, his job as *brigadir* on the *kolkhoz* was given to Kadir. Kadir was swarthy and stocky, with a pair of slender whiskers and a reputation for being a gossiper and a lady-killer. He had married Asiyam, the prettiest girl in the village, who bore him three children. Everybody wondered how he had managed to make such a catch. And when the men were called up to the front, Kadir was never called, for some reason.

"Ah, that greasy little bastard, lounging around in the rear while our men go to fight! You'll see, he'll be eyeing up the women." Such were the rumors that went around the village.

On one of the busiest working days of the season, the chairman called all the *kolkhoz* workers together. "The water's getting low," he said. "There isn't enough for the irrigation. Without proper irrigation, the yield will drop. And none of us should forget for a minute who we are producing this wheat for. So from now on, each *kolkhoz* will draw water one at a time, on a rotating basis. According to the schedule, it's our turn from tomorrow. So, comrade women, you will have to forget that you're already tired and spend the nights out here in the fields, so that you can make sure the water goes where it's needed while we've got it. The first team to irrigate is Mahmut's: Gyuli, Mervanam, Zaynaphan, and Mariyam. You will be in charge of the water for two days. After you, Kadir's team will take over. After that, we'll make the water available for your personal use."

Irrigation of the wheat began the next morning. Barefoot and up to their knees in mud, the women of the first brigade worked without stopping. They paused to wolf down a bite of food under an improvised shelter of branches, then got straight back to the irrigation. When night fell, Mervanam checked that the water was flowing freely. "It'll be dawn by the time we get back to the village. Why don't we spend the night here, and then go home when it gets light?" she said.

"Good idea," said Gyuli. "Anyway, people will have let their guard dogs out for the night by now." She started readying herself to lie down and sleep.

"But then again, maybe we should go home after all?" Mariyam said shyly.

"Forget it, Mariyam, we're all so tired. We haven't got the strength to go back. Anyway, who's there waiting for us?" said Mervanam.

"If you wanted to go home, you should have gone with Zaynaphan," added Gyuli. "It's too dark now. We won't make it back."

Going home alone in the dark would, indeed, be frightening. So Mariyam lay down beside the others. The three women, dog-tired, fell into a deep sleep immediately. The land grew quiet, and there was only the murmur of water flowing in the irrigation ditches. The old people have good reason to say that deep sleep is a cunning opponent. As it happened, Kadir had been stalking the three of them for some time. Once he was certain that they were asleep, he crept up to Mariyam, put a rag over her mouth, took hold of her hands, and dragged her away. Mariyam tried with all her strength to kick him away, but she received a sharp blow to the head and lost consciousness.

Mariyam came to as it was getting light. She looked around, trying to understand where she was. There was nobody near her. As she tried to stand up, she felt a sharp pain at the back of her head. She felt her head with her hand and sensed something wet. She held her hand up to her eyes and gasped—it was covered with blood. Her dress was torn. In a flash, she recalled what had happened that night. Realizing that she had been raped, she began to cry loudly. Her crying woke her companions, who found her not far from where they had slept.

"What's happened? Why are you over here?" They leaned over the pale-faced young woman. "My God! Look, her dress is all torn!"

Mariyam did not speak. She just sat, broken and tousled, her head in her hands. The others understood what had happened.

"Mariyam, do you know who did this? We won't say a word," said Mervanam, stroking her matted and twisted hair.

Gyuli picked up Mariyam's shawl, which was lying a little way off, and handed it to Mervanam, who in turn slipped it over Mariyam's head. Now Mariyam took her hands away from her puffy face and began to speak.

"I lay down here and fell into a deep sleep. Then someone took hold of me, stuffed a cloth into my mouth, and pulled me away. I tried to fight back, but he hit me on the head with something. I can't remember anything after that. I woke up this morning and realized that someone's abused me. So what can I do now? It'd be better to die than to live in shame." She burst into loud tears.

"I could take the head off that monster with this *ketmen*," said Gyuli, hatred in her voice.

"Any filth can humiliate a defenseless woman," said Mervanam. "Well, let's think now, who could it have been?" She thought through all the men who were still in the village. The others also started to run through the few men who had not been called up to the front.

After a while Mervanam became animated. "I think it could only be that freak Kadir," she said. "He's always telling dirty jokes in front of us. Well, you hideous man, just you wait. We'll get our hands on you yet." She shook her fist. "We'll get our revenge, you inadequate creature!"

Gyuli fetched a bucket of water and made Mariyam undress. "Mariyam, wash yourself. Make sure that not even a trace of that creature is left on your body."

Mervanam poured water from a large scoop, while Gyuli helped Mariyam, who was still weak, to wash herself. Under the collar of her sleeveless top, Mariyam always had concealed a needle and a little thread wound around it, and now these proved useful. Mervanam sewed up her torn dress and helped Mariyam to dress. When they had finished, the three friends vowed to each other never to tell about what had happened, and to take revenge on the perpetrator of the abuse.

For several days after this, Mariyam did not go out into the fields. She felt unwell. When neighbors asked how she was, she told them that she had felt dizzy at work and fallen, and her head had hit a stone. It was so bad that she still could not lift up her head.

"It's a mercy that Allah has left you alive," remarked Zaynaphan-moma when she called in to see her neighbor.

"Yes, I suppose so," nodded Mariyam, who suddenly started weeping.

"There, there, my dear. These are difficult times, I know. If the men were here, things would be easier for you."

Hearing this, Mariyam realized that had her husband Adil been here, nobody could have harmed her.

"Come on, you lie down. I'll go and make some sharp *suyuk ash*.

"Don't worry about it, *ana*. You can hardly walk, yourself."

"Remember, after my daughter died, you helped me for so many years. Surely I can at least make you some *lapsha*?" the old woman asked. She stood up with some difficulty, then taking up her stick, made her way home.

Left alone now, Mariam's thoughts went back to the events of the previous night. She felt as though she would never be able to wash herself of the filth that had been done to her.

• • •

The summer was reaching its end and preparations were under way for the harvest. The *kolkhoz* chairman Imyar-aka gave the women two days off for urgent tasks at home. They picked vegetables and fruit on their plots and took them to sell in the bazaar; with the proceeds they bought other foodstuffs, clothing, and shoes for their households.

On the first day of the harvest, everybody, young and old, took a scythe or sickle and went out to the fields. It made them happy to see the golden stalks of swaying wheat that stretched to the horizons. Now they had a single objective: to bring in the whole of the harvest without losing any of it. The old folk said longingly, "They could at least give us each a sack of grain for our labor."

The Uighur love song and music. For all the hardship of their fate, they never fail to glorify and celebrate their lives in song. And on this hot day, the reapers, sweating from the labor and the sun, filled the surroundings with their ringing voices.

> *After the harvest and the scorching heat,*
> *may your tired hands find rest.*
> *After our rare and keen embraces meet,*
> *may I remain in your heart forever.*

A breeze brought a breath of cool and caressed the fields of standing wheat. The strains of their song rose high and disappeared into the heavens.

It was time for lunch. The women washed their hands in the nearest *aryk* and sat down to rest and drink tea. Gyuli and her friends sat a little way from the others.

Mariyam, crouched and huddling, announced to them that she was pregnant. "What can I do now?" she wept. "Whatever will I tell Adil? All very well if he believes me that Kadir abused me by force, but if he doesn't?"

"Don't worry," Gyuli assured her, "Mervanam and I will be your witnesses and will explain everything to Adil."

"But Gyuli, you know what Adil's like," whispered Mariyam to Gyuli in despair. "He can hit me if his mood takes him. It would be better to die than to suffer his beating all my life and him heaping blame on me. Isn't there some way out of this? Zaynaphan, do you remember when you told me about some kind of herb that can induce an abortion. What is it? Will you show it to me, please?"

"No. I would never take that sin on myself. What if something happened to you?"

"An embryo you carry beneath your heart is guilty of nothing. When the baby's born, give it to me," said Gyuli indignantly.

"But don't any of you understand? The child will always remind me of that maniac. No! I'd rather die!"

Mervanam took Mariyam by the shoulders and turned her face to her. "Listen to me. My grandmother used to say that whatever you tell yourself in your heart will come to pass. If you die, who'll be there for your children? For Adil?"

"I don't even want to know about them anymore. I just want to get out of this mess before the gossip starts. This is what bothers me day and night."

Unsure how they could help Mariyam, the other women fell silent. After a while, the two *brigadirs* came riding up to them on horseback.

"If you've had your rest, please get up and continue your work," said Mahmut.

"Say, Mariyam, it looks like you got tired on the first day of the harvest. Or are you just not in the mood anymore?" joked Kadir.

Mariyam turned pale and began shaking.

"Mahmut, we've decided to work through to the morning again," said Gyuli.

"As you wish," he replied.

"And I'll come and keep watch over you." Kadir grinned.

"Who do we have to fear at night except for rapists? Wolves, you think?" Zaynaphan flared up.

This put Mahmut on his guard. "What's that about rapists?" he asked.

"Zaynaphan's joking," said Mervanam, looking at Kadir.

"Well, I'm off," said Kadir, turning and hitting his horse with his whip.

"Come on, then, comrade women, let's get back to work," Mahmut urged them.

After Mahmut rode away, Mervanam said, "We'll stay out here tonight. And if Kadir dares to poke his nose in, we'll give him the works."

When evening came, the tired villagers dispersed for home. Gyuli and her friends prepared food for their children and old people at home, milked their cows, and tidied up. Then they returned to the field for the night.

They worked by the light of the moon for most of the night, mowing the wheat and binding the sheaves together. Finally, rubbing themselves in the small of the back, numb from exertion, they lay down in the same spot as they had on that earlier night. With the exception of Mariyam, who could not sleep, the others fell into an exhausted sleep at once.

About an hour passed. Mariyam heard somebody's cautious footsteps. "Mervanam! Someone's coming!"

Mervanam prodded Gyuli and Zaynap, then whispered, "Let him come nearer. We'll give him something to be afraid of."

The three women pretended to be asleep. When the man came close, they jumped up, took hold of him, and knocked him to the ground. Mervanam struck a match, and they all saw that it was Kadir. Shrieking and shouting, they began to hit him. Kadir kicked at them and tried to get away, but Gyuli lashed out at him with her sickle. "So you're the rapist, you slimy midget!" she shouted. The sharp pain made Kadir howl at the top of his voice.

Other villagers sleeping in the field heard the noise and came to see what was going on. "Eh, what's all this? What's happened?" They ran up to the women. "Someone been bitten by a snake?"

"We've caught a squirming reptile," answered Mervanam with indignation.

"So who was making all that noise?"

"That was this runt, Kadir. He was stalking us," exclaimed Zaynap, glancing with disgust at the man lying tied up on the ground.

Mariyam started shaking out of fear. Gyuli threw her old vest over her shoulders. "Well, Mariyam, it's all over now. You can calm down. We've caught the swine."

When it grew light, Mahmut rode up to the women. "What happened here last night?"

"Mahmut, we can't tell you everything. During the night, this hateful man tried to rape us. I hit him with my sickle," said Gyuli with disgust.

"Just wait, I'll show you all," Kadir hissed, then groaned in pain.

Gyuli leaped up, sickle at the ready. "You don't care what you've done, do you, swine?"

Mahmut stopped him. He jumped down from his horse and went up to Kadir. "You scum. If I'd a gun with me, I'd shoot you myself," he barked, then kicked him. "The real men are out there dying in the war while you sit around here and rape their wives. You traitor! Get up, you animal!"

"I can't get up. Help me, please!" begged Kadir tearfully.

Mahmut looked at Kadir's wound. The sickle had slashed him at the waist. His clothes and the ground under him were bloodied.

"Give me a cloth," ordered Mahmut, addressing the women looking on. Gyuli held out her handkerchief. Mahmut pressed it against the wound.

"Take off his shirt and bandage him up," he ordered.

Mervanam and Zaynaphan, cursing Kadir viciously, bandaged his waist.

"You've given him a taste of his own medicine. Shall I give him some too?" he asked, looking at the angry villagers.

"That pig couldn't repay us for what he's done with his own death," said Gyuli.

"Mervan-hada, would you go and fetch Saryam with the cart. We need to get him to the village, and he won't make it on his own," ordered Mahmut. When Saryam-hada came with the cart, they picked up Kadir and lay him on it.

The next day, a rumor got round the village that the women had fought Kadir with a sickle. The news disturbed some, while others approved. "That's just what he needs, the shameless monster. The number of women he's disgraced." And now Mariyam's friends had taken their revenge on Kadir, but for her things were no easier.

Kadir lolled about in hospital for a long time, then signed himself out before he was properly recovered and came home on crutches. His wife Asiyam, outraged at his antics, did not show him any particular pity. Her children started to avoid their father. Many of the villagers turned their faces away when they saw him. And the wretched man now lived in fear, dreading the return of Mariyam's husband Adil.

After a few months, Mariyam's belly began to swell noticeably. The other women started looking at her askance. She did not know what to do with herself. She would gladly have disappeared through a hole in the ground, but the ground was hard and solid; she would have flown up into the sky, but the sky was too far away.

One day as she was returning home with a yoke on her shoulder, she overheard two women talking.

Saryam saw her and deliberately raised her voice. "Look at her. She has no shame. Having affairs while her husband is at war. Now she's going around pregnant."

"And while we've been waiting for our husbands to come home but got letters instead saying they're killed in action. I bet hers'll come back, no problem!" echoed Dzhannyat.

"It's true. They say that devils lurk in still water," Izzyat said with sarcasm to Mariyam's back.

At that moment, Mervanam came toward them. "What are you doing hanging around here? You should all be at home."

"We'll chat wherever we feel like it. What's it got to do with you?" snarled Saryam.

Dzhannyat gave Mervanam a malicious look. "Don't you go lecturing us. You'd better look after your friend. Who is it who's helped her to get better so quickly, anyway?" She broke into an evil laugh.

"What happened to Mariyam isn't something I'd wish on anybody. If you want to know the truth, she was raped," said Mervanam curtly, going into Mariyam's house.

Mariyam rushed up to her. "Thank heavens you're here. Something's happening to me. The child hasn't moved for four days!" She took hold of Mervanam's hand.

"Oh, Allah! That's bad. What should we do?"

Just then Gyuli appeared in the door, as though sensing something wasn't right.

"Gyuli, would you go and find a cart? We need to get Mariyam to a hospital."

"It's not her time yet, surely?" asked Gyuli in surprise.

"Mariyam says the child has stopped moving."

Without asking further questions Gyuli went to her sister's house, fetched her cart, and drove it to Mariyam's house. As the women were climbing on, Zaynaphan came hurrying toward them, and the four of them set off to the hospital in Zharkent.

The doctors examined Mariyam. "Your child is dead. We will give you an injection to bring on labor. Giving birth to a stillborn child isn't easy."

Her friends said good-bye to Mariyam and went home. For Mariyam, the injections brought only pain, but her labor did not progress. They repeated the procedure the next morning, and Mariyam developed a high temperature and fever. She moved between lucidity and unconsciousness. The doctor did not leave her, waiting all the while for labor to begin.

Mariyam, however, sensing that something was wrong, begged him, "Doctor, you're a kind man. Save me, don't let my children be orphaned!"

Eventually they put Mariyam on the delivery table, gave her another injection and began to squeeze the infant out by hand, aided by massage. The fetus came out, but Mariyam felt as though something inside her had broken away. The doctors, having finished their task, left the operating room, leaving Mariyam alone.

And then she found herself feeling light, rising up, and flying out through the little ventilation window of the operating room, like a bird. When the doctor came back, he found the woman lying unconscious. He rushed to massage her chest and struck her on the cheeks, but none of his efforts to revive her were any use. Mariyam had bidden this cruel world farewell forever.

• • •

"What a terrible end for Mariyam! Goodness, all your heroes have such bitter destinies to fulfill. I have to say, I feel quite shaken by the will and courage of these Uighur women." Ruth's eyes were filled with sadness.

"Yes," agreed Mehriban. "Mariyam, for one, grew up an orphan, cold and hungry. She knew happiness for a short, sweet time when she married and had her children. But then the war came. And then, her life was ruined when Kadir assaulted her. That was her lot. But how do you measure the pain caused by war? So many letters announcing that someone's father, husband, or son would not be returning. And the women and the old folk left behind lose their strength and health from the unremitting hard work. The children had to grow up before their time. For many of the villagers, the war left indelible wounds. I would like to tell you now what happened to Mahmut. For people like him, life changed completely."

10

SPECTERS OF WAR

When he was discharged from the military hospital, Mahmut returned to the village with an arm missing. Straight away he took up what work he could do, and it appeared to others as though life had returned to normal for him. All the time, however, his mind was bombarded with repeating images of his comrades dying in battle. They lay on the ground with arms and legs missing, covered in blood. No matter how he tried, he could not banish these visions, and they began to affect his behavior. He became irritated easily, flaring up over the slightest misdemeanor, and would let fly with his fist. People in the village began to be nervous of him. Not only children, but adults too.

Some said, "Oh, Allah, no girl will marry Mahmut." Others were sorry for him because he had become an invalid. Abdul-aka and his wife Adalyat-hada had only one desire once the work in the fields was complete, to find a wife for their only son.

Once autumn came with its cold rains, Kurvan-aka, Adalyat's brother, took her to the *kolkhoz* administration. They were admitted to the chairman's office, where Imyar-aka himself was sitting at his desk in front of a portrait of Stalin that hung upon the wall.

"Come in, take a seat," said the chairman, pointing to a bench by the door. The chairman had aged visibly; his hair had turned distinctly gray, and deep wrinkles had appeared on his face. "Thank you for coming. What can I do for you?"

Kurvan-aka hesitated, suddenly awkward. "Listen, this is why we've come. Mahmut lost an arm in the war, but he's working hard on the *kolkhoz*. His parents are longing to marry him off." He nodded toward Adalyat.

"Well, why not? That's good news," said Imyar-aka.

"Well, you are the man in charge of our village, and we wanted to ask your permission. We understand that this is hardly the time to be arranging weddings, while there's a war on. But if we can't marry him, Mahmut's state is going to deteriorate completely."

"I understand. You have the right idea. War or no war, you need to build a family. So who's the bride?"

"We are thinking of Aisha, Saryam's daughter. They have agreed to it."

"Good. When do you intend to have the wedding?"

"Sometime soon," said Adalyat.

"The people here are tired of weeping. Let there be some joy in the village at last," said the chairman decisively, bringing his hand down on the table.

Kurvan-aka and Adalyat stood up and thanked Imyar-aka. The chairman shook their hands and said, "If you need anything, tell me. We'll help if we can."

Mahmut's parents began to invite the villagers to the wedding straight away. And while it was modest compared to peacetime festivities, the occasion was nevertheless happy. They killed a sheep and served *kordak* to the guests. Once they had eaten, the ceremony of Nikah was performed for the young couple. The old men blessed them and said, "When the war ends, let them build themselves a house and start their family. May there be more weddings in this village! Allah, grant us happiness!" Then they all joined in prayers.

Despite his marriage, Mahmut's disposition did not change. The war had evidently maimed his psyche, and this could be seen in the rough way he treated his young wife, always finding fault with her. One day he came home, and the evening meal was not yet ready. "I can't wait all day. I'm hungry. Give me a bowl of tea."

"But I've got herbs boiling in the *kazan*, there's nothing for me to heat the water in. Can you wait a while?" Aisha continued preparing the meal.

Mahmut flew into a rage. "What sort of a dinner do you call this when it's not ready when I come home? What the hell do you do with yourself all day?" he shouted and kicked the kettle they used for pouring water on their hands to wash.

Aisha stared at him in bewilderment. "What's the matter with you?"

Going up to her, Mahmut seized her by the hair, dragged her, and began kicking her. Aisha cried out in a piercing voice, "*Ana!* Help me!"

Mahmut's mother came running and panting in from the garden and pulled Mahmut away from his wife. "Are you mad? Since when was it acceptable to hit a woman?"

The terrified Aisha stood shaking and choking on her tears.

"I come back from work, and she hasn't got dinner ready. She couldn't even give me a bowl of tea. She's useless! What would you do?" raged Mahmut.

"Son, you can't go on like this!" reproached her mother. "Who's going to live with this violence?"

"Well, you and your pot of tea, you can both go and get lost," he uttered angrily and stormed out of the house.

Adalyat took her daughter-in-law in her arms and they wept together for some time. Then her husband Abdul-aka came in. "Is something the matter?"

"*Aka, ana,* if Mahmut is going to lay his hands on me like this and insult me, I can't go on living with him," said Aisha, wiping away her tears.

"Aisha, dear, he wasn't always like this. The war's affected him. I think he'll come back to his old self with time. Try to be patient," said her unhappy mother-in-law, also wiping away tears.

Aisha did her best to be patient. She understood completely that Mahmut had fought for his people and country and that he must feel incomplete with an arm missing. She realized that he was haunted by terrifying images of the war that would not leave him. Yet in the past he had been a calm and balanced young man, a *dzhigit* with a generous heart. He used to be respected by the other villagers. But war hardens people and makes them bitter.

• • •

"I can understand Mahmut," said Ruth, "driven into the slaughterhouse of war. He sets off young and healthy and comes home handicapped and without a future. What a bitter fate." Ruth sighed sharply.

"That's the time it was," nodded Mehriban. "The war years were all the same. Always the same backbreaking work, always those heavy thoughts about husbands and sons fighting on the distant front.

"When the spring of 1945 came, it filled the world with the scent of flowers. The gardens of the village blossomed, the rosebuds in the yards swelled up, and the nightingales sang without end. The bright sunlight warmed not only the cold ground but also the people's spirits. And with that spring, again, at last, there was a feeling of hope.

"The long-awaited announcement came on the radio on the ninth of May. 'The war is over. The Soviet Union has defeated Hitler's Germany.' People had been waiting for that news for four horrendous years. They were joyful beyond measure and threw their hats into the air, hugged one another, and shouted out, 'Victory! Hurrah! We've won!' They wept for happiness. Nobody could sleep at night, but instead everybody was out, walking the streets, calling in on neighbors, embracing them, and congratulating them again and again that victory had at last come.

"Once the general rejoicing died down, life returned to its old ways. The villagers bore the painful repercussions of the Great Patriotic War for many years to come."

Mehriban glanced at her fellow passenger. Seeing her nod in anticipation, she continued her story.

11

THE HEART'S HARD JUSTICE

After victory was declared, the old people took to sitting all day outside their houses on the mounds of earth that reinforced their walls, awaiting the return of the *dzhigits* from the front. One such day, old Idris took a pinch of tobacco from his pouch and wrapped it in a piece of old newspaper to make a cigarette. He offered some tobacco to Mahpir, who was sitting beside him. Mahpir rolled a cigarette as well. The two sat there inhaling their smoke and began their usual conversation.

"A lot of men lost their lives in that war. How many do you think will come home?" asked Idris.

"I just hope they come back in one piece and unharmed, not as invalids like Mahmut," responded Mahpir.

"Once the men come back, our women will find things easier."

"We always used to think women were weak, but just look how heroically they've done all this men's work!"

"They dug the ditches, they sowed the wheat, they harvested it, and tied up the sheaves. Carried heavy sacks too." Idris-buva nodded approvingly.

"I don't think that every man could have done that, eh?"

"The title of hero should be conferred on each and every one of them," concluded old Idris. "Without the intensified work in the rear, without the women, we wouldn't have won."

They rolled up more tobacco. Mahpir inhaled, then went into a fit of loud coughing. He took out his handkerchief to wipe the perspiration from his brow. "I need to give up smoking. I can't sleep at night for coughing."

"What's the point of that? We're nearly seventy. That cough'll go with us when we go."

Their conversation was interrupted by one of the neighbor's boys, who ran up to them and jabbered breathlessly, "Good news! Some men have come back to Zharkent from the war. They say some of ours are there, from Chigan." The boy turned and ran off round the village, loudly calling out the news.

As the villagers heard the news, a wave of excitement passed through the village. Only Kadir was unhappy. If Adil was among the returnees, he would have some explaining to do. An intense fear gripped him. There were moments when he simply began to shake. He thought over his misdeeds and began, for the first time, to be genuinely sorry for what he had done. He was walking with crutches now and took this to be his punishment for his actions. But it was the return of dead Mariyam's husband that he feared the most.

Now his fear became impossible to endure, and Kadir felt that the time had come to take the step that had long been at the back of his mind. Late that night, when all his family were asleep, he went out into the yard. He sat down on the bench in the wan moonlight, lit a cigarette, and sank into thought, recollecting his past.

When he was a boy, his father had worked in the fields for a wealthy landowner, Ivrahim. Every autumn his father expected payment for his labors, but the cunning *bay* had always found a way of refusing him. In the winter, his father brought firewood for his employer on a sledge. Every morning his mother would drink a meager bowl of tea, then went off to bake bread, wash, and clean in the landowner's house. She came home late at night, her legs numb. At night, exhausted and cold, his parents' sleep was constantly disturbed by their coughing, but at dawn they were both back hard at work. In the end, they both died of tuberculosis, one after the other, still young and without having repaid their debts. The orphan Kadir quickly found himself in the company of other homeless boys. In rags and perpetually hungry, they slept in dilapidated old houses and spent their days stealing. Thinking about it, Kadir had not enjoyed a single happy day in his childhood.

As an adolescent, he started working on the *kolkhoz* and got his life into some sort of order. He was agile, sharp of tongue, worked hard, and sought attention. Later he married happily. His belly was full now, and he always wore good clothes. Hs wife Asiyam ran the household with military precision. When he came home from work, his three children would come running toward him, calling out, "Papa!"

Filled with self-pity, Kadir thought to himself, "Happiness was right here in my hands, and the only person to blame for losing it is me. I threw it away. And now I'm a cripple, no use to anybody." He broke down and cried like a child. Afterward, he smoked again. He breathed out the smoke and sat for a long time, hearing a nightingale singing in the garden and the faraway barking of some village dogs. Then with a broken sigh, he looked up at the moon and muttered, "Oh God, this is it." His eyes flashed with tears.

He got up heavily and went into the shed. He took a length of strong horsehair rope, tied one end to a high beam, and tied a noose at the other end, then went out into the yard again. The world seemed to him to be completely dark. In this indifferent blackness he felt utterly and irredeemably alone. Kadir glanced at the open doors of his house. His body began to tremble violently. Moving only his lips, he whispered, "Asiyam, children, forgive me." Then he went back into the shed, put the noose over his head with trembling hands, and with the words, "God, forgive me!" threw himself down. Startled, the cow lying nearby began to moo.

• • •

"He passed his own sentence on himself," said Ruth very quietly.

"I think his conscience finally got to him," replied Mehriban, also softly.

"And what happened after that?"

12

PEBBLES OF FORTUNE

After the war, some households experienced joy as their men returned from the front. In other houses, however, to which there came not a soldier but a notification of death in action, there was the silence of loss. Among these was the family of Kurvan-aka and Maysimyam, who longed for and waited in vain for Tursun to come home.

During the war, Maysimyam had given birth, despite her middle age, to a daughter, Mehriban. Her pregnancy had felt incongruous since she already had grandchildren growing up. On top of that, the girl was born at only seven months. Nobody thought that she would survive. They wrapped her in a fur hat to keep her warm and held her carefully in their arms.

And, glory to Allah, she survived. Mehriban was just a year younger than Tursun's son Amanzhan, and she was looked after by her two elder sisters.

Receiving no news of Tursun, Saadat prayed for him day and night. One day she took the three-year-old Amanzhan and drove to the military commissariat. They told her that some of the forces had been retained near the front to help restore the towns and cities destroyed in the war. Perhaps her husband was among them. They would look into it and notify her.

The long wait lengthened into many months. At last, the army issued a notification in 1946.

Muridinov Tursun went missing during the fierce battle for Berlin.

At this, Maysimyam began keening. "Oh my son, where did you end up? Where should we look for you, my own flesh and blood?" Despondent, Kurvan-aka grew withdrawn. And Saadat, while not losing all hope of finding him, wept when she was out of earshot of her child. But what was the use of tears? Everybody waited and hoped, not allowing themselves to imagine that Tursun might no longer be among the living.

Saadat had finished her teacher training in 1944 and came back to the village, where she took up work teaching primary school classes. Sepiyam had been working at the school for some years and taught her many things. Saadat proved a good teacher, and she soon won the respect of both the pupils and their parents. Success in her work pleased her, but she was still unsettled in her heart. She still longed for her beloved Tursun to return. She often thought of their unforgettable night before their parting. She had said to him, "If something happens to you in the fighting, I won't be able to live." What was she to do now?

She now had Amanzhan, and she knew she must live for his sake. She devoted herself to bringing up her only son and educating him well, for he was all that was left to her of Tursun.

When thoughts of this kind visited her at night, she would cry. In the daytime, the schoolchildren distracted her from her grief, and the days passed quickly.

One day Saadat decided to visit Zaynaphan-hada the fortune-teller, the only *kumlakchi* in the village, to see if she could tell her what had happened to Tursun. Often people came to consult her if they had lost animals or wanted to resolve some matter, and she would cast a set of small stones to read their *kumlak*. Those around her had advised Saadat not to trust some old soothsayer but to rely on destiny alone, yet her need was so great that she found herself at Zaynap's door. Zaynaphan heard her out, then tossed forty-one pebbles onto a *koshma* and concentrated herself in thought.

"Forget your hopes about Tursun," she said eventually. "If you know of a suitable young man, marry him. You need to perform the rite of Nikah soon. So see to it and don't shy away. Loneliness is for dogs and donkeys, not for the likes of us."

"But Zaynaphan-hada, I came to ask you about Tursun, not to hear about getting married!"

"Well, Saadat, you've come, so listen. When your son grows up, he will go to a distant place, and from there he will bring you news about his father. You will be very happy. But there will be no Tursun in your life."

Saadat was shaken by the fortune-teller's words. She wished that she had not come. She wanted to go on living with hope that Tursun would return.

"Saadat, stop waiting for Tursun. Marry somebody else. You're still young, and it's not too late to give

Amanzhan a brother or a sister," said the old woman, looking at her with pity.

"Why do you keep on about marriage? Is that all you can talk about?"

"A person can suffer even in a golden palace if she is left alone without a soul mate. All I am telling you is what the pebbles say. When your son gives you news of his father, you will remember me with gratitude." Zaynaphan picked up the pebbles and wrapped them in a cloth.

Saadat was unable to sleep that night. She dressed and went out into the garden. The moon was up, and she was reminded of that night, years ago, when she and Tursun had parted. She walked over to the apple tree, where they had talked for so long, sat down beneath it, and wept. Above her, a nightingale was singing its heart out.

"Hey, nightingale, are you missing your beloved too?"

For a moment, the nightingale was silent, then plunged back into its fast stream of music.

"You know, Tursun held me close and kissed me in this garden for the first and last time. I've still got the piece of *nan* that we each took a bite from. Tursun vowed to me that we would eat up the remains together when he returned. Tell me, nightingale, is he still alive? Will he come back to this garden?" She looked up at the tree, but the bird went suddenly silent. Saadat's heart missed a beat. But then a second later, the nightingale resumed its song, and Saadat's heart began joyfully to beat again. *He's still alive*, she sensed. And they would see each other again. That other moonlit night, he had woven a rose into her hair. Now she went over to the rose bush, picked a bloom, sniffed its scent, and tucked it behind her ear. She stood a while longer in the moonlight and then went back indoors.

After their mother had died, Saadat's sisters had all married. Now she and her son were living in her mother's house. The boy strongly resembled Tursun. Although he was still very small, he helped his mother with everything. Often Saadat took him to see Kurvan-aka and Maysimyam-hada, especially becasuse Maysimyam was frequently unwell.

The festival of Roza Khit came round, which marks the end of the fasting month of Ramadan. Saadat dressed her son up smartly. "Amanzhan, we're going to see your grandmother and grandfather."

As they walked, Amanzhan asked her mother what Roza Khit was.

"For thirty days, Muslims fast and pray to Allah," Saadat explained. "They mustn't eat or drink anything until the sun has set. In the evenings, they invite each other to the *iftar*, where they say prayers and eat together. Children go from house to house singing the holy song of Ramadan, and the people in the houses give them sweets. Before Roza Khit, people bake *zhit*, a special thin *nan*. They put the *zhit* out on the festival table together with *sanza* and all kinds of sweet things and fruit. Everybody reads the Qur'an. During the days of Khit Ayam that follow, people usually go to see their parents. If the parents are dead, the children visit their graves in the mornings and read the Qur'an over them. For three days in a row, everybody goes to visit each other. They pray for the dead, they recite the Qur'an, they eat, drink tea, and talk together."

Soon they reached the house of Kurvan-aka and Maysimyam. It was getting dark.

Maysimyam heard somebody enter the room. "Hello, who's there?" she asked loudly.

Amanzhan called out "*Assalam, moma!*" and ran to her.

"*Wa aleikhim salam!*" she exclaimed, "Come in, my dears!" She lit a kerosene lamp on the windowsill.

"Where's *buva?*" asked the boy.

"He's probably in the shed, feeding the animals."

Just then Kurvan-aka came in. He greeted the visitors warmly and invited them into the large living room.

Kurvan's house had a low ceiling. There was a covering of straw on the floor of each room, on top of which was spread a felt *koshma.* Once everybody had sat down, he gave the blessing. "*Amin, Allahu akbar!*"

"Where are the girls?" asked Saadat.

"They're with Gyuli."

"I'll go and call them," said Saadat, getting up and going out.

Kurvan-aka and Amanzhan went out to the yard for firewood. At that moment the girls came rushing in, and the atmosphere in the house became noisy and cheerful all at once. Maysimyam set one of the girls to chop some meat and the other to prepare vegetables for the seasoning. They decided to cook *laghman.*

Saadat went over to the *kazan* to lend a hand. Maysimyam was glad when her daughter-in-law felt sufficiently at home to join in the work. Modangul lit a

156

fire in the hearth, and Saadat began to warm the gravy. The pungent aroma of the seasoning penetrated all through, and after a few minutes, the *laghman* was ready. Having a daughter-in-law at home is like a gift from God.

At last, the family sat down around the long low table, and the meal began. When it was over, Kurvan-aka brought out slices of melon and watermelon, then prayed while they were enjoying them.

"Mother, what about the presents for Amanzhan?" he said afterward.

Maysimyam got up with difficulty and went into the inner room, then came back carrying a bundle. She unrolled it and took out a jacket and trousers that they had bought for their grandson. "This is for you to wear when you start school. But why don't you try it on now and let us see you in it?"

Amanzhan kissed his grandparents with delight and went to change. When he reappeared, he looked grown-up and resembled his father even more.

"Doesn't he look just like Tursun," exclaimed Maysimyam, her eyes moistening.

"Well, let's hope he'll follow in Tursun's footsteps," added Kurvan-aka. He took ten rubles out of his pocket and gave them to Amanzhan.

Saadat looked on, touched at the scene. The girls also liked Amanzhan's new suit. Amanzhan, radiating happiness, said, "*Buva, moma!* Mama has been paid, and so we also wanted to bring you a *khitlik.*"

Saadat opened her bag and took out material for the old woman to make a dress, a man's shirt in sky blue, two *togach,* and two packets of tea, and put all these things on the table. Maysimyam hugged her daughter-in-law.

"Daughter, the best gift you can give us is to be bringing Amanzhan up so well," said Kurvan-aka.

Aman rummaged about in his mother's bag and brought out a white and yellow cashmere shawl. He put it over grandmother Maysimyam's head by himself. She shed a few more tears. Amanzhan then gave his grandfather a pair of knitted mittens. "Well how about that, *buva*?" he said. "Put them on. That's so your hands don't get cold when you go out for wood. I've got a pair just like them. Now, I'll help you."

The children ran into the other room. The adults sat in silence. After a while, Kurvan-aka sighed and placed his hands on the table.

"Daughter," he began softly, "you have lived for so long, so honestly and nobly, waiting for our son to come back. Now let me say to you myself that if you find a suitable young man, you should feel free to marry him."

"One child isn't enough," added Maysimyam. "It isn't good; it isn't right to live by yourself. You should get married and produce brothers and sisters for Amanzhan. We want you to be happy." She put her arms round Saadat, who was sitting beside her, and began to weep muffled sobs.

The old couple started saying once again that they had lost hope of ever seeing Tursun again. Maysimyam went on, "When they told my sister Gyuli to marry, she wouldn't listen. And now, if her daughters marry and her son goes off to the army, she'll be left completely by herself. How do you think she'll manage when she's old and alone?"

This topic did not arise by chance. Two days before the celebrations, they had received a visit from Idris, one of the village elders. He said to them, "Greetings, Kurvan-uka. Treat me kindly, for I come only as the messenger. And in my old age, I've come to your house to propose a match for Saadat," he announced.

"Well, who have you got in mind?"

"Askarzhan has been back from his exile for a long time. For the first year, he refused to marry, saying he was too ill. But Momun and Patam have helped him recover."

"How did they cure him?"

"Momun had a she-donkey that had just given birth. Patam milked it every day before dawn for forty-one days and gave the warm milk to Askarzhan. He soon recovered. Now he's an accountant for the *kolkhoz*."

Kurvan thought for a moment. "What can I say? Saadat has been loyal to Tursun for many years. Our grandson is growing up and will start school this year. Saadat's still young and could start a new life. We agree to it."

Maysimyam, bringing bread and tea, overheard the conversation.

"Mother, listen to Idris-aka's suggestion," Kurvan-aka called to his wife. "He's proposing that Saadat marries Askarzhan."

Old Idris coughed, then sipped at the cool tea. Maysimyam sat silently, wiping away tears. She had not given up hope that her son would come back. Yet the arrival of Idris with this proposal felt to her like the final strand of hope breaking. Still, she realized, life must go on, and so she and Kurvan-aka gave their consent to the match.

"After Ramadan, we'll unite Askarzhan and Saadat, then," said Idris-aka with a measure of relief.

How many *dzhigits* and their girls had their hopes and dreams trampled by that hideous war? Saadat's heart still burned for Tursun, but now she was destined to marry Askarzhan. But life went on indeed, and Saadat had the wisdom to try to draw Askar and his children into her heart as well.

• • •

"But what if Tursun was still alive?" asked Ruth in alarm. "They hadn't received a notification that he was dead. Maybe Saadat was acting too quickly?" She looked at Mehriban quizzically.

"Saadat has a remarkable story, but that's still ahead of us," she grinned. "Shall I go on?"

13

UNEXPECTED SORROW

The years flew by. Some people reached their time and passed into the next world, while at the same time, new life was being constantly born. Children need care and supervision, demanding their parents' attention at all times. In this endless circle of cares and effort, time slips away like water through the hands. For the villagers, the post-war years had not been not easy. The war had destroyed their plans, and many lives had fallen into ruin. Still, bit by bit, the wounded country got back on its feet.

In 1954, relations between the Soviet Union and China improved. The news came that Soviet migrants to China would be permitted to return to their homeland. Many people grew impatient to see their parents, brothers, and sisters who had lived abroad for so long.

That autumn, as leaves were covering the earth in a yellow carpet, a truck pulled up outside Kurvan-aka's house. Gyuli got out, together with an attractive white-faced woman and three children. The noise of the truck roused Kurvan-aka, who came to the gate, followed by Maysimyam, who recognized the newcomer at once.

"Why, it's Rukiyam!" she cried out, flung up her arms and ran to hug her. Rukiyam was her younger sister.

"Well, what a day this is," said Kurvan-aka, "Come inside, all of you!"

Maysimyam spread out a colorful rug and sat her sister down in the place of honor. Kurvan gave the blessing. "*Amin, Allahu akbar!*" and then set to busily questioning their visitor.

"Well, my dears," she said, smiling, "at last we're with you again. We managed to leave China and made it across the border. Now we can breathe the air of our native land once again."

"And what of our mother and father?"

"They have both passed on. It's many years since they were with us."

The expressions on the faces of both Maysimyam and Gyuli changed. "Oh, my goodness... and we weren't even able to bury them!" The two women wept, thwarted in their desire to fulfill their obligations. Enmity between the two countries had made it impossible.

"All right, that's enough," said Kurvan-aka with a note of sternness. "Allah has gifted us with the chance to see Rukiyam again. When a person is sad, you treat them tenderly, and when they're tired, you offer them tea." He looked toward his two daughters.

The girls took the hint, made a pot of tea, and poured it into bowls. As they sipped the tea, the conversation ran a calmer course.

That evening, their neighbors called. They quizzed Rukiyam about her parents, looked at her and her children, and sighed. Each of them was nursing a growing hope that they, too, would see a long-lost loved one again. They did not leave until late at night. Then Gyuli took Rukiyam and the children home with her. The tired children fell asleep the moment their heads touched their pillows.

"Rukiyam, you should get some sleep too!" smiled Gyuli tenderly. "A long journey is tiring, after all."

"Seeing you all again, I've forgotten all about being tired," sighed Rukiyam, looking round at the room with its warm, familiar feel. The two women lay down but could not sleep. Having been separated for twenty years, they had plenty to talk about.

"You know, sister, what happened to us turned out to be remarkably similar," said Rukiyam. "Life was a test of strength for me as well. Ahmat and I did well in China at first, and we had three children. I worked at a school for handicrafts in Ghulja. But in 1936, the troubles began in Xinjiang, and the people rebelled against atrocities committed by the authorities. Thousands of Uighurs were killed, and thousands more ended up in prison. That spring they arrested Ahmat and confiscated our house and all our belongings. I was left on the street with three children. We hired a cart, loaded our bundles onto it, and set off in torrential rain and high winds until we reached the house of Ahmat's brother, Hashim-aka.

"When I told them tearfully about our plight, Hashim-aka and his sister Sanam wasted no time and put us up in a temporary building in their yard that had two rooms. But Hashim-aka said to me, "Rukiyam, if they've arrested Ahmat, they may be after me as well. It would be better if you leave Ghulja.

"I could see he was nervous. I said to him, 'But where can I go with three children? My parents are dead. My brother's ill and can't even feed his own children. We could go to Dashigur, but what can I do there? At least I've got a job here and an income, even though it's not much.'

"All right, you can stay here for the moment, and we'll think more about it later," he said.

"From that time, life became difficult. I regularly took parcels to Ahmat, but the guards would not take them and would not even let me approach the prison. Was my husband alive or dead? I didn't know. My earnings weren't enough for us, so at night I would sew by candlelight. We made it through to autumn that way. But in the end, Hashim gave in to his fears and asked us to leave. Once again, I found myself constantly wandering the district with three small children in my arms, trying to find some kind of place to live. Finally I managed to rent a one-room shelter from the grandmother of someone I knew, who was called Agcha. We huddled gratefully into the room, relieved to have a roof over our heads. We could breathe again a little—and then the struggle to make ends meet began once more. Oh, sister, the things we went through. I wouldn't wish them on anybody."

Gyuli quietly wiped away tears. "My goodness, our troubles were so similar!" She raised herself a little from the bed and looked into Rukiyam's eyes.

"Oh, Gyuli, just wait till you hear what happened later. I kept watch over my children with an eagle eye. I made their food for them, and I made their clothes. I got them ready for school. At night I got no sleep because I was sewing things to order. There were often days when we had no coal or firewood. I had to wrap the children up before they went to sleep in everything we had. My health began to deteriorate. One day as I was coming home from work, and I fell over, right in the street. They told me at the hospital I was anemic and needed to eat better. But how was I to do that when there were three other mouths to feed? They made me stay in the hospital. I lay there for ten days, while kind old Agcha took care of the children.

"My health improved slightly after the hospital stay, and I started working again. But then more troubles came. My little girl Madzhangul, who was seven, used to play with the neighbors' children. They were playing with matches one day, and a spark fell onto Madzhangul's dress and set it on fire. In a panic she started rushing about, screaming. One of the neighbors heard her and threw a bucket of water over her. It put the fire out, but her burns were fatal. My little girl was in agony for three days and then died." Rukiyam wiped tears from her eyes with the sleeve of her dress. "After she died, I took to my bed for a whole month. Two friends, Muniram and Pridam, took care of me and tried to comfort me. They helped look after the children."

Gyuli was no longer lying down but sitting up straight, her eyes flickering with tears.

"In all that trouble and hardship, the years passed unnoticed." Rukiyam sighed. "Seven years after they put Ahmat into prison I received notification that he was dead. When I read it, I passed out. When I came to, the children were beside me, crying on the floor. I took them into my arms and began sobbing. 'Your father's gone, he's left us forever. Ahmat! My Ahmat! Why have you left us? How will I go on living?'

"Time stopped for me. My life just stopped dead. I cried and screamed for a long time. It was frightening. It was so hard, and I was lonelier than I had ever been. I'd always hoped that the day would come when my one and only Ahmat would be released and would embrace me again and take the children in his arms. Then our lives would become easier, warmed by the sunshine of our love. But now? I had lost my husband, I had failed to protect my little Madzhangul, and I could scarcely walk any more. It never rains, it just pours— one misfortune simply bringing another in its wake. I cursed the time that took my Ahmat away from me."

Gyuli took her by the shoulders, as though she had become cold. "So what happened after that?"

"The winter that year was very harsh. It was almost as cold in the house as it was outside. We were all wrapped up in everything we had, and the children huddled together to keep warm. One day, Muniram called in. She looked pitifully at our cheerless home. I put the children to bed, and we sat down at the table to exchange news and talk about life.

"You can never get enough of a good conversation with a close friend. We talked, and the children tried to get themselves warm and to sleep. Finally, my son Bilal and my daughter Imhanam grew quiet. Muniram looked at me directly in the eyes and said, 'Rukiyam, just look at yourself. Your health is terrible. The doctors told you to eat well, but you're still giving everything to the children. You're getting weaker every day.'

"'Well what can I do? That's my lot at the moment,' I said quietly.

"'Look, I haven't come here for no reason. Why don't you marry my brother Gopur? He was in prison for five years. We spent a whole year helping him recover and get back on his feet. And now he's in good shape again. Gopur's a knowledgeable man and works as an accountant in a factory. Don't say no until you've thought it through.'

"That day, Muniram stayed the night in my cold house. Then she started coming every day to persuade me to marry Gopur. In the end, I agreed. Muniram was right. Things would be much easier with a husband. I began to get stronger and even started to smile. The children no longer just huddled together. Now we had a protector—a calm and hardworking man at home. And in due course, I bore him a son. He was happy beyond words.

"But destiny has a way of gambling with people. One moment it lifts you high, and the next it hurls you to the ground. That's what happened next with me. One day a neighbor came by and said, 'Rukiyam, have you heard? Ahmat's been let out of prison!' It was like having cold water thrown over me. My arms and legs were shaking, and the blood ran out of my face down to my feet. The neighbor was taken aback. 'What's wrong?' she asked. 'You're not guilty of anything! It's all in the past.'

"She went away, but I stood there for a long time after, unable to move from the spot. I just tried over and over to make sense of why they had sent that unlooked-for notification that Ahmat was dead. Who would have mocked us so cruelly? Now my whole life with my first husband passed before my eyes. We loved each other very much and had never imagined being apart for so much as a day. But life had forced us apart. My heart had never stopped bleeding from being broken in two. For the next few days, I could think of nothing but this piece of news that the neighbor had brought. I could neither work nor talk, and my whole world was swamped with weeping.

"Later, another woman came to me at work at the craft school, with news about Ahmat. Apparently, he was back in Ghulja and wanted to see me. Instead of answering, I burst into tears. The woman said, 'This evening a car will come to collect the children. They will be taken to see their father. After all, he has the right to see them.'

"I nodded. After work I plodded slowly home, going over in my mind all of what had happened in the last few years. Ahmat had gone to prison because he had been involved with others in an uprising. After eight years of suffering, he was hoping that his wife and children would be waiting for him at home. And then he would find out that he no longer had a family. Poor Ahmat, what would he do now? My poor heart was consumed, and I cried long and hard. How I eventually got home I don't know.

"That evening a car stopped outside our house. Bilal and Imhanam, in their best clothes and excited to be seeing their father, vied with each other to persuade me to go with them. But to see Ahmat was more than I could bear.

"Gopur came home in the evening from work. He was gloomy and did not touch his food. 'Where are the children?' he asked.

"Their father Ahmat has just been released from prison. He wanted to see the children and sent somebody to collect them. I've just seen them off.

"He was silent for a while, then said, 'Rukiyam, now Ahmat has come back, are you leaving me?'

'What are you saying? I am not leaving you,' I said firmly.

'I will not let you have my son if you do.'

"Next day when I came home from work, I saw the same car waiting in the street. My heart was in my mouth. It was getting dark. I walked toward the car, and Ahmat got out. He was thin and pale, with sunken eyes.

'Rukiyam, wait, let's talk.'

"If I had listened to my heart I would have thrown myself into his arms and cried my eyes out on his chest. But I did not have the right to do that. I was a Muslim and was married to Gopur. I stood still, crying silently. When I lifted my eyes to Ahmat, I saw his face was wet from tears. He opened the car door. 'Come and sit in here, we can talk.'

"I got into the car. The driver got out, leaving us alone. Ahmat began to embrace me and kiss me passionately.

"'Let me take you with me,' he said. 'I have been through all that suffering and humiliation in prison only to see you again. That hope is what kept me alive. Rukiyam, I can't live without you!' He clasped me still harder to him.

"I tried to free myself from his embrace. 'Ahmat, listen to me. I have also been through a lot of suffering. Our Madzhangul is dead. I can't tell you in words how awful that was. And to prevent the children from starving, I have had to marry again. I have suffered every single day, thinking about you. It has been torture and sickness to the soul. And I did not remarry out of love but to get out of unendurable hardship.'

"I sobbed so hard that my whole body shook. And Ahmat, without letting me go, cried as well. My heart was telling me to go now with Ahmat. After all these years of suffering, here was my beloved beside me once again, and happiness was within reach. But at the same time, my conscience was telling me to think about Gopur, who had rescued me in my time of need and saved the children. And he wasn't going to let me take his son from him.

"Ahmat went on resolutely. 'You're not to blame. I will love the son you bore Gopur as one of my own and will raise him and teach him. Let's go and see Gopur, talk with him and collect the children.'

"'Ahmat, how can I abandon a man who helped me at the darkest time? Our destinies have parted us forever. You're a man, you should marry another woman for love, build a family. But I have to submit to my portion in life.'

'What you are saying is killing me,' said Ahmat quietly. 'Just when I gain freedom, I lose you. Please, think again, and don't hurry to answer.'

"We hugged for the last time, kissed one another, then I got out of the car. I walked home, but in front of my eyes all the time was Ahmat, full of love and hope.

My heart was in pieces, crying out within me. 'If you break up with the man you love,' it said, 'you'll always be unhappy.' I sat down on the curb and cried like a small child. I realized that the suffering of the previous seven years was not as much as what I went through that night when I cut off the one and only love of my life.

"When I went inside, Gopur was already there. He saw my reddened eyes but did not ask what was wrong. The baby started crying, and I went to attend to him in the inner room. He took hold of my breast and started to suck, oblivious to my state. Gradually, I calmed down as I rocked him in my arms. That day, my destiny was fixed by my son Nazar," said Rukiyam, finishing her story and looking at her sister.

Gyuli, weeping and sighing heavily, said, "Nothing is fair in this world. Nobody can achieve their dreams in this life."

"When nations quarrel, thousands of ordinary people suffer. We didn't choose to fall into that mess."

"So what happened to Ahmat?"

"He did a lot for the children and went on hoping for a long time that we would be together again. But I stayed with Gopur. Two years later, Ahmat married an attractive Kashgari and fathered three children with her. He got prestigious positions at work. But when he turned forty-six, his heart failed. His suffering had worn him out. A lot of people went to his funeral. I went as well and met his wife Halidam."

"And what's happened to Gopur?"

"Gopur and I lived together for ten years. He genuinely loved me, and he got on very well with my children. But he had an illness in his liver, and gradually he lost his appetite, lost weight, and turned yellow. The doctors couldn't help him. He also died before he reached fifty."

"Oh, Allah! Just look at these broken lives!" Gyuli shook her head.

"You know, sister, there has been so much happiness and so much pain in my life that I've learned to distance myself a little. In the end, you just have to endure it. I only hope my children will be spared so much hardship and humiliation. Bilal and Imhanam are now studying in Beijing. And I regard myself as a master seamstress. I can sew anything. I've brought my sewing machine with me and can use it to feed my children."

The two sisters sighed almost in unison.

"Rukiyam, we lived in different countries, but our lives and sufferings were the same." Gyuli leaned back and added in a sleepy voice, "Let's sleep now. It'll be light soon. Get some rest now, and we'll go on talking tomorrow." She put out the candle just as the first cocks were crowing.

• • •

"Yes," said Ruth, "Gyuli and Rukiyam did have similar fates. But Mehriban, I don't understand why Rukiyam refused to go back to the man she loved. Women in the West would see that very differently."

"You're absolutely right, Ruth. But this is why I wanted to write about Uighur women. They are brought up in such a way that honor always comes first.

Still, times are changing, of course, and opinions may change too. It may be that women today are willing to sacrifice a lot for the sake of love. If that's how it is, so be it. But most Uighur women abide by their morals and sense of purity." There was pride in Mehriban's voice.

"That sounds like no bad thing," agreed Ruth. "But it's such a complex question. I'd rather you go on with the story." She leaned back and closed her eyes again.

14

A Hidden Talent

More of our compatriots now returned from China. They built new houses, and the village grew noticeably. The mood among the villagers was good; people smiled more often.

On the first of September, Rukiyam dressed her children Bazar and Gozyal smartly and took them for their first day at school. They were met on the school steps by their teachers, Sepiyam and Saadat.

"We'll put your children into the first year," said Sepiyam. "They need to master our alphabet first."

Satisfied, their mother left them at the school. The classrooms soon filled up, for most of the settlers from China had brought young children with them.

Now that Rukiyam had arrived in the village, Gyuli no longer felt lonely. Prior to her sister's arrival she had been living completely alone. Hadzhyar had died a few years earlier, her daughters had married, moved out, and had their own children, and Yadikar was serving for three years in the army.

"Here's my house, Rukiyam. Bring your children. Come and live here. I'd be very happy to have you," she said to her sister.

"Thank you so much," Rukiyam beamed. "And before your son comes back from the army, we'll buy a house of our own. How wonderful that we'll be together again!"

"Absolutely. And God forbid that any of us be lonely any more, and especially not in old age."

Early one September morning, Gyuli milked her cow and led it out to the herd. Rukiyam and six-year-old Nuraniya swept the yard and then set the *dzhoza* table out in the arbor and spread a cloth over it. The two sisters sat down at the table and dropped pieces of thin *nan* into their bowls of *aktyan-chay* to begin their breakfast. Just then Maysimyam came into the yard. She had a worried expression on her face.

"Sister, what's the matter?" asked Gyuli and Rukiyam with one voice.

"Kurvan-aka has taken a bad turn," she replied. "He's complaining of pain in the lower back and says his sides are burning, as though someone has sprinkled them with pepper. He's been working in the field for several days, trying to overcome it. But he didn't sleep last night. His body is burning like fire, and he's muttering something we can't make out. It's worrying us. Today he's sweating a bit and seems to be back to his normal self. But he can't get himself up. He just carries on lying there. Even moving a little hurts too much."

Gyuli placed some *aktyan-chay* before Maysimyam in a bowl decorated with a floral pattern.

"If only it didn't hurt him so much! He drove that tractor for twenty years without a break. But no man is indestructible."

"He probably caught a chill on the tractor," suggested Rukiyam, joining in.

"Yes, you're probably right," nodded Gyuli sadly. "He would sit on his tractor from spring to late autumn, never straightening himself up. Then in winter, he walked seven kilometers every day to the repair station and back again. He always wanted to check how the repair and maintenance of the tractors was progressing. None of that was easy for him. Poor Kurvan-aka!"

"I've started having some confused dreams recently," said Maysimyam, who finished her tea and pushed the bowl away from her. "Maybe the spirits want to be remembered. I will bake some *zhit* for lunch. Come and join us."

She got up and hurried back to her ailing husband, expecting her daughter Modangul to arrive any moment with Nadya, a *feldsheritsa,* or traveling medical assistant.

Nadya, a Russian, had helped many of the sick of the village over the years. After listening to his heart and breathing through a stethoscope and massaging him a little, she said that he should go into the hospital immediately. She wrote out a referral on the spot.

Kurvan-aka was in no hurry to get to the hospital, however. He first asked his sister Adalyat to try folk remedies, but they were to no avail. Meanwhile neighbors and relatives came to visit every day. Kurvan-aka had a high status among the locals. If it is true that everybody has a symbol that describes their nature, then in Kurvan's case this might be a great plane tree, strong and reliable. He always helped people. They came to him often for help or advice, and Kurvan-aka would do whatever he could for them. Anybody who came to his house would leave inspired. And so when this highly respected tractor driver fell ill, a large number from the village came to see him.

Kurvan-aka never gave in to difficulty. After twenty years of impeccable work, he was awarded the rank of Leading Tractor Driver. Once he was elected as a government deputy at the regional level and twice at district level, and he had been decorated with a number of medals for his selfless labor at home during the war.

So at last, at age fifty-five, he had taken to his bed. His arms and legs ached and had no strength, and then there was the pain in his lower back and the burning sensation on his sides. His body felt as if it was on fire. The illness had advanced not only because he worked so hard but also because of the worries and stresses he had endured. When Tursun had disappeared, Kurvan-aka had gone many nights without sleep. He had never expressed his grief to anybody, but could it have been easy for him to let go of one of his two sons who had grown up beside him like tall trees?

Then Kurvan-aka had gone to considerable lengths to get his second son, Turgan, into higher education. Turgan, on leaving the pedagogical institute in Zharkent, had worked for two years at the primary school in the village of Kash. After this, he told his father that he dreamed of going to Tashkent to study at university with his friends Hakim and Asim from the next village. Kurvan-aka was pleased. "Now is the time to be studying," he said, selling his cow and calf to send his son away to the city. Turgan was the first person from our village to go to university.

Once he received his diploma, Turgan wrote to say that he would have to work for two years wherever he was sent, as payment for his education, after which he intended to return to the village. His parents were proud of him. Now, however, Kurvan-aka was ill and wondered whether he would live to see his second son's return.

One day Mariya and her husband Yakup came to see him. "*Aka*, what has happened to make you so ill?" Yakup shook Kurvan's hand.

"I've worked all my life and not cared for myself, and now I'm lying here helpless," the older man grinned cheerlessly. "What does the doctor say?"

Adalyat, sitting at the head of the bed, sighed. "*Feldsheritsa* Nadya says he should go to the hospital. I've tried to treat him myself, but it hasn't worked."

"Well in that case I'll go and fetch the *kolkhoz* cart." Yakup got up. "No need, thank you," said Kurvan-aka. "Don't bother yourself."

"What are you saying? You've done so much to help me. I respect you like my own brother."

"What have I ever done for you?" asked Kurvan in surprise.

"Do you remember when we came back from Ghulja? My elderly mother died soon after. I came to you one night and poured my heart out to you. You treated me as one of your own and comforted me. The next morning, you got the people in the village together to help us take my mother on her last journey in fitting fashion. Good deeds aren't forgotten, and I'll be loyal to you until I die. So let me take care of you now." He went out to fetch the cart.

Adalyat and Maysimyam got Kurvan-aka dressed, by which time Yakup returned. They lay some straw onto the cart, on top of which they placed several *korpya*, and finally they lay Kurvan-aka on the rugs.

"Kurvan, my one and only brother," wept Adalyat, "if I die, you are the one who should bury me. May Allah grant that you get better. We'll be waiting for you at home." She hugged him.

Beside them stood Maysimyam, also in tears.

"Don't cry," said Yakup, trying to give them courage. "Kurvan-aka will recover and will go back to riding his iron horse."

The cart moved out of the yard.

When Mehriban and her mother returned home, the room felt cold and melancholy. The girl put her arms round her mother and cried. "*Apa*, what do you think? Will *dada* get better?" All night she thought about him, unable to sleep. He treated her particularly fondly as she was the baby of the family. Mehriban was also very similar to Kurvan-aka's mother. He sometimes even used to call her "mama-girl" and loved her more than anyone else. Mehriban adored him, in turn.

During the spring plowing season Kurvan-aka often did not have time to come home for the midday meal. Maysimyam would boil a few eggs and wrap some bread up in a cloth and send Mehriban to take it to him. The girl would go happily out to the fields, and when she came to where he was plowing, she would put up her hand and wave. Sometimes Kurvan-aka did not get to the appointed place in time, in which case

Mehriban put the bundle of food down on the grass and went collecting aromatic wild mint and dandelion along the side of the *aryk*, which they would later use for cooking. She also picked flowers and simply admired the view of the fields. She would stand there and bathe her face in the sun and the breeze, waiting for her father to stop the tractor and then go and wash the dust and sweat from his face in the *aryk*. Only then did she unroll the cloth like a table cloth, break the nan into pieces, and shell the eggs. After this, she would sit and watch her father eat his lunch. He would say, "Daughter, why don't you eat with me?" But she would always decline, even if she was hungry. She was always moved to pity when she saw how tired he looked.

Kurvan would then drink his tea and ask her what the people at home were doing. She would turn serious and give him a detailed report. Her father, after saying the prayer after the meal, would place his greasy sweater under his head and doze for a while. Mehriban would gather up the cloth and look with pity at her aging father. Then she would get up decisively, go over to the tractor and wipe the seat, which resembled a huge iron plate, with the cloth. Going back to her father, she watched him a while longer.

For as long as she could remember, he had worked unceasingly. He always came home covered in dust. After a short rest, he would go and tend to the garden. As the recurrent pain in his back became more intolerable, he would lie down on his front and ask Mehriban to walk up and down on his back. Then next morning he would be back on the tractor at dawn, heading out to the fields.

Sometimes Kurvan would call Mehriban to ride on the tractor with him. She saw steam rising from the newly-plowed earth. After sowing, the land looked surprisingly level. Holding her father's hand, she admired the scene. And when the field was later covered with green shoots of wheat, the beauty was indescribable.

During the winter, the villagers would drive out beyond the village fence to gather firewood. They would return in the evening, the cart piled high with branches and stems of trees. On such days, Kurvan-aka came home shivering from cold, covered in snow, his whiskers and eyebrows white with hoarfrost that made him look like Father Frost. He would come in and sit by the stove, warming his hands by the fire, while the ice on his ears melted. Mehriban would wipe them dry with her slender fingers. Her mother, spreading a *korpya* by the stove, then set the *dzhoza* with hot food. The children sat down by the table and watched their father. Mehriban, perching beside him on her knees, longed for him not to have to go to work every day and to be able to rest from his hard lot in life.

From the spring until the first snow, the villagers had so much to do, at home and on the *kolkhoz*, that they had no time to sit together and talk heart to heart. Only during the long winter nights could they do so, sitting up until long after midnight before dispersing homeward. On such evenings Mehriban used to sit beside her father and listen with bated breath to the tales of the villagers and their hard lives. Her receptive child's memory retained these stories for the rest of her life. She dreamed that one day she would write a book about these hardworking people with their light, bright spirit. It would be an interesting read, and her father would feature in it.

Never once did her father say, "I feel unwell" or miss a day at work. All the more, then, did the sight of him lying on the *kang* disturb Mehriban. She abruptly recalled a particular incident. Early one spring, at sowing time, a sore appeared on Kurvan's right shoulder. It did not give him any peace. Her mother tried to treat it, without success. One day while shaving, her father caught the sore with his razor, causing it to burst. Blood and pus ran down his shoulder. Her mother washed the area and then took a small piece of felt mat, burned it, and pressed the ashes onto the wound, which she then quickly dressed again. Wearing this bandage, Kurvan-aka mounted the tractor and set out to the fields. Mehriban was amazed at the sense of responsibility her father had toward his work. She was full of pity for him.

Seeing him now, weak and lying on the *kang*, her heart was wrenched with sorrow.

"*Dada*, what's happened?" She went up to him and looked into his eyes.

"Don't worry, daughter, I'll be on my feet again in a few days," he said with a grin, forcing himself to overcome the pain.

And now he had been taken to hospital. Mehriban was sunk in heavy thoughts and did not realize that she was dozing.

The next morning, Maysimyam could barely rouse herself from her bed. All night her arms and legs had ached, and she had only got to sleep as morning came. "*Bismillah*," she said, rubbing her knees and pulling on her soft-soled slippers. She arranged her shawl on her head, put on a sleeveless jacket, and woke the girls.

From the cowshed came the sound of mooing. Maysimyam went to milk her, took her out to the herd, then came back and fed the chickens. There was disorder in the yard now that Kurvan-aka had been taken away. Mehriban sprinkled a little water onto the ground, then swept the yard tidy and picked up the rubbish. "*Apa*, let's go in. It's cold out here," she called to Maysimyam, who had gone to attend to the garden.

Meanwhile, Mahinur was getting ready for school. In her school uniform and with her two thick pigtails she looked neat and pretty. Her mother admired her growing girl. Her friends called out to her from the street: "Mahinur!"

"Right, Mother, I'm going. I'll go and see Father after school."

"Daughter, don't go to the hospital today. Anyway, how will you get home from Zharkent on your own? Mehriban and I will make some food and take it to your father ourselves. But don't forget to send a letter to Turgan."

After breakfast, Maysimyam and Mehriban began to prepare *zhutta* for Kurvan-aka. Maysimyam chopped a carrot finely and fried it in hot butter, then added various spices and seasoning and mixed it all together. Next, she divided a piece of dough they had prepared earlier into six pieces and rolled these out as thin as paper. She spread the carrot mixture evenly onto the dough pieces and rolled them up into roulades, then placed these in the *manty* steamer to be cooked.

"*Apa*, the water's boiling in the *kazan*!" called Mehriban.

"And everything's ready here, daughter. Light the oven," she instructed, then took the *manty* steamer and placed it on the *kazan* with the boiling water.

Maysimyam poured some *aktyan-chay* into a red Thermos flask that Rukiyam had brought from China. When the *zhutta* were ready, she put them into a deep bowl with a floral pattern and wrapped it tight in a white cloth to keep them warm. Mother and daughter climbed onto the cart and set off for Zharkent.

They got there at midday. The hospital was in the upper part of the town—on Soviet Street.

"Mehriban, won't you be late for school?" asked Maysimyam anxiously.

"No, *apa*, our classes don't start until two o'clock. I'll come and see *dada* quickly and then go off to school."

They walked up to the green gates of the hospital, leaving the cart under a gigantic elm tree. Patients wandered about the yard in faded overalls. Some of them sat on benches, talking to visiting relatives. To Mehriban, the hospital yard seemed gloomy. They asked one of the patients about Kurvan-aka.

"I know who you mean, he's in one of our wards. Go and get your white coats, and I'll take you to him," said a man, taking the mother and daughter with him.

The cloakroom attendant issued them with white coats and cautioned them not to be too long. When Maysimyam and Mehriban entered the ward, six patients were lying there talking to each other.

Maysimyam greeted them and went over to her husband.

Kurvan-aka's face brightened into a smile.

"How are you feeling? Is the treatment helping?" asked Maysimyam.

"It seems this illness isn't going to clear up very quickly. Sit down." He pointed to the bed.

Mehriban did not sit down. She noticed that her father's eyes were sunken and that his face had become longer. Only his black whiskers still conveyed a sense of life.

"*Dada*, when are you going to get better and get up again?" she asked him. Her eyes filled with tears.

There were also tears in her father's eyes. "The doctors are giving me medicine and injections. God willing, they'll get me on my feet again." His tears now ran down his whiskers and onto the pillow.

"I've brought you some food. Try it now, while it's still warm." Maysimyam took out the bowl containing the slices of *zhutta* and put it on the chair beside the bed.

Kurvan-aka looked at the dish. "I can't eat all that. Divide it up and give it to the other patients; let them try it."

Maysimyam gave each of the other patients a bowl of tea. Kurvan-aka made the effort to chew a little, so as not to upset his wife, and fell back on the pillow. "I'm not hungry, I'll eat later," he said, then, with a weak hand, he pulled a tobacco pouch out from under the pillow. "The doctors told me to stop smoking. So I've stopped. I'm giving you this pouch back, daughter. You embroidered it and gave it to me."

Mehriban took the little green pouch, sniffed it, and put it in her bag.

"Now don't be late for school." He went on, "My dears, why don't you go home again? There's no need to come in every day. They give me as much as I can eat."

The other patients thanked Maysimyam for the *zhutta*. Mother and daughter looked one last time at Kurvan and set off for home.

During the half hour or so that they had been in the hospital, the weather had turned. The wind picked up and started carrying the smell of rain. "This is why my arms and legs hurt all night," said Maysimyam.

"Daughter, let me drive you to school. Then I'll go back to the village."

"No, *apa*, don't worry. If you don't hurry, you may get caught in the rain. I'll run to school by myself," said Mehriban. When her mother had climbed onto the cart, she handed her the reins. Scarcely had Maysimyam called out, "Hup, hup!" when the cart jerked and moved off. Mehriban listened for a long time to the clatter of the cart's wheels on the stone road.

As Maysimyam drove along, she fell to thinking many things over. She remembered the days she had spent with her husband and the joys and sadness that had befallen them.

The children had just begun to grow up, and life had become a little easier, when the war came. They lost their eldest son. No sooner had that wound begun to heal, Kurvan himself had fallen ill. And if something should happen to him, God forbid, what would happen to the family? Their daughter Modangul had married a good man; there was no need to worry about her. Now she would like to see Turgan marry. He would look after his aging parents and would be there to bury them. He was a man, after all. And the little ones? Mahinur had started the eighth year at school, and Mehriban was in the sixth. She wanted to see them establish themselves, to see them succeed, and help them to be happy. That would be a gift from God. But for now, their father so ill, all this was hard to imagine. These were the thoughts that carried her all the way home.

She unhitched the donkey, led it to the shed, and gave it an armful of clover. "Oh, you dear soul! I drove you hard today. Here, munch this, and I'll bring you some water." She went into the house, changed into her old *chapan*, put on her galoshes, and went outside again. She gathered up the dry dung and took it into the shed. Out of either haste or tiredness, her heart began to thud in her chest. She rested a little, then gathered the remainder of the dung into a basin, piled some firewood on top, and took it all into the house. By the time Maysimyam had lit a fire in the stove, Mahinur came in, soaked through and shivering with cold.

"My goodness, child! Go and change quickly. I'll get some tea ready."

Mahinur changed, then went and curled up into a ball by the stove. "*Apa*, have you been to see Father? Can he walk?"

"Not yet, *kizim*. He's still in bed for now. I don't know whether he'll be able to get up again. Did you send the letter to Turgan?"

Mahinur nodded. Hopefully Turgan would come soon. Maysimyam could hardly pour the tea, her hands shook so much.

There was a gentle knock at the door, and in came Rukiyam with her little girl, Nuraniyam. "Assalam, *hada.* I stopped by this morning but saw the lock on the door and guessed you'd gone to the hospital. What news of Kurvan-aka?"

Mahinur placed bowls of tea in front of her *kichik-ana* and Nuraniyam.

"He feels very bad." Maysimyam started to weep. "His eyes have hollowed, and his cheekbones are sticking out. I took him some *zhutta,* but he only took one bite. He says he's got no appetite."

"Come on, sister, calm down. You need to save your strength and make sure your blood pressure doesn't go up."

"Oh, Rukiyam. My head is spinning. The worry won't leave me alone. I've written to Turgan asking him to come quickly."

"*Apa,* I've just seen Saadat-hada," piped up Mahinur. "She said that she and Amanzhan would go to see *dada* tomorrow."

"How old is your grandson?" asked Rukiyam.

"Amanzhan's fourteen and in seventh year at school. He and Mahinur walk to school in Zharkent together. He often helps me out, doing jobs in the garden and the yard, chopping wood. And he reminds me so much of Tursun!"

"And how is Saadat getting on in her new family?"

"Our Saadat's given birth to twins. Askarzhan is very happy. His daughter is now married, and his son is in the army. Tadzhigul did not live to see these happier days. She was a gentle and humane woman."

"They were the ones who suffered that time in Chilik with Gyuli?"

"That's right. They supported each other when they were in exile. Then Askarzhan made it back from the camp, but poor Tadzhigul had died by then. Saadat married him and brought up his children like her own."

They finished their tea and said the prayer. Rukiyam finally came to the point of her visit.

"Maysimyam, Nuraniyam had a temperature all night. She says her stomach aches. Can you have a look at her?"

"Very well. Come over here, little one," Maysimyam called to her niece. She sat her down beside her and felt her head with her hand, then her shoulders, and laid her palm on the girl's stomach. "She's had the evil eye on her. Mahinur, will you fetch me a handful of salt?"

The girl fetched the salt and poured it into Maysimyam's hand. Maysimyam divided the salt into three parts. She took one part in her hand and started to move her cupped hand containing the salt over Nuraniyam's body, reciting as she did so, "*Ash kodi, chik kodi, go to the beautiful girls, go to the beautiful boys, go out to their lovely hair, go to the long roads and go to the old walls. Ash kodi, chik kodi, not my hand but the hand of the holy mothers, the hand of the mother healers, suf, suf, suf.*" She repeated this three times, and three times she ran her hand, filled with salt, over different parts of the girl's body.

After this, both stood up. Maysimyam threw a handful of salt into the fire. As it fell into the flames, it began to shoot and crackle. Maysimyam washed her hands, then went up to Nuraniyam, passed her hands over the girl's back and chest and said, "That's it, my girl, you're healed." And she began to laugh.

Nuraniyam laughed and ran to her mother.

"Thank you, sister. We'll expect you tonight for supper. Gyuli-hada is cooking. Don't sit at home thinking bleak thoughts."

"I'll come," promised Maysimyam.

After seeing her visitors out, Maysimyam lay down on the warm *kang* and soon drifted off without realizing. Mahinur started doing her school homework. Everything was very quiet until Maysimyam woke up suddenly and whispered, "Oh, Allah, save us!"

"*Apa*, what's scared you?"

"I was having some kind of nightmare. The spirits of the dead just won't calm down. It feels like something's about to happen." She pressed her hand to her chest.

"*Apa*, you shouldn't talk like that. Whatever the dream was, you should take it as good. That's what you told me."

"Yes, that's how it is. May everything be for the better," agreed Maysimyam, although she still felt discomfort and anxiety.

She drank a bowl of water and breathed deeply, then lay down again. She had no strength today, either because of the dismal weather or because she had not slept all night. When evening came and Mehriban returned from school, she could scarcely get up. "Oh, Allah!" she exclaimed. "It's dark already. Has the cow come home?"

"Don't worry, *apa*, I've already milked her," replied Mahinur. "You were sound asleep. I didn't want to wake you. You don't look very well." She looked anxiously at her mother.

"For some reason I've been so tired recently."

"You haven't forgotten that *kichik-apa* is expecting you tonight for supper?"

"That's right. I'll go. It may help me relax a little." She sighed, and then pulled on her galoshes and went out.

Once her mother had gone out, Mehriban said to Mahinur, "*Hada*, when Mama and I went to see Father at the hospital, I didn't recognize him at first. He's got so thin that you can hardly make out his body under the blanket. Just his head still stands out. It really crushed me. I cried all the way to school afterward."

"No need to cry. Maybe he'll still recover."

"But listen. Father didn't see much in his life that was good. When he was a child, he was an orphan and hungry. Then he grew up and started his family, and to make sure that we never wanted for anything, he worked from dawn to dusk on that tractor. He took absolutely no care of himself. And now he can scarcely walk at all. I dread to think what may happen to him." She broke into sobs.

"Don't invite trouble, Mehriban. You've got to trust that Father will get better." Mahinur hugged her little sister and wiped away her tears. "Why don't we clean all around the house and yard tomorrow, so that everything's spotless? Amanzhan can pick vegetables in the garden and put them in the store."

"*Hada*, are you preparing for something?" asked Mehriban with disquiet.

"Turgan-aka may arrive at any time, and then all the relatives will turn up. So we need everything to be in good order."

"I'll ask Modangul-hada and Sadyk-aka if they can help tomorrow," agreed Mehriban.

The girls gathered together the next day. They whitewashed the house and tidied the yard. Amanzhan and Sadyk dealt with the vegetables.

And the days continued to pass, various members of the family went to visit Kurvan-aka at the hospital. But his situation did not improve.

On one of those days, Maysimyam came out of the cowshed to see a tall, handsome, broad-shouldered young man coming into the yard with a suitcase in his hand. She put her bucket down. "Son, it's you! Turgan! At last!" She flung herself on him and wept.

Turgan embraced her and kissed her. "Don't cry, *apa*."

His sisters came running out of the house, shouting, "He's arrived! Our brother's here!" There was embracing all round, and Turgan was then taken indoors like a long-awaited guest. Tea was served and Maysimyam updated him on the news of his father.

Turgan listened closely and then said, "*Apa*, why don't you prepare something liquid for me to take in to him? I'll go to the hospital tomorrow and talk to the doctors. It looks as though I'll probably bring him back with me."

Turgan walked to the hospital the next morning. When he entered the ward, Kurvan-aka opened his eyes wide. "My dear son! Allah himself has brought you!" His voice was weak, and his eyes filled with tears.

Seeing his father in this state, Turgan also began to weep. He sat down by the bed and embraced his father's frail body firmly. He could hear how fast the older man's heart was beating.

Kurvan-aka took his son's hand. "Son, will you please take me home?"

"Certainly, *dada*. I'll speak to the doctors now." Turgan got up. Feeling dispirited, he went to the office where the doctors were stationed.

"I'm the son of Kurvan Murdinov," he announced. "Can you please tell me about his condition?"

A doctor of some fifty years, who was graying at the temples and wore spectacles, searched through a pile of papers. "Both of your father's kidneys have wasted away, and the medicines we have been giving him have had no effect," he said. "On top of that, the patient came too late to hospital for a chance of recovery. I'm afraid there is nothing we can do. He does not have much time left. I suggest that you take him home, so he can say farewell to his family."

Turgan brought his father home that same day. Mehriban came home from school in the evening and rushed straight into the inner room, where her emaciated father was lying. Adalyat was sitting at the head of the bed, and Maysimyam at the foot. Mehriban froze.

"Come here, mama-girl," called Kurvan-aka, barely audibly.

Mehriban went over and sat down beside him, stroking his cheeks softly. She was weeping and could see tears running silently down her father's face. The four of them sat there weeping as it grew dark outside. The light of hope was not very strong within them.

Kurvan-aka grew weaker and faded away with each passing day. On the ninth day after his return, sensing the end, he called Turgan to him. Turgan sat beside him and lay his warm hand on his father's stiffening head.

"Lay me on the ground," Kurvan-aka instructed him. The family lay out a *koshma* and spread four *korpya* and two pillows on the floor and lay Kurvan-aka on them. He looked with a steady gaze at all those around him and said, "I am dying. Don't be afraid."

Kurvan-aka closed his eyes, then opened them again. "Turgan, son, from now on, everything will depend on you. Take me well to the grave. Look after your mother. She is very ill. And your sisters are in your custody, Turgan."

He did not take his eyes off his son.

Stroking her brother's warm head, Adalyat said, "Kurvan, brother, you have honored us all, and we are pleased with you. Please be satisfied with us." She kissed his forehead and broke into sobs.

A single tear ran down from Kurvan's eye, leaving a damp trail on his hollowed cheek, falling onto the pillow. He was silent.

At that moment, everybody knew with certainty that he had departed this world. His family continued to sit around him in silence, quietly wiping their tears. Adalyat took a long piece of white cloth and tied her brother round the chin, and then tied together his big toes. After this, she slowly wrapped the whole of the body in white cloth and ordered everybody to follow her into the other room. They placed Maysimyam in the center of the room, and her daughters and closest relatives sat down beside her.

Hearing that Kurvan-aka had died, their neighbor Rihanbuvi called in. She greeted everybody quietly and then placed cushions behind Adalyat and Maysimyam. "I've brought a pot of *aktyan-chay*. I'll pour it into bowls for you to drink. People will start coming now, but you will get dry throats from lamenting." She handed bowls to the women.

Gyuli had brought a roll of white cloth. Now she tore pieces off and handed them to the neighbors and family assembled. She tied lengths of the same cloth around the waists of the men.

An hour later, the gates were open. Turgan, girdled in his white cloth, wailed loudly. "Father! My unhappy Father! Your ordeal is over, you have come to your reward!"

Amanzhan, Sadyk, and Mahmut also joined the lamenting. As people came into the yard, they all began to cry. All the villagers came to remember and pray for the dead man, and so did many from neighboring villages.

After washing the deceased and wrapping him in white, they lay him in the *tavut*, the ceremonial covered stretcher kept by the village for funeral processions, spreading the pall over it in the center of the yard. They recited the prayer of parting over the body. After this, the men picked up the *tavut* and carried Kurvan-aka away on his last journey. Turgan, Amanzhan, and

Mahmut, walking ahead of the cortege, cried and keened, "Father! Our dearest Father!"

In accordance with Uighur custom, women and small children are not allowed to follow the cortege into the cemetery. They stayed in the yard of the house and continued their lamenting. But nobody noticed Mehriban disappear among the men, following them to where she was not supposed to go.

This was the first time that she had been in a graveyard. She saw the big rectangular pit, its length the height of a man, and to one side an opening leading into a recess as deep as a seated man and as long as his full height. Two men now carried the *tavut* up to the side of the grave and lifted the body down to two other men below. They laid it out on a bed of earth that had been prepared earlier. After this, they bricked up the niche and climbed back out. Now, one at a time, each of the men who had accompanied Kurvan-aka on his last journey threw seven *ketmens* of earth into the grave and then threw the *ketmen* in as well. The next man retrieved the *ketmen,* and repeated with seven shovels of earth. Many men were present, and so the earth piled up quickly, soon forming a small hill over the grave. The mullah read the appropriate *sura* of the Qur'an and they all raised their hands in prayer, after which they dispersed homeward.

At that moment, Turgan noticed Mehriban. "What are you doing here? Children aren't allowed near the graves. It's dangerous! Come on, let's go back." He took his little sister by the hand, and they walked home.

From that day onward, Mehriban had difficulty sleeping. No sooner had she closed her eyes than she saw the niche in the grave and her father, lying on the damp earth, wrapped in white. She would wake suddenly and jump out of bed, screaming and crying. Maysimyam, who was deeply affected by the loss of her husband, was suffering from high blood pressure and spent most of the time lying down. Gyuli and Rukiyam took over all the domestic tasks.

Seven days after the death of Kurvan-aka a *nazyr* was held, as is customary. Afterward, as the various relatives who had come from far and near for the funeral, were setting off for their homes, a strong wind suddenly stirred. It threw everything in the yard into disorder, leaving it looking neglected and dismal.

Something sinister also began to happen to Mehriban. Day by day, she grew paler and weaker; she could not sleep at night and would not eat. The tearful Maysimyam tried to treat her with her folk remedies but without success.

One day, Gyuli brought her friend Zaynaphan the *kumlakchi* to her sister's house. "*Hada*, let Zaynaphan read the *kumlak* and tell us how we should treat Mehriban."

"Gladly," said Maysimyam. "As if it wasn't enough for me to be ill and mourning, Mehriban has fallen sick as well."

Zaynaphan spread a towel over the table and threw her fortune-telling pebbles onto it, then raised both hands and began muttering something softly. She jumped up suddenly. "*Allahu akbar!*" she called out. She divided the pebbles into three piles and took three from each and put the remainder aside. She finished with a row of nine pebbles, three groups of three.

"Maysimyam, don't burden yourself with fears. Your daughter will get better," announced the old woman.

She then divided the stones two more times. One turned out to be superfluous. Zaynaphan considered the pebbles and thought for a whole. "Mehriban shouldn't have gone to the cemetery. She was badly disturbed by it. You need to go to the cemetery now and fetch a handful of earth from her father's grave. Put a pinch of the soil into a bowl of water and give it to the girl to drink tomorrow morning. Do this for seven days in a row. And you should keep candles burning in seven places for one week starting today."

"We'll do everything you say," nodded Maysimyam, who stroked Mehriban's head.

Zaynaphan looked at the stones again. "If this doesn't help, you must have the girl swallow a raw sparrow's heart every morning for seven days, washed down with a bowl of water. That will certainly cure her."

She gathered up the pebbles and cast them again. Again, the result was nine stones, three groups of three. "Well, Maysimyam-hada, it looks like we won't get any further until you give me something," she commented.

Maysimyam fished five rubles out of her pocket and put them in front of the *kumlakchi*. Zaynaphan put the money into her pocket and continued her consultation.

"Your daughter is being kept alive by her father's spirit. This is very good. And Allah has granted her some kind of special gift. That will become clear later and will bring you joy. Mehriban must develop that gift in herself." Zaynaphan wrapped the pebbles in a special cloth and got up.

The session was over. They all felt a sense of relief. "Thank you, Zaynaphan," said Maysimyam. "Let's have some tea."

"No, thank you. It's time for me to be getting home. I have to see to my animals."

Just as Zaynaphan was ready to leave, however, Rukiyam brought in a pot of *suyuk ash*, sprinkled on top with finely chopped coriander. "I waited until you finished what you were doing. But please, help yourselves. *Suyuk ash* must be eaten while it's hot!"

Zaynaphan gladly partook of the evening meal with her friends and went home afterward.

From that day the women carefully performed all that had been prescribed by the *kumlakchi*. To the delight of all, Mehriban began to sleep peacefully after seven days.

When twenty days had passed since the death of Kurvan-aka. Maysimyam sat down beside Turgan. "Turgan, you have proved yourself a man. You arrived from Tashkent in time, you were able to say good-bye to your father, and you paid your respects and took him to his resting place. I'm proud of you, son. But now you should go back to work. It's not right for us to die along with the departed. We must go on living. Don't be worried about me. I've always got my sisters and my three daughters to help me, plus Adalyat, your *chon-apa*, my son-in-law Sadykzhan, Saadat, my grandson Amanzhan, as well as the rest of the village." She let out a sob.

"*Apa*, if you're going to cry, how can I leave?"

"No, son, I'm not going to cry. Your father left us, trusting that I would be strong."

"*Apa*, I'll be back in a year, and then it will be easier for you right away." Turgan pulled an envelope out of the pocket of his jacket. "This is some money for you to mark our father's fortieth day. As for the anniversary, I'll see to that when I come back."

Maysimyam took the money and gave it to Mahinur to put in a safe place.

"*Apa*, I'll send you some money every month. You must buy yourself firewood, coal, and provisions for winter."

"Thank you, son. I will pray for you day and night."

"Mama, you've got a lot of things to look forward to," her son smiled kindly. "You'll see me marry, and you'll bring up my children. Then we'll see my sisters marry. But we can't do any of this without you. You are our support, our hope, and our source of advice. You're our treasure." Turgan embraced and kissed his mother.

Watching them, Mahinur and Mehriban whispered something to each other.

"What are you two being secretive about?" their mother asked.

"*Apa*, just look at how like his father Turgan is," said Mahinur. "The same eyes and forehead. He's just as tall, and even his voice is similar."

"If he had whiskers, he'd be a copy of him!" added Mehriban.

Maysimyam looked with pride at her son and said, "May your life be a happier one than your father's was."

The next day Adalyat, Mahmut, Gyuli, Rukiyam, Saadat, Amanzhan, Modangul, and Sadyk brought

Turgan small gifts and wished him a safe journey. His *chon-apa*, the fair-skinned Adalyat, sat in the middle and spoke on behalf of all present. "Turgan, you are a deserving son and we are proud of you. So, go and work well. Find yourself a mate and marry. Then you'll come back to your village with honor. We badly need educated people here. But for now, we will pray for you." She lifted her hands and read a prayer. The others raised their hands after her. The horn of a car sounded on the street outside. Everybody went out into the yard to see Turgan off.

• • •

"You have very interesting customs for remembering the dead," said Ruth. "They are completely different to American customs. But I was particularly taken by what the fortune-teller said. Were her predictions correct?" Ruth raised her eyebrows slightly distrustfully.

"We still have fortune-tellers like Zaynaphan-ana as well as their remedies, even today. Not all of them are to be trusted. But I always believed Zaynaphan-ana," said Mehriban. "She had a genuine gift."

"The story is getting more and more interesting," smiled Ruth. "Do continue."

15

LIKE BORN AGAIN

O ne of the reasons that life is interesting is because it is cyclical. A person may grieve and weep, but later she will calm down, come round, and begin to work again. What else is there to do? After all, life must go on.

After the death of Kurvan-aka the older members of the family returned to their usual activities, while the younger members continued with their studies. On the warm days, the children did not notice the seven kilometers they walked to school each way, but in winter, those fourteen kilometers were a challenge.

One freezing morning in December, when snow had fallen overnight, the group of pupils set out to school from the village as usual. A little way beyond the village fence on the way toward the main road, a stream of water ran down and across the track, blocking their way. Surprised that any water could be flowing in such cold, the children placed stones in the current and used them to step across. Last to cross was Mehriban. She slipped on one of the stones and landed with both feet in the water.

"Oh girls, what can I do? My feet are soaked!"

Looking at her boots, which were leaking water, one of them said, "You should go home. Your feet will freeze in this temperature, and you'll catch cold."

"No, I can't. Today it's my turn to answer questions on literature. I didn't read Maksim Gorky's biography for nothing, did I? If I don't go today, I might get a two, which is poor, instead of a four, which is good."

The oldest child in the group, a boy called Seitzhan, shook his head in disapproval as Mehriban hurried on, ice forming on her saturated boots. Every minute, her feet became colder, and she regretted countless times not having turned back. At last they arrived, however, and Mehriban, frostbitten and miserable, ran into the classroom. Unable to bear the pain in her feet, she burst into tears. There was still some time before the class was due to start. Her classmates opened the stove door and sat Mehriban down beside it. She took her boots off and began to rub the frozen soles of her feet. They were in such pain it was as though needles were being thrust into them. Mehriban barely got through her six lessons. The pain in her feet did not cease. However would she get home again?

Fortunately for her, Mervanam had driven to the bazaar that day to trade some items and called in at the school on her way. And so Mehriban and two of her school friends sat on the cart and were brought home safely.

Needless to say, Mehriban was badly unwell after this. She went to bed for several days. Her mother rubbed her with the fat of a sheep's tail and gave her hot milk with sheep fat every day to drink. Mehriban began to feel better after this procedure and started going to school again, but her cough would not let up.

She coughed all through the winter, and in spring, when the other children rushed out and frolicked in the warm sunshine, Mehriban found that she could not run about with them in the school yard. Even just walking, she had difficulty breathing. The walk to and from school sapped all her strength. She got such painful stitches in her side that she was forced to sit down, tears in her eyes, and wait for them to subside.

One evening, when the girls were doing their homework by the light of the kerosene lamp, Mehriban said to her sister, "*Hada*, when I walk, I get severe stitches in my side. I'm gasping for breath all the time and have to stop."

"But why didn't you tell us this before? We'll take you to the doctor tomorrow," said Mahinur uneasily.

"Whatever you do, don't tell Mama."

"Why not?"

"She'll start worrying. Why don't I get through exams first and then go to the doctor?"

"But there's a whole month yet before exams. You mustn't ever allow an illness to take hold of you!"

"I know, *hada*, but if I go to the doctor now, he'll be sure to send me to the hospital. And I don't want to stay in the sixth year for another whole year. No, I'll go to the hospital after the exams."

Her elder sister thought for a while, and then agreed. But she felt uneasy inside. Mehriban had certainly started to look drawn and pale.

By the end of May, all the examinations were over, and finally Ayvanam, the form teacher, handed out copies of the results table for the sixth year. Ahead of the pupils now were the summer holidays. They shouted, "Hurrah!" and ran home.

As the class dispersed, the teacher called Mehriban over. "Today you must go and see the doctor. Do you promise?"

Mehriban nodded. Next day Maysimyam took her to the doctor. He listened carefully to Mehriban and shook his head reproachfully. "*Hada*, why didn't you bring your daughter in at the proper time? She has serious problems with her lungs. I'm admitting her to the hospital. You should go straight away."

Tearfully, Maysimyam took the referral and left the consulting room. She took Mehriban to the hospital and then returned home on the cart.

Mehriban was given a number of injections each day and a whole handful of tablets to take. On his morning rounds, the doctor put his stethoscope to her chest to check her lungs and shook his head slightly. Her mother and sisters visited often.

Maysimyam arrived one day and saw that Mehriban had been crying. "Why have you been crying, *kizim*? Are you feeling very ill?" she asked, concerned.

"Don't worry, *apa*. I'm a lot better. I've stopped coughing and am sleeping well at night. It's just that I dreamed about Father last night."

"What was the dream?"

"He was sitting next to my bed, stroking my head and said to me, 'Don't be afraid, daughter, you'll get better. All will be well for you.' Then he kissed me on the forehead and went away. He was wearing a black coat, and on his head was his old black hat. In the dream, he was healthy," she said, barely holding back her tears once more.

"Mehriban, your father is protecting you," said Maysimyam. "And you will soon get better and come home again." She smiled and stroked the girl's two long pigtails.

After her husband's death, Maysimyam had sunk into bleak thoughts and could not sleep at night. Her hair turned grayer and new wrinkles appeared on her face. Her eyes were always full of tears. Yet she paid no attention to how she was feeling; she kept her spirits up and tried to support the children.

Mehriban was in hospital for thirty-six days. She came out healthy and renewed. Her mother was overjoyed. When she entered the yard of her home, she exclaimed, "*Apa*, what a lovely clean yard you've got! What glorious flowers!" She went up to the velvety red, yellow, and pink dahlias. Nearby were also irises, peonies, henna, and desert four o'clocks.

All this beauty made Mehriban smile. Round the arbor pumpkin and convolvulus were entertwined and had grown high and become so interwoven that the hot sunlight could not penetrate. Mehriban touched the swelling pumpkin fruit, which they would later use to make scoops and ladles. Meanwhile, in the garden, Mahinur and Amanzhan were watering the vegetables. They dropped their *ketmens* and ran to greet their sister.

"Mehriban, did they give you a certificate saying you've recovered?" asked Amanzhan.

"What do you need that for?" Mehriban asked him.

"On presentation of the certificate, we will take you on to work. Our team needs a third worker right now." They all laughed.

"Hey, *brigadir*, look at how thin Mehriban's got. Do you imagine she could even lift the *ketmen*?" said Mahinur to Amanzhan. "We should assign her instead to helping Mama in the house." And they agreed on this course of action.

Soon after Mehriban came home, she went to visit Saadat. After sitting with her for a while, she asked Amanzhan to go with her to the cemetery. On the way, as they looked out over the fields of wheat swaying in the wind, she said to him, "This field was watered by my father's sweat."

"You're right. A lot of our parents and grandparents sweated in these fields. And for that, the fields have yielded a harvest."

"Father taught me to work on the earth and to take care of it. For me, every plant here is a living thing."

They reached the cemetery and found Kurvan-aka's grave. They stood there for a while in silence. Afterward, they sat down and prayed, then returned home. On the way back, Mehriban looked at her companion closely.

"Amanzhan, I want to tell you a secret. But you mustn't ever tell anybody. All right?"

"All right."

"Although it's already eight months since Father died, it's like he's still alive for me. When I was in the hospital, he came to me."

"What are you talking about?"

"It's true. One night *dada* came up to me and stroked my head. I told Mama that it was in a dream."

"You weren't afraid when you saw him?"

"No, I wasn't. He's always near me, just on my right. Sometimes I talk to him. Do you believe this? I would like to read you a poem I wrote for Father. But promise you won't laugh."

"I promise. Read it to me," Amanzhan responded seriously.

Mehriban looked into the distance. There her father stood, looking at her. She began to read the poem. Amanzhan listened, his eyes wide open. When the girl finished, the eyes of both of them were moist with tears.

"Mehriban," said Amanzhan with admiration, "what a wonderful poem! You must keep writing. One day you could be a poet or a writer."

"Do you know how much you need to study in order to be a writer? Father would have helped me go to university. But there's no hope of that now."

"If you've got talent, you will write. But if you haven't, no amount of education will help," the boy said with conviction.

"You're right," she smiled.

The two children ran home along the dusty path.

Once again, the warmth of summer gave way to autumn, and once again, the world was plunged into gold for a moment. This year, the autumn was dry and sunny. The villagers picked the vegetables in their plots and put them into their winter stores. The wheat harvest in the fields was completed, and work began on picking the maize.

There were not enough hands for the work, and so schoolchildren were sent to help the adults with this task. They were expected to work in the fields until November. The Zharkent middle school sent all its children, except for first-year and tenth-year pupils, to work at Nadak. They lived in a large hostel that stood beside the corn sorting yard.

Mehriban, now in her seventh year, went out to work with the rest. From morning to evening, they picked maize cobs, and then, after eating their evening meal and resting a little, they went to the corn yard to peel and sort the harvest. The autumn evenings were cold. The mornings were damp, and soon the children's clothes and footwear were soaking wet. Many of them became ill as a result. After forty days of this labor, they were allowed home, at last, and could go back to school.

Once again, Mehriban and the other children began their daily march of fourteen kilometers. She soon began to feel weak, and in the evenings, she had a high temperature. But she told nobody and did not miss any days at school.

One day as they were coming home from school, Mehriban suddenly sat down in the road out of sheer exhaustion. "*Hada*, I haven't got the strength to keep walking," she said to her older sister.

Mahinur felt her forehead. Her sister's temperature was high. "What can we do, anyone?" she asked the others, looking around for any passing cart. But the road was empty.

Then Sahinur had an idea. "Why don't we carry your bags, and you carry Mehriban on your back." Mahinur did so for a short distance but soon got tired. Now Seitzhan took Mehriban on his back and kept going for a good long time. Next was Amanzhan. Of the group of fourteen, six were senior pupils, and it was they who took turns to carry Mehriban. At last, they brought her to her gate. When Mahinur, after thanking them, went into the yard with her sister still on her back, their mother was aghast.

"Oh, Allah, whatever's happened?" she exclaimed, running to open the door and bring her inside. She and Mahinur carefully laid Mehriban on the *korpya*. Maysimyam felt her daughter's forehead. "Why, you're on fire!"

They changed Mehriban into her home clothes and wrapped her in a blanket.

"Lord, what am I going to do with this child? When I told her not to go and work on the maize, she wouldn't listen. And now look!" her mother wailed tearfully.

Mahinur then said, "Mama, let's have some tea, then I'll go for the doctor. Don't worry, she'll recover." She put out the *dzhoza* and laid a cloth on it. She poured tea into two bowls and gave one to her mother.

"Mehriban, lift your head up, and try to drink a little," said Maysimyam, putting the cup to the girl's lips.

Mehriban greedily drank the entire contents of the bowl of tea but was almost immediately sick. "*Apa,* my head hurts badly," she moaned.

Sitting beside her, her mother was at a loss for what to do. She jumped when the door opened and Rukiyam came in. "Has Mehriban fallen ill?" she asked.

"Look, here she is. Her whole body's on fire. Her head's aching, and on top of that, she's nauseous and vomiting."

"*Hada*, I've got a Chinese remedy I brought from Ghulja. I'll go and get it," said Rukiyam and darted out. She was back a few minutes later with something wrapped in paper.

Maysimyam took the package and made Mehriban take the small black pills. She swallowed them with difficulty and went to sleep after a while.

Mahinur brought the village doctor. She prescribed tablets for colds. Mehriban, meanwhile, suffered from the pain in her head all night. Her mother sat beside her all night and did not get any sleep.

The next morning, Gyuli and Rukiyam called in. Maysimyam said to them, "We need to take my daughter to her doctor in town. They've healed her before."

"Well, let's go together," Rukiyam suggested.

The two sisters took Mehriban to the hospital in Zharkent. The doctor on duty examined her, then left the office and returned with two more doctors. Maysimyam felt herself shrinking with fear.

They diagnosed Mehriban with typhus and admitted her to hospital that same day. They shaved her head bare and threw her lovely long locks into the stove. As she lay on the hospital bed, Mehriban drifted in and out of consciousness. Next morning three more doctors came and spent a long time examining and listening to her. They then discussed among themselves in Russian and finally reached agreement. "Little girl, we're sending you to Alma-Ata. You haven't got typhus, so don't worry. Everything will be all right."

They placed Mehriban on a stretcher and loaded her into an ambulance. En route to Alma-Ata they stopped to give her an injection and let her drink.

The jolts and bumps of the road were a torture to her, and in the end she fell into a somnolent state.

She sensed through her drowsiness when the ambulance came to a stop. "We've arrived, Mehriban," said somebody's distant voice. They lifted her up on the stretcher again and took her to a ward on the first floor, lying her on a bed. Gradually she came to, and when she forced herself to lift her head a little and look round, she saw that three beds next to her were occupied by small children and that their mothers were sitting beside them.

The doors of the ward opened, and the three doctors came in. Another examination began. They tapped her arms and knees with a small hammer and pricked her skin with a needle. They went over her cheeks, hands, and the soles of her feet. They pulled her eyelids wide open and looked at her eyes. After talking among themselves, the doctors picked up Mehriban and took her to the operating theater, where they lay her on the table. One of the doctors bent the girl's head so far forward that it almost touched her knees and held it there while another doctor gave her an injection into her spine. The excruciating pain made her scream. Afterward, they took the poor girl back to her bed in the ward. Now a nurse appeared and gave her another injection.

Mehriban spent the next two months semi-conscious while her doctors struggled to save her life.

Then one day she opened her eyes and saw Turgan with an attractive young woman beside him.

"Do you recognize me, Mehriban?" her brother said.

"Of course. You're my brother, Turgan-aka," she replied in a whisper\.

"And this is Rana-hada. Mahinur wrote to us and said that you were in the hospital, so we've come to see you."

"*Aka*, what illness have I got?"

Wiping away tears, Turgan looked out of the window rather than answer.

"The doctors say you've had meningitis," Rana said, instead of him.

"I've spoken to the doctors," said Turgan. "They say you're recovering. Does your head hurt at the moment?"

Mehriban considered for a moment. "No. It doesn't hurt right now. I'm fine. Will you take me home with you?" she asked, looking at her brother hopefully.

"The doctors say you need a strict regime of bed rest," he replied. "You're not even allowed to sit up. And you'd better do what they tell you!" He wagged his finger at her in a joking threat.

Turgan and Rana left, promising that they would come back next day.

Shortly after, the nurse came in and gave the patients their lunch. As for Mehriban, she sat and spoon-fed her.

The morning rounds were performed by an elderly Russian woman doctor, Polina Ivanovna. She would stand in the doorway and beam at everybody. "Well, how did you sleep?" She then visited each of her little patients, listening to them all attentively. Her hands were gentle, and her eyes radiated kindness. Mehriban cheered up whenever she came into the ward; it was as though her own mother was there. Polina Ivanovna commended her for her steady recovery. Every day, Mehriban was given four injections and a handful of tablets, and once per month, she was given the spinal injection.

One day Mehriban had another dream. When she woke, she lay a long time thinking it over. In the dream she had found herself on the lower side of her village. There was mud everywhere, and she was standing in it up to her knees. She could not even lift one foot. Everywhere was darkness. She stood there and cried, and then her father rode up to her on a black horse. He picked her up, sat her on the horse, and took her away. In just a moment, they were on their own street. Now her father said to her, "If you follow this road straight, you will come to your house." He lowered her to the ground and at once disappeared.

Now, remembering her father, she wept silently.

When Polina Ivanovna came in, she saw Mehriban's red eyes and asked her why she had been crying. Mehriban could not speak Russian well, but she tried her best to tell the doctor her dream.

Polina Ivanovna stroked her head and said to her, "This is a very good dream. It means you will recover from this illness. But for now, let me check you over." And she began her routine examination, tapping her knees, arms, and elbows with her little hammer. "It's five months today since you came into hospital. And you're getting better. Today, I'll sit you up." She helped her up into a sitting position. "Today you will eat sitting up. But you mustn't stay sitting up for long." And she lay Mehriban down again.

Another two months passed. Polina Ivanovna spent a long time every day examining Mehriban. One day she said to her, "Today, my dear, we'll try standing up. Don't be afraid. Hold onto my hand and try walking."

Together they managed to walk a few steps about the room. "Are you not feeling dizzy? Do you feel strength in your arms and legs?"

"Everything's fine. I've got strength," the girl replied in a clear voice.

"From now on, Mehriban, you will walk about the ward a little every day, and later you can go out into the yard." The doctor led her back to her bed. "It's no coincidence that you saw your father last night. That dream has certainly turned out well."

Mehriban was so happy she hugged Polina Ivanovna.

"I'm very happy for you," the doctor continued, her soft hands holding Mehriban's.

One of the mothers of the other sick children added, "Let's hope that our children will also get better and be able to walk like Mehriban."

Mehriban was in hospital for a total of nine months. Afterward, she and three other girls from her ward were sent to a sanatorium for half a year, where they could both rest and also attend school classes.

She never forgot the people who helped nurse her back to health. And in particular, she never forgot Polina Ivanovna and the sweet-natured nurses. She regarded them like family.

• • •

"Mehriban in the story ... is that you?" asked Ruth. "Were you protected by your father's spirit when suspended between life and death?"

Mehriban said nothing. Then she smiled. "Maybe."

"In which case, do go on." Ruth smiled back.

16

CHANGING TIMES

While Mehriban was in hospital, Maysimyam had been at her wit's end. She had wept so much that she began to have difficulty seeing. She turned completely gray and began walking with a stoop, like an old woman. So when Mehriban came home from the sanatorium and went back to school, her joy knew no bounds. Then Turgan and his wife Rana also came back to the village. Rana was medium height, with dark eyes, and swarthy skin. She quickly won their hearts with her kindness and friendly manner. Before long, Maysimyam was calling her daughter.

Turgan was appointed director of the village school, while Rana took a position as a teacher in the same school. When Mahinur received her school-leaving certificate, she entered the pedagogical institute in Zharkent. Now Maysimyam was happier. She was now the busy grandmother, looking after Turgan and Rana's two small boys.

Before they knew it, Amanzhan also finished school. One warm June evening, a whole delegation came into Maysimyam's yard—girls in white aprons and bows and boys in dark suits and white shirts.

Maysimyam sat on the low *bugluk* under the vine and waited. When she saw Amanzhan coming toward her, she leaped up joyfully and flung her arms out. "Ah, my dear son, what a *dzhigit* you've become!"

Amanzhan kissed his grandmother and held a bouquet of flowers out to her. "*Moma*, we finished school today," he said, beaming.

"Congratulations to you all!" declared Maysimyam. "If only your father and grandfather had been able to see this! How you take after Tursun!" Her eyes moistened.

Maysimyam handed the flowers to Mehriban and whispered something to her.

Mehriban ran into the house and came out with a tray piled with sweets.

"Today there is true joy in your lives. And these are for you, in honor of finishing school," pronounced Mehriban solemnly, holding out the tray to the graduates.

They took handfuls of sweets and thanked the old woman. They were about to leave when Maysimyam held up her hand for a prayer to be said. "Oh, Allah! Give these children peace and happiness! Protect them from pain and hardship. May they live long, and may they strive toward their goals. May their road be blessed. Dear children, may Allah keep you!"

The children filed out of the yard. Maysimyam, sitting alone under the vine, sank into reverie. How the years flew by! When Tursun went to the war, Saadat was already pregnant with Amanzhan. And here he was, leaving school and preparing to enter adult life. It all seemed like only yesterday.

Meanwhile Turgan and Rana returned from work. "*Apa*, what are you thinking about?" asked Turgan.

"Amanzhan and his friends came to see me. He's turned into a real *dzhigit*. Now he can go and study, just like you."

"If your grandson wants to learn, that's a cause for joy, *apa*."

"That's true, son, but it's terrible to let him go off to faraway places. If he could study near here, I'd feel happier. But you should sell the cow and calf that your deceased father left to Amanzhan and give him the money. It will come in handy for him."

"Of course, *apa*, if that's what Father wanted. We will act in accordance with his will."

Now Saadat arrived. They gave her a place next to Maysimyam.

Meanwhile Rana came in with a large dish of fresh, steaming *plov*. Mehriban chopped tomatoes, cucumbers, peppers, onions, and garlic and quickly made a salad, which she divided between two bowls.

"Help yourselves, children," invited Maysimyam.

After they had eaten, they moved on to *aktyan-chay*.

"*Hada*, I hear Amanzhan wants to go to study in Alma-Ata?" Turgan asked Saadat.

"That's right. And on that very matter I've come to ask you all for advice. I'm afraid of sending him there by himself. I'm thinking of moving to Alma-Ata to be near him."

There was silence in the room.

"But my child, that means we won't see you anymore?" said Maysimyam, alarmed.

"Why not? We'll come visiting often. And you can come to see us too. It's a year and a half now since Askarzhan died. I've decided to devote the rest of my life to Amanzhan and my two girls, Patam and Zoryam. So what do you say to my idea?"

"It is a very good decision, *hada*," said Turgan supportively. "But can you afford to buy a house in Alma-Ata?"

"I've saved up a little, and I can sell some animals."

"Our late father left Amanzhan a cow and calf. We will sell them and give you the proceeds," said Turgan.

"Thank you so much for everything! You've been such a help ever since Amanzhan was born."

Mehriban listened to the older people in silence. Later she became more animated, and a dreamy look appeared on her face. "Saadat-hada," she said, "if you go to live in Alma-Ata, then can I come in a year's time and study there too?"

"Certainly, come and stay with us! My doors are always open to those who want to learn," smiled Saadat.

"That's what we'll do, then," said Turgan. "*Hada*, you take Amanzhan and buy a house. Then come back here and collect your things. We will load them onto Omar's truck and take them to Alma-Ata. After that, you can concentrate on finding work."

"Yes, I'm thinking along the same lines. I'll need to find a job, otherwise how will we all eat?"

"My dear, if things get difficult, you can always have vegetables from us for the winter," added Maysimyam. "And I think Turgan will help when he's able."

"*Apa*, you've been a mother to me for the last eighteen years," said Saadat, moved. "Once we're established there, I'll take you to Alma-Ata. You can come and spend a year or two living with us. And your children can come and stay too."

Up to now, Rana had said nothing, but now she joined in. "Saadat-hada, our school's going to be a seven-year school. There'll be a lot of pupils. You'll miss this opportunity if you leave."

"But what else can I do? Of course, it's a pity about the school. I've worked there for eighteen years. It's my second home. But I'll come and visit often enough."

After they finished drinking their tea, Saadat bade them farewell and left with a sense of relief.

Maysimyam reflected on Saadat's life. *If success is not given at the start*, she thought, *it will not come later*. After Tursun disappeared without trace during the war, Saadat spent many nights crying. She later married Askarzhan and looked after him. They built a fine new house. They raised twins, plus Tadzhigul's two children, whom Saadat loved and nurtured as her own. Askarzhan's daughter Aminam had married a local *dzhigit*; his son Omar, returning from the army, took a driving course he had worked for the *kolkhoz* ever since. He had married a local girl called Halidam. And now they all lived happily in the warm and cozy house that they had built with their own hands. A year and a half earlier, Askarzhan had died, after being ill all winter. All in all, an ordinary tale.

When she came back from Maysimyam's, Saadat said to Omar and Halidam, "Children, I hope you will live happily in this house. Keep the fire that your parents lit burning in the hearth."

Omar and Halidam's eyes widened. "*Hada*, are you going somewhere?"

"I've decided to move to Alma-Ata with Amanzhan, Patam, and Zoryam."

"Really? What for? Have we offended you in some way?"

"No, of course not. What are you saying!" Saadat waved her hands. "It's just that Amanzhan wants to study at the institute there. And I don't want him to go there by himself. My girls are also growing up and will want to go into higher education. Don't you worry. I'll also help the grandchildren with their learning."

There was silence in the room.

"*Hada*, we are grateful to you. If we have upset you by mistake in any way, please forgive us. This is your house, and we are your children. Don't abandon us, we need you!" said Omar, clearly upset.

"*Hada*, we've grown so used to living together, how can we be parted now?" Halidam began to sob.

Patam and Zoryam hugged her. "Don't cry, *hada*. We will come to see you."

Saadat also wiped away tears. "It isn't easy for me to leave you either."

"*Hada*, you and Amanzhan should first go and buy a house and find a job. After that we'll get all the family and friends together and see you off in fine style. I'll take your things to town for you," said Omar. "As for the animals, leave any you like for us, and the rest I'll sell and give you the money."

They went on for a long time discussing the move, making plans, sharing joys and sadness.

It is difficult to leave one's home. What awaits in the new, unfamiliar city only Allah knows. But Saadat made the firm decision to move. Soon she was living in Alma-Ata.

• • •

"I'm glad that Saadat took that big step, moving into the city for the sake of her children's future," observed Ruth. "Having an assertive temperament, defining goals, and then going out to achieve them are characteristics of American women too." She smiled.

"Yes, for the sake of her children, Saadat was ready to go through fire and water. And yet the native earth on which they spent their childhood years and their youth goes on calling and pulling them back. You will hear about that later. But I fear I'm tiring you." Mehriban looked attentively at Ruth.

"No, not at all. Don't stop! I really want to know how the story of these people's lives finishes up," the American protested.

17

NEW FRIENDSHIPS

Saadat bought a small three-room house in the district of Tastak in Alma-Ata. Unable to find work in a school, she took a three-month course as a street vendor and began to sell newspapers from a kiosk near her home. She sat there from seven in the morning until seven in the evening.

Amanzhan succeeded in entering the agronomy program at the agricultural institute, as he had wished. Patam and Zoryam entered the seventh year at one of the city's schools.

Life in the big city was difficult. Saadat had to look for a second job. After finishing in the kiosk, she and her daughters did cleaning work in various public buildings. It was difficult for her to get used to city life. There were neither friends nor relatives nearby, and the city people didn't seem to talk to anyone, even their neighbors. This was an unfamiliar situation to her.

One Sunday, Saadat invited her neighbors Nadya, Raziya, Mubaryak, and Dzhamiliya to visit. Once they had tasted her delicious *manty* and fragrant Uighur *aktyan-chay*, they overcame their reserve and became friendly and talkative.

"Like you, I live by myself too," said Mubaryak. "I've divorced my husband. My daughter Guncham is in the ninth year at school. Why don't your girls come and visit us? Once they see each other, they'll make friends."

"Where do you work?" asked Saadat, curiously.

"I'm an engineer at a factory."

There was silence at the table for a while. Then old Nadya joined in. "I live with my husband Kolya," she said, sipping her tea. "We're pensioners. Our children have married and live away from us. We don't seem them much because they're always working. They just come to see us with their grandchildren on the big holidays."

"You're lucky to have your Kolya. For me, it's already a year since I lost my old man," said the old Tatar Raziya-apa pensively. "I've got a little vegetable plot. I grow vegetables there to sell. I preserve and pickle some for winter. You can't get by on just a pension."

"No chance without salted and pickled produce," agreed Nadya. "Just today, I bottled fifty jars of lettuce. And I've salted cucumber and tomatoes. It's hard to live in town without these things. Everything here costs money, so we do whatever we can for ourselves. Over the course of the winter, we eat up everything."

"I don't know how to bottle vegetables," sighed Saadat. "In the village, we dry tomatoes and peppers."

"We can show you, daughter. It isn't difficult," said old Nadya.

"Thank you. I'm free on Sundays. I'll come round and learn from you."

The youngest of the visitors was a Kazakh girl named Dzhamiliya. She had come with her twin sons Erik and Serik. Soon after they had eaten, noticing that the boys were growing restless, she bid her farewell and left quickly. Her neighbors said that she had a young family. Her husband Saken was a foreman on a building site and was studying at an institute by distance learning.

Her neighbors took well to Saadat. She was relieved to find that there are good people everywhere.

"You're very welcoming," Raziya-apa complimented her. "You're the first person to invite us round and to show us respect. We appreciate it." Raziya looked round at the others. "If we've all finished our tea, I will read a little from the Qur'an." Straightening the shawl on her head, she said a prayer.

From that time on, the neighbors began to visit each other and talk about their lives, their health, and their children. Saadat and Mubaryak became particularly good friends.

Every Sunday, Amanzhan had his own friends to visit—his fellow villagers Avut and Tair, who were studying at the technical college, and his schoolmate Daulet, who hailed from Dzhambul. In order to qualify for grants, the young men worked hard at their studies. Even so, the young never had enough money, so every Sunday they would do some work on the side. After eating their fill at Saadat's, they went to the railway station to unload wagons.

Saadat, for her part, was pleased to see them tucking in so heartily to the meals she prepared. She could see that they missed the food they knew at home.

Sometimes she would play the mother to them, giving them advice or an admonition.

One winter's day, Daulet's parents came to Alma-Ata to visit him. Since they knew nobody in the city, Amanzhan invited them to stay with him and his mother. Saadat welcomed the visitors warmly and said that they could stay as long as they needed. Saadat went out to work the next day, but she begged Daulet's parents to make themselves at home. And so they stayed with them for several days.

One evening Daulet's parents, Bolat and Zileyha, prepared the evening meal. They lit the stove and placed some meat that they had brought with them into the *kazan*. Zileyha kneaded dough. Outside it was cold and snow was falling, but indoors, the stove burned hot and meat sizzled in the *kazan*, spreading its delicious aroma.

After it had grown dark, Saadat and her daughters came in, shivering. They cheered up when they smelled the meat.

"Come over to the stove and warm yourselves," smiled Zileyha.

"Oh, Allah, what a hard frost." Saadat extended her hand toward the fire.

Moments after them, Amanzhan and Daulet also came in.

"Good, everyone's arrived," said Zileyha. She took the meat out of the *kazan* and placed it in a deep dish.

Saadat washed her hands, and then she chopped the thin sheet of dough finely and tossed it into the simmering broth. Once the dough was boiled, she placed it on a wide flat dish. She poured finely chopped onion into a small cooking pot and poured some of the boiling broth over it, then added salt and ground black pepper. After this had boiled a little, she poured the seasoning over the dough, then laid the meat on top and set the bowl on the table. Bolat took a *byakya,* or penknife, from his pocket and cut the meat into small pieces, giving a handful of it to each person. "*Beshbarmak* has to be eaten hot."

The big bowl of the stew was soon finished. Zileyha poured the *shorpa* into bowls and served them. Bolat, who had broken into a sweat from the hot *beshbarmak,* wiped his brow with his handkerchief.

"Saadat, thank you for your kindness to us. Staying with you has been like staying in our own home. It is good that our sons have become friends. The Uighurs and the Kazakhs were brothers from time immemorial. We share the same spirit and the same belief. May the friendship between our sons be long."

Somewhat embarrassed, Saadat replied: "I haven't been able to take care of you as well as I should have, as I've been at work every day. Thank you, Zileyha-tata, for presiding over the *kazan* all these days."

Zileyha smiled. "We have tasted delicious Uighur food from your hand. And it doesn't matter in the end who feeds whom. What matters is your openhearted-ness. You have taken care of our son, and this is precious. We are now relatives. When the weather improves, you must come and be guests in our part of the world."

While Patam and Zoryam were clearing the table, Bolat looked intently at Amanzhan. "Son, you remind me of somebody," he said eventually, unable to keep silence any longer.

"Who do I remind you of?" asked Amanzhan, surprised.

"I'll tell you a curious story."

Everybody looked at Bolat.

"When the war started, I was twenty-five," he began. "I was already married and had two sons. I was one of the first to go to fight. The war was brutal and bloody; I was injured several times and ended up in field hospitals, but as soon as I was able, I went back to the front. Then in 1945, just before victory was declared, I was my leg was badly injured. I was back in the hospital again. They amputated my right leg above the knee, and now I walk on a wooden prosthesis.

"There was a Uighur in the same ward as me. He was wounded on the head, on his face. He had terrible burns. My heart went out to him whenever I looked at him. Apparently, a shell had exploded near him and burned him and all his documents. The doctors said he would not live. He lay for many days in our ward for the gravely sick. Then one day he suddenly opened his eyes and moved his legs. When he finally regained consciousness, the doctors started asking him his name and what unit he was from, but the poor boy just lay there staring—silent. We thought he must have gone deaf. But apparently, he had suffered a complete loss of memory. He couldn't remember his name, his unit, or even where he was from.

"Then the war ended. We were discharged from the field hospital, and when the soldiers began to return home from the front, I said he should come home with me. I said that if he should later remember who he was and where he was from, I would take him back there myself. So he went with me to Dzhambul. My parents had six sons, of whom they lost two in the war. They were happy therefore to take in another young man as one of their own. They accepted him into the family and gave him the name Hudaybergen as a reminder that he had been kept alive by the grace of Allah through the hell of war.

"Ever since he was wounded in the head, Hudaybergen had suffered from epilepsy. Probably for this reason he avoided the subject of marriage, although my father found suitable girls for him. I don't know why I started telling you about this *dzhigit*. But something tells me it isn't without reason that our Hudaybergen and your Amanzhan look to me like two peas in a pod."

With every moment that passed as Bolat told his tale, Amanzhan's eyes opened wider. "I'd like to come with you and see this man," he said, his eyes ablaze.

"But Papa, if he isn't Amanzhan's father, have you considered how painful this might be for him?" Daulet looked at his father.

Now Zileyha joined in. "Yes, come with us to Dzhambul. You can be our guest and can meet Hudaybergen, and then we'll see," she said, looking at Saadat.

Saadat was in tears. Hope had arisen in her once again. No words came from her lips. There was silence in the room. Amanzhan eventually broke it.

"After this conversation, I have only one desire," he said. "I want to see this man."

"I'll come with you as well," said Saadat unexpectedly.

"And what about us?" said Patam and Zoryam as one, having been silent up to now.

"My dears, you'll have to stay here. You must keep on going to school and must do the cleaning in the evenings. Your *hada* Mubaryak will come and sleep here at night."

Had she had wings, Saadat would have set off that moment. But there was nothing for it; she would have to wait a little.

• • •

"I so hope it's Tursun!" exclaimed Ruth. "Otherwise it would be a terrible disappointment for Saadat. It's odd, but Saadat's sad story is evoking a lot of sympathy in me. It's as though I know this woman."

"Dear Ruth, our lives are capable of joy as well as sadness. And it was about time that fate gave poor Saadat a gleam of happiness. So keep listening."

18

THREE JOYFUL HEARTS

Next day Saadat and Amanzhan boarded the morning train together with Daulet's parents. The nine hours to Dzhambul from Alma-Ata seemed interminably long. Saadat looked out of the window but saw before her eyes the scene of parting from her beloved. Tursun held her; they both wept as they bade one other farewell. In her memory, he had been young and handsome. She remembered everything. His strong figure, the scent of his hair, even the fingers on his hands. She remembered how they had each, by the light of the moon, taken one bite from a piece of *nan*, a *togach*. Saadat had kept that *togach* ever since. She also recalled the words of the old fortune-teller Zaynaphan. *Your son will bring you news about his father.* And so it seemed to be turning out. If Amanzhan had not made friends with Daulet, she would not have met his parents. The thought that Hudaybergen might not in fact be Tursun seemed an impossibility to her. The heart of a woman in love cannot be deceived.

With these thoughts, Saadat arrived in Dzhambul. There was snow on the ground that crunched underfoot, and a biting wind stung the cheeks. Bolat and Zileyha invited Saadat and Amanzhan to rest in their house a while and drink some tea, after which they would go to the house where their parents lived. So this is what they did. They arrived at the parents' house just in time for the evening meal. The old folks welcomed their visitors kindly.

Hudaybergen greeted Bolat without glancing at the others, then turned to go out into the yard. Bolat stopped him and said, "Hudaybergen, look at the people who've come to see us. Do you recognize this woman?" The man lifted his eyes to Saadat. He stood motionless for a moment. Then he began to breathe heavily. Foam appeared on his lips, his body began to shake all over, and he fell onto the floor. Saadat rushed over to him and tried to bring Tursun, who was thrashing spasmodically, to his senses. "Tursun, I've found you! Open your eyes! It's me, Saadat!" She hugged her husband with all the strength she had.

Bolat's mother started weeping. "His heart has recognized you as well."

Tursun came round. He sat and looked at Saadat for a long time, and then buried his face in her hands. She felt her palms growing wet from his tears.

Amanzhan sat down on the floor next to his parents. "Father," he said in a trembling voice.

Tursun turned and embraced his son and pressed him to his heart, sobbing uncontrollably like a child.

Nobody was left unmoved by this scene. Seeing how these three people whose hearts had borne so much pain could now taste joy, everybody in the room was in tears. Destiny had given Saadat, Amanzhan, and Tursun an immense gift. They quickly began calling

Hudaybergen by his old name. Tursun's heart all but burst at finding his family again.

The following day Saadat and her son returned to Alma-Ata, taking Tursun with them. The old couple who had cared for Tursun as their own for so long said their tearful good-byes.

It was dark by the time they reached their house. Patam, who had gone out for firewood, saw her mother first. "*Apa*, I'm glad you're back. We've got people from the village come to stay—Turgan-aka, grandmother, and Mehriban-hada."

Perplexed, Saadat wondered whether her old mother and Tursun would be able to cope with being reunited after so long. They let him enter the house first and came in behind. When Turgan saw who was standing in the doorway, he stiffened in astonishment, then rushed forward. "*Aka*, is this you? Tursun, am I seeing right? My brother?"

The brothers, who had not seen each other for so many years, hugged each other and wept.

"Hey, what's going on out there?" came Maysim-yam's voice from the inner room. "Come in here."

They all went in to where she was sitting. She strained her weak eyes to look at them all. Tursun went up to his mother and dropped down onto his knees in front of her. "*Apa*, my dear mother! I've come back."

Her mother held him. "*Balam*! My precious son! Wherever have you been all these years? I've cried my eyes right out over you!"

Mother and son stayed pressed together, unable to part for a long time. Finally Saadat said, "*Apa*, don't cry, or you'll make Tursun ill." Maysimyam stopped her wailing at once.

What they were seeing seemed unreal. The members of the family stared at each other, unable to believe their luck—that miracles such as this could happen.

Eventually Turgan began to talk about the present. "We've come to town to take Mama to the eye doctor," he explained to his elder brother. "She's complaining that her eyes have gone cloudy and she can't see properly anymore. So we've brought her for an examination. We'd hardly come in and taken our coats off when you arrived. It seems we were fated to come today, that very hour."

"Saadat, daughter, can you tell us where my son has been wandering all this time?" asked her mother. Saadat retold the whole unlikely story from beginning to end. As she told it, none of the listeners' eyes remained dry. Though her eyesight was poor, Maysimyam stroked her son's head and felt where his injury had been.

"My poor son. It seems as though the bullet hit you here," she said, kissing him on the nape of his neck. "I wish it had hit me instead of you!" She burst into tears again. "I knew, somewhere in my heart, that my son Tursun was alive and that I'd see him again. And now, by the will of Allah, here you are. Your deceased father never stopped grieving for you, and he passed from this world with sadness in his heart."

Tursun froze. "Our father's dead?" he asked, shaken.

"Yes, *balam.*"

Tursun began to moan with grief. No sooner had he found his loved ones and been filled with joy and hope, than fate dealt him another hard blow. Once again, he and his mother clung to each other and wept.

The girls, who had made tea long ago, now put out the *dzhoza* in the middle of the room and invited everybody to partake.

Saadat noticed two large bags by the door. "What's in those bags?" she asked out of curiosity.

Mehriban opened them. "One's got vegetables in it, and the other contains *togach* that Rana-hada made for us," she said, giving them to Saadat.

"My goodness, thank you!" Saadat placed the well-browned round breads, sprinkled with caraway seeds, on the table.

Mehriban then took out a jar of thick cream. "*Hada*, I've brought you some *kaymak* from Gyuli-kichik-apa."

Saadat made a large pot of *aktyan-chay* and topped it with the *kaymak*. Everyone was hungry by now and tucked in gladly. Maysimyam, pouring the tea, said, "My dear children, the doctor can wait. I'd rather we took Tursun home to the village now."

"*Apa*, what are you saying?" said Turgan severely. Do you think we've come all this way for nothing? Your eyes are a serious matter. We need to have them examined."

"*Apa*, don't rush," said Saadat. "We'll take both you and Tursun to see the doctor."

"Surely you're not ill, are you? Where does it hurt?" asked Maysimyam, alarmed. She began to move her hands over Tursun's head and back as he sat beside her.

Turgan also realized that his brother looked older than his years. Then he thought for a moment. "Before we take Tursun to the doctor, we'll have to go home and find his papers in the archive," he said. "That should be enough to get him a passport. But without a passport, they won't let him into the hospital."

"You're right," agreed Saadat. "For the moment, our Tursun had better remain Hudaybergen Koshumbaev."

After tea, the brothers went outside to smoke.

"Saadat, did you notice that Tursun is only speaking Kazakh?" Maysimyam asked her daughter-in-law.

"Yes. His Uighur will come back as time goes by."

"He ought to go and thank the old folks who looked after him all these years and take them some presents," Maysimyam continued.

"Well let's let him recover a bit, and when the weather improves, we'll go to Dzhambul."

"I'd like to see his adoptive parents and to bow low before them, but with my eyesight, I can't go there by myself." Maysimyam shook her head.

"We could invite them here. Let them see where Tursun was born, and they can meet you and the others. And then we can all say thank you, don't you think?"

The door opened and Tursun and Turgan came in. Saadat and the girls called everyone to the table for *laghman*. Zoryam put out two garnishes, *lazdhzan* and *sirkya*. Patam put out two chopsticks for each person.

While they were eating, Saadat disappeared into the inner room for some time. When she came out she was carrying a small bundle.

"*Apa*, what were you looking for in there?" asked Patam. "If you'd asked me, I'd have fetched it for you."

"You'd never have found this, daughter," smiled Saadat. "Do you know what's in here?" she asked the assembled group and began to unroll the bundle.

Inside was a dried-out *togach*. "I don't know whether Tursun remembers, but when we parted, each of us took a bite out of this *togach*. I have kept it as a relic for the last eighteen years. Tursun promised that when he came back from the war, we would divide the remainder between us and finish it." She held the piece of old bread, hardened like wood, out to him.

Tursun inclined his head and thought deeply. He seemed to be trying to remember the beautiful night they shared as they parted, the last night of their carefree youth.

Maysimyam was shaken. "Daughter, do you realize that you saved my son with this bread?" She took the *togach*, broke it into two pieces, and gave half each to Tursun and Saadat. They dipped the pieces into their tea to soften them, then ate them, looking at each other.

"It's a beautiful old tradition," said Maysimyam thoughtfully. "It's a shame I didn't remember it myself."

Tursun, chewing the bread slowly before speaking. "Now I remember. It was a moonlit night. Saadat and I sat in the garden a long time. We couldn't bear to part. In the morning, when I went home, my father met me on his way out."

His memory was beginning to come back. And the family continued sharing their memories, thoughts, hopes, and feelings until morning came. Many times they expressed their thanks to Allah for this unexpected joy.

The next morning, Turgan and Mehriban took their mother to the eye institute in Alma-Ata. A doctor slowly examined Maysimyam's eyes and then took Turgan into a separate room.

"Some of the vessels in your mother's eyes have burst. She has a condition known as glaucoma. There is nothing we can do for her condition at this stage, I regret to say. Here are some drops that may help her a little." He handed Turgan a small phial, wrote down the directions for taking them, and politely excused himself.

The diagnosis deeply upset Turgan. He did not know how he would be able to tell his mother. When Saadat came home for lunch, he told her the news. "Unfortunately, I've got to go back home because of work," he sighed. "I need to organize a New Year tree for the school before the start of the winter holidays."

"Why don't you take Tursun with you and let him see his relatives and everyone in the village," Maysimyam suggested. She could not wait to take her son back to his old home.

But Saadat was not keen to be parted from Tursun. "*Apa*, why don't you stay in town another ten days or so? We'll take Tursun to the doctor, and I'll arrange some time off work. Then we can all go back together. Turgan and Mehriban, you stay here tonight as well, and tomorrow you can take the bus home."

Turgan agreed. Next day he and Mehriban went back to the village, while Tursun stayed in Alma-Ata with his mother. When the others had gone off to their various tasks, Maysimyam began to tell her son everything that had happened while he had been absent. Tursun listened carefully and then suddenly asked, "How is Gyuli-kichik-apa?"

"God is great. You've remembered Gyuli!" His mother was delighted. "Our Gyuli has grown old. Her daughters are all married. Her son came back from the army and trained as a tractor driver but now works as a joiner. They say he's a master craftsman and has golden hands. Gyuli married him off, and now she's a grandmother, but she often suffers from high blood pressure. But then, how can people who worked so many years in the fields and never rested expect to still be healthy? Thanks to Allah, her daughter-in-law's a good one. And another piece of good news—after the war, your Rukiyam kichik-apa came back from Ghulja."

"I don't think I remember her."

"She went with her father, mother, and brother to Ghulja when you were little."

"And is Adalyat chon-apa still alive?"

"Yes. She's gotten old as well. She has a weak heart and hardly walks anymore. Mahmut came back from the war an invalid, with an arm missing. He married and has children. But he's become very difficult and short-tempered. People are nervous of him. He's even got a nickname—Mahmut the Shell-Shocked. Adalyat-hada's daughters are married. Her own husband died. All the old people you knew are long dead."

She told him tearfully about Kurvan-aka, his long illness, and his death, and described his funeral. "And after your father died, Mehriban fell seriously ill. She only just came through. Your little sister Modangul is married and lives in a good family. And as soon as Mahinur finishes her studies, we'll have to get her set up in life too."

That evening Maysimyam sat Tursun and Saadat down beside her and said, "Children, we're going to have to call in a man of knowledge and have him perform the rite of Nikah for you two. We're Muslim, after all. You mustn't go on living together without it."

Saadat told her neighbor Raziya-apa about the astonishing events that had just occurred.

"God is merciful, daughter," Raziya replied. "This is a gift from him to you. Why don't you go home now and get things ready? I'll fetch the mullah Rahmitullah, who lives just a street away."

Saadat went home and, together with her daughters, prepared an evening meal and laid the *dzhoza*. Then in the evening, Raziya-apa came round with the mullah, and Maysimyam seated them in the places of honor. Once everybody was assembled, the mullah instructed that some milk be poured into a bowl and that two lumps of sugar, a pinch of salt, and two pieces of bread be added to it. Raziya-apa did so and held the bowl out to him.

Rahmitullah had Tursun and Saadat stand before him. He read a *sura* of the Qur'an and then turned to them and said: "Tursun, son of Kurvan-aka, do you willingly take Saadat, daughter of Arup, as your wife?"

"Yes, I take her of my own free will."

"Saadat, daughter of Arup, do you go willingly into the protection of Tursun, son of Kurvan-aka, as your husband?"

"Yes, I do, of my own free will."

The mullah recited another prayer and handed the bowl to Tursun. He drank a mouthful of milk and ate a piece of the bread, then passed the bowl to Saadat. Saadat whispered *"Bismillah,"* took a mouthful of milk, and the other piece of bread, then put the bowl down on the table.

"Dear children, the ceremony of Nikah is completed. I wish you a long and happy life. Congratulations on your Nikah!" pronounced the mullah solemnly.

Raziya-apa also congratulated Maysimyam on the marriage of her children. Maysimyam shed a few tears and said, "His father, may he rest in peace, always dreamed of honoring his return from the war by holding a big *toy*, a wedding for the whole village. But he did not live to see it. And now the unthinkable has happened—after so many years our son has come home from that terrible war."

Mullah Rahmitullah stroked his beard and said, "That is the mercy of Allah. The one who has departed will return, while the one who is deceased will not return. The fact that you've found your son again, will always be a joy for you."

Saadat put a large bowl of *plov* on the table, and the girls brought in salads. They invited the guests warmly to partake of all they could eat. After the food, they sat for a long time over tea and talked, as was customary. As was also customary, Saadat presented the mullah with a man's shirt and gave Raziya-apa a piece of material for a dress and some sweets.

Tursun and Saadat, who had dreamed for many years of this day, were deeply happy; their faces kept lighting up with smiles.

Amanzhan tried to spend as much time as he could with his father. They went to the shops together, choosing clothes for Tursun. Daulet often came and stayed the night with them. Tursun was proud that his son was studying at an institution of higher education.

"Amanzhan, can you find me some kind of job?" his father asked him one day. "Your mother's working from dawn to dusk while I sit around like a dependent spouse."

"*Dada*, you need to get your strength back first," said his son, smiling. "When summer comes, you'll go to the village and see your friends and family. And after that, we'll find you some work."

Tursun felt better. Amanzhan was right. Saadat, meanwhile, having taken him to various doctors, managed to qualify him for category two invalidity. He began to receive a pension.

Maysimyam was longing to go home and asked every day, "Saadat, when will we go back to the village?"

It is a wise saying that "a living soul always has hope." The spring finally came, coating everything with flowers and filling the air with fragrance. Saadat took ten days off work and started preparing for the trip to Zharkent. Maysimyam was delighted. By now, Tursun had become fully accustomed to his new life and looked healthy and renewed since back with his family.

Saadat asked her neighbor Mubaryak to keep an eye on her children while she was away, and then, prepared and calm, they set off.

• • •

"Is it normal for you to leave your children with neighbors?" asked Ruth.

"We treat our neighbors with great respect," replied Mehriban. "It goes back a long way. We expect to live on friendly terms with our neighbors, to help each other out, and to share the responsibilities of looking after children. We even have proverbs about neighbors. 'Buy your neighbors before you buy your house' and 'A close neighbor is better than a distant relative.' That's why Saadat made a point of getting to know her neighbors, inviting them around for tea, as soon as she had moved in."

Ruth nodded, surprised, and settled back to hear the next part of the tale.

19

NEIGHBORS

While Saadat was away, Mubaryak looked in on the children every day. Her daughter Guncham spent all her free time with Patam and Zoryam, who were now best friends.

One evening Patam and Zoryam came home after finishing their cleaning job. They ate their supper and settled to do their homework. Amanzhan was not yet back from the institute. Suddenly, the door flew open and Guncham came hurrying in. She was pale and frightened.

"What's happened? Is someone chasing after you?" asked the startled girls.

"Yes," cried Guncham, quickly closing and bolting the door behind her.

"Oh Lord, and our brother's late tonight. Just our luck!" exclaimed Patam.

At that moment there was a knock on the door.

"Who's there?" asked Patam tensely.

"It's us, it's us. Open up!" came the voices of Amanzhan and Daulet.

Sighing with relief, the girls opened the door. The look on each of their faces was so frightened that

Amanzhan, rather than just taking his coat off, stood and looked at each of the girls in turn.

"Whatever has scared you all so much?" he asked.

"It's my fault," said Guncham. "I came rushing in like I'm crazy."

"And what happened to you to cause that?"

"It's my cousin. He's got involved with some dubious types," she said. "They've been messing around with soft drugs. He's started asking my mother for money all the time. Sometimes I see him after he's been smoking. And now he's started injecting himself."

"Why does he inject himself?" asked Amanzhan, baffled. "Is he unwell?"

"He's become addicted," sighed Guncham. "If an addict doesn't get his fix, his whole body hurts. Then when he gets his injection, he goes stupid and loses all control of himself. They say the injections are very expensive, and so he's always after money."

"Good lord, how did your cousin get into this awful business?" exclaimed Patam with a sense of desperation.

"He came round again today. It wasn't just him this time. He had two of his friends with him. I was afraid. I bolted the door and came running here to get away from them."

"Do his parents know he's an addict?" asked Amanzhan.

"They do. His father hit him and tried to make him see sense, first by intimidating him, and then by begging him. Nothing worked. It made his parents ill with worry, in the end."

"And are their other children addicts too?" asked Daulet.

"No. Out of their five children, only one turned out like that. The other four are normal people with jobs. Only Mahsat turned out a good-for-nothing who makes life miserable for his parents."

Now that the young men were home, the girls began to calm down. The twins prepared supper, and the hungry *dzhigits* washed their hands and sat down at the table.

"Guncham, stay and eat with us," they said to her.

"No, thanks. Mama may already be back. I'll go home," answered Guncham, somewhat without conviction.

Patam shook her head doubtfully. "If Mubaryak-hada comes home and sees you're not there, she's sure to come and look here. And what if those boys are still hanging around your house? What will you do?" She stood in Guncham's way to prevent her leaving.

Guncham was a pretty girl with thick black hair and large dark eyes. She sometimes glanced surreptitiously at Amanzhan. And although Amanzhan was aware of this, he simply treated her as a sister. Now Guncham eyed the young man again, thinking that nobody would notice. And Amanzhan acted as though nothing had happened and went on eating. Shortly there was another knock on the door, and Mubaryak came in.

"Well, everyone, how's things?" she asked.

"We're fine, thank you. Come in and join us, Mubaryak-hada."

"No, thank you. I'm very tired today, so I think I'll go home. Say, girls, why don't we make *laghman* together tomorrow? It's Sunday after all. And Saadat-hada may be back."

"That's right. Nine days have already passed, and Mama needs to be back at work on Monday," said Zoryam.

"Well, that's settled then."

Mubaryak took Guncham home with her. On the way back, Guncham told her that Mahsat had been round demanding money again.

"Oh, Allah, when will that boy stop harassing us? He comes every week. I need to go and tell his parents."

"*Apa*, I'm scared of him. You know, he didn't come by himself this time. He had two other boys with him."

Hearing this, Mubaryak seized her head with horror. "Daughter, whenever you're at home by yourself, never, ever open the door to anybody. Whoever knows what's in the heads of these addicts? Tomorrow I'll go and talk to my sister. Enough! I'm at the end of my tether with this. I can no longer work in peace."

Next morning, Mubaryak and Guncham had a light breakfast, took some meat out of the refrigerator, and went over to Saadat's. By that time, Patam and Zoryam had already made the dough for the *laghman*.

"It's true what they say. These village girls are hard workers," Mubaryak said, smiling as she came in.

They decided that she would take care of the meat while Zoryam prepared the vegetables.

"Is Amanzhan still in bed?" asked Guncham, lowering her eyes.

"No, he's gone to the station to work with Daulet."

"Bravo," said Mubaryak approvingly. "We'll have everything ready for when they come back."

They prepared the *laghman* quickly and in cheerful spirits. Soon after they finished, Amanzhan and Daulet came in, exhausted. They ate the meal as one family, talking and joking together. Afterward, Mubaryak and Guncham went home.

That evening Saadat and Tursun arrived from the village. The girls bombarded their mother with questions about their friends back home. Saadat, refreshed with tea, told them whom she had seen, where she had been, and what the news was in the village.

"Aminam invited us round," she beamed. "They've built a new house, big and spacious. Aminam and Ahmat are real workers, and so things go well for them. Omar and Halidam miss you terribly and can't wait to see you in the summer."

"And our sisters, Rana, Modangul, and Mahinur?" asked Amanzhan.

"They're all well and asked me to say hello. They all said, 'Let's hope Amanzhan comes back home after his studies. We'll fix up a fabulous wedding in his own village.'"

Hearing all this, Tursun grew thoughtful. "This is all true," he said. "Why don't we go back there too? How good it would be to live among our own."

Having spent a few days in the village for which he had longed so much that it had hurt, Tursun had been reluctant to come back to Alma-Ata. He, more than anybody, felt the bond with the lands that were his home.

"Amanzhan, as soon as you get your diploma, they'll assign you to work in some village or another. So make sure you ask them to send you somewhere close to home," Tursun advised his son. "That's where all our ancestors have lived and worked. You can continue their tradition. May our home village flourish."

"*Dada*, calm down," smiled Amanzhan. "As soon as I get my diploma, of course we'll come home."

These words pleased his father greatly. "When I went back to Chigan, I walked through the gardens and fields. It was like going back to my childhood. It felt like being born again. You young people won't understand this feeling, but for me, after all my wandering, my homeland pulls me and calls me."

"*Dada*, *apa*, maybe it's right that you go back there now. Why not? Daulet and I can stay at the institute hostel."

"No, son," said Saadat firmly. "Until you finish your studies, we're staying here in Alma-Ata. And what happens after that will become clear in due course." She went out into the yard.

The days grew warmer, and the fruit trees in the gardens came into blossom. Everything around them became heightened in beauty. To keep himself occupied, Tursun decided to construct a *bugluk* under one of the spreading apple trees. His neighbor Kolya also took an interest in this project. "What is it you're building under that tree?" he asked. "You could lay out a whole vegetable patch there."

"Uighurs like to sit outside in summer on a *bugluk*, rather than in stuffy indoor rooms," Tursun answered. "And we've got plenty of room for a vegetable patch."

"Will you put up a sun shade?"

"Yes, I will. I'll plant vines around the outside," Tursun answered, working enthusiastically.

Old Nadya called out from behind the fence, "Kolya!"

"See, neighbor, my wife can't manage without me for a single minute," grunted Kolya with irritation.

"Nikolay, look how much there is to do in the garden, and all you can do is stare at Tursun!" squawked the old woman.

"Well, friend, I'd better be off," he sighed, shaking Tursun's hand and dragging himself off toward his house.

Tursun spent several days building the *bugluk*. Amanzhan and Daulet helped him in the evenings, which made the work go faster. Soon the structure was complete, and the family could sit outdoors and breathe the scent of the garden and the earth.

The summer holiday crept up almost unnoticed. Patam and Zoryam went to stay in the village. Amanzhan completed his first year at the institute. To help support his parents, he took a job in a home-building factory located not far from home.

Normally, Tursun would finish his work in the garden and then go out to sit with Saadat in her kiosk. They often talked at length after work as well, and Tursun gradually became fluent in Uighur again. Never once did he get upset at Saadat for marrying in his absence. On the contrary, he came to love Askarzhan's daughters, Patam and Zoryam, as his own. Now Tursun regarded himself as truly happy. He had a family, and his beloved Saadat was with him. He even began to forget about his illness. His wounds made their presence felt only when the weather turned.

Nonetheless, Saadat was afraid of leaving Tursun by himself. The kiosk was near their home, and so she would dash home whenever she had a free moment to check on him. She tried to cure Tursun's condition with every medicine she could get her hands on, both what the doctors prescribed and folk remedies. But the illness did not go away.

Patam and Zoryam came back to Alma-Ata together with Mehriban, who had now finished school. She was pretty, shapely, and had decided that she wanted to study Uighur language and literature. She passed the entrance examinations, and it could hardly have been otherwise, for she had applied herself day and night to preparing for them. She was overjoyed when her name appeared on the list of entrants. Here she was, the daughter of a humble villager, going into higher education! Her father would have been proud. When she came home, Mehriban called out, "*Aka*, you can congratulate me, I got in!"

"You clever girl, Mehriban!" Tursun hugged her and tossed her up in the air. "Now, to study, you need to be healthy. I wish you good health. And remember, gaining knowledge is no easier than digging a pit with a needle. So you must be both diligent and patient. And we will be very pleased for you."

The girls decided to make *pelmeni* for when Saadat and Amanzhan came home. Zoryam finely chopped meat and mixed it with finely chopped onion. They salted the mixture and added ground black pepper. She worked the mixture with her hands to create a mince.

Mehriban kneaded a dough of flour enriched with an egg. Once the dough had rested, she rolled it out thinly and evenly and cut it into small squares. She placed a spoonful of meat onto each square, and then the two girls began to wrap the dough around the meat to form individual *pelmeni.*

"Preparing food always takes so long!" said Zoryam suddenly.

"Yes, but that makes it so tasty," responded Patam.

"What Uighur dishes do you know?" Mehriban asked them as they made up the little pasta parcels.

"Well, for a start, there's *suyuk ash*—a soup with long thin noodles—and there's *kaligach tili,* or larks' tongues, with triangular-shaped noodles. There's *shintugur,* where the dough is in cubes, and *halvash,* with wide noodles, and *uzup tashlap* with torn pasta pieces, and *omach,* with hard grated noodles," Zoryam recited quickly.

"And meat *pelmeni* like *gesh chushur* and *kok chushur,* which is green *pelmeni,* stuffed with herbs" added Patam.

"And *sozup laghman,* which is stretched, and *kesip laghman,* which is chopped, and thickly stretched *guyru laghman,*" Zoryam continued.

"And how many kinds of *plov* do you know?"

"Well, there's *toy polo,* or nuptial plov, and *korma polo,* fried plov, and *goshsiz polo,* or plov without meat, and quince plov, or *behi polo.*"

"And for *manty,* there's *petir manta,* the ordinary kind, then there is *boldurup manta,* in a sour dough, and *kava manta* with pumpkin, and *dzhusyay mana* with herbs.

"So far so good... don't stop. What else do you know?" asked Mehriban encouragingly.

"There's kebab, which we call *kavap*, and *samsa*, and *hesip*, which is sheep's intestine stuffed with meat and rice; *kuygan opkya*, which is lungs cooked in flour and milk, and *gesh nan*, or meat pie, and *kordak*, fried meat with potato, and *shorpa,* or broth."

"Good grief, the list's endless," laughed Zoryam.

"Well, just think how many dishes we don't know yet," winked Mehriban.

Patam sank into deep thought and then reeled off more names. "There's also *tuhum poshkal*, like small pancakes, *piyaz nan*, an onion pastry, *shuluguruch*, which is cream of rice with meat and carrot, and *shovaguruch*, or rice soup. And we've forgotten *mashhorda*, pea soup," she exclaimed excitedly, like a child.

Talking as they worked, the *pelmeni* were soon all made up. Zoryam lit the fire, and Mehriban heated some oil in the *kazan* and began to fry the chopped meat. Once it was cooked, she added onion, pepper, tomatoes, and spices and the requisite amount of water. By the time the water was boiling, Saadat was home from work.

"Oh, what a wonderful smell! What is this feast in honor of, girls?"

Zoryam, checking the fire in the stove, explained. "*Apa*, there's happiness in our house today. Mehriban hada has got in to the institute!"

Saadat congratulated Mehriban and hugged her. Patam, meanwhile, placed the *pelmeni* in the boiling broth, and at the moment that they were ready,

Amanzhan arrived with a healthy appetite. "A good man always turns up just in time for a meal." They laughed.

Tursun was proud of his son's intellect and hard work. He often glanced at Amanzhan, seeing himself in him. The family was now sitting around the low *dzhoza* on the *bugluk* he had built outside under the apple tree. Mehriban served the *pelmeni* in large bowls, garnished with coriander and mint. Zoryam put out a bowl of each of the two familiar condiments—*lazdzhan* and *sirkya*.

Before the meal began, Tursun solemnly declared, "Today our brilliant Mehriban has been admitted into the institute to study, as she has long dreamed of doing. And now we celebrate this happy news with delicious spicy *pelmeni*." So ending his short speech, he broke into a laugh.

"I always knew Mehriban would be accepted," said Amanzhan.

Their mood continued to rise. Saadat was proud to see her girls becoming real hostesses, attending to their mother and their friends and family.

Meanwhile the summer holiday flew by, and in no time, the young people were back at their studies. They went off every morning, while Tursun went into the garden each day to pick vegetables as they ripened. One day Raziya-apay came up to their gate. "Tursun, son, it's already beginning to get cold. I wondered if I could ask you to fit secondary frames in my windows. And my doors don't shut properly. I'll pay you for the work."

"Fine, I'll do all that," he said. "But I won't take money from you. Better if you pray for our children's happiness."

And so it was that now Tursun had built the handsome *bugluk* in his garden, and how people came to him, even from neighboring streets, to ask for his help with various repairs on their houses. Tursun was pleased to feel useful.

• • •

"Wow, so many national dishes!" exclaimed Ruth. "I can see that Uighur cuisine is rich and diverse."

Mehriban grinned. "That's not all of them by any means. If I think, I can come up with another list just as long. And I was hoping to let other people know some of the particularities of Uighur food, so I have included recipes for some of our favorite dishes in my book."

"You'll whet the readers' appetites, for sure," Ruth smiled. "But I hope that this isn't the end of the story?"

20

A Prophetic Dream

With autumn came rain and mud, and in the mornings and evenings, the city was as cold as it was in winter.

One of those frosty evenings, when Saadat and her family were gathered in their cozy room, the door opened and in came Mubaryak. She was evidently in a hurry. After greeting everyone she said to Saadat, "I've been invited to a wedding tonight, but I wondered if I could ask for one of your girls to come to my house tonight. If I'm late back, she can sleep over. I'm nervous of leaving Guncham by herself."

Mehriban could see that neither Patam nor Zoryam was keen to go, so volunteered herself and left with Mubaryak.

Mehriban and Guncham did their homework together and then began to talk. This year, Guncham had completed her tenth year at school and looked certain to be in line for a gold medal. She hoped to go on to study chemistry and biology at Kazakhstan State University and to become a scientist like her father. She was going to a Russian-speaking school, so her Uighur was not fluent, but she understood everything Mehriban said.

"You know, Mehriban, I really like Amanzhan. But he doesn't take any notice of me. Maybe he thinks I'm too young," she said, rather embarrassed.

"The thing is, Amanzhan is busy studying from morning to night. And he works on the weekend. He hasn't got time to look at girls." Mehriban shrugged. "He just thinks of all girls as sisters."

Guncham burst out laughing. Mehriban looked at her with admiration. "Guncham, you're so beautiful. You'll break the heart of more than one young man."

"There are lots of young men in my class, but with them, I'm strictly good friends," she replied.

"School friends are a special case," said Mehriban. "They're always there to help you, advise you, and defend you. They're like brothers."

"Have you got a boyfriend?" Guncham asked.

"No. I'm not looking to meet anyone or fall in love. I've come here to study. But once I've got my diploma, then I can think about finding a man."

The two girls went on talking for a long time. It had grown late, and Mubaryak was still not back, so Guncham unrolled the bedding and they lay down to sleep. Mehriban was soon sound asleep, but later she had a disturbing dream. She woke with a cry. Looking round, she saw Guncham sleeping peacefully.

"Oh, Allah, save us," she whispered, trying to go back to sleep. But the dream would not leave her, and so she lay for a long time, staring into the darkness. Only toward morning did she doze off again, to be woken by Mubaryak's cheerful voice: "Girls, get up! You mustn't be late for school!"

Mehriban opened her eyes. "Mubaryak-hada, we didn't hear you come home."

"I opened the door very carefully and came in on tiptoes," she replied. "I looked in on you, but you were both sound asleep."

Mehriban stood up, dressed, and declined the offer of tea. She hurried home. She felt a strange trepidation clawing at her inside.

That evening, while they were preparing supper, Mehriban remembered the dream she had had. "Last night I had a dream that scared me so much I couldn't sleep for half the night. And it's been haunting me all day," she told everyone.

"What was it like? All dreams should be regarded as good," said Saadat.

"You tell it to us, and we'll interpret it as good," laughed Tursun.

"All right, listen. It was dark outside, or wherever it was. I had gone over to Mubaryak-hada's house for something. I opened the door, and there was Mubaryak-hada lying on the threshold, with her eyes open and her hair all tousled. I cried out loud and stepped farther inside, and there, lying on the table in the very middle of the room, was Guncham. She was pale, and her eyes were closed. I began to shiver and started crying. And just then, my father appeared. He took me by the hand and led me out of the house. Once we were outside, he let go of my hand and said to me, severely, 'Go home right now. Never tell anybody what you have seen, and never go into that house again.' And he vanished."

Everyone stopped what they were doing and looked at Mehriban in silence.

"Go on. Tell me how good my dream was," said Mehriban.

Saadat made a helpless gesture. "That was a bad dream, sure enough."

At that moment Amanzhan's friends Avut and Tair came into the room. The talk about the dream broke off. Mehriban could not forget about it though. The next day, the young people went back to their studies, and the older people went back to their jobs. The weather remained rainy and oppressive.

Every morning Saadat would give Tursun his medicine and then go to work at the kiosk. On an ill-fated day during this rainy period, Tursun's tablets ran out. It was essential not to interrupt the medication, as this could cause his fits to return. She now remembered that it had been Mubaryak who had obtained the tablets for her, as she knew somebody who worked at a pharmacy. She therefore decided to stop by at Mubaryak's and give her money for more tablets.

When she knocked on Mubaryak's door, it swung open. At once, her senses were assaulted by a nauseating smell of blood. Saadat froze in fear. Stepping to one side, she found she had stepped in a pool of blood, and then she saw Mubaryak's body on the floor, her eyes bulging, and her hair disheveled.

Saadat let out an uncontrolled scream and rushed outside.

Old Nadya and her husband Kolya were working in their yard when they heard Saadat scream. They dropped everything and hurried to find her. Saadat was unable to utter a word. Sobbing hysterically, she could only point toward Mubaryak's house. The old couple looked inside and at once recoiled in horror. Eventually, some people walking along the street found out what had happened and called the emergency services.

When Tursun saw the scene, an epileptic fit took hold of him. The neighbors helped Saadat take him home. When the ambulance arrived, the staff gave him an injection.

Once Tursun had fallen asleep, Saadat went back to Mubaryak's house. By this time, the police had arrived and erected a barrier round the house. They would not let anybody in. They took photographs of the scene inside.

"Can you tell me, please, is the girl still alive? Her daughter, Guncham. Is she still alive?" Saadat asked them.

"Who might you be?" the investigator demanded to know.

"I'm a neighbor and a close friend."

"When did you last see the dead woman?"

"Three days ago, when I came home from work. Mubaryak was also coming home from work. It was raining hard, and Guncham ran out with an umbrella to keep her mother dry. And they both went into the house together. So tell me, is the girl alive?"

"No, the girl was raped and killed. We think this was done in front of her mother, to make her give the killers money."

Saadat broke into loud sobs. After a while, orderlies brought out the two covered bodies on stretchers. They loaded them into the ambulance and drove off. By now, a considerable gathering of neighbors were standing outside the house, including Russians, Kazakhs, Uighurs, and Tatars. They talked softly among themselves, wondering who could have murdered a mother and daughter so brutally. Some of them were in tears.

One of the police approached Saadat. "If you used to visit your neighbor, then you would know where things in the house were kept. Would you mind looking now, to see if anything is missing?"

Saadat steeled herself and went with them into Mubaryak's house. There was a stifling, ominous smell that made her nauseous. She overcame the spasm in her stomach, however, and walked slowly round the room, looking closely.

"The white box is missing from in front of the mirror, where Mubaryak kept her jewelry," she pointed out. Then she saw Mubaryak's white handbag on the floor. "It looks like they took her money as well. But otherwise, everything is in its place."

"Do you know your neighbor's relatives?"

"Mubaryak herself was from Uighur District. Her father is dead, and her old mother lives with her son. Her sister lives in Alma-Ata, in Sai.

"Do you know the sister's address?"

"No, I don't. I've only met her once."

"Did your neighbor have any enemies?"

"She never spoke of any. She was very open and straightforward. A good person."

"We conclude that the occupant of this house knew her killers. There is no indication of a break-in, so it seems that she opened the door to them herself."

Saadat remembered Mubaryak's drug-addict nephew but did not dare to mention him. She wanted to get out of that house as quickly as possible.

"It's time for me to go to work," she said timidly.

"You may be needed again." The officer saluted her.

When Saadat went outside again, the other neighbors were still standing around discussing the terrible event. She slipped past them and went home. She sat down beside the sleeping Tursun. The victims of the murder kept appearing before her eyes, and her head started aching in earnest. She felt nauseous again. She could not go to work that day. The loss of her dearest neighbor seemed somehow unreal, like a nightmare. Mubaryak had been like a sister to her, and her death was a heavy blow.

Saadat lay down eventually. But once again, no sooner had she closed her eyes than the images of Mubaryak and Guncham, tousled and broken, appeared in front of her.

Mubaryak had been a beauty with a shapely figure. She knew how to dress tastefully. Her short wavy hair had suited her very well. Moreover, she was frank, cheerful, sincere, and still young, still full of plans. And at sixteen, Guncham was well suited to her name, which meant "bud." She had been clever and attractive, a lover of life. She had been in love with Amanzhan, and her dark eyes had betrayed that love. How many hopes and dreams had died with her?

Saadat held her head in her hands. How would her daughters react to this hideous news? How would they hold out? Beside herself with anxiety, she went outside again. The neighbors had dispersed. Saadat looked over at Mubaryak's house. The door had been sealed and locked.

Her head aching, Saadat went back inside. It felt as though her blood pressure had risen. She took some medicine and lay down. Moments later, she remembered that Mehriban had dreamed exactly this tragedy a few days ago. She jumped up again. *Oh, Allah,* she thought, *that dream foretold what would actually happen.* Her mouth went dry in fear, and she went to drink some cold water.

When the twins came home and heard what had happened, they burst into tears.

"This savagery could only have come from Mubaryak's nephew," said Amanzhan forcefully.

"But if he was such a bad person, why hadn't Mubaryak reported him to the police?" asked Tursun.

"She did, but they still didn't arrest him," said Saadat, her voice crushed.

Tursun clenched his teeth. "Only fascists would do something like this," he said. "When they retreated, they shot everyone mercilessly—young and old, even children. When I saw Mubaryak and Guncham lying in their own blood, it reminded me of the fascists and how they behaved."

"*Dada,* this is the first time you have told us anything about the war," said Amanzhan in surprise.

"It would be better if nobody has to know about that dreadful war, son."

Patam and Zoryam could not find solace and went on weeping over their lost friend. "And now we're afraid of going into the yard in the dark," they said.

Mehriban, who had foreseen the murder in her dream, kept her gaze focused on a single point. A single thought thudded inside her. *This is nothing but savagery, killing women and leaving them lying in blood. How can those monsters still walk free?*

• • •

"Mehriban, I can clearly remember your media telling us that there were no drug problems under socialism," exclaimed Ruth.

Mehriban sighed heavily. "The media and information was always controlled by the regime of the day, and it still is. Back then, the policy was to deny any problems. They created the illusion that all criminal activity was under complete control."

The American looked out of the window. The view of the limitless sky contrasted starkly with the terrible scenes that had just been described. Her mood was heavy. "But still," she said, shaking her head, "do continue."

<h1 style="text-align:center">21</h1>

JOY AND SADNESS

From that tragic day onward, Tursun's health deteriorated significantly. He began to wake up shouting in the night. None of the medications prescribed for him were to any avail. In the end, he was sent to the hospital for a course of treatment for one month, from which he returned a little better. And now he felt the longing to move back to his old village.

The years were passing, meanwhile. Saadat had expended a lot of effort in moving to the city and enabling the children to study. She continued to work at the kiosk, although in winter it was an extremely cold place to sit, and the constant cold took its toll on her health. Yet she gave no attention to her own well-being, for Tursun's condition had worsened again. She put all her effort into caring for him. Telltale creases formed on her face, once so soft and smooth, and her hair turned gray. She now looked older than her years.

For all that, she could say that the fruits of her hard work had been rewarding. Her children were now qualified specialists and self-confident individuals. So after asking Allah to grant her children happiness and long lives, she and Tursun moved back to the spot in which they had been born and grown up.

Amanzhan was the first to return to the village. He had been given a position as an agronomist for the *kolkhoz*. He soon found a good house for his parents to live in. By now, Maysimyam was almost completely blind, and her arms and legs had swelled badly. When Tursun, Saadat, and Amanzhan called to tell her that they had come back to the village permanently, she was overjoyed. "Now let's hope that Mehriban will come back as well," she whispered from time to time.

And what of Mehriban, indeed? Just then she was sheltering under the roof of the bus station from a heavy downpour, waiting for the bus from Almaty to Zharkent. When the bus approached, passengers rushed forward from all directions. Mehriban elbowed her way toward the door through the crowd, and as she did so, to her surprise, she heard somebody behind her call her name. She looked around to see her old classmate Seitzhan.

"How are you keeping, Mehriban?" he asked.

"Fine, thanks. I've just graduated, and I'm going home." She grinned.

"Me too. So is this a new life beginning?" He winked at her.

"You could say that," she answered cheerfully to her old school friend.

Seitzhan had been one of the boys who helped to carry Mehriban home when her feet had frozen. The *dzhigit* standing before her now was tall and swarthy, assured and cool, and with a diploma from the medical institute.

Eventually they made it onto the bus and set off. Mehriban glanced attentively at the young man as she answered his questions.

"So you've got a diploma. What are you going to do? Will you teach at our school?" he asked.

"I don't know yet. That's up to the regional schools department to decide. I'm now officially a 'young specialist,' and I'll have to work wherever they send me. And you? Will you work at the hospital in Zharkent?"

"Yes, I've been referred there."

"Doctors must work very hard and carry a lot of responsibility," observed Mehriban. "They save lives, after all."

"Well, working with children can hardly be easy either. Teachers have to pass on their knowledge to their pupils every day. People remember and respect their favorite teachers for a long time afterward," replied Seitzhan.

"My father once said that a teacher should be as pure as crystal so that he would be an example to the children."

"Kurvan-aka was an honorable and hardworking man," the young man said deferentially.

"These days, children get ten years at our school. So they no longer have to get up before dawn to be in time for lessons." Mehriban smiled.

"But do you remember how we used to walk to Zharkent every day? How many of the kids gave up school because of that!"

"I do, and four of the fourteen in our class went on to higher education, five went on to middle-level training, and five gave up."

"The ones who gave up, Karlin and Kadir, are now tractor drivers at the *kolkhoz*. Azat and Manap are team leaders for the maize crop, and Gyulpyam got married and is bringing up children," Seitzhan added.

"So everyone in our class has found their place in life."

"But they do say there's no gain without pain. Do you remember how long and how severely ill you were at school?"

"That's true. And yes, I remember. I was ill much too often. My poor mother was so worried about me."

Talking over their childhood memories and discussing their possible futures, the young pair did not notice the long journey pass. Seitzhan, looking at this attractive young woman in her simple, brightly colored dress and with her long hair thrown down her back, sensed warmth within him. When they reached the village, he walked her home.

"Mehriban, I hope we'll see more of each other now," he said warmly as they parted. And she laughed, turned, and ran inside.

So energized and joyful was she that she literally flitted into the house. Seeing the large family gathering that had assembled inside, however, she stopped abruptly before rushing forward to hug her mother, who was lying on her bed and now very weak. Tears poured from her eyes. Thoughts about Seitzhan and about how extraordinary life was evaporated from Mehriban's mind at that moment. The relatives had gathered to hear Maysimyam's last words, and her mother's voice was barely audible.

"Gyuli, Rukiyam," she said, "from now on, you will be mothers to my children. I'm proud of all of you. And you, please be satisfied with me. My dear children, live happily."

One on each side of her, Gyuli and Rukiyam stroked their elder sister. "Hada, we are all pleased with you," they said, not taking their eyes off her.

As though she had specially waited for Mehriban's arrival, Maysimyam, a woman of generosity and purity of heart, having borne all of life's tribulations and raised deserving children, now closed her eyes forever.

The old people nodded approval, saying, "Maysimyam held on to life up to the very moment that her children came home from Alma-Ata."

The death of their mother was a blow for the large family. Still, there was nothing for it. One could only acquiesce to fate and to Allah. The next morning, the whole village turned out to accompany Maysimyam on her last journey and to bury her in fitting fashion.

Acts of good or evil are never forgotten. On the day that Maysimyam passed away Yakup-ata, recalling the kindness that Kurvan-aka once showed him, rolled his sleeves up and set to work. His wife Mariya worked the traditional seven days at the *kazan*. Mervanam and Zaynaphan, despite their advanced age, tried to provide support for their friend Gyuli and the others.

• • •

"So Maysimyam finally came to her resting place, the poor thing," sighed Ruth. "I wonder how the rest of Mehriban's life unfolded from that point."

"Yes. Now she was without her mother." Mehriban sighed heavily, concealing her tears from Ruth's gaze. For some time, she could not say another word. Grief was imprinted on her face. After a while, however, she sighed deeply and recovered. She had to continue her tale.

22

THE LONG-AWAITED NIKAH

In proof of the proverb "The living must go on living," one propitious spring day Tursun and Saadat began to prepare for their son's wedding. It was a happy and enjoyable task. They went and bought all they needed and brought it home. Tursun's adoptive family from Dzhambul, Saken-ata, Halima-apay, Bolat, Zileyha and Daulet, made their long-awaited visit for the occasion. Having once taken Tursun in as their own, that family had never ceased to think about him.

On the Friday before the wedding Amanzhan's side was to take *mal-guruch*, gifts of livestock and other presents, to the bride's family, who lived in the neighboring village of Pidzhim. So they and the village elders congregated at Saadat's house, fortified themselves with *plov*, then got into cars and drove to Pidzhim. They also took a truck carrying a bull calf with brightly colored shawls tied between its horns.

When the cavalcade approached the bride's house, people ran out to meet them and called to one another. "Hey, they've arrived! Everyone come and block them!" It was customary for the entrance to the bride's house to be cordoned off, which they did with a length of satin ribbon, until the groom's side delivered the agreed bride price and suitable gifts. Selimyam, Gyuli's daughter, took the money out of her bag, and also handed over two bottles of vodka for the men and a shawl for each of the women. At this, the way into the bride's yard was symbolically opened, and the first of the party to enter were the *aksakals*, the highly respected village elders.

Now the women took their seats in the *chayhana* at little round tables groaning with tasty dishes. Across the yard, the men sat around tables under a vine. After the *aksakals* had recited a prayer and added a *duga*, Yakup-aka got up and spoke on behalf of the groom's party, in a tone of ceremonial importance. "Dear family of the bride-to-be, before we partake of this meal together, I hope that you will not object if we give you the gifts we have brought?"

Voices of agreement could be heard, and the relatives of the bride nodded approval.

"Very well, so let the *dzhigits* bring in the goods."

Young men brought in rice, carrots, and flour by the sack load and placed them in the center of the yard, followed by oil, sweets, and tea. Next, they brought a package of salt and two cases of wine and vodka and soft drinks. Rana and Modangul placed a cloth over a long table and set on it a large pan of *plov*, the boiled meat of half a sheep, a large bowl of *somsa*, ten trays laden with desserts and piles of sweets and seedless grapes, nuts, and biscuits. On another tray lay some pretty material for a woman's dress along with a man's shirt.

"Dear hosts, here are the offerings with which we have come to you today," said the groom's representatives, standing up.

The bride's parents and relatives answered them. "Thank you, honored guests and future relations. What you have brought us is sufficient. May our young pair be happy!"

Yakup-aka signaled to the mullah Ibrahim to recite the next prayer, and when he added a special *duga*, all present raised their hands. Tea was served, followed by *plov*. At once, the atmosphere grew animated, with jokes, laughter, and cheer all round.

When the *plov* was finished, Yakup-aka stood up again. "Let us say the *duga*, because then we'll need to slaughter our bullock, cook the meat, and do all the other things that have to be done before it gets dark."

Once the guests had departed, Hasan-aka, Omar, Yadikar, and Sadikzhan went to the far end of the garden. In no time at all, they killed the bullock and cut up the carcass, then placed the meat in a large *kazan* and started to boil it.

When it was time for the groom's party to leave, Rihan, the bride's mother, said to them, "Saadat, remember to send three or four women to help us tomorrow, and make sure they get here early. And don't forget the milk and the *kaymak*."

"Don't worry," she answered. "Modangul will take care of it."

The next day, the young people sprinkled the yard with water and swept it clean. They set out two rows of long tables, laid cloths on them, and spread them with trays of desserts. Beside these they set out plates of boiled chicken and beef, sheep's lungs in a white sauce, and *hesip*, a homemade sausage of sheep's intestine with meat and rice, *samsa*, spicy vegetable dishes, salads, and of course, ruddy-looking *togach* breads. Vodka, wine, and other drinks were set out.

When everything was ready, Rihan examined the generously-piled tables carefully and said to the young people who had set them, "Thank you. The *dastarkhan* is wonderful. Now I need you to go over to the *chayhana*, spread a white cloth on the *dzhoza* there, and put out the same dishes again."

"But the mullah and the elders will be in the *chayhana*, so don't give them any vodka," warned Polat.

By this time, people were arriving. A group of musicians seated a little way from the tables began to sing and play, and the mood grew festive. People strolled about in groups. The mullah and the elders took their honored positions in the *chayhana*. Once everybody was seated under the vine, they were addressed by Kurvanzhan, a well-known toastmaster from Pidzhim.

"*Assalamu aleykum*, neighbors, brothers, and all our esteemed guests who have traveled from villages far and near! We are gathered here today for the marriage of a young woman of our village, Guzyal, daughter of Polat-aka, to our brother Amanzhan, the son of Tursun-aka. The ceremony of Nikah will be performed by the mullah Ivrahim-aka shortly. Meanwhile, please welcome the bride and groom."

Rhythmic music now broke out again, and a group of young men and girls moved into the yard. In their midst, walking slowly, came Guzyal and Amanzhan.

They proceeded toward the *chayhana* and then, as complete silence descended, all present listened attentively as the mullah Ivrahim recited a *sura* of the Qur'an.

"Success and prosperity to your Nikah, my children, which has been sent to you from heaven! May you be happy," said the mullah solemnly to the pair, once they had each partaken of the matrimonial drink of sweetened milk that symbolized their bond before God.

Tursun and Polat, the fathers of the two families, congratulated the newlyweds, then declaring themselves henceforth to be in-laws, they embraced each other warmly. The young people danced to the music and then went out of the yard. They got into a number of cars and roared off in high spirits for a ride.

On this occasion, special cooks had been invited to preside over the *kazan*. They made no fewer than ten pots of tea, which young men then served in bowls to the guests. Kevir-aka, a cook renowned in Pidzhim, lifted the lid from the great *kazan*, stirred the *plov* within, and began to divide it into portions in large dishes. Two young men carried the steaming meat in a large basin and placed it on the table, and Ahri-aka placed three large pieces of the meat on each bowl of *plov*. Two spoons were laid beside each bowl.

Ahri-aka directed that the best pieces of meat be given to the in-laws. "And now, boys, it's time to serve the *plov* to the guests, starting at the far end," he instructed.

Each *dzhigit* took two dishes at a time and began distributing the meal. Once everybody had been served, the toastmaster signaled that old Saken-buva from Dzhambul should speak.

"*Assalam*, dear guests and relatives. For me, it has been a joy at long last to see the place where Tursun was born and grew up and to meet you, the fellow villagers and family of my son. I am overjoyed." He paused for breath. "After a very long wait, Tursun has finally been reunited with his family. And today he can celebrate his own son's wedding and be proud of the fact. We have traveled a long way to be here to share this joy with Tursun. May there be no more wars, and instead let people live together in peace and harmony. Let us come together for big celebrations and rejoice in one another. And may Amanzhan and his bride be happy!"

Tursun hugged the old man, and the guests raised their glasses. The music started up again, and the younger people danced in the middle of the yard.

When the music stopped again, the toastmaster invited the two fathers to speak. Polat worked at the *kolkhoz* as an accountant, and his wife was a teacher, and people regarded them as affluent compared to Tursun's family. It may have been for this reason that he spoke with particular pride.

"When our children grow up, they marry, and we form family ties with people who were previously strangers. Now Tursun and I are in-laws. For our part, we gave our daughter a good upbringing, and now she's a nurse in the hospital. I am certain that she and Amanzhan will live happily together. Should they find themselves in need of anything, we will be there for them. Thank you all for coming to share in our happiness. Enjoy the celebrations!"

Now it was Tursun's turn. His hands began to shake suddenly. Turgan went up and stood beside him, and Tursun glanced at him gratefully. "Today a wedding is taking place in the Zharkent region, in its most prosperous and beautiful spot—the village of Pidzhim. How many illustrious people have come from this place! I am very pleased to now have a family tie to Polat. Our children are happy because we are living in a time of peace and our *dastarkhan* is rich. I wish our young people happiness, good health, and peace."

"Well said, *aka*," whispered Turgan, squeezing his brother's hand.

"The guests would like you to sing 'Ilahun' now, brother," said Tursun.

"Well, if I didn't sing it at the wedding of my dear nephew, where else on earth would I want to sing it?" said Turgan, who began to sing the popular song about the revolutionary Uighur hero, softly at first and gradually growing louder.

> *No man will shoot at Ilahun,*
> *nor will he sell his fast horse.*
> *On his account have no concern,*
> *He will not be jailed in Urumqi.*
> *On the road to Kuria[2]*
> *Did your cart break down, Shangian[3]?*
> *By basely betraying Ilahun,*
> *Did you find peace, Shangian?*

------

[2] An ancient Uighur town in modern-day China.
[3] Shangian - the mayor of the town.

As the song ended, everybody around him applauded and called out for more. In honor of his brother, Turgan sang another song before the dancing resumed and the younger guests played games and held contests. The wedding was a success!

At two o'clock it was time for the women to sit down to their repast. The helpers quickly set out the tables once again. The women arrived in groups, wearing light, loosely cut dresses with white shawls on their heads. They greeted each other amiably and began to sit down on the colorful rugs in the *chayhana*. In those days, Uighur women knew nothing about cosmetics. Girls would come to these events in their best dresses with *osma* for eye-shadow and a flower tucked behind their ear, and the result was very fetching.

Tea was served to the women around three o'clock, and then the hostess, Rihan, said to them, "Dear guests, please take some of these sweetmeats home with you so that your children and grandchildren can share in our festive *dastarkhan*." And so they did, putting the leftover desserts into paper bags, and then the helpers took away the empty trays. Now Turahan, who was leading the women's part of the matrimonial ceremony, announced, "While the *plov* is being served, let us view the bride's dowry. Bring in the chest and put it in the center."

Two young women carried in a chest, opened it, and took out a small, tightly wrapped bundle containing sweets, which they gave to Adalyat-ana as the eldest kinswoman of the groom. Gyulsum, the bride's sister, then took out a mirror and held it aloft. "This mirror is for the young couple," she announced.

"And here is a suit for our son-in-law and a *dopa* to wear on his head," she continued, holding them up and then putting them to one side. Then came tablecloths, curtains, bed linens, and new dresses and outfits for the young bride.

"Now I'm not going to display the footwear, as that isn't done. But there are boots, shoes, and slippers in here." This said, Gyulsum's job was done.

The bride's mother, getting up, thanked the groom's party for their generous dowry. She then signaled to her daughters, who brought into the yard a large bed, crockery, two rugs, four quilted blankets, four long narrow *korpya,* and four pillows, which they placed on top of the chest. Turahan then announced to the women sitting in the *chayhana* that all this had been provided by Rehan-hada.

All the relatives nodded approval and complimented Rehan. Gifts were then given by the bride's relatives, her aunts, and woman friends, and once all of these had been presented, the groom's party in turn opened their dowry chest. Rana took out a small, tightly wrapped bundle containing sweetmeats and presented it to the senior relative of the bride.

"And here are three kilograms of Indian tea, a suit for her father and a chiffon dress for her mother, ten men's shirts, a length of China silk sufficient for ten dresses, a hundred shawls..." They raised the items high as they enumerated them, so that everybody could see. "These things are what the bride's family ordered from us. Please accept them. And now let me show you our gift to the bride: shawls, dresses and outfits, a coat and various items of footwear. Anything else our son will buy for her," Rana added with a grin.

Next, the bride's side presented their gifts. And once this old custom, both fascinating and practical, was over, the music started again. All the women, young and old, joined in a folk dance. And when the dancing ended, *plov* was served to the high-spirited guests, and after that, *aktyan-chay*. When the tea was finished, Saadat got up and announced, "Dear Rehan, I would like to invite you and all your guests to come to us tomorrow for the groom's ceremony, the *chilak*, at our house."

With that the bride's part of the ceremony was completed, and the attention turned to preparing for the second half of the festivities, which would take place at the groom's house. When Saadat got home, she warmly thanked those who had stayed behind to begin the preparations. She and the other women laid a long table that had been set up in the middle of the yard.

"*Hada*, would you take a look at the *dastarkhan*?" asked Mehriban. "Do you think people will be saying things about us?"

Rana and Saadat looked at the attractively laid table. "You've arranged everything beautifully. But you haven't forgotten the vegetable dishes?"

"We'll serve all the hot things once the guests are seated," said Mehriban.

Turgan, meanwhile, was asking a pair of Amanzhan's friends whether they had been at the stag party. "Of course we were there, *aka*," they grinned. "Nothing happens anywhere without us being there. Our mate Avut invited about twenty of us and put on a great evening. It was a lot of fun."

"And did you go to the hen party as well?"

"You bet. We were there for an hour or so too."

"Where did you go after the Nikah?"

"We got into some cars and drove to the Usek river. We had a great time."

"Well, tonight we'd love you to do your part as friends of Amanzhan, to help make sure that the celebrations go smoothly and are everything we want them to be."

"Why, sure! We are an honorable bunch, and we'll do anything for a friend."

"And Tairzhan, when do you think we'll be celebrating your wedding?" winked Turgan at one of them.

"We're hoping to tie the knot this autumn."

"Good. It gives parents a lot of happiness when their children build a family. But for now, let's go and help the cooks." Turgan, who together with Rana was in charge of the celebration, led the young men toward the garden.

Once it grew dark, the guests arrived. At almost exactly the same time, six cars drew up, decorated with colored ribbons, in which sat young men and girls.

"Light the fire and get the pair to walk round it three times, then have them come into the yard," said Saadat.

They lit a pile of wood at the gate that had been prepared earlier. Amanzhan and Guzyal took each other's hand and circled the fire three times. The music started, and the young couple danced into the yard, then took their designated places. They were a fine couple. Amanzhan wore a black suit and a white shirt and a tie; he had a *dopa* on his head, the Uighur national headdress, which suited him very well.

Guzyal looked exceptionally beautiful in a long white dress with a veil over her head. Seeming a little nervous, she whispered something to Amanzhan from time to time, as though seeking his support. She looked well suited to her name: a true beauty. Tursun and Saadat looked admiringly at their son and his bride and tears of happiness glittered in their eyes.

"Saadat, you and I never had the chance for a wedding like this," said Tursun quietly. "But I'm so happy for our son."

Turgan noticed their tears and went over to them. "Your greatest happiness is to see your children happy," he said.

"You're right, brother. And not everyone lives to see that happiness," Tursun replied, rubbing the area over his heart.

Mehriban, watching her brother anxiously, reminded him to take his medicine.

The celebrations proved highly convivial. Good wishes, congratulations, and gifts were showered on the couple, and midnight approached and passed unnoticed. Soon after, however, the guests began to disperse. Rana took Amanzhan and Guzyal to the room that had been prepared for them, wished them well, and left them alone together.

Not until four o'clock did the helpers finish clearing up and washing the dishes. The next day, Tursun and Saadat rose early, swept the yard, and cleaned the *kazans*. When Patam and Zoryam saw their mother hard at work, they reproached her. "*Apa*, leave this, we'll do it all. Haven't you noticed how Father's not looking well?"

"I have," said Saadat, clearly worried. "He was groaning all night long. Would you give him his injection and his medicine, please?" She was anxious that today's part of the *toy* would go smoothly.

Zoryam swept and cleaned the area around the *kazan*, while Patyam, lighting the fire in the stove, asked, "*Apa*, will there be as many ceremonies today as there were yesterday?"

"No, it'll be simpler today. Yesterday at the bride's ceremony there was all that business with the dowry and opening up the chests. Today, Guzyal will bow to the women of our family."

Now Rana and Mehriban arrived, greeted everybody, and set to work. A little while later they were joined by Gyuli's daughters, Selimyam and Saniyam. Gradually other relatives also appeared. The table was soon laid, and at midday, the male guests arrived and took their places, and the proceedings commenced. This part of the wedding was also lively and spirited, with jokes, laughter, music, and dancing; the parents of both sides were pleased.

In due course, the men dispersed, and at two o'clock the women began to arrive. Once all were present, the parents of the bride entered. They were given the places of honor, and tea was poured. After this came *plov*, accompanied by *togach* and *sanza*. The feast was concluded with *aktyan-chay* with *kaymak*. Afterwards, Nurhan stood up and announced, "Dear guests! Please welcome the young bride, who bows to you in deference and with *salam*."

A beautiful cloth had been spread out on the ground. Nurhan-ana led Guzyal, her head covered by a shawl, onto the cloth. Nurhan-ana spoke again, "*Assalamu aleykum*, the bride comes in deference and *salam* to the Almighty."

One of the mothers among the guests called out, "May God be her support!"

"*Assalamu aleykum*, the bride comes in deference and *salam* to the prophets."

"May the prophets be her support!"

"*Assalamu aleykum*, the bride comes in deference and *salam* to the grandfathers and grandmothers."

"May the grandfathers and grandmothers be her support!"

"*Assalamu aleykum*, the bride comes in deference and *salam* to the father and mother."

"May the father and mother be her support!"

"*Assalamu aleykum*, the bride comes in deference and *salam* to all who are present here, both young and old."

"May all who are gathered here be her support!"

With each of these invocations, Guzyal bowed low. As per tradition, the older women sitting in the best places took turns to offer one another the honor of delivering the marriage testament to the bride, and in the end, it was Adalyat, Kurvan-aka's sister, who read it out.

"Let the bride rise early and not remain in bed until sunrise."

"It shall be so," responded Nurhan-ana.

"Let her bow to her parents every morning."

"It shall be so."

"May the bride's house always be clean, and may she receive guests with a smile."

"It shall be so."

"May she not indulge in mindless talk, and may she always be modest and polite."

"It shall be so. Our girl has had an education and was well brought up. She has noted all that you have said and will act accordingly," said Nurhan-ana, removing the shawl from the bride's head.

Self-conscious, Guzyal went into the house. One of the women quickly gathered up the ceremonial cloth. "I'm taking this with me, so that my son hurries up and gets married," she said, putting it into her bag.

"Yes, that's an old sign," one of the others remarked.

The women's part of the ceremony was also a success, and in due course, the satisfied guests began to disperse homeward. Seeing that their visitors from Dzhambul were also preparing to leave, Tursun invited them to stay a few more days. He wanted very much to sit and talk with them.

The next day, with the wedding over, Saadat's family entertained the Dzhambul guests with *kordak*, followed by large bowls of *manty*. During the meal, they discussed how the celebrations had gone. Tursun repeatedly got up and went to help Saadat at the *kazan*.

"What are you doing here?" she smiled at him. "Go and sit with the guests."

"They are busy talking," he answered. "Saadat, I can see you're tired. Let me be with you a while."

Mehriban looked at her brother. "I think you're tired too," she said. "I'll go and get your medicine."

"Don't bother, sister. I feel well enough today. I feel light, ready to fly, like a bird."

"That's because the wedding went so well, I expect," said Saadat. "That's why you feel so light and well." She made *aktyan-chay* in a large green pot. Now Modangul came up to them and said, "*Hada, aka*, go and sit with the guests. Leave the tea to us."

Tursun and Saadat went back to the table. They talked and drank their tea, accompanied by *ashmya sanza* and *samsas*.

Tursun, sitting beside Saadat, whispered to her, "Saadat, something's not right with me." He suddenly buried his face in her lap.

"Tursun, Tursun, what's the matter? Open your eyes!" called out Saadat in panic. They lifted him up and lay him down with a pillow under his head.

Turgan and Mehriban began to rub his hands and sprinkled cold water onto his face. But Tursun's face was growing cold; his lips were turning blue, and life was fading from him rapidly. Hearing Saadat's cries, Tursun's relatives came running over from the *kazan*. They froze at the sight of the lifeless man. Tursun's heart, which had survived the war and long years of separation, bitterness, and sadness, had been unable to bear three days of wedding celebrations. The joyful smiles of one moment changed in an instant to weeping and keening.

Hearing the sounds of grieving, bewildered neighbors came into the yard. "What's happened? What's wrong?" they asked.

"We've lost Tursun-aka," answered Turgan, unable to hold back his tears.

Once again, destiny had reached out and touched Tursun and Saadat. Amanzhan and all their close relatives were shaken by their sense of bitter injustice. Now Saadat was separated from her beloved forever. A curse on that terrible war that brought so much misery to so many! Once again, Saadat was a widow.

Yet for all that, Tursun had been granted by God the possibility of living with his family, if only for five years, and to return to his home village and to see his only son marry. So they could at least be grateful for this. Now he lay at eternal rest alongside his parents. And nobody can resist destiny.

• • •

"You're absolutely right, Mehriban. Look how long Tursun spent wandering in distant lands. His strong heart tolerated all that deprivation but then couldn't endure the happiness he had dreamed of. Fate can be like that." Ruth shook her head in sorrow.

Then, however, a smile broke out on her face. "I can't help but note that Uighur weddings are fascinating and unusual."

Mehriban replied, not without pride, "We haven't been able, of course, to preserve all our folk traditions for thousands of years, but we have kept the matrimonial traditions up to now. It's so sad for Tursun and Saadat that their own wedding couldn't take place because of the war."

23

A MAGICAL RITUAL

Life, meanwhile, went on, for they do not say that life takes precedence over death without good reason. And soon the village was blessed with another happy occasion, when Mehriban and Seitzhan proposed to marry. It was not yet a year since Tursun had died, and for that reason, the wedding was modest. The formal ceremony was held in Turgan and Rana's house, after which they retired to the groom's house, where the celebrations were cozy and fitting.

Seitzhan worked at the hospital in Zharkent, so once they were married, the couple moved to the town. For two years they rented an apartment, after which they built themselves a simple house in the upper part of the town. When this was ready, they held a housewarming for relatives of both sides.

At the high point of the evening, Seitzhan's sister Pati came up to him. "*Uka*, how come you've brought this barren wife to your new house with you? You should have found another woman who could give you a boy. You've been married for four years and nothing's come of it. Don't you want children or something, eh?" Her tone was angry.

"Stop that, *hada*," he flared up. "I'm not leaving Mehri. We'll have children, I'm sure of it."

"And when, pray? Time's passing, you know. Or are you planning to rear your children in your old age?"

Of course Seitzhan wanted children. He had taken Mehriban to see specialists in Alma-Ata, who had confirmed that she was healthy and could have children. And he and Mehriban loved each other. Why would they ever dream of divorcing? This the first time his sister had admonished him, so he walked away before she had finished. Straight away, he saw Mehriban in the end room in tears.

"Why are you crying, love? Why aren't you talking with the guests? You shouldn't be hiding in here."

"I heard what Pati-hada was saying to you."

"So that's what's upset you? But you know my sister can be difficult sometimes."

"Seitzhan, she's right." She looked up at him with her tear-stained face. "I'll go, if you'd like. Maybe, if you find another woman, you can have children and be happy." She looked at him with guilty eyes through a mantle of tears.

"Mehri, what are you talking about? We will never be parted, except by death alone." He smiled back at her and kissed her. "Don't worry, we'll have children when the time is right. They'll run all over the house and get up to all kinds of mischief, just to keep us on our toes. Come on, let's go and be hospitable to our guests."

Even so, Mehriban kept remembering what Seitzhan's sister had said, and it never ceased to cause her pain.

There were no vacancies in Zharkent for a teacher, so Mehriban took a job at a kindergarten. There she watched the children playing and loved their pranks and funny speech. Sometimes she would hug them. She longed for children of her own.

Each day after lunch, the children in her group would lie down for an afternoon nap. One afternoon, looking at their angelic sleeping faces, Mehriban found the question more urgent in her. *When will I have children too?* She got up and went into the next room, leaving the door ajar, and sat down to plan the lesson timetable. As she did so, into the room came Modangul. Mehriban greeted her softly. "The children are sleeping. Come, let's go outside."

They sat down on a bench in the yard. "I came to go to the bazaar for some things, and thought I'd drop by and see you. We haven't seen you for so long!" Modangul hugged her.

"That's true, *hada*. So much to do… and the days just race by," sighed Mehriban.

"Sister, I've been sent to you by Saadat-hada and Rana-hada. They're like mothers to us now. They want to hold a ceremony of *anla chay*, the 'tea of mothers,' for you."

"What do you mean? What sort of tea is it? What's it for?"

"It's an ancient custom. If a woman can't conceive, the mothers of the village hold this *anla chay* ceremony for her and invite up to nine older women. The hostess makes *zhit* and bakes *anla nan* bread in the *tono*—this is a big, thin *nan* specially for mothers. She sets a table for the guests and puts these things on it. Then one of the women recites a *sura* from the Qur'an, dedicating it to the *zhit*, after which she recites the names of all mothers who are saints and says the closing prayer. She asks that the barren woman be made able to conceive and to give birth successfully, to be able to hold and hug her own child. After this, each guest recites a prayer and gives her own good wishes. They break the *anla nan,* and each woman is given a piece, but they keep the middle to be shared between the husband and the wife, who eat them while asking God to grant them a child. The hostess gives a shawl to each guest. They say that Allah's mercy has no limits. If they hold an *anla chay* ceremony for you, you'll become pregnant. And wouldn't that be a miracle?"

Mehriban listened closely to her sister.

"If you agree to it, they are proposing to hold the ceremony on Wednesday. Wednesday is considered to be the day of mothers," Modangul added.

"I'd love to but wouldn't it put Saadat-hada and Rana-hada to a lot of trouble?" asked Mehriban.

"What they said to me was that if Maysimyam had still been alive, she would certainly have done the *anla chay* for you. But since she's no longer with us, they said they'll invite the senior mothers of the village themselves and ask for their blessing on Mehriban."

"Very well, *hada.* You tell them that Seitzhan and I will bring everything we need for the ceremony, and we'll come to the village on Wednesday."

"Fine. I'll go now. I don't want to miss the bus," said Modangul, picking up her heavy black bag.

Mehriban saw her sister out. Modangul stopped at the gate and turned round. "And another thing, I completely forgot. The Uighur Theater from Alma-Ata have come to the village. We're all going tonight to see them perform *Anarhan*."

"Seitzhan and I went to see it yesterday," said Mehriban, becoming animated. "Brilliant play. Ahmiat Shamiev played Sait, Rizvangul Tokhtanova was Gulzarhan, Roshangul Ilahunova was Anarhan, and Mahpir Bakiev played Baki. They're all real stars. I was in tears all the way through."

"And when you see what happens to the lovers, Anarhan and Baki—I can't hold back. Their happy ending never comes. Anyway, *sinnim*, you'd better go. Don't miss the bus."

Modangul left. It was still too early to wake the children. Mehriban went into the room where they were sleeping, sat down, and sank into thought. *All my relatives have four or five children. Why am I different? Will Allah really refuse us a child? Maybe this has happened because I was so ill as a child. If the folk ceremony doesn't work, we'll adopt a boy and a girl from the orphanage and bring them up. I don't think Seitzhan will disapprove of that.*

Mehriban took the following Wednesday off work and went to the village. Saadat and Rana, who were almost mothers to her, had already made the *zhit*, baked the *anla nan*, and set the *dzhoza* attractively. Then at about midday, the invited women began to arrive.

"It won't be long, I think, before the senior women around here will be us," grinned Mervanam-ana.

Gyuli-ana laughed. "And when we are groaning and hobbling about on sticks, we won't miss out on invitations like this."

"Well after all, when you go out for company and conversation, we all grow younger, don't you think?"

The senior guests settled in the places of honor set aside for them.

"I so feel the absence of Adalyat-hada among us," said Zaynaphan. "Remember how she was, stately and serious, sitting at the center. She always supported her friends."

The others, hearing her, said approvingly, "May the earth beneath her be like down."

"Well, that's how it is. Some of us go sooner from this world, and others later," sighed Zunaryam, straightening the shawl on her head.

"But why all this talk about dying?" broke in Rukiyam. "It's not very often we get to meet like this. Better for us to talk about when we were young."

"Ah, Rukiyam, we never knew youth. We lost it working in the fields, along with our health. Look at what's left of us now," said Mervanam-ana. "And for all that heroic labor, the *kolkhoz* pays us the princely pension of twelve rubles a month."

"Your children will never let you go hungry, though," reassured her friend Saryam-ana.

As the women were talking, Mariya arrived. She was leading a stooping, elderly woman by the hand, who wore a white shawl. The others got up from their places.

"Please sit, please sit. There's no need to stand," the old woman waved her hand.

They gave her the place of honor.

"When Maryam-ana told me that she had been asked to an *anla chay*, I also wanted to come and give my blessing," said the honored guest in a soft voice.

"You have been sent by God," said Saadat with joy.

Mariya introduced the new guest to the others. "This is Zoryam chon-apa. She's over eighty. Whenever anybody in Zharkent holds the *anla chay*, they invite her. It is a great happiness for us that she has come here and agreed to give her blessing."

"Welcome, Zoryam-hada. We need you today very much," said Gyuli-ana.

Soon Seitzhan's mother Gulsumhan-ana arrived with her daughter Pati, and the women also offered them places of honor. Once everybody was settled, Gyuli-ana turned to the gray-haired Zoryam-ana, who had aged with great beauty and whose face was illuminated with an inner light. "Zoryam-hada, we entrust today's ceremony to you. You are the most senior among us, and so you should lead."

"Call in the one who is in need of blessing," Zoryam-hada said.

Saadat brought Mehriban in. "Here she is. Her name is Mehriban."

"If we are all here, then let us begin," said Zoryam-hada. She recited a passage from the Qur'an over the *zhit* and mentioned the names of the mother saints, among them Buvi Mariyam, Buvi Aminam, Buvi Ayshyam, Buvi Helichyam, Buvi Patyam, Buvi Zoryam, Buvi Zaynap, and Buvi Hadzhyarbuvi. She then blessed Mehriban and wished her success in pregnancy and an easy birth, addressing these requests to Allah. Next, Mehriban received blessings from the other nine mothers present. Each of them expressed good wishes, then said *Amen*, which the others then repeated.

"Dear mothers of mine, thank you all! Forgive me for having troubled you!" said Mehriban, who then began to weep.

Zoryam-ana raised her eyes to Mehriban and said, "Don't cry, child. I hope that our requests have been heard by God. And *inshallah*, we will all be together again in nine months' time to celebrate your *beshchuk toy*."

Modangul poured tea into bowls and served it to the guests. Saadat and Rana placed large bowls of *manty* and *zhutta* on the table. "Help yourselves, dear friends," they said.

"You really have rolled this *zhutta* dough out paper thin, said the old women approvingly. And the carrots are chopped as fine as hairs. They are delicious—and perfect for us oldies who've got no teeth left!"

Mehriban and Modangul then placed bowls of *aktyan-chay* before the guests, who sipped the tea and conversed unhurriedly. Zoryam-ana broke the *anla nan* into pieces and gave a piece to each woman present, keeping the middle of the bread for Mehriban. "You should divide this piece of bread into two, and you and your husband should eat the pieces together."

The guests raised their hands and blessed Mehriban again. Rana gave each of the women a shawl and said solemnly, "This is so your hands are not empty and so that your wishes may be granted."

Once the guests had left, Mehriban thanked her sisters. "Saadat-hada, Rana-hada! Thank you so much!

Thanks to you, I do not feel the lack of a mother. You've done so much for me."

Several months passed, and to the surprise of many, Mehriban conceived. It hardly mattered whether this was due to the prescriptions of the doctors or to the blessing of the mothers. The main thing was that she, her husband, and those close to them were happy. Mehriban prayed morning and evening that the child would be born in good health. Yet this did not come easily. She lost weight and broke out in a rash of pigment spots, and with each passing day, she found it harder to walk. In the first months of pregnancy, she had continued to clean the house and yard, but before it was time for her to go into the hospital, she was calling on her sisters to help her. Modangul and Mahinur came over and were more than happy to do washing and housework, as well as tasks such as whitewashing the house, while Mehriban prepared a tasty lunch for them.

"I've been thinking a lot about our mother recently, and I've been seeing her in my dreams," said Mehriban one day.

"That means she's helping you," said Modangul.

"Mama would be so pleased for you now, like all of us," added Mahinur.

"It's so unfair that right now, with all of us working, just when we can afford to provide them with all the clothes they need, to look after them and cherish them, we no longer have our mother or father with us." Modangul's eyes glistened.

Seitzhan came into the yard. "So what's this, the Great Flood?" he joked.

The women burst out laughing and wiped away their tears. Modangul and Mahinur got up. "We look forward to hearing your good news," they said warmly as they left.

Mehriban saw her sisters out and then came into the house, looked herself in the mirror, and said with displeasure, "Seitzhan, look what's happened to me. I've lost all my looks."

"Not at all. You're a beautiful woman who's about to become a mother," he said, putting his arms around her.

"But when can we expect our child to arrive?" She stroked her swollen belly.

"It's just a few days now. Be patient, my love."

"The closer the time comes, the more I'm scared."

"There's nothing to worry about. I'll be with you. It'll all turn out well."

One night soon after, Mehriban woke up with pain in her back. She went into the end room to avoid waking Seitzhan and paced up and down, looking now and again at the clock. After an hour, the pain had increased to the point that Mehriban began to groan. Seitzhan hurried from the bedroom to see what was wrong. "What is it? Has the labor started?" he asked, picking up the telephone.

An ambulance quickly arrived and took Mehriban and Seitzhan to the maternity hospital. The nurse on duty, Galina Ivanovna, examined Mehriban and said that there was still time, leaving the admissions area. Crying out in pain, Mehriban endured five more hours of labor pains. As it grew light, Galina Ivanovna realized that the contractions had begun and instructed her to go to the operating room. She asked that Seitzhan, since he was a doctor, to be the assistant.

They lay Mehriban down and gave her an injection. Seitzhan held her hand and wiped the sweat from her brow. Seeing his wife struggling so hard in labor, he also broke out in a sweat and began to shake. Time passed, and the contractions dragged on. Galina Ivanovna began to worry. She took a bedsheet, gave one end to the midwife and held the other, and used the sheet to apply pressure on Mehriban's belly.

"Mehri, push! Take a deep breath and push as hard as you can. Come on, come on, the baby could choke!" called out Seitzhan.

At this, Mehriban doubled her exertions, and at last the baby was born. Then, exhausted with pain and soaking wet, she realized that she was a mother. Joy filled her, and her body seemed to become very light. Galina Ivanovna cut the umbilical cord and handed the baby to its father. "Here is your long-awaited daughter," she announced, smiling.

Seitzhan carefully took the infant in his hands. "Welcome into this world, little one! Mehri, open your eyes and see our beautiful girl."

It was all Mehriban could do to open her eyes. She looked at her new child, smiled weakly, and closed her eyes again. A nurse washed the baby's mouth and nose, wrapped her in swaddling clothes, and took her away. Seitzhan said to Galina Ivanovna that he was worried about his wife.

"Well, you're a doctor," she responded. "You should know that giving birth for the first time is often difficult for women over thirty."

The nurses helped Mehriban back to the ward to lie down. She was asleep almost before her head touched the pillow. At lunchtime, Seitzhan came into the ward to see her and gently touched her to wake her. Mehriban unglued her eyelids with great effort. Her face was pale and swollen.

"My love, I've just been to the ward for the new-borns to see our girl. She weighs four kilos and two hundred grams. Well done, Mehri! How are you feeling?"

"I can't wake up. I just want to sleep and sleep."

"The birth was difficult, but you'll get your strength back in time," said Seitzhan gently. "I've already phoned the village. Mama's sent you some *aktyan-chay* in a Thermos flask and a *gesh nan*—a meat pie. You should eat, and then you'll have some milk."

Mehriban struggled to sit up. Her hands were shaking. She drank the tea greedily to slake her thirst, but she did not touch the pie. She had scarcely enough strength to sit, and soon lay her head back on the pillow and closed her eyes. Seitzhan went out quietly.

That evening, after Mehriban had fed the baby for the first time, Seitzhan came in again and gave her some food from home. While she was eating, the young father took his tiny daughter in his hands.

"Look, Mehri, she's like me," he said proudly, stroking the black wisps of hair on the baby's head. "Today's the first of September, when all children go to school with bouquets of flowers. In seven years' time we'll be sending our child to school too." He could not take his eyes off the child.

Mehriban looked at her husband and smiled. He came over and sat on the bed.

"Tomorrow I've got to go to Taldykorgan for work. I'll be back in a couple of days," he said to her.

"Well, isn't there some way you can get out of it?"

"I'm afraid not. They'll never let me. I'm going with a group of colleagues."

Their conversation was interrupted by a young nurse. She took the baby from Seitzhan and walked away. As she did so, he called out, "Nurse, make sure you look after my little daughter while you've got her!"

He kissed Mehriban, said good-bye and left the ward.

That night heavy rain began to fall. The newborns in the maternity hospital were restive; they fidgeted and cried. At midnight they were taken to their mothers for feeding. Seeing how her baby sucked at her breast, Mehriban suddenly experienced a deeply maternal feeling. She looked unceasingly at her child, studying every detail of her tiny face. When she had done feeding, Mehriban took off the swaddling and held the girl's little hands and feet and stroked her tummy. Once she was sure that all was well with her, she wrapped the baby back up in the swaddling clothes. Just as the nurse took the child from her again, a woman who had just given birth was brought to the bed next to her.

"Sister, I've got a dry mouth. You haven't got some tea or water I could have?" she asked.

"Did the birth go all right?" Mehriban asked her, pouring tea from the thermos and passing it to the young woman.

"Thank you," she said in a weak voice. She drank the hot tea quickly, and her head flopped onto the pillow.

Mehriban also grew quiet. For some reason, she had had a sense of foreboding inside her. It may have been because of the difficult birth. The folk wisdom has it, after all, that "you understand the value of a mother only when you become a mother yourself."

Early the next morning, Mehriban woke early from her own shouting. She lay drenched in sweat. Her cries also woke her new neighbor.

"Sister, you were shouting. Were you having a nightmare?" she asked with concern.

"Yes, it was a bad dream. Sorry."

Mehriban could not close her eyes again until later in the morning. The sound of the rain outside went on; even its steady pouring seemed dismal and uneasy.

Later that morning, the rain suddenly stopped. Mehriban had just managed to wash when the grinning Modangul and Mahinur appeared at the window of her ward, bearing all manner of delicious food from home. Looking at Mehriban as she stood by the window, they congratulated her and told her to eat well. Then they waved good-bye and were gone.

Two days later, Seitzhan appeared with a large bouquet of flowers. "I'm back! And why doesn't my daughter come running to meet me?" he joked, kissing Mehriban.

Mehriban felt relief to see that her husband had come home safe and sound.

Nine days after the birth, Mehriban was discharged from hospital. Seitzhan, together with Amanzhan and his wife Gyuzal, all bearing flowers, came to collect her. Seitzhan thanked the doctors and nurses and took Mehriban and the baby home, where his mother and Mehriban's sisters were waiting.

Gulsumhan-ana was holding a tray of a dry herbs, *adrasman*, and as Mehriban approached the threshold, they set the herb alight. It gave off aromatic smoke, which Gulsumhan gently blew so as to envelop the mother and child with its refreshing scent. After this, Mehriban crossed the threshold and went inside. Everybody was pleased, for a new baby brings happiness into a house.

Once they had eaten, Seitzhan's mother said, "Son, I don't know whether you are planning to have her sleep in a *beshchuk* or not, but I've brought this cradle with me just in case. Many years ago, you lay in it yourself, so let your daughter have it now, and may she grow up to be as fine a person as you."

"Thank you, mother!" he replied.

Saadat also spoke. "As the wife of Mehriban's elder brother, I would like to say that if Maysimyam-ana were alive today, she would have brought Mehriban home from hospital to stay with her for forty days, as is the custom. Then she would have celebrated with a *beshchuk toy* before sending her and the baby home. But alas, Mehriban's mother is no longer with us. So I've come to invite Mehriban and the little one to stay for that time with me. I will take care of them."

But Seitzhan had a different view. "Saadat-hada, a thousand thanks for what you have said. But we've waited a whole six years for a child, and now I don't want to let her out of my sight for even an hour. She's like a ray of sunlight to me, a breath of happiness. We'd love you to come here and help Mehri instead, though. Don't be offended, Saadat-hada—but why don't you come and spend those forty days here with us?"

The Uighur custom is to name a child twelve days after it is born. On the twelfth day, Seitzhan's mother asked him what name he had chosen.

"I've been reading a book called *Names and Their Meanings* and would like to call her Samiya."

"What does that mean?" asked his mother.

"In Arabic, *Samiya* means 'exalted' and 'respected.'"

"Very well, son, if that's the name you like, let it be so."

The next day they brought the mullah Aysa to the house. Gulsumhan and Saadat-hada prepared a *dastarkhan* of *plov*. Once they had eaten, the mullah stood up and began the naming ceremony. "When a child is born, the first duty of the parents is to name it. That is the obligation you are performing today," he said solemnly.

He took the baby from her father's hands and recited a *sura* over her. "Seitzhan, what name have you given to your daughter?" he asked her anxious father.

"Samiya."

The mullah formally called the baby by her name, then said to the parents, "Congratulations. I hope that your daughter will have a long and happy life." He returned her to Seitzhan, and she grew calmer.

All present greeted the parents, who were visibly moved, with smiles and thanked the mullah. Seitzhan took the baby to the other room and lay her in her cot.

That evening Gulsumhan-hada asked whether they would mind if she went home. She was needed to help in the home of her daughter-in-law.

"Of course, Gulsumhan-hada. If you need to, you should go," said Saadat. "I'll stay here for another forty days with Mehriban. You don't need to worry."

As it always did, autumn brought the first morning and evening frosts. It rained, and so the maize harvest was difficult. No sooner than the sun peeped out briefly again and began to dry the land did the villagers get back on the job. On one of these days, Mehriban's daughter reached forty days of age. The Uighurs have marked this day since time immemorial, so Seitzhan and Mehriban prepared everything they needed for a *beshchuk toy* and invited female relatives and friends from both sides of the family.

When everyone had arrived and taken their place, Pati spoke. "At long last, my brother is a father. I never would have believed it!"

"Congratulations! Congratulations!" came voices from all round.

"I have to admit that I'd been nagging him over and over to find another wife, not to spend his life with a woman who was as barren as a dry stick."

She was cut short by Imhanam-ana, who was sitting in the place of honor. "Oh, Allah! Patyam, don't talk like that. Everything is in God's hands, after all."

A woman sitting next to Pati gave her a look of disapproval. "Mehriban will bear him sons as well, just you wait and see."

"Sounds too good to be true." Pati jerked her shoulder.

Mehriban's aunts, Gyuli and Rukiyam, arrived bearing sizzling dishes of food wrapped in cloth. They greeted Mehriban, handed her the dishes, and removed the rubber galoshes from their soft leather *myasya* boots and placing them underneath the *bugluk*. They then came into the main room and were offered the places of honor.

Gyuli-ana had grown older and thinner. Her face had become more wrinkled, and her eyes hollower. She walked with difficulty. And now, when they had settled again, Gulsumhan appeared in the doorway.

"Good, so we're all here," she said welcomingly. "Let's pour the tea."

Modangul, Mahinur, and Gyuzal poured tea into bowls and passed them round on trays. The guests began to sample the *sanza, samsa,* and various sweet items on the table.

Gyuli glanced affectionately at Saadat, sitting opposite her. "Thank you so much for looking after Mehriban for the forty days in place of her mother."

"When Samiya grows up, I hope she'll call me grandmother and will come to visit me," joked Saadat.

Once they had finished their tea, Gulsumhan invited the guests, as was the custom, to take any of the leftover sweet dishes home with them. The women wrapped them in bundles. Meanwhile, the time had come for giving gifts to the hostess. First to do so was Gulsumhan-ana. She presented Mehriban with a large dish of *samsa* and a length of material for a dress, a suit for Seitzhan, and some castoffs for her little grandchild. "I've also brought the *beshchuk,* in which my own son used to sleep," she added.

"Thank you, *apa*. You needn't have —" began Mehriban, but she was interrupted by Pati.

"Because I made *plov* for the celebration but didn't manage to make anything special," she began to gabble, jumping up from her place. "My brother Seitzhan, although he's over thirty, he was still waiting for a child of his own. And so I'd like to give him a jacket and a costume for Mehriban and a pram for Samiya."

"Thank you, *hada*, these are wonderful presents," said Mehriban, delighted.

"And now you need to give my Seitzhan sons," his sister added.

It was clear that Gyuli did not like the way Pati spoke. "We will be grateful for what God gives us," she said. "If Seitzhan and Mehriban stay in good health, they will have sons."

Next, Gyuli-ana placed a big bowl of *manty* on the table, together with a shirt for Seitzhan, a pretty length of cloth for Mehriban, and a pile of children's clothes for the baby. Gyuli was followed in turn by Rukiyam.

"Thank you all, thank you!" Mehriban said over and over, not trying to hide her tears of gratitude.

When all the presents had been given, *plov* and fresh salads were served. Plates of the *samsa*, *manty,* and *zhutta* brought by relatives were also put out. The guests tucked in and sampled them all willingly, all the while joking, laughing, and singing songs. Gokharbanum began to play on the *dutar,* and the younger people danced. When they had all danced their fill, the *dutarchi* moved to the room where the older women were sitting.

"Ladies, what shall we do? Shall I play for you to dance, or shall I sing a song?" she asked them.

"Sing us one of the old songs," the senior women requested. They knew that Gokharbanum could make their folk songs sound particularly beautiful.

When at last the celebration was at an end, somebody recited a short prayer, the *duga*. Saadat then gave presents to the women on Mehriban's behalf. The older women each received a length of bright floral material, a shawl, and a man's shirt. The younger guests were given shawls.

"Saadat, you haven't forgotten to prepare the water for the ceremony?" asked Gulsumhan.

"No, I haven't forgotten. We can start now," replied Saadat.

She left the room and soon returned with two large bowls. One of these was empty, while the other contained a small quantity of butter, tea, salt, sugar, and *adrasman* herb. Also in the bowl were coins, earrings, a finger ring, and some beads. Saadat poured some water into this bowl and then placed both bowls in front of the oldest of the mothers present. This was Imhanam-ana, who wore a white dress of China silk. Rolling up her sleeves, the old woman announced solemnly, "In the name of Allah the Compassionate, the Merciful," taking a spoonful of water from the full bowl, "Mehriban, may your daughter's life be long, and may she be honest, conscientious, and intelligent."

She poured the spoonful of water into the empty bowl, then took a coin and a bead from the filled bowl, and passed both bowls to Gyuli, sitting beside her. Now Gyuli repeated the procedure, transferring a spoonful of water to the empty bowl and taking a coin and a bead for herself, then passing the bowls on; and in due course each of the mothers performed this ritual. With each repetition, they made a wish for the forty-day-old Samiya and the life ahead of her. When the ritual ended, Rana brought in a large dish with forty freshly-baked *togach* and another piled high with sweets. When invited, they each took a bread and a handful of sweets. Then a prayer was said, and the gathering began to disperse.

"Gyuli, Rukiyam, would you stay behind for a while?" asked Gulsumhan-ana. "The three of us can wash the child and clip her hair and nails for the first time."

They took the bowl containing the forty spoonsful of water, over which so many good wishes had been said, passed it through a gauze, boiled it, and let it cool. They then rinsed Samiya in this blessed liquid, then wrapped her again in swaddling and placed in her cot.

Just then Seitzhan arrived. "How was the *beshchuk toy*?" he asked.

"It all went beautifully," replied Gulsumhan. "A lot of very good wishes were made for your daughter."

Gyuli looked at her horny hands and said to him, "Seitzhan, son, why don't you cut Samiya's hair and nails instead of us? Our old hands shake too much. And it's good if the child takes after its father and mother."

Seitzhan nodded agreement. Mehriban, sensing that her aunts were anxious to leave, asked them to stay at least for that night. But they got up from their places, saying that they were tired. So Seitzhan saw them out and hailed a taxi for them.

Now the guests had all gone, and the happy parents were left alone. "Mehri, will you hold Samiya while I cut her hair?" asked Seitzhan. She did so, and he trimmed her hair and nails. The baby sensed her father's tenderness and stared at him, making no sound. "Look, Mehri, she's got a tiny mouth, just like you, but her forehead and brows, her eyes and nose are from me."

"They say that a child will grow up to be like whichever person is first to cut her nails and hair. So now she'll become the mirror image of you, Seitzhan," smiled Mehriban, noticing that her husband's face was lit up with joy.

At that moment, she felt herself the happiest person in the world. And why ever not? She had shed so many tears before living to see that day of sweetness. Now she took Samiya in her arms and softly rejoiced.

• • •

"Mehriban, I was very interested in the *anla chay* ceremony for curing infertility," said Ruth.

"Yes, and we still perform that ritual."

"Do you think it was because of the ritual that Samiya was born?"

"I believe in omens," Mehriban replied.

"Your stories so often end in tragedy, but this story has such a happy ending. It's even cheered me up," smiled Ruth.

"Well, the story isn't over yet," said Mehriban in a mysterious tone of voice. "The rest will follow."

24

A Farewell in Spring

Time races on, sparing nobody,
None can draw even with those thundering hooves.
All things pass away, grow old irrevocably;
Time was created to steal life away.

As the Uighur poet Lutpulla Mutellip wrote, the years pass quickly, and indeed, the life of that promising poet was itself cut tragically short. As for the senior women of Bolshoy Chigan, all of them mothers with saintly souls, in the last few years they had begun, one by one, to pass away. This included Gyuli-ana, who was central to my tale. So Rukiyam, left without a sister, brought her children to join her in Alma-Ata, and they remained there even once their studies were finished.

The times were also changing. It was the era of *perestroika*, and people were becoming noticeably more selfish. The shelves in the shops were empty, and factories stood idle for want of orders. Thousands of people found themselves unemployed, while those who still had jobs did not receive their wages for months on end. With each passing day, the problems grew more complex. Zharkent, a town considered sacred by many, lost much of its former beauty at this time and gained an air of desolation and neglect. People did not know how to make ends meet or how to feed their families; many lost heart.

One day the border with China was opened. And as they say, "If the mountain will not come to Muhammad…" Many of those without jobs poured into the Celestial Kingdom, where they obtained Chinese goods that they could bring home to sell and so maintain some sort of an existence. It was the women, rather than the men, who quickly learned the secrets of making money in this way. They kept their stalls from early morning until late in the evening. Fathers no longer had time to keep an eye on their sons, nor mothers their daughters.

Along with the general chaos, a flood of low-grade foreign films came into circulation. The behavior of the young people changed noticeably. Embittered by unemployment and desperate for something to do, young men began copying nasty American fighters from the films. They lost all shame; they began using narcotics, drinking heavily, and living by stealing. Girls started smoking, drinking, and selling their bodies. This kind of life became a commonplace, while warmth, humanity, and kindness seemed to be quickly forgotten.

At this difficult time, Seitzhan fell seriously ill, and all the cares of the family now fell on Mehriban's delicate shoulders. Seitzhan told her what had caused his illness. "Do you remember, Mehri, the day after Samiya was born I had to go to Taldykorgan? It was pouring with rain, and when we arrived there, our driver could not cope with the traffic, and we had an accident. The car rolled over, and we all sustained minor injuries. The emergency services acted fast, thankfully, and doctors were soon seeing to us. But something happened to the small of my back. It had hit something made of metal. There has been pain there ever since. Ever since that time, I've used medicine and injections to keep it at manageable. And now—seventeen years on—that injury has forced me to bed."

Mehriban, when he had finished, said pensively, "That day when you went away, I had a dream and saw that all this would happen. But I never told anyone."

There was a knock at the gate. Mehriban went out, and a postwoman handed her an envelope. Mehriban showed the letter to Seitzhan. "We've got news from our daughter." She opened the envelope.

Samiya had enclosed a photograph of herself along with the letter. Mehriban kissed the photo and handed it to Seitzhan. "Just see how much she looks like you. Her curls, her forehead, eyebrows, her eyes and nose—they're all yours. If she'd been a boy, we'd have had two Seitzhans!"

In the picture, Samiya was smiling happily. Seitzhan looked closely at her features, and his own face filled with tears. Mehriban started reading the letter. "Dear Papa and Mama, I hope you are in good health. How is *perestroika* affecting you? In Alma-Ata a lot of factories have closed, and people have lost their jobs. Even people with degrees are unemployed. And we students are afraid of even thinking about the future. But I don't want to write about sad things. All this will pass, I'm sure, and things will turn out well in the end. I'm finding English hard to learn, but I'm persisting. There are four of us in my room—a Russian, a Kazakh, a Tatar, and me, a Uighur. We get on well and help each other with our work. We take turns to cook, and we make our national dishes for each other. I really miss you! Dada, Mama wrote to me about your health. I'm worried about you. As soon as I get a chance, I'll come and visit. I ask Allah to watch over your health and well-being. If things are well with you, I can live my life happily."

The telephone rang. It was Modangul. "Thank you, *hada*," Mehriban said to her. "I wasn't able to go to China for things myself. I'll come and find you tomorrow at the bazaar at six." She hung up.

Unable to find other work, Mehriban had been compelled to take up buying and selling Chinese products in the bazaar. They needed money so that Seitzhan could go to Alma-Ata for a diagnosis of his condition. Modangul and Mahinur brought goods for her from China. On her first day in the bazaar, Mehriban noticed some people she knew coming past and shrank back, hiding under the counter and staying there until they had moved on.

This upset Modangul. "Come on, there's nothing to fear. You're not a thief. You're an honest trader. There are doctors, teachers, medics, and engineers all doing this, trying to put food on the table. What are you afraid of?"

Mahinur reassured her sister with a chuckle. "*Hada,* I used to dive under the counter at first as well, out of real shame. But now I've got used to it. By the way, they say there are four busloads of Uzbeks coming to market today to buy things. God willing, we'll do well from it."

"I want to make enough for Seitzhan to get to Alma-Ata and have his treatment," said Mehriban.

"But hang on, you know your problems don't end there," said Modangul, trying to make her see sense. "You've got a daughter who's a student. It'll be fine if Seitzhan recovers, but—well, who knows?" She went quiet.

The Zharkent bazaar had grown larger. Chinese goods lay heaped up along almost all the aisles. From a casual glance, you might be forgiven for thinking that the whole town was there, buying and selling.

When evening came, the sellers put their unsold goods into bags and sacks and flagged down cars to take them home. Mehriban did so too. When she reached home, she struggled to drag her enormous bags of goods out of the car, almost rupturing her lower back as she did so. Seeing her from the window, Seitzhan felt pity for her.

"Mehri, why don't you give up this bazaar business? We won't starve. And you're shattered. What if all this makes you ill? What will we do then?"

"No, just give me time. I'll get used to it." She answered him in a voice that was artificially cheerful. "Today a lot of Uzbeks came, and we did well from them. I made some money. If that happens every day, I'll be able to save up enough. Anyway, we need to send Samiya some money too. Her grant barely covers her food, and you can be sure she'll want to wear something nice."

Seitzhan was astonished at the willpower and persistence of his wife, despite her frail appearance. After a while, he forgot about his pain.

Mehriban soon picked up the subtleties of doing business in the market and raised enough money for Seitzhan to go to Alma-Ata. She sent him along with his elder brother. He was referred there to the oncological institute. The results of the diagnosis were far from encouraging. He had a malignant growth on his spinal column on the exact site of the impact he received in the road accident.

When Seitzhan understood that his life was hanging by a thread, he broke out in a cold sweat and almost fainted. He was so shaken that he did not hear the rest of what the specialists were telling him. Coming to his senses with difficulty, he asked them, "How much time have I got?"

The two oncologists exchanged glances. "We can't say for certain. But you're a doctor yourself, so you can surely understand how serious your condition is. We're drawing up your treatment regimine now."

They wrote something out at length, then, handing the paper to Seitzhan, said to him, "You must take the medication and injections as it says here. Come and see us in a month's time so we can check the results."

He went out in a depressed mood. How much time did he have left to live? Nobody could give him an answer to that. He said nothing to his brother, who was waiting for him outside. They went together to see his daughter in her student hostel.

The visit to Samiya was not altogether successful. She was delighted to see her father, of course, and he did all he could to avoid revealing how disturbed he was. As he left, he handed his daughter an envelope containing money.

"Dada," she said, "tell Mama that my grant is enough. It's more important for you to eat properly."

"We're not going hungry. And who's going to look after you, if not us?"

"Dada, I'm thinking about changing to a correspondence course, so I can work as well as study."

"Good grief, my love, don't even think about that," he said, agitated. "What are you saying? And you can't learn English by correspondence anyway. Much better that you get on and study now, while we're all still alive."

Samiya looked at her father and became thoughtful. Seitzhan sensed that she suspected something; he got up and left with a hurried good-bye. As he and his brother sat in the car they had hailed for the ride home, Seitzhan spent the whole of the journey with his eyes fixed on the road ahead, vanishing to the horizon. His thoughts were bleak. He was aware that his death would be slow and painful. How would those close to him survive that ordeal? His own thoughts frightened him. It would be a sore test for his wife and daughter. Samiya would get her diploma and return home. At least Mehriban would not be on her own. Maybe that would make life easier?

Working in a hospital, Seitzhan had seen death often enough. Whether the dying were old or young, they would tell him about the hopes and dreams that they would not live to see. And now he was in their place.

Seitzhan arrived home at dusk. Mehriban had prepared the evening meal and was waiting for him. Seitzhan tried to put on a brave face as he washed his hands and came into the kitchen, where steaming dishes stood on the table.

"What did the doctors say?" asked Mehriban, looking hopefully at him.

"What would they say? They told me to take care of myself at home and wrote out a heap of papers."

"Did you buy your medicine?"

"Yes, I've bought it all."

"Do they say your illness is serious?"

"All illnesses are serious."

"My heart's uneasy about you all the time."

"Then take medicine for a heart condition." He grinned. "You're at that bazaar from dawn to dusk, you heave those heavy bags around, no wonder your heart's not happy. I went to see Samiya at her hall of residence. We talked for a while, and I gave her the money."

"How is she? Has she lost weight?"

"No. She's living well. She said she wants to change to distance learning, so she can work too. I didn't approve of that and said she should go on studying now, while we're all still alive."

"Good. You said the right thing. I pray to God that our daughter doesn't have to spend her life at the bazaar. Did you see the other girls she's living with?"

"No, they were at the library."

As she talked with her husband, Mehriban watched him attentively. "I think there's something you haven't told me."

"Come off it, Mehri. Don't tell me you've had another dream?"

"No, I haven't. But I sense that something's not right."

"Well if you choose to think of what's good, then all will be well, but if you start dwelling on bad things, bad things will happen. I woke up in the morning and saw the light of day. I walked upon the earth… that's how we need to think of happiness."

"Yes, that's how it is. And we aren't starving, and we've lived well for twenty-three years. For sure, that is reason enough to be happy."

"Well, think on that. There's nobody who can be happier than we are." Seitzhan hugged her.

After supper they drank some *aktyan-chay* and talked for a long time.

The next morning, Mehriban went to work at the bazaar, and Seitzhan went to the hospital. When he showed his colleagues the notes and prescriptions he had been given in Alma-Ata, they understood that he had cancer. They began his treatment that day and began collecting together the documents he would need to submit to the medical board to receive disability benefits. For half a year, Seitzhan was in too much pain either to sit, to stand, or to lie down. He was admitted to the day hospital every day for treatment, and in the evenings, they took him home. Seitzhan tried to maintain his brave face, but realizing that his bravery would not last, he began to intimate to his wife and the others close to him that he would not be in this world for much longer.

He tried to live every remaining day as fully as he could. Whenever he felt well enough, he would visit the sick. He often invited friends and relatives to visit, and for half a year he conversed with them and asked them to sing their favorite songs. He visited his parents' grave to recite the prayer of remembrance over them.

He began to make suggestions to Mehriban about how she should manage if she were to be left on her own. She was aware of what was happening to Seitzhan, and her eyes never dried from tears. Once she had realized that his illness was terminal, she had given up working at the bazaar in order to spend every possible minute with him. Family members helped her and gave her support. Samiya often came to see her parents to spend a day or two in their company.

Seitzhan received treatment for three years. He went to Alma-Ata several times, but to no avail. He aged fast, and with his sunken eyes and protruding cheekbones, he began to resemble a skeleton wrapped in skin. The hardest was the last four months; his suffering in this time was indescribable. Yet even then he found it in himself to communicate with others. His colleagues came to see him every day to give him his injection of pain medication.

Spring came around again, and again the trees blossomed, the flowers opened, and fresh scents drifted through open windows. Seitzhan was lying and listening to the song of a nightingale that came from an apple tree nearby when he noticed voices. It was two of his friends, Hakim and Alim, come to visit him. Seitzhan welcomed them and said, "There's one thing I'd like to ask of you."

"Just tell us. We'll do anything we can for you," said Hakim.

"Take me to the Usek river. The willows there will be looking good now that it's spring."

"Certainly. We'll get you in the car and go there right now." They carefully sat Seitzhan in the car and set off.

They soon reached the river. And while every season has its charms, the beauty of spring surely cannot be compared with any other. Branches of the weeping willows trailed in the water, enchanting it. Seitzhan did not want to get out of the car. He drank in the beauty of the place and whispered, "What tender willows! Tell me, are there any trees in the world more beautiful than you? If I were a poet, I'd put your gracefulness into verse. But I've come to say good-bye to you now forever. And to bid farewell to youth and to my whole life."

Hakim and Alim clenched their teeth to hold back their tears.

"Alim, my dear friend, will you sing the song about the Usek for me?"

Alim began softly:

> *By Zharkent runs the free-flowing Usek,*
> *to that river all manner of us come.*
> *My friends are in Zharkent and along the Usek -*
> *without you, my brothers, I pine in my love.*

Before Alim had finished, however, Seitzhan abruptly asked them to take him home. When Alim and Hakim brought him back indoors he asked

Mehriban for some water. He drank, then lay back on the pillow and groaned: "I've no strength any more for this misery. If Allah wishes to take me, I'm ready to go."

As if in answer, the trill of a nightingale came through the open window.

"That nightingale sings outside my window every day, as if it's saying good-bye."

"It wants to bring pleasure to your soul," said Hakim.

"There's no more pleasure for my soul. I loved the spring so much! And spring is the time I'm fated to die."

Mehriban got up to make tea, but Seitzhan stopped her. "Mehri, never mind anything else, please will you sit here with me?"

Mehriban sat down beside him. Seitzhan looked around him. The big clock was ticking on the wall. Alim and Hakim sat watching him.

"Tomorrow I will leave this house forever," he said, not taking his eyes off Mehriban. Tears ran down his face onto the pillow. Mehriban's tears burned her cheeks.

Husband and wife were holding each other tightly by the hand at the moment that Seitzhan finally expired. His friends and relatives, sitting with him, wept silently. Mullah Aysa recited the *sura* Ya Sin and then said, "This child of Allah has reached his eternal rest. Don't cry." He tied up Seitzhan's chin and covered his face with a white cloth.

Long ago, the death of her father had left an indelible impression on the eighteen-year-old Mehriban. And now the passing of Seitzhan pierced her to the core. Their hopes and dreams had been cut short in mid-flight. The world had grown tarnished, dull, and uninteresting; Mehriban had no desire to live without Seitzhan. She cried without ceasing. Eventually her *kichik-ana* Rukiyam, who had come over from Alma-Ata with Saadat, sat her down and said to her, "Mehriban, my dear, Saadat and I have been weeping with you for more than a month. But why don't you let me tell you about the life I've lived?"

She told Mehriban about the hardships she had endured, and as she finished, she wept once again. "Don't you see, Mehriban, compared to what happened to me and the other older women—Saadat and Gyuli *kichik-ana*—surely your life has been happier? You were lucky! You were able to live with the man you loved for twenty-five wonderful years. Your daughter is about to graduate. Who will give her support in life?"

Saadat now joined in the conversation. "And weeping will only increase your suffering. Tears won't bring Seitzhan back. They say that if you cry too much, the soul of the person in the next world becomes engulfed in water."

Mehriban slowly composed herself. Now Seitzhan's sister Patyam came in.

"Well, how are you?" she asked.

"We're talking with Mehriban," said Rukiyam. "Forty days have passed, and she's still weeping buckets. I've been reminding her of how much harder it was in my day."

"My brother Seitzhan and Mehriban had a good life," said Patyam. "Seitzhan was ill for three years and four months. Mehriban took superb care of him, we know that for sure. And now my brother's soul has found peace. Mehriban, I want to tell you how grateful I am to you." Patyam drew breath and shook her head sorrowfully. "I married Nurum when I was seventeen. A month later, the war broke out and Nurum was called to the front. Then the war ended, and on the day that the whole country was celebrating, I found out that he had been killed. I could have spent the rest of my life crying over him. Allah alone knows where Nurum's body was left lying. So I want to say to you that we have to approach even grieving with a calm heart. At last Seitzhan's suffering is over. Now all that remains is for us to pray for him."

The others looked at Patyam with sympathy. They could see that her soul had been wounded when she was still very young.

"Our dreams in this life are often broken," sighed Rukiyam.

Four months after Seitzhan's death, Samiya came to see her mother. She showed her her diploma certificate and told her that she had found a job with a tourism company.

"*Apa*, I'm going to rent a two-room apartment in Almaty, and you can come and live there with me," she promised.

"I'm not going anywhere until a year has passed since your father passed away," said Mehriban stubbornly. Rukiyam and Saadat voiced agreement.

"Fair enough, Mama. You stay here until the anniversary of Father's death. I'll send you money each month, and I'll come and see you."

Samiya stayed for a week and then returned to Alma-Ata.

For a year, relatives from both sides, friends, colleagues, and neighbors all visited Mehriban and helped her and relieved her loneliness, praying for Seitzhan. When the time came, they marked the year since Seitzhan's death. After this, Samiya sold the family home and took her mother to live with her in the city.

• • •

"So it seems I jumped to a premature conclusion," sighed Ruth. "The fate of this heroine was tragic like all the others. So sad that Samiya, the child they'd waited for so long, should lose her father."

"In this life, happy days alternate with sadness and grief. And after moments of sorrow, the soul cannot become happy again because there is always a place inside that is full of inescapable sadness."

Two tears trickled from Mehriban's eyes. And she alone knew how fiercely the fire burned in her heart.

<h1 style="text-align:center">25</h1>

THE GREAT FLIGHT

During *perestroika* the price of apartments in Alma-Ata fell sharply. Samiya and her mother bought one in a four-story building on Oktyabrsky Street. After moving in with her daughter, Mehriban began to feel a little better. When she came home from work each day, Samiya would try to take her mother's mind off her grieving and despondency. They went to concerts and performances at the Uighur Theater and often sat talking together before they went to bed. Having been used to living on the land, Mehriban was not altogether comfortable living in two first-floor rooms. She often walked the streets, thinking of her village, and of her parents and their hard lives.

One day in late autumn, Samiya came back from work holding a big white envelope. "*Apa*, sit down, I've got some good news. A few months ago, one of my work colleagues showed me a notice in the *Karavan* magazine. It was a prize draw for a green card that allows the winner to go and live in the USA. Anybody interested in entering the draw was invited to send their documents in. Some of the girls and I entered it. And this envelope is a reply from America. Look, *apa* - I've won a green card!" She whooped with joy and ran to hug and kiss her mother.

"What are you talking about, *kizim*? Why on earth do you want to go to America?"

"Mama, can't you understand? You're well educated, after all! This is a message sent from heaven. I can speak English now. I could go to America, study, and work there. These days all the rich people are sending their children to school abroad. Do you remember when Papa called me a tomboy? Well, since that's what I am—a girl-*dzhigit*—then I want to have things my way. And it would please my father's soul."

"So you're going away and leaving me on my own?" whispered Mehriban, horrified.

"*Apa*, what I'm thinking is, let me go there, get settled down, and find a job, then I'll send you a visa and money so you can come and see America."

"But I don't know English. What's the point in me traveling to the ends of the earth?"

"I'll write a letter for you in English. You just show the letter to the consulate, and they'll help you," said Samiya, looking hopefully at her mother.

"But daughter, you've got plenty of work here already." Mehriban began to weep.

"I'm not leaving today, *apa*. It'll take six months to get the paperwork ready."

"Why's that?"

"Well, first I've got to go to Moscow—to the US embassy—and show them this letter. Then there'll be an interview, after which they should give me permission to travel. Then I'll come back to Alma-Ata, get ready, and finally fly."

"Samiya, I've lost your father, and now I'm going to lose you as well. What's the point in me carrying on?"

"Mama, that's the logic of an illiterate peasant woman. You're still young. You've got plenty of life left ahead of you! You've got to live your own life and find your own way in it! I will do everything in my power to help you." She was holding her mother in an embrace and stayed there a long time.

Hearing this, Mehriban thought again. That evening, mother and daughter talked at length over dinner. And eventually, each of them thinking about Samiya's future, Mehriban gave her consent.

A month passed. Samiya came back from the US embassy in Moscow with permission to enter America. She also began searching for people already living in the USA with whom she could make contact and found a telephone number for a certain Polat and his wife Farida, both Uighurs who had settled in Los Angeles.

Before she left, Samiya visited the places that were dear to her. She went to her father's grave for a blessing and said good-bye to her relations. And now the date of departure was drawing inexorably closer.

Mehriban, preparing to see her daughter off on her long journey, baked *zhit* and asked Rukiyam *kichik-ana* and her daughters Guzyal and Nuraniya to accompany them for the send-off. They were all naturally worried about sending the girl away to the other side of the world. They wished her a good journey and prayed for her.

"Mother is now in your care," said Samiya to the two sisters. "It would be good if you keep in touch with her, telephone her often, and ask after her health. In a year's time, I'll send her a visitor's visa. May God help me."

"And can we come and visit you? We'd like so much to see America," said Guzyal and Nuraniya, excited.

"If I can settle in properly, I'll certainly help your children get an education in America," Samiya assured them.

"Samiya, did you phone America on the number I gave you?" asked Rukiyam.

"No, but I'll call them tomorrow."

"But how will you manage on your own in a foreign country?" Mehriban grew agitated again.

"There aren't many Uighurs in America, so the ones that are know each other and look after each other," said Rukiyam. "And here, we'll take care of your mother. Today Modangul's youngest daughter Rosa is coming to stay with us to study. She could go out and stay with you a while," she suggested.

Guzyal pulled an envelope out of her bag and held it out to Samiya. "Samiya, this isn't much, but take it, from all of us. It may come in handy."

"Thank you," she said. "You're all so wonderful to me."

Guzyal and her sister said good-bye and left. Rukiyam decided to stay with Mehriban for a few days. Samiya started to gather the books, clothes, and other things she needed into a large red suitcase. While she was busy packing, the two mothers sat and watched the frail-looking young woman, amazed at her fearlessness.

Next day, Samiya phoned Polat in Los Angeles. "Assalam, Polat-aka. My name is Samiya, I'm calling from Kazakhstan. I won a green card and am coming to the US. I can speak good English, but I don't know anybody there yet. Rukiyam-ana gave me your number, so I'm calling to ask for your help."

"Are your documents in order?" asked a distant male voice.

"Yes."

"When do you fly?"

"The thirteenth of July."

"And how can I help you?"

"If it were possible, would you be able to meet me at Los Angeles airport?"

"That's fine, we'll meet you and do what we can to help. Don't worry, we look forward to your arrival."

Samiya came into the room, unable to conceal her delight. "*Apa*, they're going to meet my flight. There are lots of good people in the world!"

After this telephone conversation, Mehriban felt a little calmer. "Glory to Allah," she said, smiling at Rukiyam.

"Well, let me tell you about Alahan, who came from Urumqi," Rukiyam said. "I didn't invite her home for nothing. She went through enough in her life. She has a younger brother, Polat, who graduated in Beijing and got married. He then went to study in America. He's now been there for five or six years. He's been home a few times since. Anyway, everything turned out well for him. He's got a good job and a single daughter. Alahan gave me Polat's phone number so that Samiya could call him and talk."

"Thank you, *kichik-apa*, I feel less nervous now," sighed Mehriban with relief.

Samiya left for America the next day. When her silvery aircraft climbed into the sky, her thoughts took her back into her distant childhood, which yet seemed so near.

Her parents had loved her very much. When she was little, they took her every spring to the mountains, where they would enjoy the clear air. They gathered herbs and flowers and went for walks. And sometimes her father took her to the Usek. They would sit for a long time on the bank, watching the moving water and the soft fronds of the weeping willows.

One hot June day, her father decided he would teach little Samiya to swim. Holding her up, he explained how she should move her arms and legs. Just then an unexpected wave hit them, and Samiya slipped out of her father's hands. She was washed downstream by the fast current. Her father rushed after her and quickly rescued her. All the time, her horrified mother had been running along the bank, shouting and wailing. As he brought her out of the water, her father held her tightly to him and whispered, "Daughter, today you were born for the second time."

Later, when the girl had grown a little, her father took her several times to see the mosque in Zharkent and told her about it. She could still remember what he had said. Proudly he had related that the building was already more than a century old, that it had been erected by the order of a Zharkent merchant, Velivay Yoldashev. The construction was supervised by the Chinese architect Hon Pik, and not a single nail was used. Today, the mosque was the cultural legacy and crowning glory of Zharkent.

Her father had been very pleased with her success in her studies and called her a "girl-*dzhigit.*" He probably did this because he had no son. When he had a moment free, he would read a book to her, but such happy moments came all too rarely. As a rule, her father used to work from early morning to late evening.

In the summer holidays, her parents would take Samiya to Alma-Ata. They strolled in the parks, visited attractions, and went around the museums. Her childhood had been happy, indeed. And how happy would her father be if he knew that she was on her way now to America. Tears prickled her eyes at the thought.

She landed that evening at Los Angeles. At the immigration desk, however, the officer examined her documents and said, "You have not given a permanent address of residence in the United States, and because of this, we cannot let you leave the airport." Samiya was at a loss. Not knowing what else to do, she tried to telephone Polat, but nobody answered. After five interminable hours of waiting, a woman of officer rank came up to her. "You have come a long way. How come you don't know the address you are going to? Your green card will be sent to that address in one week's time. We need to know where you will be staying."

"Let me try telephoning one more time," said Samiya in a trembling voice.

She dialed, and thankfully a woman's voice answered. "Hello, is that Polat Iskander's residence?" she asked in English.

"Yes, it is."

"Do you speak Uighur?"

"Yes. Who's speaking?"

"I'm Samiya. I've just arrived from Kazakhstan. They are holding me at the airport because I don't know your address."

"Well, write it down. I'll dictate it to you."

Samiya quickly wrote down the address and handed it to the officer.

"Polat and my daughter have gone to the airport to meet you," the woman's voice continued on the line. "You'll see them when you come out."

"Thank you so much, *hada*," said Samiya with relief.

And indeed, when she emerged from the airport, she saw a swarthy man of medium height coming toward her. He smiled welcomingly. This was Polat. "Welcome, *sinnim*!"

"Please forgive me for making you wait so long."

"Don't worry about that. Let me introduce you to my daughter Halida."

Halida was a girl of average height with short hair and beautiful eyes and brows. She was wearing a blouse and trousers. They all got into the car and drove off, speaking in English. As he drove, Polat looked at the newcomer from Kazakhstan, impressed by the ease and fluency of her English. It seemed that she and Halida had found a common language.

The streets of Los Angeles gleamed with hundreds of illuminated billboards. Seeing them for the first time, Samiya could not take her eyes from their dazzling, almost bewitching effect. They drove for a considerable time and eventually drew up at a gateway marked "Park La Brea." A security guard came out and pressed a button, and the gate opened. The car moved into the spacious courtyard, skirted a large fountain, and stopped in front of a twelve-story apartment block. "This is where we live," said Halida, getting out and pointing at the row of multi-story blocks.

Polat and the girls picked up their baggage and took the elevator to the sixth floor. There, smiling, was the woman with whom Samiya had spoken by telephone. "My name is Farida-hada," she introduced herself.

Their apartment was spacious and neat. Nothing was superfluous. Halida showed Samiya the guest room. "You're probably tired after your journey. Why don't you take a shower and change, and then we'll have dinner."

When Samiya emerged from the guest room, radiant and fresh, the family sat down to eat. Polat asked Samiya to tell them about herself and her family.

"My father worked for twenty-three years as a doctor. It's now just a year since he died. My mother is a teacher, but she's out of work at the moment. I'm their only child. My mother had problems with her kidneys, and the doctors forbade her from having any more children. I went to the middle Russian school in Zharkent and to university in Alma-Ata. I graduated and worked at a tourism agency for a year. That's when I won the green card. And now here I am, sitting here as your guest in America." She smiled. "My mother's living in Alma-Ata. We sold our house in Zharkent, and that's how I was able to come here."

"As soon as you receive your green card, you should apply for a social security number," said Polat when Samiya had finished her story. "In two weeks, you'll have the necessary documents to be able to work here, study here, and get bank credit. You should get a credit card. That will allow you to go to the shops and buy whatever you want," he explained to her.

Farida joined in. "You should put any money you've brought with you into a bank account. It's not done here for people to walk around with huge amounts of money in their purse. All payments are made using bank cards," she added.

Samiya listened carefully. "So I'm not allowed to work until my documents arrive?"

"Nobody will give you a job that's paid with a monthly salary. But there's nothing to stop you working as a waitress at a restaurant, say, where they pay you on a daily basis for the hours you work."

Samiya became thoughtful. Halida noticed this and said, "People who come to America can't just start working in their line of expertise. My father, for example, was a professor, but he had to work for his first year as a restaurant cook. My mother cleaned rooms in a hotel, and I helped her. But now my father teaches in an institute, and my mother works for a bank. I'm studying at college and hope to get into university later. But it's the holidays at the moment, and I've taken a job. People in America strive to be independent. You'll learn to live that way too. Oh, and one other important thing: as well as a job and a place to live, you'll need a car."

Samiya felt worried and uncertain, though the thought of going back home never entered her mind. Her new acquaintances told Samiya a lot of interesting things about America and promised to help her out. By now it was late, and Polat got up from the table.

"It's time to rest," he said. "Halida, will you bring Samiya up to speed on what she's got to do? As far as I can see, she's intent on achieving her goals. And that's how it should be." And the father went off to his room.

• • •

"The fact that Samiya won the green card and could go to live in America was pure destiny," said Ruth. "And as you said earlier, there's no escaping what's in store for us."

"How many times has life demonstrated that that's how it is?" Mehriban nodded.

26

TWO DESTINIES

After Samiya left, Mehriban began to spend time with one of her neighbors, the elderly Polina. Polina was short and thin, with sad eyes. She frequently came to see Mehriban, and one day she decided to tell her about her son.

"Sasha was born when I was over forty. What a fidget he was! Still, he did well at school. He didn't get straight into an institute because he had to serve in the army. He was handsome, tall, and had a cheerful nature. But they sent him to Afghanistan, and he came home with both his legs missing. Since then, he's just sat within his own four walls, watching television, and reading. But sometimes he gets such attacks of depression that he takes it out on me. Of course, I understand. It's hard to accept being crippled for the rest of your life. And he often wakes up in the night, shouting, then just sits and smokes until morning. He says, 'Why make me live like this? Why couldn't I just die in the fighting?' and starts crying. If I die, my son will be left within those four walls, like in a prison. The pension he gets from the state just covers cigarettes and medication. There's nobody else to look after him, you know. And that's my tale of woe, neighbor." Polina wiped away a tear with her handkerchief.

"Have you got other children?"

"I've got a daughter, but she's married with small children and hasn't got time for us."

The two neighbors sat talking for a long time over their tea. Eventually Polina got up. "I'd better go and see how Sasha's doing. I'm so glad that we're neighbors." She smiled and went out.

Left by herself, Mehriban thought about Samiya. "Thank God she's alive and in full health. And she sends me letters often." She did not notice that she was speaking aloud.

In one of her letters, Samiya described the beauty of Los Angeles, hoping that she would be able to show it to her mother one day. And Mehriban sensed that going abroad was perhaps not so frightening after all.

Not wanting to languish on her own, Mehriban found work at a kindergarten once more. Working from morning to evening, she did not notice the time passing. On top of this, Modangul's daughter Rosa had entered one of the institutes and was staying with her. She was glad of the company.

One night Mehriban woke suddenly, startled. She got up and went to the kitchen for a glass of water. Turning on the light, she noticed a notebook and a pen on the table. What were those doing there? Was she still dreaming? She opened the notebook. The pages were blank. She drank the water and sat down, took the pen and notebook, and started writing out the names of all the women she had known since she was a child. Then she wrote out what had happened to them in their lives.

That night, Mehriban sensed that she had found a vocation—the very thing her daughter was always urging her to do. "*Apa*, you've got to find your place in this world."

When she was a child, Mehriban had written poems dedicated to her father. Now, however, her desire was to write about the mothers she knew, the mothers whose lives had been filled with fleeting joys, immense suffering, and unassuming heroism.

The next day, she stopped at the bazaar on her way home from work and bought ten exercise books and a number of pens. At that moment, she noticed a girl leaning languidly against a tree. Their eyes met.

"Hello… You aren't Aynur from Zharkent by any chance, are you?" asked Mehriban.

"Yes, that's me. And Mehriban-hada, is that you?" she asked quietly.

Aynur did not look well. Her red eyes stood out against her pale face, and she seemed too weak to be able to walk.

"What's the matter? Are you ill?" asked Mehriban.

"My head's spinning, and everything's gone dark," whispered Aynur through pallid lips.

"Well, that's not good. Why don't you come back with me?" said Mehriban decisively. And ignoring the girl's protests, she took her home. She made Aynur some tea, after which she seemed a little better.

"Have you been in Alma-Ata long?" asked Mehriban, pouring her another bowl of tea.

"Yes. I worked at the maize plant in Zharkent, but when *perestroika* came, they closed that and the meat processing plant too. None of us had jobs anymore.

Some of us who had some money started buying and selling things from China. I tried that for a while. But it seems that market trading isn't as simple as it looks. I got nowhere with it. Not only didn't I make money, I got into debt. Around that time my father also lost his job and started drinking. My mother fell badly ill and ended up in the hospital soon after. We didn't have the money for medicines. The money we borrowed from relatives and friends was barely enough for anything. So a friend and I decided here to find work in the city. We looked everywhere and were turned down. Meanwhile my mother needed medicine desperately to survive." Aynur began to sob.

Mehriban took the girl's hand in hers. "I understand, Aynur. I've been through hard times as well."

"No, Mehriban-hada, you have never been where I've been. The humiliation and abuse that I've suffered I wouldn't wish on anybody. After wandering for so long, hungry, and of no use to anybody, my friend and I eventually resorted to soliciting clients on Saint Street. Even before we got there, that street was full of women and girls of all nationalities. And so I began to sell my body, and the money I made from that occupation I sent home. That was all that my parents and five little brothers had to live on. They believed I'd gotten a decent job. Oh, Mehriban-hada! Even in a nightmare, you couldn't imagine the sorts of things we were forced to do in that rented apartment..."

Mehriban, gasping for breath at what she was hearing, could say nothing. Aynur, her face wet with tears, continued with her story.

"I put food on our family's table for five years. I tarted myself up, then got into smoking and drinking. The days dragged on, each the same as the one before. But I couldn't go on living like that for long. One day I got a temperature and a sore throat. I started coughing badly. My friend got me some medicine for colds, but I came out in red spots. I didn't pay much attention to it at the time, and as soon as I felt a little better, I went back to work. But I was getting weaker every day, and I soon realized I couldn't go on working. And now I'm losing weight so fast, I'm afraid to look in the mirror. I've no appetite. Just the other day, at long last, I took myself to see a doctor, and they analyzed my condition. It turns out I've got AIDS. So God has punished me by giving me this awful illness. They say there's no cure, so I'll just have to wait until it kills me." She choked on her tears.

Shaken, Mehriban sat and thought. She did not know how to help the unfortunate girl. Then she said, "Aynur, let me tell you this. You sacrificed yourself to help your mother recover and to feed your brothers. And I'm sure that the other women who wait on that street for business aren't doing it out of choice either. There is absolutely nobody who can blame you for what you did."

Aynur thirstily drank up the tea, which had cooled. "Mehriban-hada, I'm twenty-five years old. I haven't got a home, a husband, or a child. I am dying like a tree that has rotted from the inside. And I think there's very little time left for me."

"You've got a fever," said Mehriban, feeling Aynur's hot brow. "You should stay here tonight, and tomorrow I'll take you to Zharkent to your parents. OK?"

Aynur begged Mehriban not to tell anybody about her illness.

"Nobody will know except us two. I can keep secrets," she replied.

"Thank you, Mehriban-hada. It was Allah himself who sent you to me. Please take me home. I want to die at home." She sobbed.

The next day was a Sunday. They flagged down a car and set off to Zharkent, and by evening, they reached Aynur's family home. It was drizzling slightly. When they walked up to the gate, nobody came out to meet them. Aynur stood at the gate, hesitant, until Mehriban picked up her bag, took the girl by the hand, and led her into the yard. The yard was tidy but deserted. They went up to the house and at once saw a fat man in a vest, sprawled drunkenly on a *bugluk*. Seeing Aynur, he grimaced, then knitted his brows.

"Well look who it is! Needing a rest from the street, is that it? Or are you crawling home to die, you slut?"

Mehriban flared up. "Don't you dare talk to her like that! She's your daughter, after all!"

Hearing the noise, Aynur's ailing mother came out of the inner room. She feared her drunken husband so much that she could not speak and simply stood shaking. The right-hand side of her body was paralyzed.

"You're no daughter of mine!" shouted the father. "They say in Alma-Ata you were a prostitute. Get out of my sight!"

Aynur summoned all her strength, looked her father in the eye, and said firmly, "And was that not thanks to you? Just look. Instead of trying to put food on the table, you, father of the family, just took to drinking! As far as I remember, all you've ever done is get drunk and get into fights. And driven my mother to paralysis. You got us into debt, just so you could drink yourself senseless. Yes, I made my living by my body. And I did it to feed your family. You didn't disdain the money I sent you, did you? No, you took it and spent it. Well, I'd rather die than live with someone like you."

At this, her father goggled drunkenly. "Shut it, whore! Think you can teach me what's right, do you?" He cursed Aynur abusively and lunged at her menacingly. Her younger brothers held him back, pulling at him from all sides.

"What's this?" she carried on, looking provocatively at her father, "Ddon't you like hearing the truth?"

Her poor mother, hugging her with her one good arm, said to her with difficulty, "My poor dear daughter! You've sacrificed everything for us." She broke into sobbing.

Mehriban meanwhile felt as though she was suffocating. She said good-bye to Aynur and hurried out. Her heart was pounding, and she sensed that no good would come from that house.

Now the rain had stopped. Once she had had her fill of fresh air, she hitched a ride to Bolshoy Chigan, where she spent the night with her elder brother Turgan. The next day, the unhappy news reached her that Aynur had hung herself. The pain breaking out in her chest, Mehriban looked up at the sky and whispered, "Oh, Allah, forgive the sins of poor Aynur."

She returned to Alma-Ata that day. She brought *nan* from the village to give to Polina, and when she got home, she went to knock on her neighbor's door. The door was open. Going cautiously in, Mehriban saw Polina's son sitting in a wheelchair. He was wearing a cap that had fallen forward, covering his face. Mehriban greeted him, but he did not respond. Just then Polina came out of the kitchen. "Hi, Mehriban! When did you get back?"

"Just now. I've brought you some of our village *nan* to try." She put them on the table.

Unexpectedly, Sasha started to yell, pointing at the door. "Well so much for you and your village *nan*. I'll tell you where you can stick it. You Muslims are all filthy black-arses. I hate you!"

"Sasha, for crying out loud, stop that! What's this got to do with our neighbor?" Appalled, his mother looked guiltily at Mehriban.

Mehriban turned and went toward the door.

"I hate you! Go and shove it, bitch!" bawled the young man again, and hurled his tea bowl at her. It missed.

Mehriban hurried back to her own flat and took some cardiac drops. When Rosa came home in the evening, she told her about what had happened.

"But why did you go to hers?" said Rosa, "You should have invited her here instead and given her the bread here."

"But I wasn't to know how much he hates Muslims."

"He hates them because he was in the war. All the same, though, some of our own soldiers killed Muslims in that war. I expect that the Muslims there hate the Russians just as much."

"Oh, Allah, this hatred is terrible. No doubt that poor boy still sees his dead comrades before his eyes all the time. That's why he's become so angry. But then, there were Uighur boys fighting the Afghans too, and they're Muslims as well."

Mehriban remembered how the Afghan tragedy began. It had been a golden autumn, when the work on the harvest was at its peak, when they announced on the radio and television that war had broken out in faraway Afghanistan. Those older people who had not yet forgotten the horrors of the Great Patriotic War were uneasy. When it became known that Soviet soldiers were being sent to Afghanistan to fulfill an international obligation, the parents of many a young man felt their hearts contract with dread; the conscripts were effectively being sent to their slaughter.

The call-up for the Afghan war reached Zharkent before long. Young men were summoned to the enlistment office and given a medical examination. A meeting was organized on the village square for parents, war veterans, and fellow town and village dwellers. The chairman of the *kolkhoz*, Ivrahim-aka looked round at the new recruits standing in a line.

"We have registered you all as members of the *kolkhoz* and created work record books for you. If you decide that you want to study when you come back from the army, you will have a record of two years' experience. We hope you return safe and sound. The whole village will be waiting for you!"

Next, the war veteran Mahmut-aka spoke. "My boys," he began in a firm voice, "when we were young we also had to go and fight—in our case with the fascist German occupants. Many *dzhigits* gave their lives for their country. We will never forget them. War can never be easy. So be vigilant! Do not forget that your parents are waiting for you at home. And do not taint the name of your village."

After Mahmut came an old woman, old Sherhan, one of the holy mothers. She leaned on a stick. "I sent my four sons off to the war and not one of them came home. I grieved for so long over the four letters I received that I nearly lost my sight. So why is Brezhnev now sending our raw grandsons to a foreign land to their inevitable deaths? If this has to be, then let me go along with my grandson. I can protect him."

The others present laughed, and the chairman of the village committee replied, unruffled as ever, "Grandmothers are not allowed to serve in the army, *chon-apa.*"

"Hey, son, what's the use of weeping in an empty house? It would be better to go with the boy and cook his food for him."

Nobody dared to pull this venerable old woman into line. Everybody understood that having lost four sons, she had no desire to part with her sole grandson.

Now Turgan's son Murat spoke on behalf of the recruits. "Dear mothers and fathers! Thank you for your kind wishes. We also hope to return home and to work alongside you. We will not let you down. Meanwhile,

while we're away fighting, you look after yourselves and wait for us to come back."

"He speaks well, that son of Turgan and Rana," said the elders. "And he's so well-built, stately, and full of respect for the older generation. It's a real pleasure to watch him."

"Well, both his parents are teachers. He had a good upbringing."

Hearing this, Rana whispered anxiously, "Oh, Allah, protect my son from the evil eye."

The recruits bade their parents and friends good-bye, got into waiting vehicles, and were driven away. Their parents went home and waited, constantly anxious. Happily, all nine of the men from our village came back from the hell of that war. They looked much older now than their peers, having survived for two years between living and dying in the Afghan mountains. They rescued wounded comrades and witnessed the deaths of many at the front. The nightmare they had endured remained before their eyes and did not let them live in peace. There were Soviet soldiers in Afghanistan from 1979 to 1989. And some of the soldiers sent from our region, Panfilovsky, did come back in zinc coffins, bringing grief on their families. How many must have wept over those cold coffins! And how many hopes and dreams were buried along with those young men… But there was nothing anybody could do.

Mehriban and Rosa sat for a long time talking about the war. And of course, Mehriban understood that Sasha's abusive outburst toward her was due to the scars he had sustained in the war. And yet, after his shouting and foul language, she did not feel fully herself. She would have gone on feeling out of sorts had Rosa not suddenly jumped up, slapping her knees. "*Hada*, I completely forgot! There's a letter from Samiya!" she exclaimed, handing it to Mehriban.

Mehriban could not conceal her delight as she hurriedly opened it. The letter read:

> *Please don't worry about me, apa. I've already grown accustomed to the way of life here. I'm working in two places. It's not easy, of course, but I'm not afraid of difficulty, and you and Father brought me up to be fearless! I've put the money you gave me in the bank. I'm renting a one-room apartment. Polat-aka, Farida-hada, and their Uighur friends have provided me with everything I need for the place. Whatever small things remain I can sort out for myself. I'm also learning to drive. As soon as I get my license, I will buy a used car. Here you can get a license from the age of sixteen. Everybody observes the rules of the road very strictly. And the roads here are as smooth as mirrors. Later, I'll drive to my classes at Santa Monica College. The only thing is, my English isn't good enough yet. I'm planning to learn to use a computer and to take courses in business and economics.*
>
> *Halida and I have become close friends. I've also met some other girls, they're very nice and very normal. Apa, I've been missing you so much. You tell me you've been working on a book about the lives of the mothers. That's brilliant! I'm sure*

that you can become a writer. I'm proud of you. Good luck! And Father would have supported you in this undertaking. His spirit is helping us all the time. Give my thanks to Rosa for relieving your loneliness! Now I can feel that all is well.

It's probably already winter with you. Here, winter is just rain - rather like our autumn.

I kiss you and send my love, your daughter, Samiya.

The letter brought her a whiff of energy and lust for life.

One evening a few days later, Polina called by. "Mehriban, I'm going to see my daughter and will stay there overnight. I want to see my grandchildren, as I haven't seen them for ages. I'll be back early tomorrow morning. Here are the keys. I've told my son that if he needs anything, he should knock on the wall and that Mehriban would come in and help."

"But your son hates me. How can I be of help to him?" asked Mehriban, taken aback.

"Please don't take that personally, neighbor. You know he's not right in the head. He insults everyone. Ever since he was disabled, he's just changed completely. Once upon a time he had a kind heart." The old woman wept.

Saying nothing, Mehriban took the keys. Later, in the middle of the night, she woke suddenly, as though somebody were shouting, "Get up!" An acrid smell of smoke hung in the air. She looked carefully for the cause, but everything seemed to be in order. Then she realized that the smoke was coming from Polina's flat.

She woke Rosa and the two rushed out onto the landing. When she opened Polina's door, the inside was filled with thick smoke. Mehriban went inside and found Sasha lying unconscious on the sofa. She laid him on a blanket and pulled him outside. Meanwhile Rosa contacted the emergency services.

Mehriban closed the windows and switched off the television. Seeing that the carpet was smoldering, she filled a large bowl with water and drenched it. It seemed that Sasha had fallen asleep with a cigarette in his mouth. The cigarette must have fallen onto the carpet and caused it to smolder and give off smoke. Sasha must have inhaled carbon monoxide and lost consciousness. Now an ambulance arrived and took him away.

Other neighbors woke up and came to see what the noise was about. When they learned of Mehriban's resourcefulness and courage, they thanked her. "But where's Sasha's mother?" asked the elderly Dzhamilya-apay.

When Mehriban told her that she had gone to see her daughter, Dzhamiliya-apay inhaled sharply. "The poor thing! And she can't go anywhere, she just has stay forever tied to her son. And live with his swearing and his fists."

The neighbors checked Polina's flat once again, then bolted the door and went home.

Next morning when she returned, Polina learned what had happened. "Mehriban, thank you so much," she said with tears in her eyes. "If you hadn't been there, my son might have suffocated and died."

"It seems that your son is a handsome young man. I noticed that as I was pulling him out of the room in the blanket," said Mehriban, not without a note of humour.

"He's good-looking all right, but ill-fated."

Several days later, Polina called again. "I've just brought Sasha home from hospital. He would like to see you," she said, taking Mehriban with her into the apartment.

The young man in the wheelchair looked up at Mehriban with his handsome face. "Thank you, neighbor," he said laconically. His eyes radiated happiness. And at that moment, a pretty, dark-blond young woman walked in, greeted everybody and stood awkwardly at the threshold. Sasha's eyes flashed.

"Mama, this is Irina. She's a nurse at the hospital where I've just been," he said, turning to Polina. "She's agreed to marry me."

"That's right, we've decided it," said the girl, coming up and standing next to Sasha.

"Mama, did you hear?" he exclaimed.

"Yes, I heard you, son. If you're going to be happy, then I'll be happy too," she said, embracing them both.

Mehriban also congratulated the two young lovers. That evening she told Rosa. "Just think, a burning carpet has brought happiness to Sasha. And I came away feeling happy myself."

"Well, I think Sasha will change now," Rosa suggested.

"Definitely! And for the better," nodded Mehriban.

• • •

Ruth seemed intrigued by Mehriban's account of the war in Afghanistan. "So your folk perished in Afghanistan for reasons we don't understand. And many of our soldiers died in the same way in the Vietnam War. Hundreds were crippled. My brother's a Vietnam veteran. He was disabled by spinal injuries, and he's confined to a wheelchair. He became short-tempered and caustic after the war. His wife couldn't stand it and left him.

"In America, though, families that have suffered from the Vietnam War receive good pensions. In my brother's case they pay for a home help and a nurse. Still, almost everyone who took part in Vietnam curses that war."

"There are so many conflicts in the world," said Mehriban ardently. "How I long for peace. Why can't the leaders of the nations come together and agree on peace and tranquility?"

"Isn't it odd how people fight, while everywhere they are longing for peace?" added Ruth. "Dear Mehriban, we'll be landing soon, but I'd love to hear the rest of your long story. Please go on," she asked.

So Mehriban came to the final part of her narrative.

27

IN A FARAWAY LAND

Mehriban was becoming more and more absorbed with the book she had started to write. In her mind's eye she saw her childhood, the difficult years her parents faced, and the bitterness of their poverty. When she dwelled on these memories, all sleepiness vanished from her. She would settle in the kitchen each evening and put her thoughts down on paper.

On winter evenings Rukiyam *kichik-apa* came round and told Mehriban her stories, to which she listened with great interest and which she later wrote down. Sometimes she would read passages of her work to Rosa, seeking her response and listening to any comments or observations. The process of writing so took over Mehriban that she no longer had time for grieving over Seitzhan. With each day that passed, she felt better, and the pile of written pages grew thicker. Eventually the book was finished.

Not having the means to publish the book, Mehriban wrapped the manuscript up and put it in her storage chest, where it lay for five years. Though the book had not reached its public, Mehriban felt a sense of lightness and joy, as though she had fulfilled her duty of rememorating the mother saints. Then early one summer's day the door of the house opened, and there stood Samiya. Mother and daughter ran into each other's arms and wept. They looked at each other and hugged again. "I haven't seen you for five whole years, *kizim*," said Mehriban. "Why did you go so far away?"

"Don't cry, *apa*. In that time, I've learned so many new things and how to stand firmly on my own two feet," her daughter replied, smiling brightly through her tears.

Now Rosa, who had fallen asleep, came out of the next room and joyfully greeted Samiya. Samiya wandered round the apartment. Nothing had changed in five years.

Half an hour later, they were all sitting at table, eating little *bliny* made by Mehriban and talking about America. Samiya showed the others photographs of her friends. "*Apa*, these are Polat-aka and Farida-hada, and this is their daughter Halida. And these are the American students I'm studying with. And this is where I live."

"What a lovely building!" exclaimed Mehriban and Rosa as one.

Samiya showed them one picture after another of the sights of Los Angeles and told them at length about life on that distant continent. Rosa's eyes shone with fascination. "Samiya-hada," she said, "you're so lucky. You live in a wonderful city, you've come to grips with a different country and made friends there. What an interesting life you've got!"

Hearing this only made Mehriban prouder of her daughter. "You can see why her father called her a "girl-*dzhigit*." She hugged Samiya again.

"It isn't easy to be successful in America straight away," Samiya pointed out. "At first I missed Almaty terribly. The city seemed so foreign. There are an awful lot of incomers there, all looking for jobs. To begin with I had to get whatever work I could. I even worked as a waitress for a while. That's a hard life too—you're on your feet until the last customer has gone. Sometimes I didn't get away from work until one in the morning. My next job was cleaning in someone's house."

Mehriban's eyes moistened again. "You went all that way just to do housework and be a waitress, right?"

"*Apa*, people there are happy to be able to sweep the streets," smiled Samiya. "Anyway, after that, I took driving lessons, got my license, and bought a car on credit."

"You can drive now?" said Rosa, amazed.

"Yes, I drive every day to Santa Monica College. Soon after that, they offered me work as a teacher's assistant. The students are off at the moment, so I took ten days' vacation. I'd like to take my mother back with me."

"But why is your holiday so short?" asked her mother.

"Nobody there gets a whole month's vacation like we do here. It's not their way."

Mehriban could see that her daughter had changed a lot. Her speech and gestures conveyed determination and a sense of self-confidence.

The next morning, Samiya took her mother to the US embassy, and they joined the queue of applicants. People were called to interview by their surname and admitted one at a time. When Mehriban was called, Samiya went in with her. A middle-aged woman invited them to take a seat. Samiya talked to the woman in English for some time. At length the officer examined Mehriban's documents and asked her, "Have you been to the United States before?"

"No," said Mehriban, "I've never been abroad."

"What is your reason for traveling to the United States?"

"My daughter wants to show me the country."

"Are you intending to remain in the United States?"

"No, I will come home after my visit."

"Do you have family remaining here in Kazakhstan?"

"Yes. A brother, two sisters, and other relatives."

"Do you have somewhere to live in Almaty?"

"Yes, I've got a two-room apartment. And I've got a job here."

"Very good," the officer nodded. She signed the papers and placed a visa in Mehriban's passport. "You may travel to the United States."

Once they were outside, Samiya asked her mother, "*Apa*, did you notice the questions she asked you? They are designed to make sure people don't stay in America."

When they got home, Samiya thumbed through her notebook and said, "*Apa*, let's not lose time. Let's go straight to Zharkent and see the relatives and visit Father's grave."

"But daughter, why don't we say good-bye to Rukiyam-ana tonight?"

"OK, let's wait for Rosa and go to see Rukiyam-ana this evening. I'll go and get some presents," Samiya agreed.

That evening, Rukiyam-ana and her daughter Nuraniya received their guests for dinner. Rukiyam-ana had aged a lot. She stooped and had become gray and wrinkled. Yet her loose-cut dress and snow-white shawl still suited her, as they always had. "Well, well, just look at our girl-*dzhigit*, surfing the big waves of life!" she exclaimed, kissing Samiya on the forehead.

When they sat down to the meal, Samiya said to Rukiyam, "*Ana*, thanks to the phone number you gave me, I've been able to meet some good people. Polat-aka and Farida-hada have helped me enormously. They're like family to me now." She went on to tell her about her five years in America.

"Well they say, 'no pain, no gain,'" said Rukiyam-ana. "And you didn't have an easy time of it. But now you've got your own home, a job, and a car. These things are rewards for your hard work and lack of fear."

"You say you want to go on studying," Nuraniya chipped in. "So when will you get married?"

"I'd be so happy if you could find your other half," added Mehriban.

"I hardly think about that at the moment," replied Samiya. "I'm putting all my efforts into getting into university. That is my main goal. Anyway, I haven't met a boy I like yet." She chuckled.

Rosa was showing a distinct interest in following in Samiya's footsteps. "Samiya-hada, could you help me go to America?" she asked. "I'd love to study there."

"Well, I've met students from Kazakhstan in LA. They get financial support from the Kazakh president's state fund and the "Bolashak" program. Why not try doing it that way? If it doesn't work, I'll have a word with Polat-aka and try to get you a student visa."

"Rukiyam-ana, Samiya wants to show me America," said Mehriban. "This girl-*dzhigit* has come all back here for just ten days so she can take me with her as a visitor."

"Well you know the saying: for as long as you have sight, go and see the world. Find out about new places. Is there anything wrong in that? How long will you be away?"

Laughing, Nuraniya said, "*Apa*, you're still full of life. But don't scare the ones who are preparing for their final journey!"

"Well, they say that where there's life there's death," the old woman said. "I've already reached the end of my time. It's your turn now. Go and see those amazing places, and don't worry about me," she added.

Next morning Samiya and her mother went to Zharkent. They spent two days there, saw various relatives, and visited her father's grave before returning to the city.

Samiya's ten days of holiday passed in a blink. Then Mehriban, who had never traveled anywhere, found herself on an aircraft for the first time. Samiya gave her a seat by a window and showed her how to fasten her safety belt. There were various announcements from the crew as they prepared for take-off, and then they heard the roar of the engines building up. Mehriban whispered to herself, "In the name of Allah the Compassionate, the Merciful," then peered out of the window. Its silvery wings gently rocking, the plane was already climbing higher and higher. And taking her farther and farther from home.

Once they had reached cruising altitude, a friendly stewardess offered the passengers lunch. Mehriban selected chicken with rice, while Samiya opted for fish and chips. The stewardess placed trays before them that included, in addition to the main dish, small bread rolls like gingerbread, and sugar for tea.

Picking up her bread roll, Mehriban was reminded of another event from her childhood. She told Samiya, "After our fourth year at school, we were working for the summer on the *kolkhoz*. We worked so well that my friend Rimma and I were sent to a Pioneers camp, in a beautiful spot beside a river. We stayed in big tents. There were meals three times a day, and at four o'clock they gave us tea and *pryaniki*, little gingerbread cakes. But I didn't eat the gingerbread; I put it into my bag to take home afterwards. We were at the camp for twenty-four days, and so by the end I had twenty-four gingerbread pieces. When I got home again, I put all the *pryaniki* on a tray and put it on the table, pulling a mysterious face.

"Everybody at home was delighted and took one, but there was a problem. The gingerbread had hardened; they were like stone. I started crying. But Mama came up and hugged me. She said, 'Oh you poor thing! You wanted to give us a treat and it went wrong. But don't be upset. Let's dip these Pioneer *pryaniki* in our tea. That'll make them soft again.' And that's what we did. How delicious they were! I was sitting next to my father and noticed how much my brothers were enjoying theirs. My tears soon dried."

"But didn't they sell them in your village already?"

"Maybe they did, but my parents never had the money for them."

"*Apa*, that story shows how much you cared for others when you were small. It's no coincidence that you were called Mehriban." Samiya looked tenderly at her mother.

Once they had eaten, mother and daughter lowered the backs of their seats and covered themselves with the thin but warm blankets the stewardess had provided.

Mehriban's thoughts went back to Seitzhan. "How young he was when he died. If he was still alive, we'd be flying to America together. But this world is unjust. What can you do?" She looked at her daughter, who was fast asleep.

After nine hours of flying, they landed in Amsterdam. There they waited for six hours before their flight continued to Los Angeles, a further seven hours away. By the time they landed in the USA, tired from the long journey, Mehriban realized that Samiya really had moved to the end of the world.

At the passport control point, Samiya took out their documents and requested permission for her mother to stay for six months. This was granted, and a stamp was put in Mehriban's passport. The two women took a taxi to Samiya's apartment.

Mehriban was astonished at how wide and straight the city's streets were. The pavement was lined with trees and flowerbeds, and behind them rose tall buildings with striking architecture. The car took them to the Park La Brea district, where Samiya lived in a townhouse near the apartment block in which Farida lived. Mehriban could not take her eyes from the lush surroundings of trees, bushes, and flowers around the dwellings. They took their baggage and went inside. Mehriban looked carefully round the house. "It's all so new and shiny! What a wonderful, clean place you've got!"

Samiya showed her mother around. "This is the dining room, and in this room, you can also eat and watch TV." She took her upstairs. "There's just one room up here, the bedroom."

"But you said you lived in a one-room apartment," said Mehriban, bemused.

"Yes, because here the number of rooms means the number of bedrooms."

They sat down together on the big bed upstairs. The room was filled with light. Samiya opened the door of a built-in wardrobe. "This is where I keep my clothes. And through that door are the bathroom and toilet."

These too were spotless and gleamed white.

Having seen the apartment, Mehriban gave her verdict. "Well, daughter, apart from the distance, you've found a place in paradise here! This is the reward for your success."

"*Apa*, why don't you freshen up and have a rest, and I'll drive to the shops for some food. Then we can make supper." Samiya went downstairs.

Left by herself, Mehriban looked at the photographs on the wall. In one of them Samiya was sitting between her mother and her father. In another, Seitzhan and she were swimming in the Usek. A third picture showed Samiya and her parents standing in front of the Zharkent mosque. Then there was another picture in which Seitzhan, in white overalls, was attending to the sick. Mehriban sighed and went to take a shower.

After an early supper, Samiya promised to show her mother the local area. "People here have very little free time. They only meet and talk at weekends and on holidays. It's hot outside at the moment, so let's wait until it gets dark, and then we'll go for a walk."

When dusk came and the streetlights began to come on, Samiya and her mother set out to explore. "There are English classes for immigrants in one of these buildings. They are free of charge, and all kinds of people go to them, old and young. Why don't you rest for two or three days and then I'll take you along. It's right next to our house."

"But what's the point of me learning English if I have to leave in six months?"

"*Apa*, I'm not going to be at home with you all the time. If you learn English, you'll be able to make friends with other women here. Surely that would be a good thing?"

"I don't want to, Samiya," said her mother, "I don't know a syllable of English."

"In this course, people start by learning the alphabet, then they start writing and speaking. I'm sure you'll enjoy learning." Samiya hugged her. She took her hand and led her toward the fountain. Elderly people were sitting around it on benches, some reading newspapers and others talking together. Samiya and Mehriban also sat for a while, then continued their stroll.

"And here," Samiya pointed, "Farida-hada lives on the fifth floor. This is a huge housing complex. It's surrounded by a metal fence. You can go for walks inside the area while I'm out working. But you shouldn't wander too far. Use the fountain as a landmark."

Mehriban was surprised at the number of flowers around the buildings. "Doesn't anyone pick these?"

"Anyone who picks these flowers gets a fine," grinned Samiya.

She showed her mother the building in which the language courses were held. "*Apa*, you'll come here five times a week and study until two o'clock."

Mehriban was unhappy at this. "Samiya, don't make my life miserable by forcing me to study."

"Don't be so resistant, mother" her daughter said firmly. "If you learn the language, you can live freely in a foreign country."

They walked for another hour and returned home. The apartment was air conditioned, and this was pleasant after the heat of the outdoors. Only now did the two women realize how tired they were. They went to bed and were asleep straight away.

Two days later Samiya took her mother to the English class. The group included people of many nationalities and different ages. Samiya went up to the teacher. "My mother has come from Kazakhstan. She doesn't know any English and is quite nervous. I hope you can help her. She would like to make some new friends."

The teacher smiled warmly. "My name is Nancy," she said to Mehriban in English, holding out her hand to her new student. "What is your name?"

Mehriban shook the hand extended to her, then turned helplessly to her daughter.

"*Apa*, she's asking you your name."

"Mehriban."

Nancy gave Mehriban a place in the front row of desks and addressed the class. "We've got a new student. She is from Kazakhstan. Let's help her."

Samiya slipped quietly out of the room. Mehriban meanwhile opened her exercise book and drew a vertical line to divide the page into two columns. On one side she wrote down the English letters that the teacher wrote on the blackboard. On the other side she made notes about their sounds. The two-hour lesson passed quickly. Then, since she did not know any of the other students, Mehriban slipped out unnoticed after class. When she got back to Samiya's apartment, she opened her notebook and began repeating the names of the letters. This took quite a long time. "Good heavens, I hardly imagined I'd be starting to learn English at fifty-seven," she grinned, looking at herself in the mirror.

When the weekend came, Samiya decided to take Mehriban to the Huntington Library garden in Pasadena.

"Is it far away?" asked Mehriban.

"About half an hour's drive. Anyone who enters this garden doesn't want to leave. You'll see for yourself. You'll soon understand what I mean."

In half an hour, they reached Pasadena, as Samiya had said. They parked the car and walked toward the big gates bearing the words, "Huntington Library." Samiya bought tickets and took her mother inside. Immediately, they were among fragrant red yellow and blue flowers. Their scent was pungent and refreshing. From the vast number of plants in the garden,

Mehriban found the ones she recognized from her village.

"*Apa*, let me tell you a bit about this garden. It contains fourteen thousand plants from all the continents of the world, in different specialized areas. There's a Japanese garden, and there's a "desert garden" for plants that grow in dry regions. Here we can see cacti, which grow in arid zones," Samiya explained after reading the names of the plants shown on their name plates.

The cacti had the strangest shapes. Many of them had big, bright flowers. The aloe were tall, like trees.

"*Apa*, just stand next to those gorgeous blossoms, and I'll take your photo," said Samiya. She took a number of shots.

There were many visitors in the garden looking at the plants, taking photographs, talking quietly, and strolling through the greenery. Ducks and ducklings swam in a pond at the center of the garden. In another pool, wondrous lilies in white, yellow, and even red captivated the gaze of visitors. "*Apa*, these flowers are called water lilies. And now we're coming to the Japanese garden."

The Japanese garden featured wooden Japanese houses around which grew tall flowering trees. The ground was thickly strewn with soft petals. A stream chuckled through the garden, and from a small bridge, red carp could be seen darting about in the clear water. Neither Mehriban nor her daughter could have described the beauty they saw here. It was like a real taste of paradise.

"And this is the Shakespeare Garden," said Samiya, moving on and pointing to some bright red roses that seemed to glow from within. One of the entrances to the garden through a vaulted tunnel whose metal latticework supported red and white climbing roses, and the whole effused a delicate, soft yet stirring scent. After passing through the tunnel, the two women came to the Palm Garden.

"Let's have a look round the gallery. It's got old paintings from several centuries ago," said Samiya, leading her mother into the grand white building ahead. Looking at some of the pictures on display, Mehriban seemed to see the people portrayed in them brought to life and surrounding her. The creative energy they induced in her even caused her head to ache. She asked Samiya to take her outside.

They sat down on a bench, and Samiya offered her water and began to rub her hand. "*Apa*, do you need medicine? You've gone a bit pale."

"Don't worry, daughter. It's all clearing now. It seemed as if I was being surrounded by spirits in there," her mother replied, sipping the water.

"Well, *apa*, shall we go home?"

"Have you shown me everything you intended to?"

"Yes. The only thing we haven't seen is the library itself. It has over a million rare books."

"Huntington must have been a wealthy man," Mehriban said.

"Yes, he was a merchant with good connections. He traveled all over the world and collected a huge number of tree and flower specimens. He created this extraordinary garden. He also collected the best-known paintings by famous artists, as you've just seen in the gallery. And, of course, he found and bought the rarest books in the world, and on that basis, he founded a library. The Huntington opened in 1919, and it has flourished ever since and now attracts millions of visitors."

"The person who bequeathed such an immense cultural testament wasn't only rich, he was wise as well. What Huntington did—his generosity—are examples for his descendants," observed Mehriban, solemnly and seriously.

They went on sitting there for a long time, listening to the birdsong. "To really sense the beauty here, you need a heart as well as eyes," Mehriban observed.

When the time came to go home, Mehriban quickly looked around the garden one last time. She was reluctant to leave this glorious spot.

"When I came here for the first time with Halida, I straightaway wanted to show it to you. And today my wish has been granted."

The next day, Samiya took her mother to see the ocean. It was a hot day, and the beach and the water were crowded. Whole families lay sunbathing or swam—a human sea of children, young people, and old people. There was nowhere for an apple to fall, as the saying has it. And to their surprise, everything was clean and orderly. Once people had eaten, they put away the leftovers and disposed of litter in bins provided for the purpose. "So it's true, as you say. People here observe the law one hundred percent," Mehriban said to herself.

"This is the Pacific, *apa*," said Samiya. She undressed, went in, and swam a good distance.

Watching her, Mehriban thought of the time when Seitzhan had taken Samiya swimming in the Usek. Samiya could not yet swim, and Seitzhan was trying without success to teach her. Now, thousands of miles from home, on the shore of the Pacific Ocean, she recalled these events fondly. Those days could never be brought back, she realized.

After they had seen the ocean, Samiya showed her mother the college where she studied and worked. Students were sitting on a bright green lawn, talking, eating, or reading. After looking around, Samiya cheerfully suggested, "*Apa*, since we're in Santa Monica, why don't we have a wander around the shops?"

They came to a row of shopping malls, large and small side by side. "Here you can buy anything your heart desires," said Samiya, showing her mother inside. Indeed, the shops were filled with all manner of goods, and friendly assistants offered them help. "Let me buy you some trousers, *apa*, and a couple of thin summer blouses."

"Just a minute, what makes you think I'm going to start wearing trousers?" Mehriban was flustered.

"Just see how fine and light they are. You can't go around in your warm dress in this heat," said her daughter firmly. She purchased the lightweight clothes for her mother.

They walked round the shops until they began to feel hungry. They took lunch in a Chinese restaurant in one of the malls. There were people of various nationalities sitting there around them.

"Samiya, I'm so proud of you. You've found your place in this big city among thousands of people.

Although this is a great country, it's still not your home. Don't you sometimes miss your own language, our songs and music, our weddings, and your relatives and friends?"

"*Apa*, in this country I can live freely. Nobody here asks me what nationality I am or tells me about the color of my skin. There's real freedom here for the individual."

"You've changed a lot in five years. There's a saying, and it's for good reason: 'Don't let your child wander too far, or she will become a stranger to you.' That's how it is."

"We're living in a different time now, *apa*, and our lives are different. People want to live independently and to stand firmly on their own two feet. We don't depend on others. We don't go to cry on their shoulders or ask for their help. We've learned this from life."

"You're full of ideas, so I see," said Mehriban, looking her in the eye, "but as they say, nobody is immune to illness or misfortune. How will you manage by yourself?"

"*Apa*, please, let's change the subject," said Samiya, who asked the waitress for the bill.

They drove home in silence, each of them thinking their own thoughts. They were expecting guests that evening, however, so when they got home, they cheerfully set to preparing the meal.

Their guests, Polat and Farida, were Mehriban's age and she quickly found a common language with them. Mehriban placed a large dish of *manty* on the table and deferentially invited the guests to try them.

Polat bombarded Mehriban with questions about Kazakhstan and the Uighur diaspora. Mehriban was happy to answer them. "Kazakhstan became independent in 1991. We went through a lot of big changes over the next ten years. At the initiative of the president, Nursultan Nazarbaev, the capital was moved north from Almaty—the new name for Alma-Ata—to Astana. Astana now has a lot of unique buildings, and it's growing more impressive every year. There are over one hundred thirty nationalities living in Kazakhstan now, including us Uighurs, and we can preserve our language, our customs, and our songs and dances. We've got the Uighur Drama Theater and a newspaper, *Uigur Avazi*, and schools that teach in the Uighur language. So we're living there on good terms and moving forward with the rest of the country."

Mehriban also mentioned Polat's sister Alahan and that she had met Rukiyam-ana. And of course she thanked the couple heartily for having been so kind to her daughter, helping her during her first days in America and supporting her.

"Your daughter has a strong spine, for sure. She came here to study. She's brave and not afraid of difficulties. She'll be getting a full US passport soon, and she's hoping to be accepted into UCLA."

Mehriban felt pride at hearing such words from a senior academic about her daughter. They sat up late talking. Finally, glancing at their watches, the guests got up and made a move to leave. Farida invited Samiya and Mehriban to come to dinner, whereupon they parted.

The next morning, Samiya got up and left for work. Mehriban tidied up around the house and then took her notebook and pen and went off to her English class. In the course of a week she had learned the whole of the English alphabet and memorized a few words. She now felt her interest in the language increasing. As each student entered the classroom, the others called out, "Good morning!" and when they left they wished each other "Good-bye", and after another ten days or so, Mehriban had learned more than fifty words. Samiya was pleased that she was doing so well.

One evening, Mehriban felt a sudden bout of longing for the familiar places of home. All at once she felt cramped in the apartment and hurried outside. She began to pace thoughtfully along the paths within the residential complex and did not notice how far she had walked. By the time she realized that she had gone farther than usual, she did not recognize her surroundings. Anxious and afraid, she looked about her in growing desperation. A little way away, she noticed some Hindu men playing volleyball, their womenfolk sitting on benches nearby with their children. Mehriban hurried over to them and asked them in English where the road with the fountain was. The Indian women did not understand a word of English, however, and cupped their hands in front of them and shook their heads. Mehriban then saw a Chinese woman walking with her children and rushed to her. They mumbled something that indicated in various ways that they could not understand her either. Now it was also getting dark, and the streetlights had just come on. Mehriban was becoming really afraid. She stood rooted to the spot, with no idea in which direction to move. Shortly a young man came running past in a white cap, a white T-shirt and white shorts, and indeed white running shoes on his feet. Mehriban moved herself into his path and asked him, in a loud, clear voice: "Where is the fountain?" To make sure, she used the language of gestures, using her hands to imitate water coming out of a fountain. Then she almost cried out, "Water, water!" and looked imploringly into the young man's eyes.

The runner, sensing that Mehriban was in a very anxious state, walked with her a considerable distance and showed her the way she needed. Hoping that he had understood her question right, Mehriban smiled gratefully and put her hand to her chest. "Thank you!" she said, and hurried home.

She went so fast that her heart began to thud against her chest. She began to weep as she went into the apartment. Her daughter would soon be home from work. She washed quickly in cold water and warmed up the evening meal.

Samiya arrived shortly and noticed her mother's red eyes. "*Apa*, what's happened?"

Mehriban described her adventure. Now it did not sound as frightening as it had seemed at the time. Samiya laughed. "There, you see, *apa*, how useful it is to know a bit of English," she said, wiping away tears of laughter. "In the end, you found your way home. I'm proud of you!" She kissed her mother.

"I'm ashamed for having gotten lost in a strange country, like a little girl," said Mehriban with tears in her eyes. "In my own country, this wouldn't have happened."

"You've only been here a month, but you're already missing home?" asked Samiya gently.

"Yes, I am. It's not easy for me here. I'd like to have somebody here to talk to, but I'm like someone who stammers. Learning a new language in your old age—what sort of a life is that?"

"*Apa*, it would be silly to go home now just because you've gotten lost on a walk. Do you think it was easy for me to get used to living here? I endured everything, didn't panic, and kept moving toward my goals as best I could. And now I've got a job, a place to live, and a car—but I need to do more studying."

"So the studying you did in Almaty, was that not good enough? Was it not good enough for you to marry, to have children and set up home?" exclaimed Mehriban.

"So far in these last five years I haven't achieved anything," Samiya replied sadly. "I thought that you would support me, but no, you give up straight away. I'm sure that my father would have supported me." There was hurt in her voice.

"No, daughter, I said what I said because I thought it might be easier for you in your own country," said Mehriban in a conciliatory tone.

"*Apa*, everybody has to choose their own path in life. The one I chose isn't the easiest, but I'm not changing it."

"Well, fair enough, Samiya, you can see more clearly what you want than I can. If you want knowledge so much, I can only admire you." She kissed Samiya on the forehead.

"Once I get my diploma, then we can decide where I'll live and work."

One day when Mehriban was coming home from her studies, she heard two women sitting on a bench and talking in Russian. She was so delighted, it was as though they were members of her own family. She hurried over to them. "Are you from Russia?" she asked.

"Yes, we're from Leningrad," said an elderly woman with a walking stick in her hand.

"Well, I'm from Kazakhstan. My name's Mehriban."

"I'm Sofia," answered the older woman.

"And my name is Dina," said her companion, a stooped old woman with glasses.

They began to talk as if they were old friends. "We've lived in America for twelve years. When the persecution of the Jews became intolerable, we went to the US embassy and asked for asylum. They gave us refugee status and put us on a plane. We had to give up everything—our homes, our belongings and our friends," said Sofia. "There were four families who came over. Dina's my husband's sister."

"So if you've been here twelve years, you must have adapted to America?"

"We've gotten used to it, of course, but we still miss home," sighed Dina.

"We think about Leningrad all the time, about when we were young. Sometimes we cry." Sofia smiled and asked, "So how did you end up here?"

Mehriban told them about her husband's death and that she was here to visit her daughter.

"So you're lonely too, like us." Sofia shook her head with compassion. "Our husbands have died too, and Dina and I have been left by ourselves."

From that day onward, on her way home from classes, Mehriban would sit with her two acquaintances and they would talk for hours. One day Sofia told her about her childhood.

"One day, after I'd gone to school, they gathered all the Jews of our district together, crammed them into trucks, and took them to an unknown destination. They shot them dead without trial or investigation. My parents and sister were among them. I survived only because I'd been at school at the time they were rounded up. I was afraid to spend the night in our house after that. I thank our neighbors, grandfather Vasya and grandmother Galya. They hid me in their household. Then during the Siege of Leningrad people were dying of hunger. As it happened, my new guardians had a large bottle of cod-liver oil in their cupboard. Each of us—old Vasya, Galya, and I—took a spoonful of the oil every day. Even so, my two old guardians eventually died of exhaustion. We were all emaciated, like skeletons. Because we were so hungry, we were always desperate to sleep. And so it happened, one day Baba Galya went to sleep and didn't wake up. Before he also died, Vasya gave me the bottle containing the remains of the fish oil and told me not to take too much of it—just one spoonful per day. Then he closed his eyes and died. I was on my own again. Thanks to God and to the cod-liver oil, I survived. Decades have passed since then, but I can remember it all."

After Sofia finished, all three women sank into reminiscence. "We were hungry and destitute during the war as well," said Mehriban thoughtfully. "We didn't have an easy time either."

As she grew accustomed to her life in America, Mehriban told her daughter something new every day. She made friends with her fellow students: Fatima the Turk, Mimi from Japan, Indira from India, and a number of Koreans. All of them were uprooted from their home countries, so they quickly became close. Samiya was pleased that her mother was mixing with others and improving her conversational English.

One evening when Samiya and her mother were walking near their home, they saw a young woman playing ball with her little daughter and noticed occasional words of Russian slipped into their speech. Samiya went up to her and addressed her in English, then introduced her to Mehriban.

"*Apa*, she's one of us. She used to live in Almaty!" cried Samiya, delighted.

"We're from there as well," said Mehriban joyfully.

"My name is Aliya. I graduated in Almaty from the Foreign Languages Institute. I met an American called Henry, and we married. I've lived here for nine years now. We've got two children—a boy, who's nine, and Aya here, who is three. I want to go out and work, but I can't find a nanny to look after Aya."

They talked a while longer and then parted.

The next day was the eleventh of September 2001. That morning, after Samiya had gone to work, Mehriban switched on the television. All the channels were broadcasting one and the same thing—footage of two aircraft crashing into the Twin Towers of the World Trade Center in New York within a short interval. The skyscrapers soon collapsed and sent up immense clouds of dust. Terrified people were screaming and running in all directions. Of the commentary, Mehriban understood only "New York" and "September eleventh," and she wondered whether what she seeing was from a movie that was being made in the area.

Samiya came home soon after, and in her eyes was a look of fear. Glancing at the TV images, she said in a trembling voice, "*Apa*, I think a war's broken out."

"What are you talking about, Samiya?" asked Mehriban, horrified.

"Well, you've seen the pictures, haven't you? A group of terrorists have destroyed the Twin Towers, killing thousands of people who were inside. They sent us all home from college right away, both students and teachers. Nobody's working today."

"Oh, Allah, what's going to happen to us? Why don't we go home, daughter," she implored, badly shaken.

"There won't be any flights anywhere today or tomorrow. How do you propose to get away?"

On the television, the same footage was replayed over and over. Mother and daughter did not leave the apartment, afraid to miss some important piece of news, but no new information was given.

When night fell, the residents of the tall buildings gathered at the fountain. Each was holding a lit candle. They put the candles round the fountain to remember the dead and in prayer for peace in the world. Mehriban and Samiya were there, along with the two old Leningrad ladies, and Aliya and her husband. At some point they all sang the American national anthem and then began to disperse.

When they got back to the apartment, Samiya telephoned Polat-aka.

"They're hunting for the terrorists everywhere. There's a thorough search going on. Everything will be back to normal in a few days," Polat comforted her.

But for now, nothing was normal. Americans started killing Muslims in the street out of hatred. There were disturbances in the major American cities. "The police are monitoring the streets. The instigators of fights and disturbances are being arrested," ran the television commentaries. The government urged the people to be calm; the people, for the most part, were living in fear.

Mehriban noticed that the two elderly Russians had started to express hatred for the whole of the Arab world. She tried to give them her view. "It doesn't make sense to make a whole people your enemy because of a few terrorists."

She was due to return home in November, but after the events of September, she was afraid to leave her daughter behind. One hot Sunday in autumn, Samiya took her mother to the Chinatown district, with its crowd of banks, restaurants, its large bazaar, and many shops. Chinese people were talking loudly in their language, and Mehriban was taken aback. "They're behaving as if they were in their own country. Goodness, I feel like I've landed in China."

Samiya nodded at some stooping, wrinkled old women. "*Apa*, look, even these old Chinese women have left their home behind, so their children and grandchildren can grow up free." She smiled.

Mehriban thought for a while. Then they went into one of the Chinese restaurants for lunch. In the evening they returned home. Samiya seemed to be unable to say anything to her mother. Eventually she spoke but began from far away.

"*Apa*, do you remember how you cried and wanted to go home after your first month here?"

"Yes, of course I remember."

"But now you've gotten used to it, you can speak English, you've got friends. You've found out about the customs and cuisine of other nations, haven't you?"

"That's true. I've given my friends Uighur cooking several times. They liked it."

"And at first you didn't want to wear trousers, but now you wear nothing else. You go around in lovely blouses and look much younger. You've already started getting used to freedom. And now it's time for you to leave me and your friends…" sighed Samiya.

"And what else is there to do? It's not like you're coming back with me. You've gotten used to the life here," sighed her mother in turn. A few teardrops ran from her eyes.

"*Apa*, your visa is only for six months, but I could write to the immigration department, and they'll give you another six. What do you think of that?"

"I'd happily stay here if I felt needed. But you never have a minute to spare. You work from one Sunday to the next."

"Of course I love you being here. It makes me so happy to come home from work and see you coming to meet me—and can smell my favorite food waiting."

Mehriban thought for a while. She had telephoned Almaty only a few days earlier and spoken to Rukiyamana and Nuraniya. They told her that everybody was well at home. So she knew she could stay on with her daughter if she wished.

"All right, daughter, if they'll give me permission, I'll stay another half-year."

Samiya jumped up and down like a child. "You're the greatest mother in the world!" she exclaimed.

That evening they watched a TV show devoted to women, a project created by the African American journalist Oprah Winfrey. Mehriban was glued to the program until it ended. Noticing her mother's interest, Samiya told her a little about Oprah. "She's a famous journalist, and she's very rich. She invites the most celebrated actors, writers, and artists—anyone with a successful career—and introduces them on air. She also buys good books and introduces their authors to her viewers and gives out free copies to the studio audience."

Mehriban sensed a vague idea begin to develop. She thought of the manuscript she had left in her trunk at home. "Samiya, what do you think? If we translated my book into English and sent it to Oprah, would she like it?"

"It's perfectly possible," Samiya replied. "The Americans are always interested in the customs and traditions of other nations. Right, here's an idea. I'm giving private English lessons to five Chinese boys. I can save the money they pay me and give it to you to help publish the book."

Mehriban now felt sorry for her daughter. "Samiya, you mean to say that as well as working and studying, you're still tutoring people as well? You need to take more care of yourself."

"*Apa*, it's hard to manage here on just one job. I'm still young and healthy. But when I finish university, I'll be able to work in just one position because it'll be well paid."

"Very well, daughter, I'll get work as well and we can both put money toward publishing the book. But who'll give me a job?" she wondered.

As she said those words, Samiya's mobile telephone rang. It was Aliya.

"Let me talk with my mother and get back to you," said Samiya and hung up.

"What is she saying?" asked Mehriban.

"*Apa*, there's work for you right here. It's for Aliya. She wants someone to look after her little Aya five times a week from two to six. She'll pay you weekly."

Mehriban was delighted at the proposal. "Like they say, if you ask something of God, he will give it. And it's much better to have something to do, like looking after a child, than just wandering about," she said with a tone of certainty.

So now Mehriban studied English in the mornings and then from two to six she looked after the three-year-old Aya. Her experience of working in a kindergarten proved its worth; not only did she play with the little girl in the outdoor playground, but she also taught her a little. Aya quickly got used to Mehriban, and Mehriban, like a real American, no longer had any spare time.

Now that she was busy with work, the days passed quickly. Winter came, which in Los Angeles brings no frost, but frequent rain, more reminiscent for Mehriban of autumn. And soon Christmas and New Year were approaching. Shops, government buildings, and cinemas all decked themselves out with tall fir trees decorated with toys, ribbons, and shimmering garlands of various colors. Samiya took her mother and Halida for a drive along Los Angeles' wealthiest streets to enjoy the sights. Then they parked the car and strolled along Rodeo Drive in Beverly Hills, taking in the boutiques full of costly clothing, shoes, jewelry, and gold. Pointing the items in the shop windows out to her mother, Samiya said, "*Apa*, these shops are expensive. When I finish studying and get a good job, I'll buy you things from here—but for now we're just window shopping!"

"Just a minute, daughter," grinned Mehriban. "What do you think I've got to dress in these fancy brands for? I'm from a poor family in some isolated village. And suddenly I'm strolling along the wealthy quarters of LA, just like that. And it's a real delight!"

"Maybe God is rewarding you for all the suffering you endured and for all the good you've done for others," said Samiya with conviction.

"There are plenty of people in the world who suffered like that."

"But you've said yourself that happiness is given to one in a thousand. And you're that one in a thousand."

They visited more shops and later ate in an Italian restaurant. As they talked about what they had seen,

Halida told them how hard it had been for their family when she moved to America. "My parents couldn't find work that suited their experience and qualifications. My mother eventually got a job as domestic help, and I used to help her. We earned just enough to pay the bills. We bought our groceries at the cheapest possible shops. I used to cry with envy at the sight of children who could enjoy ice creams and other treats.

"One day, my mother got work once a week in a certain household. As usual, I went along to help. And I bumped into one of my classmates because it was her mother who had hired us. I was so ashamed that I ran into the bathroom and burst into tears. My mother followed me, apologizing for putting me in such an awkward position, and then she cried too. When we left, my classmate's mother secretly gave me money, so I could buy myself an ice cream. Next day I went to school, dreading that my classmate would tell everybody. But she simply said hello to me as though nothing had happened. I was so relieved. But my mother and I never went to work in that house again."

"You have been through hard times too," said Mehriban.

"Yes, we have, though thankfully things are good now. We are US citizens and have gotten used to living here."

"*Apa*, in March I can get a US passport. And then they can give you a green card," said Samiya.

"What would I want a green card for?"

"It'll let you come to America whenever you want. You won't need a visa."

"Do you think I'll be coming here again?"

"Of course I do! Remember you had your dream of appearing on Oprah's show?" laughed Samiya.

Halida looked bemused at Samiya, understanding nothing. Samiya explained to her about her mother's manuscript and her desire to meet Oprah.

"If you desire something, it must necessarily come to pass," said Halida.

The days raced by. Soon it was spring, and on 19 March 2002 some seven hundred people gathered in the city of Pomona, California to receive their American passports. They had their relatives with them; Samiya took along her mother and Halida. A representative of the state of California announced the purpose of the occasion and handed off to a judge, who called upon the new citizens to vow to observe the laws of the land. Next, each of the new citizens was given their passport and their name was read out. Among the hundreds of people of diverse nationalities who received their certificate of US citizenship was Samiya, the young Uighur. Once the issuing of documents was completed, a singer took the stage and began to sing the national anthem of the United States. The thousands of people in the hall stood and joined in, and then applauded warmly and at length. When the ceremony ended, they filed out of the hall full of hope and happiness.

This was a big event for Samiya. Mehriban and Halida congratulated her joyfully; Polat and Farida called her, inviting mother and daughter over that evening to celebrate.

Soon afterward, Samiya sent off her mother's documents so that she could be issued a green card. She meanwhile sat the Graduate Management Admission

Test (GMAT) that would entitle her to apply to UCLA. Her university entrance application had to be accompanied by two essays, of which one could be on a subject of her choice. The title she chose was "The Lives of My Ancestors." As soon as she heard that she had passed the GMAT, she sent the essays and application off to UCLA. Now she had only to wait.

Mehriban shortly received a summons to an interview with the immigration department. On the appointed day, she and her daughter went to the office and were called into an interview room. The officer, an African American, examined Mehriban's documents and asked her a series of questions. Samiya acted as interpreter. After the interview, they photographed Mehriban for her document.

As they came out of the office, they saw a long queue. "Are all these people waiting for a green card?" asked Mehriban.

"Yes. But yours will be sent to my address," sighed Samiya with relief. "We've just done something very important."

"What a huge building, and how clean it is inside!" observed Mehriban. "Hundreds of people in that queue, but nobody is pushing or arguing."

"Well, when you get back to Almaty, you can tell everybody about the things you've seen here," laughed Samiya.

"I definitely will, it'll be like telling them a fairy tale. Samiya, all the good things I've seen here are thanks to you. It's only a pity that your father didn't live to see this." Mehriban's eyes filled with tears.

"I think of my father's short life like a bright star that burned out early. His spirit is with me all the time."

On the way home, Samiya parked near the intersection of Pico Boulevard and Beverwil Drive. "*Apa*, I wanted to take you to a Japanese restaurant here," said Samiya in a solemn tone of voice.

A Japanese waitress of about fifty in a black apron and with short hair met them as they entered. She showed them inside and ushered them to a table by the window, all the while smiling and bowing low to the guests. The small restaurant was busy. Mehriban looked around her attentively. "Why are the curtains, tablecloths and even the aprons all black?" she asked.

"That's the house style," said Samiya.

The middle-aged waitress came up to them again, smiling and handed them the menu. She bowed and moved away with soft, small steps. When she saw that Samiya was ready to order, she returned with a notepad and pen. Samiya ordered miso soup, sushi, salmon in teriyaki sauce, and for dessert, fried ice cream.

The waitress came back almost immediately with two cups and a pot of a rich green tea. Also on the table were soy sauce, a red chili dressing, and salted soy beans, all in tiny ceramic dishes. As they were sipping the tea, the miso soup arrived in two wooden bowls. Samiya saw that Mehriban was peering at the thick soup with its green garnish. "*Apa*, the black bits are seaweed, it's very good for you. And this is *tofu*, made of soy." She took a spoonful of the soup and began to eat.

Mehriban liked the miso soup. When they had finished it, the waitress brought two square dishes and placed a serving of sushi in front of Samiya and the salmon teriyaki in front of Mehriban.

"What's that bright green paste you've got there, the size of a teaspoon?" asked Mehriban.

"This is a very strong garnish called wasabi. And this is finely chopped ginger that they serve only in small amounts. And the black here is nori, which is dried seaweed. They lay this out and put rice, fish and cucumber on top, then roll it up into little tubes. And look at this—it's nigiri sushi, rice pressed into little balls by hand, on top of which they put thin slices of raw fish," Samiya went on.

Samiya poured some soy sauce into a small ceramic dish, added a little wasabi, and mixed them thoroughly with a small rod. She then took a piece of sushi, dipped it into the sauce and put it into her mouth with relish. Meanwhile Mehriban was enjoying her tender piece of salmon in teriyaki sauce. "This is delicious. It just melts in the mouth. The cooks here must be from Japan."

"When anyone opens a restaurant here serving a national cuisine, they invite top-class chefs who are the best at preparing their national dishes. All these restaurants are competing for customers. Did you see the sign on the door with the letter A? That means that this restaurant was awarded the highest grade by the California food hygiene inspectorate," Samiya said.

The waitress took away their empty plates, then brought desert in two small dishes—each with three balls of ice cream the size of walnuts. "I've never seen ice cream fried in butter before," said Mehriban, looking at it with amazement.

"They roll the balls of ice cream in soy meal and drop them for a moment into very hot butter, then quickly take them out again. The soy meal is done in a flash, but the ice cream doesn't have time to melt. It doesn't lose its shape. Try it."

Mehriban liked the taste of the ice cream. Afterward, the waitress brought the bill and then showed them to the door, smiling and bowing all the way. "Arigato," she said.

Samiya responded in kind. "Arigato!"

"See, that's real Japanese culture for you," said Samiya. "Not only do they thank you, but they go with you right to the door, as though you were esteemed personal visitors."

"It will be a long time before we reach that level of service culture in our country," said Mehriban.

When they got home, Samiya found the letter she had been waiting for. She tore the envelope open, quickly read the contents, and leaped for joy. "*Apa*, they've accepted me for university! And I'll get a state grant to pay for it!" She threw herself onto her mother's feet and shed tears. Her mother stood up, hugged her, and also wept.

"It's true, you know. They say that God takes care of orphans," said Mehriban over and over.

Samiya telephoned Polat at once to tell him the good news, then began ringing round all her friends.

Next day Mehriban prepared a meal and invited Polat's family over for dinner. Polat, sitting in the place of honor, said slowly and in a calm voice: "When I talked to your daughter for the first time, I could see that she was clever and also brave, and I realized straight away that she would do well in America. It seems I was right."

"And in the past six years, Samiya has done an awful lot," added Farida. "She arrived in a strange land, found work and started studying, and now she's made it to university—and with a grant to pay for it. Not everybody's capable of this. It's a great joy for us, and indeed for all the Uighurs living here."

"And I couldn't have done all this without you," said Samiya, trying not to cry.

"I'm so pleased that my daughter lives in this great city among such kindly people, and that she's got her own place. I will be leaving soon, and I leave my daughter in your care," said Mehriban, unable to hold back her tears.

Polat smiled as he looked at the women, so deeply moved. "Don't cry, Mehriban. As soon as you get the green card, you can come here again. You've already got used to America." He smiled.

"*Hanum*, you've become so much younger since you came here," said Farida jokingly. "They may not recognize you back in Almaty."

They went on talking for a long time about the Uighurs, their history, and destiny. Polat had an expressive way with words and could talk beautifully and in depth. Mehriban was amazed at his intelligence, and at the simplicity with which he spoke. Later she served them all *aktyan-chay* and hot *samsas*.

"However many good things we are able to eat, if you don't drink *aktyan-chay*, something's missing," said Farida, gulping the hot tea.

"I do love your flaky *samsas*," said Halida, tucking in hungrily.

Samiya put on a recording by the "Dervish" ensemble that her mother had brought from Kazakhstan. The singer Dulmat Baharov sang Mehriban's favorite song: "A Mother's Legacy." They all sat listening.

"It's a wonderful song. The words are very moving," said Farida. "Mehriban, can you write out the lyrics for me?"

It was evident from her sad eyes that Farida was missing the lands of her home and the people she was close to there. Halida noticed this too. "*Apa*, I'll give you a copy of it, and you can listen to it in the car," she said.

That evening Mehriban thanked Polat's family many times for having shared their good fortune and been a support to Samiya.

The time for Mehriban's departure was drawing near. She filled her big black case with clothes, plus gifts for her relatives. Samiya kept her word and gave her the money she had saved so that she could publish her book.

Samiya and Halida went with Mehriban to the airport. The closer the hour of departure came, the greater was the longing and pain in Mehriban's heart. She did not want to be separated from her only daughter. But finally the time came. She hugged Samiya and kissed her. "My clever, clever daughter! Take care of yourself! I hope you will achieve all your goals."

Then she kissed Halida and said to her: "Look after each other, be like family. Don't drift apart."

Mehriban turned and walked off to her terminal. Samiya, suddenly forlorn, stood still, watching her go.

Toward evening on the next day, Samiya telephoned Almaty. When she knew that Mehriban had safely arrived home, she felt better and was able to throw herself back into her work again.

• • •

"Many people dream of living in America, but you went back home. Didn't you like it?" asked Ruth.

"I loved it, of course, but all the same, my roots are stronger in my home country," said Mehriban. "Los Angeles is amazing. I made friends there. I found out about life for ordinary Americans, and I could be with my daughter. But there's a Uighur proverb: "Better to be a poor man in your own country than a sultan in a foreign land." After living in America for a year, I understood what this means," said Mehriban.

"You may well be right," said Ruth thoughtfully.

28

RECOGNITION

While Mehriban was spending her year in America, considerable changes took place at home. Many of the young people had children, and some of the old took their leave of this world and closed their eyes forever. On her return, Mehriban learned that Rukiyam-ana had died. Less than forty days had passed. Mehriban went at once to see her children, Nazar, Guzyal, and Nuraniya, to offer her condolences.

A few days later, she traveled to Zharkent. She fell into memories during the journey, and when she reached Bolshoy Chigan, she went straight away to Turgan-aka's house. She saw that her brother and his wife Rana-hada had grown older. Two pretty little girls came out to greet Mehriban.

"The grandchildren have grown up and are already helping us around the house," said Rana.

"Goodness, are these Murat's girls?" Mehriban could not believe her eyes.

"Yes. Murat's living with us. And our daughter-in-law's a quiet, good woman. The youngest has moved out, but his house is nearby, and he often calls in. As for us, well, we've gotten older, as you can see," sighed Turgan.

Rana sent one of the girls to fetch her family, while she and the others set the *dzhoza*. While they were drinking tea, in came Saadat, Modangul, and Mahinur. They greeted Mehriban warmly. "You look very well. I see your daughter's taken good care of you."

"So how is my granddaughter that I used to look after?" asked Saadat.

"Samiya's doing very well. She's working and studying. At the moment, studying is her only focus. She sends heartfelt *salams* to you all."

"She probably wants to get to the cutting edge of knowledge," said Turgan in admiration. "If she goes to university and studies well, she may stay in America."

"Well, it wouldn't be bad to have at least one educated person among us," said Saadat approvingly.

Mehriban meanwhile opened a large bag and handed out gifts that Samiya had sent to her relatives.

"Oh Lord, we should have sent her presents as well," exclaimed Modangul.

Surprised and delighted, the women looked at what they had been given. Mehriban felt so happy to watch them that it was as though the gifts had been for her.

"I hope you'll be staying with us here for a couple of weeks?" asked Mahinur.

"Of course she'll stay! We haven't seen her for a whole year after all! said Saadat firmly.

"Yes, please, I'd love to stay a little," said Mehriban. "Then I can go and give my sympathies to the people who've lost folk and congratulate the ones who've married."

"None of the old people are left now. Now we're the old ones," said Turgan.

At this point, Amanzhan and Guzyal came in, greeted Mehriban, and hugged her. It seemed to Mehriban that Amanzhan had grown a little older as well. Which was only to be expected; people in this village still worked hard and without concern for themselves. They had to look after their animals and tend the vegetable gardens, and nobody would survive the winter if they did not prepare for it.

"How are you keeping?" she asked her favorite nephew and childhood friend.

Amanzhan replied without hurrying. "We've set up our own agricultural venture. We're growing maize at the moment. Our Guzyal's getting her pension now. The grandson is growing up at home."

"But what a joy, to be bringing up a grandchild!" exclaimed Mehriban.

Guzyal gave Mehriban an admiring look. "Los Angeles has made you younger. I see the climate has been good for you."

"Well yes, for sure, and I didn't have to milk a cow or grow vegetables. For the first month I couldn't get used to life in America, and I really longed to see your faces," admitted Mehriban. She went on then to tell them about what she had seen and learned while abroad.

"You don't mean to say that all Samiya's doing is studying?" asked Amanzhan. "We thought you'd gone to give her away."

"Samiya hasn't the slightest interest in marrying yet. And I've been longing for grandchildren," sighed Mehriban.

"When the right time comes, she won't ask anybody," Saadat observed. "She'll marry herself to whatever fate may have in store for her."

"Tell us about the Uighurs living in Los Angeles," said Modangul.

Mehriban described Polat's family and how hospitable and kind they had been. Polat, she said, was both a very learned man and very generous. She described the Uighurs who kept up their customs and language. The others listened with interest.

"And when will you publish your book, Mehriban?" asked Amanzhan abruptly.

"I'll be working on that as soon as I get back to Almaty, *inshallah*."

"If you need money, I'll help you."

"Thank you, Amanzhan. Samiya's already given me some money for publication."

"Seitzhan was right to call her his 'girl-*dzhigit*'," said Saadat. "See how brave she's been to cross the ocean in pursuit of her path."

Hearing these compliments about Samiya, Mehriban felt proud of her. But she was hoping that Samiya would marry soon and give her a grandchild.

Ten days later Mehriban returned to Almaty and took her manuscript to a publishing house. She was instructed to discuss the text with some experts, make some amendments to the text, and perform a few preparatory tasks. These visits and discussions with people proved more tiring for Mehriban than the writing itself had been.

When she was able to hold an advance copy of *A Mother's Testament* in her hands, however, all her difficulties disappeared. The tiredness of many days evaporated in an instant. One night she reread the book from cover to cover, and again she wondered at the courage of the heroes and heroines of the story, their dedication and bravery. Once more she saw the old Uighur women, selfless mothers, in their old dresses, with *ketmens* on their shoulders, going out to the fields. Overwhelmed at the feelings that now rose in her, Mehriban wept softly. She felt as though the spirits of the women she had written about were pleased with her.

That same day, Amanzhan came to dinner. He picked up the book, examined it, leafed through it and read a little. Then he took an envelope out of his pocket and handed it to her. "Brilliant, Mehri! Here is a *korumluk* for the book," he smiled.

"Thank you so much, my dear!" said Mehriban, a little embarrassed. "If everyone who reads this gives me a present, I'll soon be rich," she grinned.

"Well, you've achieved the objective you set yourself," said Amanzhan. "And thanks to you, the mothers of Bolshoy Chigan are forever inscribed in the history of our people."

"That all sounds very well," said Mehriban, "but first read the book through, and then tell me what you think."

"I'm here in Almaty for a couple of days for work. I'll read it through while I'm here, then I'll give you my views."

They sat and drank tea, continuing to talk about the book.

"Amanzhan, I'd like to organize a *nazyr* at the village, an evening for remembering our ancestors, and give copies of the book to them. What do you think?"

"That's an excellent idea. But why don't I organize the evening while you concentrate on publicizing your book."

"That would be wonderful, thank you. In a few days, I'll send Samiya a few copies in America."

Amanzhan took the copy of *A Mother's Testament* into the end room and began to read. He read through the night, finishing the book just before dawn, by which time he could not fall asleep. The book stirred up memories in him. Many images and events candidly and vividly described, drew him into deep reverie. When Mehriban began to prepare breakfast, Amanzhan followed her into the kitchen.

"Mehriban, I hadn't imagined that you could write so well," he said, looking at her with new eyes. "It felt as though I was there in those times and saw those heroes with my own eyes. At times, I was moved to tears." He hugged Mehriban and kissed her.

Mehriban was touched. "Well, I hope that the book will become a testament to the women of Bolshoy Chigan for future generations. May it be an example to the young."

After breakfast, Amanzhan left for work. Left by herself, Mehriban again and again pressed the book to her bosom. How much effort had she put into that book, how much love had she poured out!

The final edition of the book came out a short while later. Mehriban took part of the print run with her to Bolshoy Chigan, and on the appointed evening, Amanzhan held a big *nazyr* in the village club. Mehriban gave copies of *A Mother's Testament* to all who came.

The greatest acclaim an artist can receive is recognition by the public, and this is what Mehriban received from her fellow villagers. Many of those who read it telephoned her later in Almaty to thank her and wish her success. This gave Mehriban inspiration to pursue further artistic endeavors.

Back in Almaty, Mehriban was also waiting for another joyful arrival—a letter from Samiya containing a green card with which she could visit the USA again. Samiya wrote that she had enjoyed the book very much and thought that it should be published in English as well. She would then try to arrange for Mehriban to come and meet Oprah Winfrey. At the end of the letter, Samiya wrote:

> *Apa, now you've got a green card and you can come to America whenever you wish. I miss you and can't wait to see you again.*

She picked up the green card itself and examined it. Now she would have to save up the money to go and see Samiya again. She realized that since her stay in America she had also changed. She missed not only her daughter and her other friends in Los Angeles but also the dynamism of American life.

Her thoughts were interrupted by Rosa. "Mehriban-hada, tomorrow I start teaching English!" she said, unable to contain herself.

Mehriban had come to love this pretty, black-eyed girl with expressive eyebrows like her own. "And it's time for me to get to work as well," she said, looking at the window.

"Hada, there's a *muqam* evening tonight at the Uighur Theater," Rosa went on. "I've got us both tickets."

Mehriban acquiesced with delight to going to the theater. She had been missing her favorite melodies and songs.

The curtain went up at seven o'clock. On the stage sat a group of musicians in bright national costume. They were holding Uighur folk instruments: the *dap*, the *bas hushtar*, the *gezhyak*, the *satar*, the *chan*, the *ravap*, the *dutar*, the *tambir*, the *nay*, and the *dolan ravap*. Mehriban was proud that her people had always been considered musically gifted and had a rich artistic heritage. The players accompanied various singers who came on to perform the *muqams*, their names well known to the Uighur audience: Nuralyam Kurbanbaki-eva, Sahibyam Myashryapova, Tolunay Aysarova, Dilbirim Burhanova, Luiza Rosahunova, Martazhan Mametbakiev, Nuralim Varisov and Parhat Davutov.

The men had brightly colored embroidered *dopas* on their heads and wore satin shirts with stand-up collars. Over them they wore short *chapans* in red velour, embroidered with Uighur patterns. All this was completed by black trousers and gleaming calf-leather boots. As for the women, also in skullcaps, they wore fine chiffon dresses richly decorated with floral and leaf patterns, with sleeves glinting with golden threads. Over the dress, they wore a sleeveless blouse. Big gold crescent-moon earrings hung from their ears, and beautiful beads and *tumars* covered with precious stones adorned their necks. Coins flashed and jingled in their hair, and their shoes had high heels. Each performer's costume was inimitable.

Now the musicians struck up and the series of *muqam* commenced. Mehriban was transfixed; she opened herself completely to the music. The whole audience, indeed, sat rapt and transported to the distant past, when those ancient melodic forms were created. For Mehriban, they represented the music of the centuries. Her eyes filled with tears. The lives of her ancestors had been filled with suffering, and so their songs reflected sadness and human tragedy.

When the *muqam* "Mashrap Nyagmisi" began, little girls flitted onto the stage like white swans and began to dance. They were all of the same height, and all had their hair pleated. Their clothes were light and colorful, and it was impossible to tear one's eyes from their graceful movements.

At the end of the concert, loud applause filled the hall, and flowers were presented to the performers. Mehriban and Rosa were so thrilled by what they had heard and seen that they continued talking about it as they walked home. "The twelve *muqams* are the pride of our people, the legacy of our forebears," said Mehriban proudly.

"But how old are they? When did *muqams* start to be composed?" asked Rosa.

"Well, Azat Burhanov, an academician of the International Informatization Academy, an NGO linked to the United Nations, who directs the "Nava" ensemble, said that the roots of the *muqam* lie in antiquity. In the sixteenth century, during the rule of Abdureshid Khan in the city of Yarkand, his young wife, the *muqamchi* and poetess Amanisa Khan, formed a group of musicians, together with Kidirhan Yarkyandy. This group collected together and sorted all twelve of the *muqams*. Later, in 1950, the government of the Xinjiang Uighur Autonomous Region commissioned a group of composers to write the *muqams* down in musical notation. They used the songs of the Kashgar *muqamchi* Tudahun Alnagma as a model. And that's how this priceless musical treasure has been preserved.

"Then in 2000, the "Nava" ensemble, under the composer Ikram Masimov, learned the *muqam* "Mushavryak" and performed it at a festival in Turkey. They played for an hour and a half! I don't know whether the audience could understand the words or not, but our music certainly made an impression. The applause at the end was thunderous, and all the performers were given flowers."

"Do other peoples have *muqams* too?" asked Rosa.

"Yes, but not as many as we have," said Mehriban.

The two women, one old and the other young, went on sharing their impressions long into the night, until they fell into the arms of sleep...

• • •

"So Uighur musical culture seems to be highly developed," observed Ruth. "It's great that you have preserved the *muqams* and can transmit them down the generations." She spoke with admiration.

"Well, the book I wrote is my small contribution to the development of that same culture—my testament for future generations," replied Mehriban.

29

THE BOOK OF LIFE

As soon as Samiya graduated from university, she and an American friend, Melissa, opened a tourism bureau. The first two years were difficult; the girls worked hard to find paths to develop their business. They studied and went on doing other work. Gradually the agency grew in popularity; the number of staff increased, and eventually Samiya was elected the president of the young company. She was attentive to her colleagues and treated them calmly and considerately. They respected her for this. And now that things were running more smoothly, Samiya began to look for a literary agent who would arrange for *A Mother's Testament* to be published in English.

She began by contacting agents with a query and placing few posts online. Several people responded almost immediately. Samiya was particularly interested in a reply she received from a young woman called Danielle and proposed straight away that they meet.

Danielle lived in Malibu, California. She had been born in Ogden, Utah into a white-collar family. She had a younger brother. She had been educated at Pepperdine University in Malibu. Since then, she had worked in a PR agency. Samiya liked Danielle straight away. She was tall and thin and had straight hair and open features. From what she told her it was clear that her parents were also open and honest people.

"Would you read my mother's manuscript, please, and let me know what you think?" asked Samiya, handing her a folder containing the text. "It would mean a lot to me to be able to publish this. Firstly, because it would enable American readers to learn about our people, and secondly because it would make my mother's dream come true."

"OK, I'll read it through, and then I'll call you. Then we can discuss things in detail," promised Danielle.

They parted warmly, like old friends. Once more, Samiya felt certain that she was surrounded by good people. A few days later, Danielle telephoned and suggested that they meet in a coffee shop. As they sat together over their coffee, Samiya could not restrain herself any longer. "What do you think of the book? I really need to know."

Danielle swallowed, thought for a moment, and then smiled. "That book has opened my eyes to a lot of things. Although my culture has different religious beliefs and customs, we are all in this world to love and be loved, and we are all trying to find our path to happiness. We raise children and teach them wise things, and dream of watching them learn to stand on their own two feet and realize their own dreams." She looked into Samiya's eyes. "Samiya, I need to say that your mother is a very loving woman. As a writer, she tries to understand and communicate the interior state even of the 'bad' characters. Books like this touch the heart. I'm sure that this one is dear to more people than just your mother. It will be much loved by a lot of people."

Samiya felt immense joy on hearing Danielle's comments. "Danielle, this makes me so happy," she confided, not hiding her feelings. "The opinions of a professional are very important, and because of what you have said, my happiness knows no bounds. You are the first American to have read the book, and so everything you say is valuable." She stood up.

Danielle stood up too and they hugged one another. "Now, I'll find an editor and give them the manuscript," she said in a business-like manner. "They may print just a small run of the book to start with."

"Will I need to meet the editor?" asked Samiya.

"No, I'll take care of the whole process from now on. That's my job after all. As soon as the book is ready, I'll call you," said Danielle, who then hurriedly took her leave.

Months went by, but Danielle did not call. Samiya felt awkward about reminding her or asking about progress, so she refrained and waited. Then one morning, just as Samiya was arriving at her office, her mobile rang.

"Samiya, guess what news I've got for you!" It was Danielle, her voice was excited.

"Hurry and tell me. Don't torment me," implored Samiya.

"We have a publisher for your book! Congratulations!"

Samiya stood dumbfounded for a few seconds, then felt a tide of exultation. "Thank you, Danielle, so much. I'd like to invite you to join us tonight at Il Fornaio in Santa Monica. Can you come?" she asked, her voice ringing with joy.

"Yes, I can come. How about at seven?"

Samiya invited Halida and Melissa to join them. After work she went home, took a shower, set her hair, and put on white trousers and a white blouse, black high-heeled shoes, and to complete the ensemble, she carried a small black handbag. Before leaving the house, she glanced at herself in the mirror. On the way, she stopped at a florist and bought an elegant bouquet of roses.

The restaurant was not far from the ocean. Danielle arrived almost immediately after Samiya. She was also holding a bouquet of flowers. They looked at each other and burst out laughing. Danielle was first to give her bouquet of flowers to Samiya, congratulating her.

"Danielle, it was you who made this project happen. It was so important for me. So I congratulate you too," said Samiya, holding out her bouquet to her.

A waitress showed them to a table and put both bouquets into a vase of water. Without further ado, Danielle took the sample book out of her bag and handed it to Samiya. "Your dream has come true!" she said solemnly.

"Thank you again, a thousand times, Danielle. This book has made us friends for life," she said with emotion.

"Agreed—we're friends forever now," she answered, clearly similarly moved.

Halida and Melissa now joined them. Samiya introduced Danielle to them. "From today, Danielle is a friend of all of us," she announced. "May our circle of friends grow larger."

A waiter, tall, swarthy, and handsome, came up to them. "Good evening, *signorini*. My name is Mario, and I'm your waiter this evening," he said, handing them each a menu.

"OK, everybody, choose whatever you'd like," said Samiya excitedly. "I'm inviting you all."

"But what's the celebration today? It isn't your birthday, is it?" asked Halida, bewildered.

"I'll tell you later." Samiya smiled, exchanging glances with Danielle.

"Are you ready to order, *signorini?*" The smiling waiter came up to them, notepad in hand. There was a distinctly Italian accent to his English.

"Let's begin with salads and water," said Samiya, then turned to the others. "Well, girls, what would you like to drink?"

"Why don't we order a bottle of Chianti?" suggested Danielle.

"And have you chosen your dishes?" asked the waiter.

"I'd like *linguini more chiako*," said Samiya.

"And can I have my favorite, *turtei con aragosta?* asked Danielle.

"Well, I'm on a diet, but tonight I'll break it and have *cannelloni al forno*," added Melissa.

"As for me, I always have *lasagna ferrarese* when I'm eating Italian," said Halida.

"And would you like to order desserts?" asked Mario.

Samiya ordered her favorite *tiramisu*, while the others opted for Italian ice cream.

A few minutes later, Mario returned with a large tray with the salads and four pieces of *bruschetta*, rubbed with garlic and browned in the oven. The bread was garnished with pieces of tomato and sprinkled with finely chopped basil. Mario divided the salads onto two plates and poured water into their glasses. Into another glass he poured a little red wine and offered it to Samiya. She sniffed the wine, then sipped it, rolling it about her tongue. She swallowed and nodded agreement. Now Mario poured wine for the other three at the table.

Eventually Samiya decided it was time to announce to her friends the reason for having invited them. She took the book out of her bag and showed it to them. "This is my mother's book. It's just been published in English. This has been made possible thanks to the professionalism of Danielle here, who acted as my mother's literary agent. I wanted to invite you tonight in order to share my happiness, and of course, to express my appreciation to our new friend."

A little stunned by this news, the girls all raised their glasses. "Samiya, that's a wonderful gift for your talented mother. I congratulate you from the bottom of my heart," said Melissa, hugging her.

Halida gave Samiya a significant look and added, "Now that the book's been published, Samiya has another task—another of her mother's dreams to fulfill."

"You mean your mother has another dream?" asked Danielle.

"She's wanted to appear on Oprah's TV show as the author of this book for a long time."

The waiter brought the main courses, wished them *buon appetite,* and moved away. Samiya enjoyed her dish, which reminded her of chopped Uighur *laghman.* It contained seafood, cheese, and a creamy sauce and was sprinkled with finely chopped basil. Danielle's, in turn, consisted of large round *pelmeny* stuffed with lobster meat and poured over with onion, seafood, and tomatoes in a creamy sauce. A sprig of green basil lay to one side. Melissa had wide tubes of *cannelloni* filled with chicken, spinach, mushrooms, dried tomatoes, and mozzarella. Again, this was all baked in a creamy sauce and sprinkled with basil. As for Halida, her *lasagna* consisted of rectangular sheets of pasta, between which alternated minced meat with mushrooms and a tomato sauce with parmesan.

Eating and drinking with relish, the girls did not stop talking. Danielle gave Samiya a look. "I'm still thinking about your mother's second wish. Why don't we invite her over here before we start selling the initial print run."

"What for?" asked Samiya.

"We could organize presentations of the book at universities. People will buy it and ask your mother to sign it. And after that, the publisher could print a bigger run."

Melissa now joined in. "And if Oprah saw a copy, she'd probably be interested."

"If she got interested in the Uighurs living in Kazakhstan, that would be incredible," exclaimed Halida.

The deserts arrived. "Well, girls, too bad you didn't order the *tiramisu*. It's just heavenly," teased Samiya.

"Alas, we're on a diet." Melissa affected a sigh, picking languidly at her ice cream. The others laughed.

The waiter brought Samiya the bill. "Leave the tip to us," said Danielle. "The service was very good."

"No," said Samiya firmly, "you're my guests tonight." She added a tip of twenty percent to the bill.

"That's a lot for a tip," said Halida, shaking her head.

"It's reasonable. I used to be a waitress, and I know how hard the work is."

"But I know why you gave Mario twenty percent. It wasn't for his service but because he's gorgeous!"

They all laughed again. The waiter thanked Samiya and handed them their bouquets. The girls bade their fond farewells, then each got into her own car and drove home.

As soon as she got home, Samiya telephoned her mother and told her the news. "*Apa*, you need to come to America again," she said persuasively.

"But Turgan-aka is very ill. How can I leave him? Suppose something should happen?" said Mehriban sadly.

"*Apa*, you don't need to be here for very long. But it's essential that you come," said Samiya, and then explained the situation.

Once again Mehriban put aside her cares and duties to travel to Los Angeles. Danielle arranged a presentation of *A Mother's Testament* at Pepperdine, where she herself had studied, and then at UCLA, where Samiya had studied, and finally at Santa Monica College. The small print run sold out in a flash. Never had Mehriban been so happy. She felt like a bird soaring in the sky with her wings spread wide.

But her joy turned out to be short-lived.

• • •

"Presentations and meetings like that must be hugely inspiring," said Ruth.

"Absolutely! I got a huge creative stimulus."

"And maybe, if I told you my life-story, would you feel like writing another book? What if the heroine of your next book was me?" Ruth asked cautiously.

"Well it's entirely possible that the story of your life could be the subject of my next book," Mehriban nodded. "Everybody has a life that is worthy of an absorbing book. But I'm not making any rash promises. Time will tell," she said thoughtfully.

30

THE AMERICAN'S SECRET

It was after midnight when the mother and daughter were woken by the telephone call. Samiya spoke briefly, then hung up and said quietly, "*Apa*, Turgan-aka has passed away."

At these words, tears began to run from Mehriban's eyes. Samiya hugged her and said, "Don't cry, *apa*, calm down. If you like, I'll get you a ticket tomorrow and you can fly back. But even then, you won't make it for the funeral, because they're burying him tomorrow."

"I'm going anyway, Samiya, even if I do miss the funeral. For us, Turgan-aka was like a father. Oh my Turgan! He never let the fire go out that was lit by my parents, and so I must certainly go."

"*Apa*, don't be cross with me, but I'm worried about you—and I need my mother as well. Eighteen hours of flying isn't easy. If you add the waiting time at the airports, it will take you twenty-four hours to get there."

"Well, come what may, I'm used to flying now, so don't you worry. Your mother is a strong woman," she said and again burst into tears.

Realizing that her mother was not going to back down, Samiya helped her prepare for her journey. Mehriban did not close her eyes all night, but instead talked to her daughter about the hard lives of her parents and relatives.

Samiya bought a ticket the next day, and at seven o'clock that evening, she put her mother on her flight. Late that night she telephoned Rosa and asked her to meet her mother and go with her to Zharkent.

Mehriban waited at Amsterdam for about four hours for the flight to Almaty, where she arrived at five in the morning. She and Rosa took a taxi bound for Zharkent and set off straight away. The journey from Los Angeles to Zharkent had taken twenty-eight hours, and they arrived at her brother's house at ten o'clock. So what they say is true, "When you hear of death, you'll travel from the ends of the earth."

Turgan and Rana always used to come out smiling to greet Mehriban at the gate. This time, however, the gates were flung wide open, and there was no brother to greet her. Unable to contain her sorrow any longer, Mehriban broke into loud sobs, then went into the house to greet the women, relatives and close friends, who were sitting there with white shawls on their heads. They were already preparing for the memorial meal for the third day after Turgan's death. The three sisters, now parted from the brother who had always been a mountain of support to them, wept long and hard. But what could they do? No matter how much we try to comfort ourselves, telling ourselves that the world is unjust, we can never extinguish the flame of longing for a person dear to us, however much time may pass.

Several months passed. One day, Samiya telephoned from America, saying, "*Apa*, your dream is coming true. You need to come back to the States." Mehriban understood at once. Although she did not feel happy, she thought to herself, *How right it would be if my parents—my father and my mother, who went through such hardships to raise and educate us—and my two brothers, Tursun and Turgan, who were such supports, could hear about my successes and could see my happiness.* Tears poured from her eyes. And in truth, had they been alive, surely, they would have been pleased for Mehriban? With these thoughts and dreams foremost in her mind, Mehriban found herself once more on a plane bound for America.

● ● ●

Ruth was silent for a while, and then she spoke. "Mehriban, for the whole of this journey I've listened to your story, and I realize how much you've been through. You know the price of life, and you've overcome every obstacle. I think that you have found happiness. Compared with yours, I had a cloudless childhood. But a different misfortune awaited me. I lost my happiness because I was proud and stubborn. I always thought that my opinion was the most important, and I alienated the people who were close to me because I did not respect them." The American looked out of the window, where white clouds were drifting past. "So now, let me tell you my story."

"When I left university I started work and thought more about my career than about getting married.

But after I turned thirty, I decided it was time to start having a personal life. I married a very wealthy man. A year later, we had a son, and his father called him Peter. But I soon got bored sitting at home with the child and just a couple of days after he was born, I went back to work. We hired a nanny to look after Peter, just as we had a cook to prepare our meals and a housemaid to do the cleaning. My husband and I went out early in the mornings and came back late at night. Occupied with our business, we did not notice Peter growing up.

"He grew into a tall, handsome, clever young man who got into university easily. He wanted to become a lawyer. I noticed that he had his own opinions about everything, and that he stuck to them obstinately. Well, one day our housemaid left. To replace her, I hired a girl from Mexico. Soledad was dark haired, with big eyes and dark skin. She was quite pretty. Admittedly, her English was not very good. None of this would have mattered, of course, but I noticed that Peter was developing feelings for her. We tried to explain to him that an uneducated Mexican girl would not be his equal. He openly confessed, however, that the girl was expecting his child. Now there was a serious conflict. We gave our son an ultimatum: either he give up the Mexican girl, or we would close his bank account and stop paying his university fees, and on top of that, we would remove his name from our will. All this was an attempt to scare him. But Peter got seriously angry.

"I don't need anything from you. I will not leave Soledad and my son. You took care of me, and now it's my turn to take care of my son." Saying this, he walked out of the house.

"My husband and I were left by ourselves in our huge house. Still, we didn't try to find our son or bring him back. We were sure he would soon ditch the Mexican and return to his normal life. But it all turned out differently. Pete gave up his studies. He and Soledad moved to New York. He took a two-year course and became a firefighter. They called their son Alex. They wrote to us when he was born, but we did not respond to this news. As ever, we were indignant and were living in hope that one day he would come to his senses.

"You can see, Mehriban, how stupid we were. Because we were so arrogant, we rejected our own grandson, we didn't try to understand our son, and we wouldn't share our money with their family. Goddamned pride! We heard rumors that Soledad improved her English, went to college, and then got a job. But we had no idea of the difficulties Pete and Soledad went through in setting up home and raising their son. As always, thinking only about ourselves and our business, we forgot about Peter.

"You probably know what took place in New York on September 11, 2001. That day we were informed that our son was among the firefighters who died saving the lives of others. And only after that did my husband and I come to our senses and realize that we had lost our son forever. I cannot forgive myself for this. We don't respect the people who are dear to us while they are alive, we don't listen to their inner longings, and we do not value their thoughts. And then, no matter how much you cry, no matter how much you reproach yourself, there's no bringing them back.

"We flew to New York to be there for the funerals of the firefighters. And that is where we saw Alex, our four-year-old grandson, for the first time. How much he looked like his father when he was little! As for Soledad, she was no longer the girl who had come over to us from Mexico. She had become still more beautiful. With great dignity and composure she was telling the people about Peter and about his hopes and dreams. From time to time, her eyes filled with tears, and then she would simply sit down and hold her son. Her English was flawless. We went over to them in tears, wanting to hold our grandson in our arms. But Soledad wouldn't let us touch him.

"You've come too late for that. Pete had been waiting for all this time," she said with tears in her eyes.

"We were unable to take Alex in our arms or to tell him that we were his grandmother and grandfather. We realized that the time for that had passed. Had we paid attention to Peter's feelings and listened to him with understanding and respect, our son might not have been killed. He would have become a lawyer and lived a completely different life alongside us. We would have been able to hug his grandson and indulge him. And we would have all lived happily. But that dream will never come true. We have lost the dearest person to us in the world. All that remains for us now is to live out the rest of our days and grieve." Ruth sighed and stopped talking.

"Well, it's no good torturing yourselves over it," Mehriban said quietly. "There are conflicts between parents and children in every family. In my view, you gave Peter a very good upbringing. It was because of his love and because of his son that he came into conflict with you. And it turns out that he was right, because everything in his life turned out well. He proved himself a hero, giving his life to save others. Not everybody is capable of that. For you that isn't a punishment, but rather a lesson. As Soledad said, Pete was waiting for you. In other words, he had never stopped loving you." Mehriban stopped, bewildered, suddenly noticing a tall young man sitting next to Ruth.

"My sorrows don't end there," Ruth continued. "Not long after my son's funeral, my husband died of a heart attack while driving. And so I was left alone with all our money. Of course I invited Soledad to come and live with me, but she refused. I think she still blames me for Peter's death. And now, in old age, I'm completely alone." Ruth sighed heavily. "All I've got left now is my work, which often takes me to Kazakhstan. You know, sometimes I don't feel quite myself. I forget things and can't figure out where I'm going or why. At those times, it seems to me as though people don't notice me at all. Well, what about right now? Only you are looking at me and listening to me. Nobody else seems to be bothered about me."

This made Mehriban break out in a cold sweat.

"Mehriban, I would like to ask of you a big favor," said Ruth suddenly.

Mehriban raised her eyebrows in surprise. What favor could a fellow passenger, a stranger met by chance, possibly ask?

"It's no coincidence that we met, Mehriban," Ruth went on. "I'm asking you to find Soledad and tell her everything. I ask for forgiveness from Soledad and from my grandson Alex. And may they indeed forgive me. I leave my estate to Alex. On official documents, his name is Alexander Killian, and he has our surname. When the boy is eighteen, he will have access to his inheritance. Dear Mehriban, I have told you a secret that nobody else knows. I am glad to have met you. Now, make a note of Soledad's address…"

While Mehriban was repeating the address to herself, she heard her own mother calling. She started and turned round. In the seats behind her were her father, her mother, Gyuli, Rukiyam, Mervanam, Mariyam, and other people from her village who had long departed this life.

"Oh, Allah! I thought you were all dead?" Mehriban was astonished but not afraid.

"Of course we are dead," their voices responded, "but through your book we are alive again."

Chuckling, old Zaynaphan said, "Do you remember what I said to you when I cast the *kumlak*?"

Kurvan-aka smiled into his whiskers: "My dear daughter, we are pleased with you, and we are with you always."

And now Mehriban felt the stewardess's hand on her shoulder. "Excuse me, would you please straighten your seat back and fasten your seatbelt. We're on the approach to Los Angeles."

Mehriban glanced at the seat next to her. It was empty. She asked the stewardess, "Where is the woman who was sitting here?"

"Which woman? You were sitting by yourself," she replied.

"The gray-haired woman in the white sports outfit. Ruth Killian. I've been talking to her for the whole flight."

The stewardess squatted down beside Mehriban and quietly asked her, "Did you really see her?"

"We were talking for the whole of the flight."

The stewardess's eyes opened wide. "We are not supposed to tell people this, but I'll tell you. That woman, Ruth Killian, was on the flight to Kazakhstan, the flight that emptied before you got on. As it happens, she was in the seat next to yours. And during the flight, she had a heart attack and died."

At that moment the stewardess was called away. She went off with an expression of bewilderment on her face. Before she disappeared behind the curtain, she turned and looked at Mehriban, and at that moment Mehriban remembered how, many years ago, as she cast the *kumlak*, Zaynap-ana had predicted, *You have a gift from God. You do not feel it now, but you will discover it later.* Cautiously, Mehriban turned and looked again at the seats behind her. They were occupied by passengers who had boarded at Amsterdam. "So where are the spirits I saw?" she wondered. "Oh, Allah, what's happening to my mind?" Then another thought occurred to her: *I must certainly carry out Ruth Killian's request, because only then will her soul find peace.*

Once again, Mehriban thought about her childhood and about the hard lives of her parents and the other villagers. She thought about the mothers she had written in her book for. *Maybe I have survived only in order to carry the testament of our loving, all-suffering mothers to the hearts of our readers*, she thought. *And yet it seems that my mission has not ended with the book. I still have to meet with Soledad and Alex to pass on to them Ruth's last words.*

Reflecting on all this, Mehriban thought again, *Nobody has eternal life in this world. We are all fleeting guests. And yet each of us has their own mission. It is good if we are able to fulfill it. We should live with beauty and depart with beauty, so that our consciences are clear. Our descendants do not need heaps of gold; what is important is that we bequeath them good actions, care, and love.*"

Beneath them lay Los Angeles. The aircraft was gently descending. Peering at the downtown skyscrapers, Mehriban whispered to herself, "How much more work there is for me here? Samiya said that she had some kind of surprise for me. Maybe she wants to introduce me to her husband-to-be. If Samiya decides to marry, then I will finally see my grandchild. And that would be wonderful!"

GLOSSARY

Most of these expressions are Uighur unless noted otherwise. A few Soviet usages and words from Russian and Arabic are also included.

adash	"friend," "comrade," used between men
aka	brother; also appended to a name as a term of respect toward an older man
aksakal	a village elder, lit. "white-beard," consulted on important matters and respected as wise
atkyan-chay	black tea with milk, cream, and salt. Usually served after a meal or for breakfast in large bowls known as *apkur*
apkur	a large tea bowl in which *atkyan-chay* is often served
Alma-Ata	The name given to the city of Almaty during the Soviet period. In the novel, the name changes to Almaty after the collapse of the Soviet Union. The city was the capital of the Kazakh SSR and of Kazakhstan until the capital was moved to Astana in 1997
ana	mother; also appended to a name as a sign of respect toward a woman older than the speaker

anla chay, *anla nan*	a special ceremony for women unable to conceive, in which older women prepare a special tea and special *nan* (bread) to encourage conception
apay, apa	grandmother; also appended by the Kazakhs to a name as a sign of respect toward an elderly woman
apkur	a large drinking bowl for tea or soup
aryk	an irrigation ditch to carry water to crops; digging and maintaining these was highly labor-intensive
ashmya sanza	a type of *sanza* made from a single large round of dough, rolled out thin
azan	the Muslim call to prayer, usually called from a minaret by the *imam*
balam	"my son," address of a parent to his/her son
bay	wealthy landowner or stockbreeder in pre-Soviet Central Asia
beshbarmak	a mutton stew containing strips of unleavened dough
beshchuk	a wooden cradle for nursing infants
beshchuk toy	"cradle celebration," held forty days after the birth of a child, to which only women are invited

Bismillah   "In the Name of God," part of the Arabic invocation *bismillahi ar-rahman ar-rahim*, "In the Name of God, the Compassionate, the Merciful" with which the Qur'an begins, often also said when beginning a new undertaking

bliny (Rus.)   small pancakes, with a sweet or savory filling

brigadir   gang or team leader of *kolkhoz* workers

bugluk   a wooden platform, similar to a bed, on which people sit to drink tea and rest outdoors or indoors

buva   grandfather; suffixed after name as a sign of respect

chapan   a long coat (variant of kaftan) worn by either sex, usually worn in winter, often with embroidered decoration

chayhana   a place for gathering and drinking tea; in *A Mother's Testament* it generally refers to an outdoor space in the yard or garden of a house, often on a raised platform and with a roof or vine overhead for shade

chon-apa   an older mother; used to address one's mother's older sister

chugun, chugunok   a cast-iron pot for cooking

dada	father, dad
dastarkhan	the place where food is eaten and shared; the table or *dzhoza*, if present, the cloth covering it, and the food placed on it; the setting of tables for a feast
dopa	a type of skullcap worn by various Central Asian peoples and known by various names. The Uighur men's *dopa*, considered the national headdress, is usually square in shape, black and with a white leaf pattern embroidered on the four sides. Women's *dopas* can be more varied in color and shape
duga	a prayer in Uighur often added on after formal Arabic prayers. May be a blessing or thanks after a meal, or it may be dedicated to specific situations or individuals
dutar	a lute-like musical instrument with a long neck and two strings that is found in Central Asia, Iran, and elsewhere; *dutarchi* – a *dutar* player
dzhigit	a brave young man; often, a fighter or horseman
dzhoza	a low table used for serving food when sitting on the floor

feldsheritsa	Russianised feminine form of *Feldscher*, originally German, meaning a field or military doctor
Great Patriotic War	the name in the USSR and its successor states for the Second World War, in which they were active between 1941 and 1945
hada	sister; also appended to a name as a term of respect toward an older woman
hanum	lady, madam; term of respect for a woman
hina	henna, a plant traditionally used for dying and cosmetics
imam	the leader of prayers at a mosque, and to a certain extent the spiritual leader of a Muslim community; recites prayers at weddings, funerals, and other occasions
inshallah	God willing; if God wills (said when stating a plan, hope, or intention)
kang	the flue from the stove, made of brick and routed through the house, often under the sleeping platform, to give extra warmth
kapak-chumush	a scoop or ladle made from a dried, hollowed-out gourd

kaymak	thick cream, similar to clotted cream, made by simmering milk and leaving it to stand and ferment slightly. Served to honored guests in *aktyan-chay*
kazan	a large metal cooking pot with a lid for stews, rice dishes, soups etc. Expressions such as "working at the *kazan*," "looking after the *kazan*," etc., are understood to mean taking on the food preparation and cooking duties of a household, typically after a death in the family or for a big celebration
ketmen	a large L-shaped hoe used for digging, particularly for maintaining irrigation ditches (*aryk*)
Khit Ayam	the days following Roza Khit, the end of Ramadan, in which families and friends spend time with each other celebrating and contemplating. May last up to a week
khitlik	a gift given at Roza Khit, the celebrations at the end of Ramadan
kichik-apa, kichik-ana	a young(er) mother; used to address one's mother's younger sister
kizim	girl; lit. "my girl"
kizyak	dried cow dung used as fuel for heating

kolkhoz	a type of collective farm common in the Soviet Union, in which most inhabitants of a village worked together in the fields; the produce was usually submitted to a centralized authority. Sometimes a number of *kolkhoz* from different nearby settlements would jointly manage the surrounding land. Most of the villagers of Bolshoy Chigan were employed by the local *kolkhoz*
Komsomol	the Communist Party's youth movement, created to foster strong political convictions and social skills in young people, and thereby form worthy Soviet citizens and future Party members
kora	a cooking pot or saucepan
kordak	a dish of finely chopped fried mutton or beef with potato and other vegetables
korpya	a long, quilted blanket, stuffed with wool, used as a cushion when sitting on the floor, also used for bedding
korum shova	a meat-based broth or soup
korumluk	a custom of giving a gift of money on the occasion of a major acquisition or achievement

koshma	a felt rug made from sheep or camel wool
kulak	in pre-Communist times, comparatively wealthy small farmers, often serfs who had made good after emancipation. The Communists treated these "petty capitalists" with particular brutality
Kulja	town in Xinjiang, China – today called Yining
kumgan	a metal bucket used for personal ablutions before the ritual prayers
kumlakchi; kumlak	a fortune-teller or clairvoyant who tells fortunes (*kumlak*) by casting pebbles
kurt	balls of dried, salted *kefir* (a type of fermented yogurt)
laghman	from Chinese "lamian," a noodle-based dish usually in a lamb or beef broth
lapsha	a meat stew with noodles, such as *suyuk ash*
lazdzhan	a hot sauce of ground red pepper in sunflower oil, seasoned with garlic
manty	Turkic-style dumplings, thought to be invented by the Uighurs in China, in which a meat and onion filling is wrapped in a dough parcel, cooked by boiling or steaming

medrese, also *madrasa*	a school, generally with an Islamic curriculum including Qur'an studies as well as general subjects
moma	grandmother; also appended to a name as a sign of respect toward an elderly woman
muqam	a musical mode and a set of typical melody forms used in Uighur music (by which improvisation is guided). They may contain several parts and be extensive and elaborate. Similar *muqam* (or *maqam*) are found in other parts of the Turkic and Arab world
namaz	the prescribed ritual prayers in Islam, performed at five times of the day
nan	bread; typically, round flatbreads as baked by various Central Asian and other peoples in *tono* ovens
nazyr	a wake held in memory of the deceased on the day of death, then again on the seventh and fortieth days and the anniversary
Nikah	Islamic marriage ceremony, performed by the *imam,* often in the bride's house with only close family present. A big wedding party (*toy*) would normally be held soon after

omach   a soup that features small pieces of
                       dough

osma   a plant whose juice is used to give the
                       eyebrows a dark coloring

pelmeni   meat dumplings; minced meat wrapped
(Russ.)   in dough and cooked in a broth

perestroika   "restructuring," an economic policy
(Rus.)   introduced by Mikhael Gorbachev in
                       an attempt to modernize Soviet
                       communism in the second half of the
                       1980s, introducing elements of the free
                       market and arguably leading to the
                       eventual collapse of communism, and
                       with it, the breakup of the USSR

place of   in a traditional household, a particular
honor   place at the table or on the carpet that
                       was kept for the head of the household
                       or for honored visitors

plov   any of various Central Asian types of
                       pilav or pilau—a rice-based dish to
                       which various ingredients, meat and/or
                       vegetables, are added depending on the
                       recipe and occasion

porya   a large, thin-fried pastry containing
                       onion or spring onion

pryaniki   small dry gingerbread cakes, similar in
(Rus.)   texture to German Lebkuchen, often
                       flavored with honey or poppy seeds

Roza Khit	Uighur name for Eid al-Fitr, the celebrations that break the fasting at the end of the month of Ramadan in Islam. See also *Khit Ayam*; *khitlik*
samsa	Central Asian type of samosa; a baked or fried pastry parcel containing a filling (typically lamb and onion)
sanza	thinly-rolled strips of fried dough
segiz	a small bush whose stems give a white milky substance. This is often dried and then used as a chewing gum
shashlyk	kebab; skewered grilled meat
shurpa; shorpa	chorba; a type of soup based on a meat stock, found in many countries
sin chay	black tea without milk, served at the start of a meal in small bowls
sinnim	sister; lit. "my sister"
sirkya	soy sauce
sura	a chapter or section of the Qur'an
suyuk ash	a soup or stew with finely chopped noodles, lamb, and vegetables
talkan	ground roasted wheat; this was often paid to *kolkhoz* workers as a wage
togach	a small *nan* baked in a *tono* oven; if allowed to dry out, it will keep for a very long time

tono	a tandoor oven (tonur, tamdyr): a clay oven with a beehive shape and an opening in the top, in which flatbreads and other items are baked, typically pressed onto the walls
toy	a big celebration such as a wedding
tumar	a small, decorative triangular container worn round the neck on a chain, as a talisman. A *sura* of the Qur'an is contained inside
uka	"little brother," added to name when addressing a younger man
zhan	lit. "soul"; suffixed to names as a term of endearment (e.g. Tursun-zhan, Tairzhan)
zhit	a special commemorative flatbread (*nan*) made from a thin unleavened dough and fried in vegetable oil
zhutta	a dish based on steamed carrot or pumpkin